LIGHTNING
PEOPLE

A NOVEL

LIGHTNING PEOPLE

CHRISTOPHER BOLLEN

 SOFT SKULL PRESS • AN IMPRINT OF COUNTERPOINT

Library of Congress Cataloging-in-Publication Data

Bollen, Christopher, 1975–
Lightning people : a novel / Christopher Bollen.
p. cm.

Summary: "Joseph Guiteau is a working actor who moved to New York to escape a tragic family
history in the Midwest. Wandering through a city transformed by the attacks of September 2001,
he frequents gatherings of conspiracy groups, trying to make sense of world events and his own
personal history. Looming over his life is a secret that threatens to undermine his new marriage to
Del, a snake expert at a city park, whose work visa is the only thread keeping her from deportation
back to her native Greece. The new marriage influences the lives of those around them: William, a
dark and troubled actor whose sanity is fading as quickly as his career, leading him to perform increasingly desperate acts; Madi, a young entrepreneur who will have to face the moral complications of
a business made successful by the outsourcing of American jobs to India; and her brother Raj, Del's
former lover, a promising photographer whose work details the empty rooms of an increasingly alie-
nated city. Christopher Bollen's first novel captures the atmosphere of anxiety and loss that exists in
Manhattan. It is a story of the city itself, and the interconnected lives of those attempting to navigate
both Manhattan and their own mortality." —Provided by publisher.

ISBN-13: 978-1-59376-419-7
ISBN-10: 1-59376-419-7
1. Manhattan (New York, N.Y.)—Fiction. 2. September 11 Terrorist Attacks,
2001—Influence—Fiction. 3. Psychological fiction. I. Title.
PS3602.O6545L54 2011
813'.6—dc22
2011025049

Cover design by Joseph Logan and Christopher Bollen
Interior design by Neuwirth & Associates, Inc.

Soft Skull Press
An imprint of COUNTERPOINT
1919 Fifth Street
Berkeley, CA 94710

www.softskull.com

Distributed by Publishers Group West

Printed in the United States of America

10 9 8 7 6 5 4 3 2 1

This is for my father and my mother

"The truth will set you free. But not until it is finished with you."

—David Foster Wallace

PROLOGUE

WE HAD LIGHTNING strikes all summer but no blackouts. Through May and June lightning came without rain, rising out of New Jersey like a laser concert and slicing east in white tracers through Manhattan. Storms were a huge attraction for those of us who moved here from the Midwest. We'd climb up to the rooftops as ritual to watch them roll in from the west, feeling momentarily connected to the cereal-grain prairies and humid river valleys that we had worked so desperately to escape. For a long time we did this without worry or risk. After all, in the years when we were still new to the city, rooftops served as our twenty-four-hour parks. They were our unpoliced drug lairs, our water-tower jungle gyms, our love nests for random hookups with enough of a romantic panorama not to feel ashamed when groping through underwear near a bed of moldering trash. Every building had one, junked with cables and rusted lawn furniture and billion-dollar views. For many years we were drunk and happy, loitering on these hot tar gardens, adding our slender bodies to the skyline. The storms, however, were different. They were a private matter, a religion best observed alone, and maybe only for the Midwesterners, because they were the ones who were killed.

First it happened to a twenty-three-year-old from St. Louis on a rooftop on Broome Street, then to a twenty-seven-year-old from Indiana on a sixth-floor tenement on the Lower East Side. Another lightning death occurred a few weeks later, also to a Midwesterner. The victims were all young men and women who had moved to the city within the last few years, scrounging for jobs or fame. And they had all been struck by a single bolt that ripped the shoes off their feet and melted the coins in their pockets. Although the newspapers never bothered to draw more than a cursory connection, each victim was described as "happy" or "ambitious" or "starting to make a real home in New York." "I don't know why the weather would take her," one grieving mother was quoted as saying. "You expect murders or burglaries. But you don't think your daughter is going to be killed by lightning in the middle of Manhattan. It makes no sense."

Most people will tell you that such deaths don't make sense. Lightning strikes contain all of the inexplicable characteristics of coincidence, no reason, just a dice roll—like a tornado rummaging through one house and leaving the next unbothered. Then there are tougher cynics like Del, who says that because crime is down, New York has to find creative ways to stay dangerous.

But I know the real explanation for these deaths—there is one for those who are willing to listen. The answer lies in the landscape itself. The Manhattan skyline has changed since I moved here from Cincinnati at the age of eighteen. What no one seems willing to mention is that before the World Trade Center fell, lightning rarely struck any parts of Manhattan other than the towers themselves, as they were the highest conductors in the city. But they are gone, and now we have taken their place, little conductors in our tight jeans and unwashed T-shirts, easy targets in a city that was supposed to hide us.

Tonight I poured whiskey into two glass tumblers and watched snow fall across the television screen. Outside, taxis sped south toward the bridges, and Del and I kissed on the bed as close as we could to the air-conditioning. Her tongue was dry and her neck heavy, our faces blue in the television light. After she smoked her last cigarette, we took our clothes off. We did not have sex. We were nervous, and Del was tired. "Get the lights, will you?" she said, as she reached over and set the alarm clock for 8 AM. I thought the final moments of our single lives might turn us into feral sex partners, but we stuck to our routine. Tomorrow morning we are getting married at City Hall.

I wish I could say that I am marrying Delphine Kousavos, a beautiful Greek woman with long black hair and a bad smoking habit, only out of love—that we bumped into each other on Seventh Street near Tomkins Square Park eight months ago and, clinging to each other's arms and sentences, are about to spend thirty dollars for a two-minute ceremony. That also isn't the correct explanation of events. It's just the easiest story to tell.

Many of us came to New York to get away from the stories of our childhoods, hoping here they would no longer apply. For a long time I thought I could shake the predictions told to me about my family, the ones my mother raised me on in a darkened house in Cincinnati that took each death as evidence, each year as a clue. There is a pattern that runs through the generations, a conspiracy in the bloodstream that kills with perfect timing. For many years, I thought nothing from back there could find me. Those stories could be wrong. But they could also be devastatingly correct.

If I am right, I won't live to see our first anniversary.

For a while I was very young here and didn't need to give in to the paranoia. I remember a lot of first days in this city: how a morning could lead to a fist fight with a homeless woman, a request by a model scout on Broadway to come in to an agency for pictures, an offer of a part-time job cater-waiting for a group of Chinese diplomats, or a four-milligram Klonopin shared with a failed child actor hiding from Hollywood before riding bicycles around an empty loft in Tribeca until our minds became unglued at dawn. All of those first shiny details told us that we had gotten very far from where we started, and that there was good reason to expect more.

We still go up to the rooftops. We still look at the storms dragging in from the west. At some point, we stopped thinking of our time here as an open story that would only end well. Lightning doesn't strike the same place twice until it does. Behind every senseless tragedy there is a careful logic. At some point, the weather changed when no one was looking, and we were no longer so young in New York.

PART ONE

CHAPTER ONE

JOSEPH GUITEAU MARRIED a Grecian snake charmer.

Not from Greece immediately, not by a long shot. There was hardly an accent to her vowels. She was a woman with a penchant for 1970s American rock, two credit cards in her wallet, and an alumni library card issued from Columbia University. She didn't carry her United States work permit with her, but she had it to show when necessary. It was never necessary. The Bronx Zoo ("world's greatest animal park in the world's wildest city") made sure to keep the noses of their Bengal tigers, adult Congo gorillas, and white alpine owls clean as far as the INS went by staying up to date on their employee files. Delphine Kousavos, sanitizer of anaconda cages, nurse to the irritable copperhead, specialist of the western diamondback, loved Joseph Guiteau. She had real feelings for him. As a child on her tiny island of Amorgos, she'd never dreamed of marrying a star of shaving cream commercials in a foreign municipal building at the age of thirty-two. But Del understood the facts as they were dealt. She had lived with Joseph in their Gramercy apartment for five months. She handled beasts far more venomous than actors. She married him on the morning of June 14, 2007.

Joseph was so nervous he couldn't get the ring on her finger. Quiet seconds passed inside Marriage Chapel #2 as he shifted his weight on his left foot and then his right, jamming the ring against Del's knuckle. The silver-haired Puerto Rican court official, who must have seen every combination of man and woman that ever existed swearing eternal love before her, swallowed hard and closed her eyes. "It's not . . . " Joseph stuttered, glancing up at Del and then back at her hand, his hairline breaking in green sweat beads under the ticking green fluorescents. Del suppressed a small laugh and fixed her eyes on the New York City emblem painted on the wall behind him. A pilgrim and an Indian stood side by side, staring blankly inside a ring of wheat; the two looked very much like a lonely immigrant couple taking their chances on matrimony just like everyone else.

Del's finger started to swell.

"Let me," she said quickly. Before Joseph could stop her, she grabbed the ring and slipped it cleanly over her knuckle. The judge clenched the edges of the podium and, in a mangled Spanish accent, pronounced them man and wife.

"You shouldn't have done that," Joseph said later, when they walked through the metal detectors and out into the downtown sidewalk frantic with bike messengers and secretaries in the noontime rush.

"Done what?" Del replied. "I hope you don't mean marry you."

"I mean the ring. You shouldn't have had to put it on yourself."

"Did you notice the poor girl who came in after us was eight months pregnant and bawling her eyes out? I think it went beautifully. Considering."

Joseph reached for her hand and held it for a second as they crossed through the stalled traffic on Centre Street. Office lights glared faintly in the windows surrounding City Hall Park. The sidewalk was canopied in magnolia branches, hanging low from the weight of brown buds. Joseph unknotted his necktie, and Del pulled the white gardenia from her hair, loosening a braid that unraveled in a tangle down her back. She made only a perfunctory attempt at working out the knot. Her fingers were still shaking, and she saw that Joseph's were too. Her heels on the cobblestones were as loud as their breaths, and neither of them spoke or looked at the other. She threw the gardenia into the park's dry fountain well and scanned Broadway for a taxi that would take them the thirty blocks home. Del noticed that nearly every bench and tree in this part of town was decorated with a small chrome plaque, a few engraved with commemorations of the dead, others blank and shining in the sun, waiting to be filled with the names of future ghosts.

"It's going to be impossible to get a cab," Joseph said, stepping out into the traffic with his arm raised. "We should have booked a car."

"Why don't we take the subway? It's only six stops, and we can pick up some wine at Nico's—"

Joseph cut her off with an aggravated sigh.

"I'm not bringing you home on public transportation."

Now that they had gotten married, they were suddenly talking to each other like strangers. Del watched Joseph try and fail to flag down an off-duty cab. Right then, he looked less familiar to her than he had in all the months that they had been living together. His blue eyes seemed lodged in deeper sockets, and the sunlight located hidden strands of red in his dark blond hair, which matched the color of his lips. His face was tired and more angular than it had been that morning, but his body jerked restlessly in his pinstripe suit. She noticed his skinny ankles peeking from under his pant cuffs. She stopped herself from telling him that he was being ridiculous to care about how they were getting home—what about the convenience of a ceremony at City Hall did he not understand?— but she knew that his pride was at stake. First the ring and now the likely prospect of no ten-dollar fare to see them back. Del followed him into the street and slid her arms underneath his suit coat. She rubbed her lips lightly against his neck, until an erection grew in the pants she had hung in the bathroom that morning to smooth the wrinkles with the shower steam.

"Come on, Joe. It doesn't make any difference to me." She turned in her blue crepe de chine dress to start off for the entrance to the 6 train, leaving Joseph no choice but to stumble after her. As Del reached into her purse for her pouch of nicotine and rolling papers, she smiled, indulging an old habit for generalizations that she had worked to control over the years. *Americans*, she thought, *those consummate tourists even in their personal lives, always needed their photo ops and rented limos with streamers icing the hood to ensure that an event was marked by happiness.* But as soon as this thought crowded her mind, she realized her own people were far worse when it came to weddings—perhaps the guiltiest on earth in celebrations of love.

"Fine. We'll do it your way," Joseph grumbled as he searched his wallet for his MetroCard.

"Believe me, you're getting off easy. If we were married in Greece, you'd want an annulment after four days, and my family would still be parading around drunk, pelting you with rice every time you stood up to use the bathroom."

"Please don't tell your parents I took you home like this," Joseph pleaded, pausing at the steps leading down to the subway platform. The whole day was greasy with June light, and he pinched his eyes to acclimate them to the darkness underground.

"Only you couldn't get an annulment," Del continued, lost in the imaginary picture of her relatives dressed in white linen to the backdrop of the Aegean Sea. "Because my grandfather is the only judge on the island. So at a certain point it would stop being rice thrown at you and start being stones."

"Christ," he laughed uneasily. "Exactly what kind of family have I married into? Is there anything else you want to tell me?"

Del shrugged, left her cigarette rolling for Gramercy Park, and passed through the teeth of the subway turnstile. Her muscles relaxed in the cool, dirty winds brought by a train coming through the uptown tunnel.

IN THE COMPARATIVELY modest month of wedding preparations in the Kousavos-Guiteau household, Joseph had suggested early on that they rent out a bar on the Bowery to celebrate. They could invite a hundred friends, serve crustless triangle sandwiches smeared with anchovies as a hat tip to tradition, and encourage everyone to speed dance and drink gallons of champagne for maximum elation—"until we're all just one pile of melted plastic by the end of the night," he had said enthusiastically. "That's how you make it official." Joseph had tried to sell this plan to Del in part to ensure that their post-wedding lives wouldn't be a descent into the particularly agoraphobic form of hibernation new couples tended to take on. But Joseph also suspected that there was a reason for receptions. They provided the necessary distraction from realizing that you had just entered a binding legal contract with one of its chief clauses stipulating eternal unity. Too much time alone with the eternal leaves even the most dedicated wanting to jump through the nearest window, eyes on any escape route.

He remembered Del's response. "No," she had said flatly. "That sounds so exhausting."

"Well, how do you suggest we mark the occasion?"

Del hadn't answered him. She had let the plan drop and for weeks had avoided the issue. Now, alone in the silence of their apartment two hours after the ceremony, Joseph felt justified in the wisdom of his instincts. He slowly took off his coat and hung it in the closet off the bedroom. He walked back into the living room and leaned against the windowsill to pull his shoes from his feet. He rubbed the indentations that the leather left on his ankles and looked out the window, where a crew of undernourished skateboarders sped under the fire escape. Del was locked in the bathroom, removing her dress and makeup, as she had been for the last forty minutes. He occasionally heard the click of a lighter followed by the smell of smoke to indicate that she was in no hurry to return to him. He sat on the sofa to stare at the afternoon light slanting across the floor and then stood up to find the bottle of wine that they had bought on their walk home. He unpeeled the foil but didn't open it.

Joseph didn't know what he was supposed to do to fill the hours after the wedding. The nervousness of the morning continued to hang over them. As soon as they unlocked the front door, he felt like they were moving awkwardly around each other, touching only by accident as they passed down the hall. As a professional actor who earned his money by the amount of repeated airings of his commercials rather than by the hours it took to film them in the first place, Joseph was accustomed to filling up free time. Hell, it was an art form the way he could transform an unaccounted day into a nonstop rush of errands, phone calls, Internet searches, masturbation, and previously uncharted routes through side streets in the East Village to discover novelty bookshops and second-hand stores whose only purpose was to distract the armies of artists and drifters who made up much of the city's rudderless population. Even before they had agreed to get married, Del took on the tone of a disgruntled wife a few weeks into their cohabitation. "What the fuck do you do all day?" she'd ask him with her arms crossed over her chest in judgment. He'd always provide the same answer: "I've been thinking." Del seemed to regard "thinking" as an activity equivalent to playing the lottery—lots of irrational hope with no net results—but it was true that in the last year Joseph consumed whole hours lost in thought. He thought on a bench in Madison Square Park about his family, about the people who had lived and died before him in Ohio, about the coincidences that ran through his bloodline. Sometimes, to waste an hour, he even attended certain meetings filled with paranoid cases who thought out loud about government plots and impossible cover-ups. Those voices made his own thoughts seem less crazed, almost normal by comparison. Joseph never shared what he was thinking with Del. He guarded those secrets the same way that he protected his most personal possessions when Del first moved into the apartment: in small closed boxes as if to say, *some items are just mine. Even though we live together, you aren't allowed in.*

He stood as still as he could in the middle of the living room. He heard the shower run in the bathroom and Del's voice humming along to a song stuck in her head. For a second, as his fingers began to undo the top button of his shirt, he wondered if it was fair to marry a woman whom he couldn't let in completely. Jitters too late infected his mind: *You, Joseph Guiteau, wearing a pinstripe suit, are only an actor playing the part of a happy groom.* What right did he have marrying a woman whom he blocked and shielded from his worst secrets, who had only learned scattered pieces of his life edited and scoured of their grimmest details? He often went silent when Del threw her hands on her head in exasperation and said, "Doesn't anyone in this city have a nine-to-five job anymore? Am I the only person who has to wake up in the morning?" Work had been her signal complaint since they met. He knew she hated her job at the zoo, stuck giving tours and cleaning snake cages to stay in the country on her visa. But as of today she wouldn't have to worry about that anymore. She could be free now. Joseph loved her enough to give her that.

"It's just jitters," he said out loud to drive them away. He inhaled deeply and walked to the bathroom door. "Del, you almost ready?"

"A minute," she yelled.

He returned to the sofa, unbuttoning his shirt and wiping the sweat from his chest. A bleating car alarm in the street mixed with the muffled motor of a garbage truck, all the ordinary echoes of the city telling him that it was still a normal day, and soon the nerves would pass and he and Del could go on, living like they had, in their rented apartment five flights above the sidewalk behind the matted branches of the elm trees.

It occurred to him to call someone with the news. Isn't that what someone was supposed to do when they married, tell the ones they loved? Joseph reached for the cell phone in his pocket, unsure of whom to call. He hadn't spoken to his only relative in nearly fifteen years. He was amazed that he still remembered the ten-digit number of the house in Cincinnati and was so taken with his immediate recall that he only regretted dialing when he heard the first ring. After three more rings a voice answered tiredly, distrustfully, like the vocal chords were out of practice.

He had not heard that voice since he left Ohio, and he remembered it now, how it had deepened in pitch after his father's death. He struggled to return the simple greeting, but his tongue shut down against his teeth. His mother was the last person who would celebrate the news of his wedding. She had already given up all belief in the value of such eternal commitments. That low Midwestern voice had been the one to tell him all through his childhood that there was only one thing he could count on with certainty: ending up like his father, and the father before him. Maybe she had changed, he thought, as he tried again to say hello. But he waited through the silence of the receiver.

The bathroom door opened, and Del walked out with a towel knotted over her breasts. A wet rolled cigarette hung clumsily from her mouth. She smiled and then squinted her eyes when she noticed the phone at his ear.

"Who are you calling?" she asked as she tapped her cigarette into the ashtray on the dresser.

There was no reason to tell his mother the news. There was no reason after so many years to tell her anything. Maybe he just wanted to know that she was still there in the house in Cincinnati, with power lines connected to the utility poles along the street as if keeping the whole house moored to a world that his mother had long given up. Joseph closed the phone and dropped it on the coffee table.

"No one," he said with a smile. Del picked up the wine bottle and rammed the corkscrew into the bottle. Her hands were wet, and the handle slipped from her grip. He grabbed the bottle to open it for her, and she walked past him into the bedroom. She returned a minute later pushing a pair of faded gray jeans over her hips. A black bra hung over her shoulders, unfastened in the middle, and her breasts slapped her thin freckled arms as she fought the unwilling zipper.

"Hey," he said, "We're married." Del looked up at him with her eyebrows lifted, and in that moment Joseph no longer felt waylaid by the anxiety of the morning. Yes, they really were married. The day had happened. He just needed to say it out loud to someone. Del laughed and pointed to the stereo on the dresser.

"Put on some music then," she said. She patted his left cheek as she made her way toward the kitchen. "I'm sorry I didn't agree to a party. I guess you're just going to have to forgive me."

He was relieved to see her easy, ungraceful walk in the shadows of the hallway. Maybe love was the closest thing to feeling safe in the world. As safe as two people can be anymore.

"You love me, right?" he yelled to her. He didn't want to stop talking now that they had found their foothold in each other again. He knew it was stupid to ask that question on the day of their wedding, but the sound of his mother's voice had brought too many doubts to circle in his mind. "You're happy. About today, I mean."

As he put one of Del's favorite records on the stereo—an erratic '70s rock ballad that reminded him of drilled cavities and reminded her always of molten romance—she stepped back into the hallway.

"Of course I love you. More than anyone ever. Christ, what a fucking question."

BUT WAS THAT the absolute truth? The day had been filled with questions, but they only asked for answers in the present tense: I do. Not I will. Not I did. Del made moussaka for dinner from the recipe her mother had given her, a list of ingredients and baking directions typed on a piece of paper that proved its merit in its thick wax of ancient, corroded grease stains. They ate the meal at the table under candlelight, where Del made excuses to return to the kitchen to splash cold water on her face and take sips of whiskey from a glass on the counter. At the table she drank wine and reached her hand out to stroke Joseph's arm with her knuckles. When there was nothing left of the moussaka in the pan, nothing left of the day but the last hour to midnight, she followed Joseph into the bedroom. They kissed on the bed as her fingers dug below the waist of his pants, tracking the scant hairs of his stomach until they flowered around his penis. Enough light from the street shone through the diamond grates of the window for Del to see Joseph clearly. His straight white teeth and the solid architecture of his face always managed to astound her. She appreciated how handsome, how disturbingly and un-menacingly *Midwestern* those features were, how they matched some old idea of what American men looked like when she had imagined them at night on her bed as a child. She pulled herself away with a final kiss and told him she needed a glass of water. The temperature was nearing a hundred degrees in their apartment tonight.

She loved Joseph. More than anyone. But the unconditional "ever" might have been a bit of a romantic leap. In truth, there were other men that filled up the dark island in her head reserved for those names and faces she had once felt certain she had loved. Del had a habit of returning to that island, of sitting with those ghosts for concentrated minutes, desperate to resurrect details—accents, dinners, states of circumcision, arguments, intimate conversations that felt like walking over a cliff together—that made remembering them worth the price. What was the value of holding on to someone if she couldn't hold them again later in her mind? As she walked quietly through the apartment on the night of her wedding, slightly drunk on the combination of whiskey and wine, she allowed herself to remember the first time love had inhabited human form to unbalance the contents of her heart.

Dash Winslow had been as striking and ridiculous as his name implied. Dash had seduced Del at Columbia on the grass lawn next to Rodin's *Thinker* simply by standing before her one afternoon, cutting a shadow over her *Anatomy of the Human Brain* reader. He had long red hair that descended into brown as it reached his elbows and a thick red beard that brought out disturbing green eyes, which made him look possessed by a marauding homicidal Viking. What he was possessed by, in their senior year at Columbia, was a family who had the audacity to name their second son Dashiell, owned a huge chunk of commercial real estate on Long Island, and bankrolled an entire hall in the Islamic wing at the Met. Thus Dash's ripped heavy-metal T-shirts and piled-on silver chains and even the yellow daisy that he tucked thoughtfully behind his ear could easily be written off as an attempt at low-grade rebellion while attending a middlebrow Ivy. But Dash really was possessed. His pupils held a dilation that could only be seen in others during the peaks of an intense acid trip. He brought Del back to his off-campus apartment and fucked her three times in two hours. He spread a bedsheet out on his balcony and, naked, they watched the sun cinder into New Jersey and the homeless build their tents in Riverside Park. They drank whiskey and smoked pot as they leaned against each other. That was the night she first fell in love with single malt scotch, a lasting indulgence, and also with him.

Like someone who came from extreme privilege and unlike someone tied to the responsibilities it obligates, Dash carried a reckless confidence that she had never seen in a man her age. She was used to settling for the occasional half-hearted orgasm with one of the cerebral loners who didn't have her work-study obligations, waking up at seven on weekend mornings to pack bags of fetal pigs in the biology freezer, which she favored to churning out collated color copies for the junior faculty. Dash claimed her as his girlfriend right away, picking her up most nights in front of her dorm on 114th Street, placing his gray wool fedora over her head, and taking her to underground clubs on the Lower East Side that he had frequented since he was thirteen. She couldn't believe this side of New York had always existed without her ever tapping into it. Somehow, like most Columbia undergrads, Del had been left stranded inside the wrought iron of the Upper West Side, living on the cool sophistication of subway rides down to Soho for student-teacher cocktail parties in renovated lofts with Abstract Expressionist prints the color of urine on the bathroom walls.

Dash was naked so often when they were together, the red curls covering his nipples and matching the flaming tuft above his hooked erect penis, a part of her felt detached when running into him on campus and seeing him dressed in camouflage pants with absurd yellow handkerchiefs tied around his wrists—like he was dressing for a world outside of the one they shared. Yes, she considered herself a feminist. Yes, she held a lit candle on the march down Amsterdam Avenue to take back the night and attended seminars on the brutality of fashion magazines and female genital mutilation in remote West African villages. But Dash could hand her a blade of grass that he picked on his way to meet her and she'd keep it preserved in the gold locket she wore around her neck. He played bass in a band called Splatter Pattern. She had briefly tried out as a backup singer, but, as Dash himself said, "You sing like you're being electrocuted for a crime you didn't commit." Instead she sat behind the curtain at their shows smoking a dozen cigarettes and throwing death glances at the girls who assembled around the stage—models or junkies or wannabes of either camp who looked pretty and lost under the colored lights. Alas, she'd found her type: He was an artist. He bought Marcel Breuer metal chairs and twisted them into useless piles of junk.

Del and the red Viking had fallen so hard for each other that the morning after they graduated—she magna cum laude in biology, he a "walking degree" until he finished a full summer semester of classes and a mandatory gym requirement—he asked her if she would consider living with him and having a baby. "Isn't that what all this money I've got is for?" he asked, while kicking a combat boot toward the ceiling fan that circled slowly above his bed. "Let's make a child because we have so much love it needs to spill into something else." What he didn't know—and what she did—was that her stomach was already carrying a dark secret. What she didn't know—and what he did—was that he was about to embark on a two-month tour with his band. They were both twenty-one.

Her parents were a furious chorus of answering-machine messages. She tried to stop drinking the scotch in his apartment for the baby she hadn't yet told him about. She had moved her clothes into his closets and spent evenings camped out naked on his balcony when she received the news that Dash had been with his two bandmates in a blue Mustang at 12:30 AM on Summerlick Highway outside of Boston when they were hit head-on by a semi traveling at seventy miles per hour. The driver was alive but in serious condition. The man in the front seat had been beheaded by the truck's grill. The passenger in the back had sustained such grave injuries that he bled to death as the police tried to cut him out of the Mustang's chassis. Dash had not said anything to the officers as they worked to pry him out of the skeletal backseat, but one of them got the sense that he had, for a while anyway, been conscious. Del's college roommate and best friend, Madeline Singh, held her hand for twenty-eight days. Madi held it when Del was not invited to the funeral by the Winslow family, held it as Del agonized about whether or not to have the baby, tried to hold it as they waited on the plastic bowl seats at the Planned Parenthood clinic, and used every inch of her hands to clasp on to Del at John F. Kennedy Airport before her flight back to Greece, to go home, to get away from New York, to be embraced by a family that had already framed her diploma over their living room clock, encased in glass to keep the sea salt from infecting the gears.

Del spent a year on Amorgos before returning to New York. In those four seasons drifting in the quiet Aegean she gained pounds and invested her afternoons in her own studies, first in the heart muscles of the human anatomy and then, with a strange interest in toxins and circulatory structures, in herpetology, reptiles, the cold-bloods. The western diamondback drew her particular interest, fangs on one end, a rattle on the other, swerving through the deserts of America, reminding her of the country she missed. Madi kept a bed waiting for her return in an apartment on the edge of the East Village. By the time Del climbed out of a taxi on Avenue B with two pieces of luggage and a box of vinyl records—the only item she took from her dead boyfriend's apartment before she slipped the key under the door—the pain of losing Dash Winslow had pretty much dissipated into the heartbreak of failed possibilities. Or rather, Del saw him for the distortion he had always been, a gorgeous kid who had been amplified in the head of another as the perfect, all-answering, money-backed future. He had finally been consigned to a blade of grass hidden in a locket at the bottom of her jewelry box.

Eleven years later, she stood at the kitchen counter filling a glass with water from the faucet, and she could actually blame Dash's death as the reason she had tumbled out of permanent citizenship in the United States by leaving that summer for Greece. If she had stayed, gone to graduate school or landed a job in biology research, she would have been granted one of those passes that the INS bestows on students who remain in the beneficent kingdoms of the educated working class. Instead, she had to apply all over again for visas, collecting letters from employers and friends on her merits every few years, paying cash for immigration lawyers who said "the chances are good, Ms. Kousavos. You work at one of the city's top tourist attractions. Now when are you going to get that panda pregnant? My son loves pandas. Do you think you can swindle free weekend passes?"

The last thing her father had said to her when she was home for Christmas three years ago was, "Don't you do something drastic, young lady. Don't go marrying some fool American for the papers, for the citizen card. You do a wedding here with your mother. We decorate the whole town for you." She hadn't phoned them yet to give them the news, and part of her wondered if she needed to tell them at all. Families far away are allotted such small windows into the lives of their children, wasn't it best to let them imagine her world the way they wanted to, as if every day the Statue of Liberty drifted behind her shoulder and cops cleared her path at night until she was safely locked behind her door? It amazed her that she had survived fifteen years in the city, for much of that time staying out late enough to see dawn break through the yellow night sky, and still her parents cautioned her to be careful if she told them she was visiting a friend in Brooklyn. "Take a taxi," her mother would plead. "We will send you the money if you cannot afford it." (This from a woman who felt spending more than twenty dollars on a dress constituted financial delusion.)

Her parents would not have approved of the scant fifth-floor apartment she and Joseph called home. The ceiling in the kitchen had turned a septic brown from water leaks, and scabs of paint dangled over the table, ready to drift like dandruff over their meals. The dark oak floorboards in the living room were severely warped, sprouting loose nail heads that left the soles of her feet in a constant callus. But the worst was the heat. Even when she moved into the apartment in the bitter January cold, carrying box after box up five flights and tracking snow across the wood until most of her belongings sat in puddles, the rooms hung to their fever. That winter the windowpanes shriveled until they no longer sealed out the wind. But a few feet from the frosted glass, Del and Joseph danced to her collection of old records, sweating in shorts and stretched-out T-shirts, as if they alone had fallen into a billboard advertisement for a tropical time-share while the rest of the city was submerged in ice.

They used the air conditioner sparingly all summer. The mayor and the evening news warned of tri-borough blackouts. "They'll pull the power whether we use it or not," Joseph said, fingers threatening to engage the on-switch. "They're telling us this because Con Edison's already worked a few well-timed blackouts into their yearly budgets." "Don't be stupid," she replied. "They are afraid of mass revolts in the street. Can you imagine what crimes would go on if this city were left for a night in total darkness? Do you want to be stuck in an elevator for ten hours? It's serious, Joe."

She carried the glass down the hallway and into the living room, where she noticed the stereo's needle skipping on the last grooves of a record. *Her* stereo. Now *theirs*. The stereo had been one of her chief contributions to the mingling of appliances. She wondered how long it would be until those distinctions would dissolve, possessives failing to modify, *his* and *hers* being *ours* without the slightest impulse to claim. They never argued over drawers or closets or cabinet shelves. The fights they had about the heat or his juvenile actor friends could hardly be classified as arguments. Often when her voice hardened into the first signs of irritation, Joseph would draw a slow smile, nod his head in quiet concession, and let her opening assault be the last words on the issue. Madi always said that silence was the male form of hysteria, "All that quiet is just another way of screaming their dicks off." But Del couldn't help but be impressed by Joseph's composure, and usually her highly charged rage would suddenly transform into a hungry adrenaline, her lips guiding toward his mouth and her hands wrapping around his ears, and then she'd go hot for him, because he was so attractive when he didn't realize he had done anything to stop her dead in her tracks.

"Del," he called from the bedroom.

It amazed her how quickly the evening had returned to normal. The night she asked Joseph to marry her almost a month ago, she walked into the living room ready to supply him with a list of incentives. She had spent her subway ride home from the zoo merging love with legalities—"You see, I don't have to be tied to a working visa," she rehearsed, "You see, they can't kick me out of the country just because I feel like quitting. You see, I'd only be tied to you"—until those words almost reduced her to tears. She imagined him looking at her like an extinguished bulb, two eyes with popped filaments, skin the shade of gray glass, and her teeth chattered and her throat went dry. Why the hell would he agree? Why would anyone get married if they didn't have to? She asked him while she straddled his lap on the couch, unable to keep a cigarette from her mouth, and for the first time in all of their months as a couple, Joseph answered immediately without a single pause coming between them.

She entered the bedroom, letting go of that island where Dash still dwelled, climbing on to the warm, open stretch of their mattress. Joseph pulled off her clothes and lifted her pale, skinny body with its moles and snakebite scars on top of him. He put on a condom before he went into her, and she shifted her weight to trigger the little beast that goes loose in her brain. She wondered what made her think of Dash Winslow from eleven years ago, because he hadn't been the only love of her life. At one point, that had been Madi's older brother, Raj, who was even more disposed than Joseph to prolonged silences. It didn't matter who found her first or who claimed her the hardest. What mattered was who stayed on.

She watched Joseph's face contort, and she pushed her tongue between his teeth to fill his mouth with thanks. *This is home, this is my husband, this has been decided*, she thought.

CHAPTER TWO

"RUINED," WILLIAM ASTERNATHY said, hand propping the heavy weight of his head on the bar of the Hairy Bishop. He lifted a beer to his lips and took a slow sip, waiting for the impact of the word to register on his friend's face.

"Ruined," William repeated, licking the Heineken from his lips for added emphasis. "By a single decision. You don't leap over your mistakes and come off clean each time. You're going to have to pay the price."

Admittedly, this reaction to the news of Joseph's marriage did not go down as a high point of their friendship. But if love had sent Joseph bounding into the bar that afternoon, his grin the only warm pocket in the establishment, the more obdurate propeller of depression had brought William shuffling through midtown traffic to their once-a-week hideout. If he could convert depression into a form of electric energy, William figured he could generate enough power to run Hairy Bishop's greasy, time-lapsed jukebox clear into another decade. That his good friend, main competitor, and occasional scene partner chose to break the news of his marriage exactly three months to the day of William's own wife walking out on him did not help matters. Nor did it help that Joseph had stopped attending their Monday night acting class, thinking himself sufficiently schooled in his badly workshopped Brutus across from William's Cassius. What William had wanted to say when Joseph threw a rock through a perfectly decent afternoon of drinking was, "You think you can succeed where I failed? Good luck."

The ruined-life philosophy had come to him that morning by way of a PBS documentary on the dangers of scuba diving. William had woken at eight with the sunlight beating on his eyelids. His bedroom windows faced east, gathering greens and the first rays of dawn—an exotic and expensive luxury for most residents in the gargoyle-tiered building on Central Park West. But most residents weren't suffering from a tequila-shot hangover, trying to piece together the choppy memories of the night. William had attended a party in Tribeca. The host, Reef Mourasani, the sedentary shipping heir of a family that actually paid him not to embarrass them, had chosen to ring in his thirtieth birthday by inflating a giant neon-orange Moon Bounce castle in the center of his loft. William dutifully unlaced his shoes, climbed into the plastic air chamber, and somewhere between leaps became entangled with a young woman who worked at a Brooklyn recording studio. Fighting gravity and nausea, they jumped in lunar orbit and kissed until the entire structure began to deflate. They tumbled out onto the hardwood floor with keys and pocket change in their hair. William had been drunk enough to ask her back to his place, but by the time he ripped the condom wrapper open with his teeth and felt soft thigh muscles clamp around his waist, he had lost all interest in the intended goal. Which was to prove to himself that he still had this in him—sex or intimacy or at least the ability to be enveloped for extended minutes in another human being. His penis had already curled up for a night of unearned sleep, so he said as politely as he could muster, "Do you need cab fare back to Bushwick?"

"Use your finger," she had replied.

In bed that morning, his head hurt more when he closed his eyes, so he focused them on the blue underwater TV world of crenulated anemones and glistening fish. The controlled movement of the black-suited divers weighed down with oxygen tanks on the television was utterly quiet and delicately unhurried. They had settled into a slow breathing pattern that William copied, inhaling and exhaling as if preserving air for his own ascent into the day. Then the documentary flashed to the body of a female diver lying on the ocean floor, her wetsuit covered in white sediment like she had sunk decades ago and was being surveyed for whatever treasure remained in her hold. The voiceover explained that most scuba divers met their end from panic over a loose mask or a momentary chink in their breathing apparatus. "One simple mistake one hundred feet below the surface, and an inexperienced diver in a bout of panic, like this Caribbean vacationer, pays the ultimate price." For a second, the screen glimpsed her face, a skeletal jaw clenched in determination. In his hangover state, William figured the lesson to be learned was not to give in to panic. Brushing his teeth and glancing in the mirror at the broken blood vessels strung like Christmas lights under his eyes, he reassessed the scuba diver story, deciding that it definitely meant to be careful about making stupid mistakes. No mistakes = no panic. Although, fear of mistakes = possibility of panic all along. William rested his forehead against the mirror. For a man whose self-esteem relied so heavily on the power and performance of his body, he felt like time was finally grabbing hold of him and shaking him out for unsettled debts.

When he returned to the bedroom, divers were collecting the woman from the ocean floor, and he turned to the view of Central Park to prevent having to look at her face again. He smoked a joint while standing naked against the window, letting the ash fall on the hardwood, letting the sun warm muscles that still flexed under his tan, unwashed skin.

Right now, staring at Joseph on the neighboring barstool, his friend's clean, shaven skin and bright eyes the color of suburban swimming pools were resurrecting the hangover nausea of the sunlight that morning. Wasn't the premise of drinking in the daytime a tacit agreement not to feel ashamed for failing in the basics of personal hygiene? William could actually smell the flannel shirt he was wearing, the fetid armpits mixing with the nicotine stink of other people's cigarettes. No doubt, Joseph's new wife did his washing for him. She probably stood over him making sure that he brushed and moisturized. Certainly she picked out the cloyingly ironed polo shirt that was tucked into his jeans without the rumple of a gut, because, he could swear, Joseph actually looked like some glossed three-dimensional version of the headshot he carried to commercial auditions. Maybe Joseph had just come from an audition. That thought roused him with added resentment. As fellow actors living off any chance paying role that magically came their way, they could gauge their success off of each other. William mistook the fact that his friend wanted to drink a few beers in the middle of a Tuesday afternoon as a sign they were still on even ground.

"What part of your life with that woman was so lacking that you needed to fix it with a wedding?"

Joseph made a show of rolling his eyes. He slapped, not punched, his hand down on the counter. William always found a hint of effeminacy in Joseph's gestures, a result, he figured, of his friend growing up without a father.

"Nothing was lacking," he shot back. "She asked, I replied. As simple as that."

"Wait, she asked you? Jesus." William slammed his glass down in frustration. "I'm telling you this as a friend. The worst mistake I ever made was getting caught up in a few months of decent sex and free dinners. I did the math. I admit it. Jennifer was loaded. I had, what, about two hundred dollars in the bank? Of course I signed a prenup. They don't tell you in college that you're going to need to eat one day. There should be an obligatory minor in napkin folding, a seminar in flirting with older women. If those teachers had an ounce of responsibility they'd run into those acting classes warning everyone to quit and save themselves right away."

"If that's your concern, you can stop worrying," Joseph said, wiping strands of hair from his forehead. "Del's broke. Or just about. She works for the parks department. She makes me look rich."

"Where did you get money?" William asked, suddenly alert to a second indication that Joseph might be landing auditions that he hadn't even been called in for.

"Nowhere. What I was saying—"

"I know what you're saying." William tapped his fingers on Joseph's knee to prove that this sermon wasn't meant to provoke anger. "Look, I'm not trying to dampen the moment. If you two can make it work, I'd be the happiest. All I'm saying is, I've seen the other side. I know you think that this won't come back to bite you—"

"Don't you think it's time you got over it?"

"What's that?"

"Your divorce." Joseph said this so coolly it upset the balance of the room.

"We're separated," William clarified irritably. "Not divorced."

"If you don't like Del, that's fine. She isn't that fond of you either. But is it too much to ask for a simple congratulations?"

William struggled through the insult. He wasn't used to lectures from Joseph. In all the years of their friendship, William prided himself on being the wiser, street-minded one of the pair, the darker, tougher specialist in weathering setbacks and surviving the leaner years living as an actor in the city. The unchecked confidence in Joseph's voice suggested a sudden change in that dynamic, and William was not going down without at least dispensing some unwanted, utterly unpleasant advice about relationships. William had learned one essential fact about love: it always goes bad in the end. On this point, he was an expert.

"Think of your favorite song. What if someone told you that if you played it backward, a bizarre satanic message instructed you to blow up a children's hospital? Could you ever listen to that song the same way again? That's what coming through the other side of marriage sounds like—you can't forget the way it plays backward and the whole horrible message underneath. Love song, mutilated children, love song, children's body parts exploding through emergency room glass . . . "

Joseph grabbed a lime wedge from the garnishes on the bar and flicked it into William's chest. "You forget, it's already happened. So please shut up. At least now you know why you weren't invited."

William could remember clearly the moment he first met Joseph and how quickly he had become his confidant and, more importantly, his competition. They had turned the dark, septuagenarian-haunted

Hairy Bishop, with its patched plastic stools and permanent smoke halos around the stained-glass hanging lamps, into their hangout. William and Joseph only came to the bar together, and they had done so ever since they were introduced six years ago on the set of a low-budget horror movie. William had played the love interest of a biochemistry grad student who, for reasons not entirely clear in the script, had disturbed the forces of nature so drastically that it wiped out her friends with maniacal ease before spending a second hour having unprecedented difficulty doing away with her. At twenty-five, William's curly, black hair and brooding, angular face got him cast as the ultimate boyfriend with few speaking lines and gratuitous locker room scenes. Joseph had not been so lucky. Covered in Karo syrup, wearing a bodysuit sewn with stuffed birds, he sat drinking soup through a straw waiting to be pecked to death in front of the camera by a flock of crows springing out of a closet.

"At least you can see what kills you," William had said that night so many years ago when they bought each other consolatory rounds on these very same Hairy Bishop barstools. "I get murdered in a foot-ball field by a single gust of wind."

"There are no small death scenes," Joseph had offered feebly in reply.

But there were. Jennifer had left him bleeding from the nose the minute she cut from their relationship. They had spoken by phone twice since the breakup. Jennifer hung up the instant he started crying into the receiver. The second time, she used his name after each sentence. "I'm doing fine, William. I have a new place. Unlisted. Good-bye, William."

As long as he had known her, Jennifer had saved everything, packing it away—train tickets, matchbooks, postcards from college friends scattered into the sunsets of Yemen or Alabama to raise children or funds for women's rights organizations. Not just personal items, either. Her family had made its money in advertising, and she spent her inheritance on high-grade auction antiques. It was also Jennifer Ruben's money that floated them twelve flights above Central Park in a two bedroom decked out like Ali Baba's cave with an alarm system that spit out a litany of beeps the minute he opened the door. She always knew when he was coming home late. Jennifer, with eyebrows waxed and redrawn, with the high-school nose job that didn't hide her Jewish ancestry but revealed her family wealth, with her initials curled on her yellow robe, had saved everything. She kept her grandmother's pearls, the bridle of the horse she jumped as a child in Connecticut, the first flower that her second boyfriend had pinned to her prom dress right before he pinned her in the back seat of the limousine (that memory too was preserved with the boy's red cummerbund). But in those final moments, after William had decided to come clean about one sexual episode with an actress in a backstage bathroom, forming sentences carefully and then whining them stupidly and out of order, understanding as her knuckle hit his nose that those seconds would be the last of their marriage, he realized he had mistaken his wife for what he always thought her to be: someone who could never let go.

Now he lived alone surrounded by the debris of Jennifer's twenty-eight years, in an apartment that still technically belonged to her.

"It's really Jennifer who ruined my chances for all of the good parts," William said, waving a finger at the bartender who made no hurry to provide his regulars with refills. "I think that's what killed the marriage. She wouldn't give me any room to breathe in her own damned perfect life. She would read every script summary that came over the fax, checking it for sex scenes. Sex scenes! I was responsible for the sexual life of characters I hadn't yet tried out for."

"Of course, cheating on her had nothing to do with the split," Joseph intoned. He was no longer listening, exhausted by the information he already knew by heart. Sirens called his attention away as they swam across the windows.

"Men cheat. Women cheat. You'll cheat one day, or Del will. It's like death. You can't prepare yourself for it, you just have to accept that it's eventually going to happen."

Joseph downed the last of his beer. "Come on, aren't we both tired of feeling sorry for you? If you think your career is such shit, do something about it."

"I intend to," he said. The intoxication of two pints had marshaled some emergency supply of hope: beyond all of the sunlight pouring through the oily windows of the Hairy Bishop, opportunity did exist. His doorman was still accepting script deliveries, wasn't he? His e-mail account was still collecting messages. He and Joseph had the same agent. She was at her desk right now, wasn't she, presumably digging into projects invented fresh every hour?

"The problem is," Joseph said, as if this observation had been building force in his throat for a while, "you like to be taken care of."

William let that comment hang between them, pretending to roll it over in his head. What did Joseph know about women anyway? Del had pulled Joseph off of a market that had little interest in him to begin with. The guy hardly dated. His stories of one-night stands were so hopelessly banal, so cut and run, that William had to rethink his long-held opinion that the people who acted the most prudish in public were the world's dirtiest perverts when given a few hours alone. He had once checked his e-mail on Joseph's computer and covertly searched the Internet history expecting to find a flock of addresses guiding him to hardcore porn sites. All he found were conspiracy-theory chat rooms. It seemed so out of character for a man who listened to the stories William told without ever bothering to question their veracity that the discovery of 9/11 sites and Kennedy-mafia plots took on a more extreme perversion than snuff films would have. William chalked it up to boredom. Except for those Web sites, William's file on Joseph was so clean it was almost unnerving. Almost. He did know one thing, and he never dared to mention it. Joseph kept a loaded gun in a metal box underneath his bed. He found it the same way he found those Web sites: by snooping.

William wondered if Del knew about the conspiracy chat rooms. Or the gun. But maybe Joseph was right. Maybe William liked being taken care of too much. And maybe Joseph had simply learned how to take care of himself.

"Will you be honest with me?" William said, entangling his feet around the legs of Joseph's stool. His brown eyes were faded with worry. "Are you getting work? I mean, are you going out for auditions? Because I've got nothing."

"It's slow for everyone right now," Joseph replied. He must have understood that William's complaints had merely been a preamble to this admission of failure. "I'm up for a spot or two."

"Well, that's something." William once confided his deepest fears in Joseph, but over the years there had grown some kernel of distrust, of jealousy, a little seed that could almost be classified as hate. While William's career had sputtered and stalled through the last of his twenties, Joseph's had taken shape. His bland, generically handsome looks had suddenly found an interested audience, while William's darker, arrogant features started to read as too malevolent for toothpaste or greeting card spots. Like he was the kind of guy who couldn't be counted on to remember birthdays or dental appointments. There were carefully concealed moments of joy when Joseph failed to land a role he had worked hard for. For William, jealousy was a survival instinct. He didn't want Joseph destroyed, he simply wanted to beat him, to reach his arms out farther, to take what was there to be taken.

He paused, shaping his next thought while staring at the foam at the bottom of his glass. "What would you say if I told you I was thinking of moving to L.A. to start my career over?"

"You'll never leave," Joseph replied. "You've been living here too long to know what to do anywhere else."

"That's not what I wanted to hear," William said, suppressing a whimper that would have summarized all of the panic he felt since he saw the dead scuba diver on the television set that morning.

Joseph seemed to sense that panic anyway and stretched his arm out. "Come here," he said softly.

Two men hugging in an empty dive bar in the West Forties at 3:15 PM on a Tuesday afternoon was a strange sight even in a city of nine million. But they held on to each other briefly for dear life, like locked wrestlers taking a moment to catch their breaths, until the bartender carried over two cold beers and told them in a slow, incurious drawl that "this isn't that kind of place."

CHAPTER THREE

ONE MORNING FIVE months earlier, Joseph walked into the kitchen, poured a glass of water from the tap, and found a rat sitting on top of the stove, licking burnt cheese off one of the metal rings. He dropped the glass of water in the sink and sprinted down the hallway to alert Del. "A rat. In the kitchen. On the stove."

Del pushed the blankets aside and stumbled to the kitchen before his arms succeeded in rescuing her from the infestation of the floor. She returned a minute later wiping her palms.

"What happened?" he asked.

"I caught it between two pans," she said.

"And?"

"And threw it out the window. It was so drugged up on poison it barely fought me."

Joseph had hugged her tightly. He later realized, with deep embarrassment, it had been the first time he had pledged his love to Del. Whether or not the rat had brought on the confession, he meant what he said. He felt safe with her. Joseph had always felt safest by himself, but Del possessed a toughness emphasized in her dark, narrowed eyes and black sweep of hair that concentrated rooms to the rhythm she gave them. She didn't nag him. She took simple compliments as if he were speaking in tongues, throwing them off with a wave of her hand, only for him to find her a few minutes later smiling with the eraser-wide gap between her front teeth fully exposed. He knew himself to be lucky every morning he woke up next to her, astonished that she agreed to be lying in bed with him day after day. He tried to learn a few words of Greek, but she said the nasal of his Ohio accent was like a blanket thrown on a fire.

He had no intention of marrying her. In fact, his intention was to not get married. He simply liked that they were striving together, far more than two strangers operating on a survivalist's arrangement of shared groceries and rent. When Del asked him to marry her a month ago, Joseph understood that it wasn't just love that brought the question to her lips. He had witnessed Del in the midst of her darkest, most restless moods. She often sat on the sofa with her knees pressed against her chest, staring out of the window as the buildings across the street turned from blue to black. "Another day," she'd whisper to herself. "There it goes." He'd turn on music, pour her a drink to shake her from her thoughts, and only in the worst moments—usually two days into a work week—did she push him away and say angrily, "You can leave a job without walking out on the rest of your life. Why can't I do that?"

That was why he said yes to her that night a month ago. He didn't need Del to confess her reasons, just as he hadn't told her everything about himself. What Joseph wanted to say to William at the Hairy Bishop when his friend whined about his own wife walking out on him was this: "Did it ever occur to you that you shouldn't have told Jennifer everything? Did you ever think that once you told her the worst she had no choice but to leave you over it?" Of course, Joseph did want to tell Del everything. But he knew there were some secrets so damaging they blew holes in even the toughest terrain. He had read a story a year ago about a suicide bomber with explosives taped to his chest under his coat. At the last minute, the bomber changed his mind and was taken into custody by the police, who naturally had asked him to remove his coat. The bomber refused. He knew that if they saw the explosives they would shoot him on the spot.

Once the coat was opened, there would be no difference between the bomb and the man. Joseph purposely stopped reading before he discovered what had happened. But he could already guess. The only safe secret was one that remained concealed. He raced through midtown, sidestepping tourists and trying to fix the slight lurch from four beers with William. He was late for a meeting that he was very careful never to tell Del about.

"I SAVED A man once." The woman identified herself in the chat rooms of prisonersofearth.com as Miss Trust. At the basement meeting, under the buzzing fluorescent bulbs, she went by the less cryptic name of Rose. "He was crazy. A real lunatic, only you can't tell that by two arms waving in the water." She cleared her throat, attempted eye contact with the fourteen bodies slumped in metal folding chairs forming a loose double circle in the center of the room, and continued. "It was out at Coney Island last summer. I ran into the ocean and pulled him out of the waves. He must have weighed two hundred pounds with the water filling his pockets. I got him onto the beach and that's when I saw the donkey pin on his lapel and under it, a T-shirt that read A LEADER, FOR A CHANGE." Rose laughed nervously and wound a ringlet of her brown hair around the tip of her nose. "He thought he was Jimmy Carter. No kidding. Looked like him too, you know, that tender face of an overripe apple. He kept swearing on and on about Kissinger and embassy hostages in Tehran. 'Unfair,' he kept saying. 'Shame. They'll know Henry made a backdoor deal with Iran not to release them. They'll know I had no way out.' He started quoting some 1979 reelection speech and said he finally lost faith that our children would have a better tomorrow, and, when belief in the future died, why continue? Then he dug into his pocket and offered me a piece of paper with circles and arrows running all over the place. Said it proved the whole thing, you follow one arrow and you get around to all of them. Israel selling arms to Iran to destabilize Iraq, America selling arms to Iran to support the contras, Iran promising a payout totaling twelve billion, Israel angry about being strong-armed at Camp David, but mostly, all them—Begin, Reagan, Bush, the clerics, and

Kissinger conspiring to knock him out of office because he didn't get the greedier picture, because he just wanted fifty-two men to kiss their home soil again. By that time, a crowd on the beach had gathered around us, and an ambulance drove right onto the sand. Before the paramedics took him away, he grabbed me hard by the neck and said, 'There are no children of tomorrow. I was wrong. They grow up to be just like those monsters we call men today. I lost the election by telling the truth everyone knew. They won by telling lies nobody believed.'"

The audience shifted uncomfortably in their seats. A few worked their teeth on splintered fingernails.

"I guess you could say I saved a president," Rose said. "I brought that paper home, hung it with clothespins on my shower curtain, and put my blow dryer to it. In the end, all I got was a dry piece of paper with all of the words washed off. Here's the worst part. I called all the hospitals and the ambulance companies. There's no record of anyone being picked up in Coney Island and taken to the emergency room that afternoon. But I have that paper. They forgot to take that from me."

An elderly man who sat next to Rose placed a sympathetic hand on her knee, and all eyes drifted to over to Tobias X, leader and soothsaying blogger of prisonersofearth, to gauge his reaction. The verdict wasn't good. He puffed a quick channel of air from a graying beard that hung like an awning over his lips. The beard, along with a loose T-shirt soaked with chest sweat, gave Tobias the hybrid appearance of an American hostage or the late Jerry Garcia—a prisoner of enemy insurgents or an icon of bohemian freedom. He crossed his legs and gathered his small belly between his folded arms. "*They, they, they*. Who are they, Rose?"

"Tobias." A young man in a sleeveless Princeton sweatshirt raised his arm to reveal a mound of ginger pit fuzz. "They could be the current administration. They could be the Israeli secret police. Wouldn't be so credible for Israel to be supplying their enemies with—"

"Stop," Tobias yelled. "I will not have this meeting turned over to nonsense tales as a cheap form of entertainment. That pollutes our message. We are here specifically to posit conceivable detours,

possible ways in which our own government and their media development arm is purposefully deceiving the citizens of this planet. We
present truths against fiction. Not blank pieces of paper. That is how
you escape the prison."

"But all I have are my stories," Rose cried, pushing away the
calming hand. "You tell us not to trust the newspapers and the
commentators. Well, what the hell is left but our own stories?"

Still slightly drunk from the beers with William, Joseph sat
quietly in the second row where the suspicious stares of regulars had
less chance to settle on him. He had heard this debate erupt so many
times at the meeting—whom to trust, where the information was
coming from, what counted and what didn't. Those questions could
clog his brain for the rest of the afternoon. Joseph had been attending
these clandestine meetings—always in underground rooms of
community centers, locations changing but the bare cinderblock
walls with bulletin boards covered in flyers for dog-grooming classes
and substance-abuse hotlines predictably the same—for so many of
the years he had lived in New York. It wasn't because he believed
every irrational intrigue that got touted around these anonymous
circles. It was simply the value in the questions themselves—the
notion that the world turned with more sinister complications and
betrayals than it seemed to in the sober light of day. The conspiracies
lulled him. He found a strange consolation in these meetings.
Perhaps because they reminded him of home.

Joseph's mother had been a prophet of paranoia throughout his
childhood. She had once been a Catholic and had raised him the
same, but the religion that ruled their house was hardly monotheistic.
Joseph's mother prayed to conspiracies, making patron saints out of
plots and cover-ups and, as a tenured professor of American history,
the bizarre predictive pattern of dates. She had been a regular speaker
at conspiracy seminars, and Joseph could still remember attending
one of her speaking engagements when he was only six or seven, in
a small side room in Cincinnati's convention center off of Fountain
Square. The concrete walls had been covered in maroon muslin that
left the thirty dazed audience members holding weedy library books
and tattered newspapers synthetically pale under the bright overhead

lights. A flower show had just decamped, and the room must have been used for last-minute floral arranging because bits of green foam, plastic fern branches, and wilted white carnations littered the carpet like the aftermath of a summer storm. Joseph sat quietly in one of the foldout chairs by the emergency exit. He remembered his mother taking the stage, walking confidently toward the microphone in a brick-red dress. The applause flooded the room, and his mother fought a smile as she introduced herself. "Facts can suggest almost anything," she had begun. "But for those of us who make it our duty to study them carefully, they can tell us something very specific indeed. I am proposing that history does not simply illuminate where we have been. Logic does not come only in the backward glance. It can also shed light on where we are going. Definitive light. To misquote a fellow conspiracist, I say to you today, don't follow the money. Follow the years."

Joseph's mother thought years could predict what was to come. Joseph had left Cincinnati to get away from those voices predicting worst-case scenarios. But those frightening possibilities she had force-fed him too early started to accelerate in his mind until he couldn't outpace them, even in this city, hundreds of miles and years beyond her reach. That's when he started sitting in on these subterranean gatherings to listen to other men and women whose lives had been picked apart by questions that could only be answered by turning every fact upside down.

Joseph had never told Del how many hours he clocked listening to conspiracies. Del was not the sort of woman to take insanity with appreciation. She might have found the normalcy of these conspiracy theory regulars even more threatening: middle-aged men and women dressed in mismatched sweat suits with greasy hair, clinging to their notebooks and watching from their corners with squinted eyes as if badly in need of prescription glasses. A few college students— arrogant, supple faces with vehement nods that they had learned to perform in their undergraduate seminars—filled out the number. Joseph figured that a few decades ago this faction could have taken to the streets in a Vietnam protest but now existed mostly in the freefall of Internet space, typing their dissent and waiting to voice their exposures in secret unrecorded meetings where full names were not allowed.

Tobias had begun as he always did. "We are a small group willing to ask questions," he said. "There are some new faces here, and we must try to be welcoming. When so few in the American population are willing to ask questions and remember the answers supplied, we are thankful to gain participants. That said—"

"We don't want strangers sniffing around for trouble," Tobias's ruddy-faced second-in-command interjected. He went by the code name Gorilla, and dense black hair covered his body where his denim overalls did not. "No tape recorders. No cameras. No last names."

The group nodded with complying smiles.

"Asking questions can be dangerous," Tobias continued. "Unfortunately, in this time where identifying real from unreal is so crucial and explosive, we are forced to keep ourselves far from direct sunlight. Personal privacy is a necessary safety measure for public examination."

Rose had waited a good ten minutes to tell her Jimmy Carter story, during which Gorilla reported at length his six-year research into the morning of 9/11. He counted the exact number of Arab-owned newsstands that had been inexplicably closed in the hours before the attack and compared it to the number of Jewish-owned stores in the Financial District that had also been shuttered (side note: three gay video stores in the West Village, forming a tight geometric triangle, had all mysteriously been closed that morning). Defeated by the outcome, which suggested that neither camp knew an attack was imminent, Gorilla explained that he was now accumulating new statistics on why certain flights from JFK to various South American capitals had been heavily booked in the weeks before the collapse. "One name. Chavez. And his Bohemian Grove of capitalist pseudo-socialist Latin leaders sitting on their own oil reserves, happy to see blowout in the Middle East. No one has bothered to look in that direction yet."

Tobias scratched his chin despondently, sensing derision in his own derision camp. "That's an interesting perspective. But please do not stop thinking about an inside job. I'm convinced about the smoke clouds in the lower part of the tower. I'm convinced about explosive devices. Does anyone have any new findings on the engineering studies coming out of MIT?"

The mantra of prisonersofearth was that the U.S. government had planned the attacks. The White House saw those two New York towers as a tuning fork that needed to be struck in order to bring the entire country in key—and, of course, that key was a hymn of patriotism disguised to start new wars. Joseph heard many skeptics joke behind Tobias's back that it was just like the bloated American ego to try to take credit for even its own national disasters. But Tobias wouldn't hear any of it. The problem with Rose's story, Joseph realized, was that it pulled focus away from 9/11, the massive expanding subject that had recharged the conspiracy community and shelved all tangled, over-farmed theories on Kennedy, Vietnam, and even the New World Order as tired riddles no longer worth dissection unless they pointed to that bright September morning. Tobias clearly did not want to get bogged down with Kissinger. But the Reagan-Iran nexus, in such little circulation and thus as rare as two-dollar bills, suddenly caused a wave of alert voices and craning necks among the prisonersofearth.

"It brings up a good point," said a woman sitting just behind Rose whom Joseph hadn't noticed before. "Isn't there talk that Ahmadinejad was a leader of the radicals who held those Americans hostage in 1979? If he had an underground connection with Bush Senior—"

"Bullshit," Tobias wheezed, glowering angrily at this unfamiliar visitor. "We're getting off point here."

"That's hardly off point," the young man in the Princeton sweatshirt argued, emboldened by another voice in the wilderness. "If we've had secret deals with Iran in the past, and we have, then it could be said our sworn enemies could actually still be in the government's corner. I've seen things on the Web, listings of dates and locations where members of the president's cabinet have been in the same hotels in Madrid and Prague at precisely the same time as key foreign ministers in our Axis of Evil. That's a mighty fine coincidence."

"Did you bring that information with you?"

"No . . . I, uh, just read it online somewhere."

Tobias slammed his foot against the concrete floor and launched into his warning about the duplicity of coincidence. "I don't give a fuck about coincidences unless they lead us to something real. The history of the world is draped in coincidence. That is what separates the brothers and sisters of prisonersofearth from the other mind jockeys trying to discredit the movement with unverified information. Do I have to spell it out for you? We must remain skeptical jurists. No, we must take every report and read it as if it were a lawsuit filed against us. This and only this is the way to escape the prison."

Joseph stopped listening. He was watching the newcomer behind Rose's shoulder who had spoken once, clearing the graying blond hair from her face before retreating back into its shadows. Her features were small and fragile, with traces of makeup carefully applied to preserve the beauty that must have come to her naturally in youth. Not so unlike his mother, he thought, who had cut such a striking, fastidious figure in the hallways of the Catholic college where she taught—her own red lips and black eyes drawn with a surgeon's precision amid her straight brown hair—that it took the deans far too long to suspect the fanatical lessons she was bestowing on her students. Joseph could see a fitted beige suit coat and, from behind Rose's legs, two high heels that didn't read of nights spent in a cramped tenement apartment memorizing heretical plots by disgraced history professors. The woman put her fingers to her eyelids as if they ached from an earlier strain. A small wine-stain birthmark peeked from under the collar of her shirt when she stretched her neck. She had the polish of money and social obligations. When she opened her eyes, Joseph tried to smile at her, lifting his eyebrows in empathy, but by then Tobias had stormed from his seat and everyone was getting up to leave. Joseph grabbed his bag, tripping over the metal chairs in his path, and saw the woman tossing a quilted black purse over her left shoulder. He felt some urge to follow her, maybe even introduce himself or at least watch her slip into the crowds that ascended up Broadway in the rush for the subway. She looked too sane to be here and maybe also in some other part of the city her life was simple and complete. Her presence made the group seem redeemable and also, by comparison, less so.

He scrambled around the side table to make a break for the door, pushing by one of the college students who gathered leftover coffee cups into a ziploc bag. At the end of the table, he found a slender white hand covered in freckles opening to meet him. Disappointingly, the hand belonged to Rose.

"You were staring at me," she said, as she grabbed Joseph's fingers tightly and held on to his thumb. He didn't know how to tell her that he was looking behind her. "I appreciate you supporting me like that. Tobias can be terribly cruel, and I wouldn't come here at all if he weren't also so terrifyingly correct. But you know what I mean. I've seen you here. A few times."

"Nice to meet you," he said, forcing a smile while once again looking past her at the woman in the beige jacket who was now retreating into the hall.

"He's really good about the pharmaceutical companies, too bad we didn't get to them. I told him he should write a book. He says they'd try to kill him if he ever published anything they could trace."

He sighed and looked down at her, the poor hopeless woman with yellow teeth and corkscrewed hair going in every direction but down. She wore a pilled wool pullover, which left her skin flushed. She smelled of the smoke that clings to bedsheets.

"What brings you here?" she asked.

"Curiosity."

She shook her head.

"You don't have to lie to me. Something must have spooked you. Do you have a relative in the military? Did you meet someone on the roof of your building one night who said they were just fixing the cable? No one comes to these things, unless they've touched something invisible." She coughed and wiped her mouth. "Do you know what that feels like? To touch something invisible?"

"I really have to run," Joseph said with a faded smile. "My friend's outside."

"It feels like teeth on the back of your neck."

He glanced again at the doorway, disappointed to find no trace of the woman lingering behind. He now understood the real danger of these meetings. Lonely people came to them.

"So, what's your name, if you don't mind?" she asked coyly. He might have read her eagerness as flirtation in any other environment than this one. "Unlike Tobias, I don't think strangers tell better secrets."

"My name?" he replied, stalling.

"Yes. I'm Rose Cherami."

He paused as she waited expectantly.

"William Asternathy," Joseph said, realizing how much William would detest counting himself among the lost company of prisonersofearth. But it was the first name that came to his lips. The lights went dark in the basement conference room, and Joseph scrambled past her, escaping up the stairs to the street. He hailed a cab and gave his address, watching the blurred sidewalk as the car traveled south into the quiet sanctuary of the Village. He could be Joseph again now, the simpler version, an actor with nothing to hide.

CHAPTER FOUR

GOOGLE DELPHINE KOUSAVOS. An Internet examination of her life comes down to three entries. One cites her and Madi attending an alumni cocktail reception together two years ago at Columbia's Schermerhorn Hall in the Class of 1997 "What Are You Lions Up To?" pages. Another leads to a picture of her with Joseph at the opening of an independent film festival in Tribeca. It's not a bad photo either. She's standing next to Joseph in a cream Balenciaga dress with beige leather heels that elongate her legs, and her skin is tan from an afternoon lying in the Central Park sun. She's not really the focus of that photograph, Joseph is, stopping in front of the flurry of cameras in the lull of far more famous arrivals. Isolate Delphine Kousavos's career hits, and she appears on Google once. She's listed under the junior staff for the Bronx Reptile Department, a title from which she was promoted a year ago to "staff," although it had yet to be acknowledged on the zoo's "About Us" pages. Del often used the lab's communal computer on her lunch breaks to type in the names of lost friends and previous coworkers to find some clue of where their lives had taken them. But she sincerely hoped that no one from her past bothered to hunt for her name in return. Forget Google, she finally decided. Who cares about immortality in Internet space? Del refused to waste her free hours searching for herself anymore.

She usually spent her lunch hour out of the cafeteria, preferring the luxurious frostbitten rooms of the "Animals of the Antarctic" exhibition. She waited the hour in the shadows, opposite the penguins mating on plastic ice floes and a baby elephant seal resting his chin on a pile of fish carcasses. Before the exhibition opened, even before the cooling systems had been turned on high, she enjoyed watching the set designers reconstruct the cold barren arctic in silver paints and mesh netting. Assembled out of high-school art supplies, this brutal Ice Age gave her a moment of peace as if she had temporarily slipped beyond the reaches of the clock and its slow count to closing time.

Del had never ridden the African Safari Train that threaded the entire geography of the zoo, but she knew enough about the institution to promise, after her first month there, that she would not remain bound by a working visa and a critically low paycheck for more than a year. "I know when I'm being taken for slave labor," she had confided to a colleague from Louisiana who was the department's authority on water moccasins. Her friend eventually quit after being bitten not by a snake but by an inner city youth caught spitting in the crocodile pond. That was seven years ago, and Del was still in the same exact place. She had not told her boss, Dr. Abrams, that her visa status had changed in recent days, and he had naturally not noticed the ring. Abrams did not notice how late she stayed at night in the department lab balming the cracked epidermis of a diseased corn snake named Welbutrin. In fact, all Abrams ever noticed besides her thighs and breasts was the disproportionate amount of time she spent mothering the rattlesnakes.

"I hope those notes are for *our* files," Abrams would say, creeping up behind her to try to catch a glimpse at her notebook. "Because I'm sure you're aware we have a policy against independent studies. I don't need to tell you that it's not in the interests of the animals here to double as guinea pigs."

"No, you don't," she'd respond, snapping her notebook shut.

"We're a team in this department," he'd lecture, grabbing his raincoat from the communal rack. "It doesn't matter what college you went to. We all abide by the same rules. They're maintained for the safety of the collection."

In her years at the zoo, Del had perfected the fine art of the sarcastic smile, which, if executed properly, punctuated every sentence with "asshole" just before the period. "Have a wonderful evening," she said, smiling.

In the late afternoon, Del returned from fake Antarctica, pressing send on a text message to Madi: "I need the number of that green card specialist ASAP. Losing my mind." Madi swore she had the contact for the best immigration lawyer in town. As Del barreled through the darkened rooms of the reptile hall, she felt the vibration of a reply: "Sending now," Madi wrote. "Want me to phone in a bomb threat?"

Del hurried toward the staff door marked DANGER LIVE LAB in the carpeted black shadows of the exhibition hall. She avoided eye contact from visitors who often stopped anyone wearing a canvas jumpsuit to lodge a complaint about stroller accessibility or to demand detailed explanations on the feeding procedure of carnivores. Del used her hip to open the heavy metal door, and the bright fluorescent lights of the lab scrambled her vision. She pinched her eyes, and that was when she heard a scream rising from the inner offices.

Not a soft scream, not a token gesture. A scream that meant what it sounded like.

Del rushed down the hallway, broke through the lab's set of swinging doors, and saw five of her coworkers slowly backing away from something on the other side of the center island. Her eyes then passed to Francine Choi, standing glued to the far wall with her left leg raised almost to her stomach. The scream came from Francine, and her mouth had kept the shape of that cry, with eyes open so wide her black irises were marooned in lakes of white. Something was keeping her frozen there. Del whistled at Kip, the playboy of the junior staff with his vertiginously stiff red pompadour. He turned his head and mouthed, "Get the shovel."

Del lifted the heavy, steel shovel from its wall hook and held it upright, gripping the handle, as she darted around the island. There Del saw what everyone was staring at, the beautiful four-year-old

western diamondback, curled in a writhing figure eight on the linoleum floor, her head coiled back in the pre-striking rhythm less than
a foot from Francine's ankle.

"I can get her with the hook," Del said, about to drop the shovel,
but Francine screamed again—almost angrily now, because she must
have guessed that Del would rather save this animal, this particular
specimen of any other in the entire collection, than lose her if
there was any chance of recovery. The diamondback's neck jutted
backwards. That move was unmistakable. It's the backfire just before
the bullet leaves the barrel. Del could feel her own heart rip inside
of her—*fuck, fuck, fuck, fuck, no, no, no*—as the snake's fangs arched
out from the lower jaw, and the neck hurtled forward. Del swung,
crashing the shovel's weight down on the diamondback's head. She
had no choice.

The blow shattered the skull, her mouth oozing puss and broken
teeth across the linoleum. The shovel fell away from Del's hands.
Francine's left sneaker returned to meet her right one on the floor.

"Oh my god, Del. I'm *so sorry*," Francine wailed as she tiptoed
around the dead snake and fell against the chest of one of the older
keepers. "I was just holding her. I wanted to feel the babies in the
stomach, and she dropped."

The fact of the babies came to Del in a flash. Leto was seven months
pregnant, not the prize of the department, but Del's favorite and the
subject of her many notebooks intended to be used one day to create
the backbone of a book on rattlesnake mothers. She stared down at
the snake's bloated body on the floor and dropped to her knees in
front of it, pushing away the tears that clotted her eyes.

"It started striking. You had to do it." Francine looked around at the
other keepers for support. "That's code. Well, she had to, didn't she?"

Del glared up at her.

"Why were you holding her without a hook?" she yelled. "Why
were you holding her at all?" But Del didn't wait for those answers.
Her fingers massaged the soft, limp stomach, still wet and glistening
with the pattern of sand-blown diamonds, feeling for the pouch of
eggs in the oviducts. Even with her fingers shaking, Del knew what
she had to do. She would try to save them. She would try to rescue

the embryos trapped in the uterus that, even if alive, would never find their own way out of their mother by themselves. Kip reached over the counter and handed her a scalpel, and she sliced Leto down the side, cut the damp distended belly open, and wedged her fingers inside.

"They're coming," she said to Kip. "I can get them."

Ten babies were cut from Leto's side in ten minutes. Ten frail slivers lying like ribbons on the linoleum floor. Nine dead fetuses to be burned in the zoo incinerator along with their mother, according to code. But one, at the breaking of its egg, bright as a yolk, slipped gradually from its sac and started breathing, a mere three inches of black cord. Del lifted the baby with her fingers into a small plexiglass terrarium that Kip held out in front of her. "Be careful," she warned him. "This one has all the poison he needs already in his cheeks."

When Del stood up, wiping the snake's amniotic fluid off her hands and staring at the baby coiled at the bottom of the clear container, the tears returned. She didn't know if the tears were for killing Leto or for saving something counted as lost. She looked around for Francine, but the young zookeeper had disappeared, running for fresh air outside in the park. Kip stretched the department phone, tethered to its extra-long cord, over the counter and handed it to her. Suddenly she was speaking to Abrams, who was demanding a full account of the matter and belching in anger over the loss of a specimen.

Abrams didn't congratulate her. Instead he railed on about the canker of his dwindling staff, Francine Choi. Had she not followed regulations? Had she not heeded the signs, learned the drill, used a metal clamp instead of bare fingers to transport a viper? Didn't she know a pregnant mother was particularly susceptible to distemper? Did she know what kind of politics were involved with killing an animal on zoo grounds? "It's an embarrassment," he moaned. Del considered ratting out the young keeper who had entered the department a month ago and had since failed in pretty much every way possible. But her allegiances were not with Abrams, not even in this moment of silent acknowledgement that passed over the telephone. She knew that Francine was an immigrant too, brought over from Korea on the promise of an American visa. Once they have you, they have you. And if you mess up, there's the airplane home.

"It didn't go down like that," Del replied, trying to sound impartial, even though Kip was already wrapping Leto in a plastic tarp with her nine dead infants. "It was an accident, and there was no way of saving her. I'll talk to Francine about it."

He said he'd see her Monday early. He'd want to inspect the baby himself.

When she hung up the phone, Kip grabbed her by the arms while he made the sound of an arena-sized roar.

"You're amazing, you know that?"

"I killed an animal that belongs to the zoo," she replied tiredly. "I'm not feeling too exhilarated right now."

"You know what's funny? If this were any other department except maybe insects, we'd be on the news. If you shot a pregnant tiger, the public would care, and there'd be red tape for days."

"I cared. Leto was mine."

"You should have let her take Fran out," Kip joked. "One good bite would have taught her a lesson."

"Shit, what time is it?" Del searched her pocket for her cell phone. "I have to change. I've got a date."

"I thought you already had a boyfriend," Kip said, while fondling her hand. "You trying to make me jealous?"

"It's not that kind of date."

Before Del left that evening, she took a note card from the cabinet and wrote APOLLO, CROTALUS ATROX in black marker before attaching it with tape to the plastic top of the terrarium. The sticky little body curled against the corner, but she was relieved to see it breathing. No matter how traumatic her day had been, it didn't match his. You can see it in animals better than in human babies: that stunned, determined look of taking up space in the world. *Apollo*, she thought, tapping her nail against the glass. *Welcome to the Bronx.*

WHEN THE SETTING sun gutterballed between the East–West streets of downtown Manhattan, Del had to be careful about keeping her head in check. It wasn't just the speeding front bumpers of taxis she had to watch out for while crossing the street, it was the past that could slam into her and send her spinning violently through the air.

It occurred to her that only the ring on her finger separated her from a phantom version who had walked these same blocks after work every evening through Chelsea almost a year ago. As always, her eyes traveled through the windows of the brownstones between Ninth and Tenth Avenues. The flower boxed frames were surprisingly free of curtains to allow full-on flasher views of oak bookcases, crystal chandeliers, Ed Ruscha single-word paintings, and all the fine possessions that Wall Street executives made it their hobby to collect. She heard the chime of plates being dealt across tables and saw housekeepers plugging white candles into thick, silver sticks. It amazed her that these West Chelsea lives could be so clean, so secure in their own habits, that they didn't find the constant stares from outsiders a threat. At Columbia, she had spent her sophomore year in one insanely small L-shaped dorm room, whose single window opened onto an apartment building of competing rectangles. It had taken her months to remember to keep her shades closed when she dressed. Once she saw a hirsute young man masturbating in a window across from hers, and she stood there watching him, hoping he'd see her but also fascinated by the furious arm pumping his fantasies through an afternoon rainstorm. When he did finally look over, perhaps searching for a glimpse of naked bodies compartmentalized in university housing, teenage torsos glowing in their lit windows like insects trapped in amber, she waved.

She wondered if Joseph masturbated when she wasn't at home. If he chain-locked the front door and walked into their bedroom with his pants cuffed around his ankles. Sex with Joseph. The urgency of his pale body fumbling over her as if constantly trying to find a better position like a nervous mountain climber unsure of the distance to the summit. She had no complaints. Even if a guy was a disaster in bed, she could usually find a meeting point with him, learn to adapt to the geography of his body, discovering the softness of his chest hair or the sensitivity of his neck, because everyone took on extra dimensions when they were naked. Everyone had secret avenues and unwelcoming slums and unexpected detours of scars and muscles hidden when the clothes went on.

But to be honest, she had preferred sex with Raj.

This familiar walk to the West Side Highway where the brownstones dissolved into car washes and art galleries reminded her of their old routine: entering his studio with the wood floors glowing purple at sunset and Raj sitting shirtless at his desk, staring at photographs with a glass loop in his hand. Del would creep over to him, prizing the silence, the slight weep of the floorboards under her shoes, the clink of her keys on the dresser, the echoing motors speeding along the Hudson River. She'd slide her fingers over his collarbone, sharp as a coat hanger and strangely hot, his skin was always so relentlessly warm, and he'd drop the loop and soon they would be naked on the floor glowing purple themselves. Raj had what she always called *doomed eyes*. They were delicately ice blue, encased in baggy brown lids from his father's Indian ancestry, almost fluorescent but filled with a sadness so disarming that she often wondered, even as he worked his penis into her, if pleasure for him stemmed more from a sudden lack of pain than from the spasms firing down his back. Maybe that's what made sex with Raj so memorable. There was a sense of temporary relief, a sense that she was helping him.

She stepped over a collection of cardboard boxes and blankets on the sidewalk, unable to determine whether someone was sleeping underneath them. She did not use the key Raj had given her when they had been a couple, although it still drifted somewhere at the bottom of her purse. Instead she rang the buzzer—a sure marker that their relationship had turned a corner in the year since their breakup.

"Hello?"

"It's Del," she said, and the door gave.

Raj was not shirtless. He was dressed in a yellow button-down with a coffee stain smeared on the collar and loose khaki pants worn to holes in the knees. His hair had grown long and curly, fraying over his ears like a man much younger than his age. As he leaned into her at the door, she deflected a kiss that landed on her left ear.

"Well," he said, recovering from the rejection with a grin. He waved his arm back to welcome her in. "Late as usual. Glad to see some things don't change. You don't come over this way much anymore."

"There aren't many reasons to."

"Has it been too long to ask how your day was?"

She considered telling him about the rattlesnake as she paused for a moment just inside the hallway. She didn't know how to begin and felt that Raj was already studying her, probably determining how different she looked from the last time he had seen her almost a year ago. She swept her hand over her forehead, intentionally blocking a direct view of her face. But she was also looking for what had changed as she walked past him into the studio. His place had undergone a few renovations since she last visited. A black couch replaced two broken armchairs by the window. A bulbous metal light shone on a number of photographs tacked to the wall—interior shots in Raj's style: cold uninhabited rooms of chilly modern design. A wire bird-cage and two empty leather trunks were stacked in the far corner. Sentimental junk was not his aesthetic, and she wondered if someone else had been around the past few months renovating his room with her own sense of what a home should look like.

"My day?" she said to pick up a strand of conversation. "I texted with Madi."

"Texting with my sister is wiser than talking to her on the phone," he laughed. "She won't shut up. Right now she's big on trying to talk me into going with her on a business trip to India. 'Come on, Raj,' she whines. 'Let's go see our homeland. I'll pay for you. You can take pictures.' I keep telling her, 'Madi, we were born in Ft. Lauderdale. If you want to see where we came from, turn on MTV *Spring Break*.' Anyway, how's work? You still unhappy?"

"Of course," she said and instinctively reached into her purse for her rolling papers.

"Ah, the slow cancer of a nine-to-five." He put his hands on her shoulders, and she felt the heat of his palms through her shirt. "You want a drink? I still have one of your whiskey bottles around here saved just in case."

"No, I'm fine. I'm afraid a drink might knock me out."

He shook his head and retreated into the kitchen to pour her a glass of water.

The studio was still organized in Raj's maniacally clean but dusty fashion. Photographs, contact sheets, and blunt red pencils flooded his desk. A sagging pole that hung across the ceiling created a waterfall of sport coats, wrinkled shirtsleeves, and pant legs. His sunken mattress still lay without a frame on the floor.

She licked the sweat from her upper lip and stared out the window at the cars, half in headlights, rushing in both directions along the West Side Highway.

"Could it be any hotter in here?" she yelled. "No wonder you don't get many visits." She wanted to say *why don't you move*, but this was an old complaint that she no longer had the right to make. One of the reasons she had broken it off with Raj was the agony of having to spend all of their time together in this tiny rented studio, as if stepping outside for dinner or a drink would have wrecked Raj's delicate sense of reality. The entire duration of their relationship consisted of actions in this five-hundred-foot square—a cliche of a bachelor pad that she had endured to constitute coupledom. It was here that they slept and ate and mixed toiletries like warring chess pieces. Once, on an off chance, she had brought up finding a new place, something together, and Raj had turned and stared at her with those cold, blue eyes and said it would be difficult for him to live full-time with someone, even her, but he'd consider it. She knew he never would.

The day she broke up with him, she had picked up his camera, focused the lens, and snapped three shots of Raj rubbing his hands in one of the now absent armchairs. She thought that when he developed those pictures he might recognize them as his last moments with her, right before the inevitable, before she grabbed the bras and underwear and tampons she kept in the top drawer and blew out once and for all. She wondered now if he had ever bothered to look at those pictures of himself—a thirty-five-year-old adolescent defending his own space against any intrusions.

She pulled a rolling paper from the packet and sprinkled the tobacco grains.

"You can't smoke in here," he said when he returned from the kitchen, setting the glass of water on the desk.

"Since when?"

"New rule. Sorry." He smiled.

"God, you're just like the mayor now. Can't smoke in bars, can't smoke in subway stations. Can I ask, why do they even bother selling me these cigarettes if there's no place I can smoke them?"

"It's bad for you," he said softly, placing his dark, calloused fingers over her own. "You should quit."

She placed the cigarette in her mouth, squinted defiantly at him, and went for the lighter in her pocket. Before she could free her hand, Raj snatched the cigarette from her teeth and replaced it with his lips. She let his tongue move across her own. Just for a second. His fingers reached for her bra strap, and that enormous warmth he stored inside of him hit her.

"Stop." She wrestled her hands between their bodies and shoved him back. "What was that for?"

"Did that bother you?" he said, spinning around to gather his balance before dropping onto the couch. "It hasn't been that long, has it?"

"Yeah, it has."

"Don't tell me you're still dating that actor."

"Raj," she said, and it took courage to complete the next sentence but there was no escaping it. If she didn't tell him right now, she would never summon the nerve. "We got married."

"Married." He clenched his fingers on the armrest.

"Things change," she said, hating the triviality of those words as soon as she heard them leave her mouth. "You and I haven't talked for a while."

Raj dug his tongue into his cheek and then brought his chin back up to face her.

"You did it for the green card. I get it. So you did find a way to quit your job."

"I figured you'd hear about it sooner or later from Madi, so I thought it would be better to hear it from me."

"God, that was fast."

"It wasn't only for the green card, Raj. And I didn't pay him, if that's your next question. You don't have to be insulting."

"I'm insulting?" His voice had finally caught up to his anger, but it was louder than she expected, as if in all this time alone in his studio he had forgotten the advantages of keeping his feelings close to his chest. "Is this why you came over?"

"I don't know why I came over. You called and asked me to, so I did."

But she did know why. She had come over to do what adults can do to each other: behave like children. She wanted Raj to feel the extent to which things had changed. She wanted him to understand that people can walk out one day and be lost for good. Because relationships never end, do they? All that built-up energy has to go somewhere. But now, as her presence in his apartment felt even more intrusive, she hated herself for the weakness of wanting to tell him the news face to face.

She moved to pick up the cigarette off the floor, but it signaled a faster reaction in Raj. He lifted himself from the couch, struggling harder than a man of his age should, and stood looking at her with those two magnificent glaciers of ice on either side of his nose and his lip snarled upward. He reached his arm out and for a second she thought he might be moving to hit her. Instead he grabbed the cigarette from her mouth and snapped it in half with his thumb.

"You can't smoke in here. How many times do I have to tell you?"

"Fine," she said in a restrained tone she hoped he would copy. "What about you? Are you seeing anyone? Is there a girl hiding in the stairwell, waiting for me to go?"

Madi had told her a few months back that Raj had gone on a few dates with an Italian translator at the U.N. with long black hair much like her own. Nothing had come of it, but Del had been touched with the thought that lovers were as compulsive as serial killers. They couldn't help tripping over their own patterns, falling for the same type.

"Don't ask me a question like that," he said harshly. "We all don't have to be happy, and I'm not going stand here trying to prove to you that I am."

The last rays of sun were throwing him in shadow against the window, and Del resisted the urge to step closer to gauge the expression on his face.

Instead, she walked over to Raj's mattress resting on the floor in the far corner under the canopy of his clothes. She sat on its edge with her knees bundled against her breasts. "I don't know what I'm doing here. I'm sorry. I had a terrible day."

"Don't you have a husband you should be telling this to?"

The same faded green quilt still covered the bed. It was torn so that the patches hung from their stitching like a collection of unsealed envelopes. Raj always said the quilt smelled of gasoline because his mother had sewn it while working nights at a twenty-four-hour service station outside of Miami when he was a kid. Del leaned back and pressed her face into the thin fabric. The quilt smelled of curry, not gasoline, the bed being the closest thing to a dinner table Raj owned. When they dated, he even lit candles and set silverware across it, using the wedge between the pillows as a bottle holder. They had sex on wine stains. She often stopped mid-foreplay to wipe crumbs off of her ass.

"I'm just tired," she said.

"Didn't anyone warn you about married life? It makes you old fast. My mom always said that. But only after the divorce."

She stood up and reached for her purse. She waited for him to stop her from leaving, but he didn't. He leaned against the window-sill watching her go with his arms crossed over his chest. The smell of gasoline filled her nostrils. Engines burned along the highway outside the window. She had made her peace with Dash on the night of her wedding. Now she was saying good-bye to Raj. She was extinguishing the past one ghost at a time.

CHAPTER FIVE

ONCE, RAJ TRAVELED the world. Call Vienna, he was there two days ago. Try to reach him in Berlin, he'd just left. He'd be on the stopover in Shanghai, ten hours of airport shopping and a nap in the passenger's lounge and then a small turbojet over the Himalayas where the gas masks fell from the ceiling and every tooth filling jittered but no one panicked because they were all staring down at the face of Mt. Everest. He hit São Paolo, the Amalfi Coast, home for two days, then Dubrovnik, Bahrain, back home as a pit stop to pay the electric bill before Vancouver, on to Fairbanks, skirting over the cocaine-line Straits into Russia. Raj had become a photographer, he so often thought, from a love of stillness. Vases, trees, dust—whatever the camera caught, it held. But, in supreme artistic irony, the job of photography offered few similarities with the final product. His twenties had been spent in constant mule-backed motion—lugging his equipment all over town, wheezing up five flights of stairs for an assignment to shoot three piano progenies in a Queens living room, hanging over the ledge of a roof to snap a suicide from the vantage point where a mother of four, now splayed under a nylon tarp on Seventy-Second Street, lost her balance on purpose. Then the world came calling—bigger tragedies, better heartbreaks, prettier views. He shot for an extravagant travel magazine and a human interest periodical, carting his camera all over the globe, sweeping through exotic locales on two-day timetables, shooting, here, children holding glue bottles caked in snot, and, there, a waterfall descending into mist. Raj had devoted all of his muscles to freezing images, until his thirtieth birthday, when his muscles froze, his agent screamed, and he stopped.

On the morning of his thirtieth birthday, three years before he started dating Del, he sat on his mattress with a box of granola, a pint of skim milk, and a plastic spoon. Two days later he could be found in practically the same position, the milk sour, the cereal stale, and the answering machine blinking on overdrive. He shook uncontrollably at the thought of boarding a plane. He refused to let go of the spoon in his hand. He refused to let an open window wipe the dust from the air. He sat in the frame of his bed, matted with his own green quilt. He had taken his picture, and there he hung in his apartment indefinitely.

On day two, the front door opened, and feet stomped worryingly down the hallway. He was discovered by his then twenty-six-year-old sister, who wore a red sari layered around her shoulders and white denim pants flared like yacht sails at the ankles. She walked into the studio, at first overtaken with the smell of rotting dairy, went directly to the windows where she freed the trapped air and lost a fight with the metal blinds that refused to gather, and screamed when she turned to find her older brother lying as still as death in his bed.

Madi wrestled the utensil from his grip, threw a glass of cold water on his face (she admitted later that she had always wanted to do that to someone and she couldn't resist the opportunity), and then, with a corrective smile, wished him a belated happy birthday. She opened the greeting card envelope, still wet from her tongue, and placed the card in his hands. Then she blew up a purple balloon and tossed it wobbling into the air.

"Raj," she sighed from the edge of his bed. "This can't be your response to turning thirty. Tell me there's a better reason for the crack-up. I mean, you were never really fun the last decade anyway, so this can't be some fear about your youth slipping away."

"I have decided . . . " They both waited, but he couldn't finish the sentence.

"Decided? To urinate in your own sheets? Did you get my messages? I've been calling for two days. I finally got a hold of your agent so I could reach you wherever the hell you were on assignment and she said you never showed. 'That's not Raj,' I said. She must have disagreed because she hung up."

"I was thinking about crowds," he managed through a dehydrated tongue. "Whole packs of people all together until they spread out like a sea . . . "

"Ugh."

She actually said "ugh." Madi was all for the romance of mental breakdowns, but not when it involved her own bloodline. She threw the cereal in the trash, ran a shower for her brother, and touched up her makeup in the reflection of picture glass, behind which a line of soldiers cut a human curtain across Red Square. By the time Raj had returned to the land of the living, or at least dressed the part, she promised never to mention the "birthday granola incident" again.

Raj didn't mention it either. But after that birthday, he stayed in more. He became less visible. He kept to his studio as much as he could, and the laugh lines around his mouth began to diminish. He dated Del from the comfortable reaches of his set of broken armchairs and let her go without a single romantic chase down the stairs. Now at thirty-five, he watched summer mornings fade into gray after-noons without once stepping foot outside of his apartment. In the past week, he had managed to go four days without leaving the building. When Del had shown up that evening, he had kissed her in part because he was ready to touch the world again.

When they were together, Del asked more than once why he never took her picture. And in fact, in all the portfolios that lined his shelf, in the sealed canisters of film yet to be developed, and in the stacks of mustard Polaroid boxes, he did not possess a single photo-graph of Delphine Kousavos. He tried to explain, "I no longer take photographs of things I find beautiful. Not anymore." She snorted sarcastically, piling her hair on the top of her head while posing to judge her beauty in the mirror. "You took one of Madi," she replied. "I saw it hanging in her bedroom. Wait until she hears that you don't find her beautiful."

"Please don't use my sister against me."

"Sorry we aren't all Le Corbusier conference rooms. You must be disappointed. Some of us have a little sun damage. A few of us even breathe."

He had shot Madi because he knew the geography of her face as intimately as the bend in the West Side Highway outside his window. Underneath the lip gloss and bronzing cream, Madi was still the sister who had slept in the bunk above his own as a child before they graduated to separate rooms. Their parents: a white, reed-thin mother and a chubby Indian father splashed in black body hair. From those polar opposites, the two had come, and as kids, each had prayed with religious fervor to grow in opposite genetic directions. But puberty failed prayers. Raj had taken his mother's skinny frame along with her electric blue eyes, while Madi, refusing to give in to the inevitable, bandaging herself in tight stonewash jeans and compulsively tearing out her eyebrows with tweezers, had inherited the thicker bones and paternal proclivity to sprout dense black hair along her forearms. They were the two wobbling melting pots molded by a couple who should never have married and who crashed their progeny against each other whenever possible—a cheaper alternative to smashing their set of kitchen plates. A very pregnant Vicki Birch Singh had delighted in the exotic foreignness of her turbaned husband when she agreed to let him pick out the firstborn's name by flipping pages at random in the Guru Granth Sahib to the first letter of the first word of the first hymn according to Sikh custom. R made its chance monumental trek to Rajveer. But three years later, the kiln had cooled in the Birch-Singh household. A more disillusioned mother, smoking two packs of Newports per day and secretly attending Bible meetings at Southern Crossroads Gateway House, stuck to her guns and Birch family tradition, naming the second baby Madeline. "Screw your Guru Granth," she had wailed an hour before bringing their daughter into the world.

"Let this kid have a real chance of fitting in. Now get her out of me, or I'll drive to the hospital myself."

Raj and Madi had been raised in a pink aluminum-sided household of warring religions, Raj's red–black hair descending inch by inch free of scissors or razors, wrapped and bunned in the stiff white folds of a miniature Sikh turban. His grade-school classmates nicknamed him "The Turbinator," spraying him with invisible machine-gun fire in the stone corridors of PS33, offing the enemy Arab boy he denied being in class assignments on cultural heritage. When faced with twenty-one reports on the Irish potato famine, the Cuban exile experience, and the yuletide meaning of dreidel, the verdant Punjabi territory between the Indus and Yamuna Rivers, with its lush gardens and flowering crops, might as well have existed in Saudi Arabia under the anorexic belly of a camel. Meanwhile, Madi, heavier in body but lighter in psychological load, wore plastic jelly shoes and Bermuda shorts and permed her hair according to the statutes of *Sassy* and *Seventeen*. Taking him by the arm on the first day of each school year, with the sun lifting above the singed Ft. Lauderdale palms, she acted as his American ambassador, his crop top liberator to the bleached blondes, freckled noses, and unmanageable cowlicks of the late summer playground. Madi had tried—how much can an eleven-year-old do?—to calm international hostilities. But there were two kinds of headgear worn at PS33: those bought at the Hat Hut at Palatial Gardens Mall and his, worn at all times, indoor and outdoor, for devotion and purity, which hid hair that was longer than any brushed by grade-school girls.

The day his mother finally kicked his father out for being a lazy, emotionally inadequate non–Jesus freak, she picked him up from school in her rusted Rabbit convertible and threw down ten dollars at the closest barbershop to get his hair cut "proper."

"Cut it off," she told the barber, as tears welled in her eyes and her fingers fumbled over her cigarette lighter. "The shorter the better. Real normal."

"But, miss?" the barber had said nervously, dipping a comb in a vat of amniotic blue gel, as if afraid he were about to commit a divine transgression. "Are you sure?"

"Of course I'm fucking sure. I'm his mother." Then through an eruption of nicotine smoke and tears, she patted Raj's shoulders as he felt the cold scissor tips on the back of his neck. "You want something fun, angel? You can have whatever cut you want."

"WHY DIDN'T YOU tell me Del had gotten married?" he said in lieu of a hello into the phone. Madi made three ticking sounds with her tongue, the hold music of a brain searching for an appropriate answer.

"Raj, I'm in a meeting. There's something of a crisis here, so don't be upset if I settle Bangalore before I tackle your broken heart." He checked his watch and imagined his sister in her Tribeca office, shuffling through documents in her loud silk sari and pinstriped pants. "I realize your infrastructure is also a little volatile right now, but I'm on a conference call with stockholders."

"Did you think you could just keep it from me?"

She moaned. "I'm hanging up. Let's talk about this later." He heard a door close and then an angry whisper drive through the receiver. "So what? Isn't she allowed to? You'd think you were still dating her. Some advice. Leave your damn apartment. Go for a walk. Let the air in your place do without your lungs for a while. Wake up, Raj. I can get you on a plane to Delhi in twenty-four hours if you'd be willing to take some pictures for me. I know it's not fine art but . . . "

He returned the phone to its cradle and slicked his hair down on the sides with water from the kitchen tap. Madi had spent the first twenty-five years of life playing the all-American girl to hide the father she didn't want to look like. In college, she dyed her hair blonde and pierced her ears with seven holes. Somewhere around twenty-five, she let her natural black grow against the yellow until her hair hung like a flag splitting factions evenly down the middle. By the time she started wearing saris over her business suits, she had been promoted to vice executive in a corporate firm built on outsourcing IT departments to regions in Karnataka. "When you start calling yourself Madhavi instead of Madeline, I'll know you've really lost it," he had warned her. "I've been talking a lot to Dad," she had responded. "He thinks India would be good for you too."

Mrs. Vicki Birch had been fired for smoking on the grounds of the gas station, when missing cartons were found in the form of brand-in-question butts sprinkled near the fuel pumps at dawn. "Poor Mom," Madi had said in response to the news and then cancelled her round-trip ticket to Florida for Christmas. "She reacts to her own faults by comforting herself with bad habits. Let's not be two more of them, Raj. She needs to get her own life together without burying herself in lost children." Madi was the only person he knew who still believed that the world, so fresh out of unclaimed land, was up for anyone's grabs. Mostly her own. She was the sibling of airports now.

Raj turned the knob on the apartment door and walked across the West Side Highway to the park along the river. He sat in the grass for ten minutes as sailboats tipped against the blue sky and couples leaned over the railing to bring themselves closer to the spray of the chop. He thought of that vision on the day of his thirtieth birthday. For some reason it had always remained there on the other side of his eyelids—a field of people stretching in all directions until their various heads and shoulders dissolved into an indistinguishable blur. To remove one or to add another would make no difference. In that crowd was everything at all times, hunger and expectation and filth. He wasn't certain whether that vision had come as a nightmare or a relief. Raj had purposely turned his lens on studies of modern architecture, allowing no trace of those who lived between the walls to infect his work. So why should it surprise him that Del had finally moved on with her life? Why did it hurt to hear that obvious conclusion? He grabbed two clumps of grass and twisted the blades. The world belonged to those who kept moving in it. Del had been the one to call off the relationship. But Raj had let her go.

CHAPTER SIX

OCCASIONALLY WILLIAM'S AGENT, Janice Eccles, actually managed to do her job. And when that minor miracle occurred, a mixture of fright and euphoria overtook him, similar, he assumed, to the feeling a hostage must experience when finally freed from an escalating standoff. Suddenly, he was a free agent, no longer a pawn in a waiting game between forces beyond his control.

William slipped his arms through a white Oxford, applying a dab of cologne to his neck and leaving the top buttons open to reveal a nest of black chest hair. He hoisted a pair of jeans around his waist and laced a pair of battered loafers. William inspected himself in the mirror and was startled by his own reflection because he found he was smiling. He had been smiling ever since he had heard the message on his phone from Janice that someone with money and a script looking for a male lead had asked for William by name. Aleksandra Andrews at the Carlyle hotel, 12 PM sharp.

William had stepped quietly out of his twenties with the composure of a married man, accepting of his age. For a little while, anyway. He could see the changes every time he looked in the mirror. His younger face, a puddle of dark eyes and fattened-calf cheeks and a jaw that was tinted blue from shaved whiskers, had solidified into a slightly pissed-off grimace that only a forced smile could expunge. There was also a droop to his eyelids as if his forehead had lost its war with a heavy, distressing thought. But what surprised him more was how his brain had failed to follow the same holding pattern. He expected mood swings and hopeless indirection in youth but believed age would nail down those beating wings into solid, tenable anchors. The truth was that he felt even more lost than ever—like he was easy prey to whatever chemicals and errant hormonal secretions decided to unleash their tempers on him on any given hour. Where was the certainty that comes with the years? Wasn't that the consolation of age—some peace of mind, some getting of the joke?

He did not get the joke. His marriage had failed, his career had cooled, and he had inherited from his younger self a love of the late nights and the substances that drew those nights out further. Lately, pleasure was like a tropical island glimpsed from a plane window, almost there, in proximity, but never quite under his feet.

William entered the unfamiliar hush of the marble lobby at noon sharp, checking his watch to make sure he was on time, and was directed by the receptionist to suite 706. He used the mirror in the elevator to fix his hair and examine his clothes, the bland shirt and pants, tricks of the actor's profession to look as generic as possible so a casting agent can easily drop any identity onto his shoulders—murderer or amnesia victim, gladiator or car salesmen, gentle father or hotdog vendor or gun-toting marine. He would nail this audition, whatever it was. He would go in and bag the role, reading any clip of bad dialogue like the words dripped from his veins. He stepped onto the seventh floor and followed the medallion carpet pattern to room 706. He pressed his ear to the wood to catch a fragment of a script being read by some hack competitor and, hearing nothing, knocked on the door.

"Come in."

The suite was dark, the lights had been left off, and what little sunlight there was broke in horizontal slashes across the beige carpeting. For a moment, even though he had been asked to enter, William thought he might be in the wrong room. He opened the door wider to allow some of the hallway light to make sense of the room.

"Shut it," a woman's voice ordered.

She sat in a whicker chair in the frame of double doors that led to the bedroom. Her legs were crossed and her elbow rested on the back of the chair, allowing her hand to play with a strand of hair twisted around a finger.

"Hello," he said. "Touchpoint sent me. I'm here for the audition."

"You're William Asternathy?"

"Yes, ma'am." He tried to make the words sound like a kiss blown through the dark into her heart. You had to flirt with these casting agents, male or female, make them want to take you out to dinner if they could. He was better at it with women and felt his chances rise when he saw her head nod approvingly.

"Do you want me to read?" he asked.

"Come so I can see you," she replied, loosening her index finger from her hair and pointing toward the window. William sucked air through his nose and walked until the sunlight blinded him. He squinted, trying not to wrinkle his skin, and watched her stand up and take a step forward. She had blond hair, soft and washed but not combed so it hung clumsily over her ears. She was older, early fifties maybe, with tight, small Connecticut features that would read as pretty in soft focus, but she was pale underneath her tan. A scarlet birthmark shot up her neck almost like an arrow. She wiped her mouth.

"You're not him," she said.

"I'm not who?"

"You're not William Asternathy."

"Really? Are you so sure about that?" he stammered, almost laughing.

"You're not right."

"Well, you don't know that. Let me read."

"I said you aren't right. You're not the right man."

"Look," he snapped. He backed up a step to get out of the sun and considered moving toward her, but his fingers were bunching in anger and he didn't want to come across as threatening. "Let me read the script and then make your decision."

"Get out." She retreated behind the chair as if she also guessed he might be threatening, and suddenly the phone lying on the floor near her feet took on a larger presence than a non-ringing phone should.

He squeezed the air in his fists and walked toward the door.

"You're a fucking waste of time, you know that?" he screamed. "You bring me all the way here and you don't even let me read. Who the hell do you think you are?" But as William turned to catch one last look at her, he found that she had already disappeared into the bedroom, taking the phone with her. The double doors slammed shut and the chair fell over on its side.

"CAN YOU BELIEVE that?" William lifted his arm from his eyes and stared up at the consoling face of Brutus Quinn.

"You should complain."

"What do you think I'm going to do as soon as I leave here? I can't go on like this. I haven't gotten one thing thrown at me in months. Haven't got a single part in beyond a year. God, it's been two years now. Who am I kidding? And then this woman, this bitch, all she says is, 'you're the wrong man.' You should have seen me. I almost murdered her."

Quinn rolled his eyes and grabbed a towel from the dish rack to dry his hands. "Will, come on."

"No, I won't come on. I'm broke. Why is it every time I say I'm broke to anyone, all they do is roll their eyes?"

"It's part of the business," he said, wiping his hands roughly on a black, paisley rag. William rotated onto his stomach and picked up the tea that Quinn had placed in front of him. He had come for fatherly advice and now no longer wanted to hear it. "You can't hate people for not falling in love with you," Quinn said, throwing the towel over his shoulder. "You can't blame the world for not dropping everything they're holding just because you're walking by."

"But I do," William struggled to laugh. "I don't care if that sounds narcissistic."

"Well, I still love you," Quinn said sarcastically, but his face reddened from the truth of the sentiment.

Brutus Quinn hibernated year-round in a piteously small stucco cottage tucked behind an apartment building in the West Village, a single square of white bricks fitted with a thatched Hansel-and-Gretel roof that was so well hidden in its back garden of ailing oak trees that co-op boards and residential developers must have entirely forgotten about the thirty-year inhabitant shelling out eight hundred dollars per month to keep his stronghold in a neighborhood that was once crowded with affectatious gay men just like him. "Where have all the freaks gone?" was the title of one poem that Quinn had written on the subject of white, fertile, hetero gentrification. The answer to that question was easy: they had died. Quinn had tested positive in 1987, but his white cells somehow never bore the diminishing returns of those blood results. He persevered, heavier and more near-sighted as the years went on but still surprisingly healthy, as he watched most of his closest friends pass away within a matter of five years. William often thought of that disease as a bomb going off, leaving Quinn to carry on in the shrapnel of his former life, which decorated the cottage in the form of old photographs and dusty bric-a-brac arranged chaotically like a garage sale. Quinn had been an actor himself, and then, when his muscles lost their lean efficiency and his gray hair began to fall from the roots, continued on as a set designer for under-attended avant-garde plays. Quinn and William had met in one such production that had all the popular momentum of a six-day run. But their friendship had lasted, mostly on William's insistence by his dropping in at the cottage four or five times a month, lying on the couch covered in dirty Turkish batiks, and listening to Quinn's stories of New York in the '70s and '80s, which always involved young boys in constant need of drug money, suicides from swallowing razor blades, ACT-UP rallies at political conventions, kleptomaniacal models, and heavy doses of anonymous sex in the Meatpacking District. He couldn't walk with Quinn anymore through the West Village streets, because the old man hissed at baby strollers and whistled at deliverymen. But William loved the quiet sanctuary of the cottage, a fallen museum devoted to Quinn in the prime of his days.

"Does that say AIDS IS MAGIC?" William asked, staring at one of the many politically motivated magnets on the mini-refrigerator.

Quinn looked over and grabbed the towel. He always had wet

hands and was always drying them as if he had a nervous habit of twisting fabric.

"Oh, yes. We made that when Magic Johnson went public. We thought it would de-sensationalize the disease. You know, AIDS is magic. It's okay to have the high-five."

"High-five?"

"HIV."

"But it's not okay, is it?"

"Hush. One night, this is when the Mudd Club was really going and none of us worked, the point was not to work in those days, twenty of us dressed up like bankers, all suits and ties we got from a clerk we knew at Bergdorf's, hair slicked back prep school style by my friend Diane. Diane later jumped off the Brooklyn Bridge because MoMA didn't buy one of her paintings. She wrote her suicide note on a canvas, and after they pulled her body from the river, MoMA bought the note painting. Anyway, we went down to this Wall Street bar called Bubbles. We mingled with the usual broker clientele and then at midnight we started making out with each other, half the room French kissing and grabbing crotches. You should have seen the look on their faces. God it was beautiful. It was the end of the world for them."

"Quinn," William said, burying his eyes in his arm. "I'm sick of hearing about how great New York used to be."

"But it was," Quinn moaned happily. "It really was something. The secret got out and too many of the wrong kind showed up. I thought we were being liberators. Now I realize when everything's too free people just get lazy and safe. And all the best liberators died. They took it up the ass, because they were the most adventurous, and we lost them. That's why the gay movement is basically a joke of what it used to be. They don't know what it's like to spill your guts out and scream for your life."

"I want to live in my own time, if that's all right with you. Right now. When your parents were wilder than you are, you feel like you should quit."

Quinn froze, looking injured. He tossed the towel on William's head, tapped his legs on the couch to indicate their eviction from the pillow, and sat down next to him.

"You've got your youth. That trumps every old story from perverts like me who spend all their time on the Internet."

"I've barely got that."

"You can take my car if you ever need a day in the country. Lord knows I never drive it. The keys are in the desk."

Quinn kept his beat-up blue Cressida parked on West Twelfth Street, his main exercise consisting of waking up at five every other morning to repark it a block north to avoid the street cleaner.

"Be careful," William warned. "I might drive it to Los Angeles and never come back."

"You can't do that," Quinn said, petting his ankles. "It's the only thing I've got to sell when they kick me out of here and I'm living in a retirement village in Queens. Serves me right. I'll probably have to act straight when I'm trapped up in there at eighty. Back in the closet just so I can play bridge with a few vets who don't remember what to do with an erection but know that they still hate fags."

William wondered if Quinn really thought he would live to see eighty.

"I'll visit you. You can tell them I'm your son."

"I don't get your generation," Quinn huffed. "If I had your body and face, I'd be out having fun. Think of all the sex you could be having. I wish old age were wasted on the old, but I'm warning you now that isn't quite the case."

"What is it with you and sex?" William groaned. "It's really not that great. Half the time, it's the loneliest thing I can think of. But it's like a religion with you. Sex and horror movies. Why do gay men love horror movies so much? The only fan letter I ever received was from a gay guy who watched that stupid slasher film I made about eight hundred times."

Quinn laughed, collecting William's teacup to run brown water over it from the kitchen sink.

"We like to see the clean lives get what they deserve. Punishment for all of our years pretending to be normal. Normal's a bad thing, Will. It means you really are soulless."

"You're full of shit. I've seen the young men you go after, the ones you look at on the Internet. They're the normal ones, not the skinny art kids running around with high voices. You say you hate normal, but that's precisely what those high-school jocks and gas-station attendants are.

"We aren't superior beings," Quinn said, placing his hands on the kitchen counter and dropping his chin in frustration, as if William had missed the point. "I'm sorry if you got that impression. We're just like everyone else. We want what we can't have."

William slid his legs off the couch while Quinn turned to study him with a disappointed, bitten lip. Quinn always looked defeated when William cut his visits short. William knew that he provided a slowly closing window into youth for his friend. "I'm off to face my agent and demand an explanation."

"You'll hold things again, I know it," Quinn replied, referencing a joke they shared. Quinn had a terrific homily on the world's low evaluation of actors. The way he figured it, most of life was consumed standing around holding things. If actors managed to be paid ridiculous amounts of money to perform that service, they were the clever ones. William kissed Quinn on the cheek and opened the front door.

"I'll see you in a week."

TOUCHPOINT AGENCY'S NEW York headquarters were located in the West Thirties, a black onyx building surrounded by discount jewelers and exotic plant nurseries. Above and below sat real estate ventures, but on the seventeenth floor the elevator opened onto a long hallway of portraits in red lacquer frames—autographed black-and-white headshots gridding the wall in chronological order. The bowl cuts of television stars in their butterfly '70s collars lost ground to '80s cigarette cowboys and chubby-faced babysitters with their flowered, hairspray-stiff bangs. A black Knoll ottoman, where three young men nervously sat pinching glossy photos of themselves, drifted like a raft somewhere in the tattoo-and-piercing parlor of the mid-'90s. Farther down, the '00s hung like "after" shots in a plastic surgery clinic. William wondered what horrible new specimens the 2010s would bring.

He brushed past the young men on the ottoman. Each one couldn't be more than twenty, and two looked like Nebraska ranchers straight off a Greyhound. It was painful for William to see youth so hungry and ready in this town, so eager to take the places of those who had come long before them and who were still hungry if less assured. William made his way to the receptionist's desk and, like a famous man who did not need to speak his name, assertively asked the woman reading *In Touch* for "Janice Eccles. I'm one of her clients."

"Name?" she asked, turning a page limply and pressing a button on her telephone console.

"William Asternathy. She's not expecting me."

Janice didn't appreciate surprise visits. She didn't baby her talent, and often told her actors when they broke into tears that she already had her own kids and didn't feel the need to adopt full-grown versions at work.

"She's not expecting you," the receptionist said.

He whispered. He would not let the twenty-year-olds on the couch hear what he was about to say. "Tell her I called her ten times last week. Tell her I just had a nightmare audition that she set up. Tell her I need to see her. It's urgent."

"Two minutes. Three doors down on the left."

He continued along the hallway as the young men on the ottoman followed him with their eyes.

Janice rotated in her chair. Behind her perfectly slicked hair, buildings and steeples and pigeons filled the polished window.

"You know never to come in like this." A hard candy pivoted between her teeth.

"I'm sorry, but I called you how many times?"

"I don't know. You'll have to ask my assistant."

On her blouse, she wore a silver pin glued with bones and turquoise feathers that looked like the curious remains of a cult sacrifice. William slumped into the chair across from her.

"If you aren't calling, something's not working," he said in defeat.

"You're not working," she responded. "And you're here because you think I'm not doing my job."

"I know the summer can be slow. But the fact is the only audition you've sent me on was the one this morning and that was a joke."

The candy shattered in her mouth, and she crunched the debris.

"I make money when you work. I don't make it lying to you and giving you auditions you wouldn't get. I'm going to treat you like a man, Will. Did you see that hallway full of headshots out there? Did you see how many faces stared you down as you decided to take up my lunch hour with this crap? And those are the Touchpoint actors who had a millisecond of something that could vaguely be defined as success. Take a look." She pulled a manila file from the stack on her desk, a file that he sensed remained there permanently for just such occasions. "Patricia Savage. She made twenty grand on a *Friday the 13th* spin-off. In 1984 she had a dozen national magazine features and even went on *Good Morning, America*. What do you think she's doing now? She's a journalist in Knoxville, Tennessee, writing on insecticides. This one." Janice held a photograph of a handsome sand-skinned surfer whose hair curled like a coral reef. "Tal Kidd. He played Tom Hanks's best friend in that comedy ten years ago about the woman who turns out to be an alien. MIA. I heard he went to Portland, where, last we know, he ran a children's daycare center." Janice returned the photograph to her file and dropped it with heavy purpose on the floor by her feet. "You've had a nice run. I'm not saying it's over, Will. But what if it is? You're thirty-six."

"I'm thirty-two."

"Forty. No difference." She smacked her palm on her desk. "Wait for my calls. Let me do my job. But think seriously about other options. Hell, get married to someone with a career and see where that takes you."

"I already tried that."

"Try it again." She pulled the lid off a canister of egg-shaped candies and offered him one. "Think it over. I tell you straight because I like you. I can't help you if you sit here wasting my time waiting for lightning to strike. You want to kill me, don't you?"

"Yes."

Janice smiled at this. She rose from her seat, trudged around her desk in a swaying Aztec-patterned skirt, and patted his shoulders, the first time in their professional relationship he could remember that more than their hands had touched.

"Life is long. For better or worse."

"What about that audition today?" he asked. "Why did she ask for me if all she wanted was to kick me out?"

"She thought you were someone else. She was very particular. I wouldn't worry. She's not a director. Just a rich lady with a few important friends in the industry and some sort of first-time script. She called me up blind."

"Who did she want?"

"Not you, William. That's all that matters."

Janice opened the door for him, and he accepted the hallway. And with a hard slam, the real Janice Eccles transformed into her chrome nameplate.

Jealousy must be a survival instinct, because it spilled so naturally from his mind and caught every thought on fire, wiping out whole neighborhoods of sense and memory. Another actor, someone his own age, maybe even Joseph for all he knew. William walked four blocks pounding his fists through the midtown air. That motherfucker. He dodged bicycles and taxis, peeling around tourists frozen under street signs doing complicated logarithms with street numbers in their heads. He broke into a light run, blowing into shoulders through Times Square. Sweating, lungs wheezing like a furnace, William finally stopped ten blocks from the agency and hailed a cab. "That's it then," he sputtered to himself in the backseat. "That's the sign I was waiting for. It's over. Fine."

Inside his apartment filled with Jennifer's belongings, he tried to wrestle himself out of anger and got down to the business of getting drunk. Five bottles of vodka—"fresh soldiers," his father had called them—lined the kitchen counter. He stood at the window drinking. By nine o'clock, he had killed the remainder of one soldier and started on the second.

He thought of Jennifer stepping out of the shower with her mustard robe branded with cursive initials, her wet hair wedged in a towel. She smelled of bee pollen, her skinny thighs shuffling between the scrolling terrycloth. He tried to remember what Quinn said, about a world of sex out in the city waiting for him, about New York being wild and sarcastic and young. He culled up the short list of women he had slept with since Jennifer had left, their sweaty bodies hanging off his own, their legs open and their fingers tense, without being able to recite any of their names.

But Jennifer kept stepping out of the shower, her moist arms and neck holding her scent, her face so smooth it looked like she had never known a second of desperation.

He packed his pockets with keys, driver's license, and a silver money clip loaded with six twenty-dollar bills.

By eleven, William barreled out of a taxi and into a club called Kaos, met two friends in the second of the establishment's two crystal bars—Jesse and Ed, actors and drinking buddies. Their faces glowed with feverish consumption. Or maybe it was from the lights that rained down from above, skimming over the hundreds packed on the dance floor. Flashes of metallic wrists shaking in the air, calves muscling up and down as if taking long flights of stairs, the music so solid that it hung like a metal vest over his ribs. So much electricity to keep the club dark and loud, so much energy exerted by bartenders to fill drinks.

William felt young in his blood. It was midnight. He was alive and in loud company.

"Why do you look so happy? You get a job or what?" Ed asked, throwing his arm around William's neck. "Haven't seen you out since that night we were trapped in three feet of snow at Michael's. Nothing to do but drink. Michael's gone, you know."

"He died?" William looked at Ed with horror.

"Practically. He works at a Home Depot in Hoboken. Poor man. Says he wanted to do some soul searching. I'm not so sure Home Depot carries that."

"So where are we going next?" William asked, grinning with neon teeth. The deejay slurred the record into a new track.

"He's asking where's next," Ed screamed. "Jesse, tell him this place is enough for the next hour. Isn't it?"

Jesse offered a joint, thinly rolled, burned down to a quarter inch. William suctioned it with a deep inhale before passing it on to blue fingernails.

The woman's name was Myra, and she came with friends from the damp forest of the dance floor. Nothing hurt, not even the shine of a flashlight directly in his eyes from a bouncer who was looking for a man that did not match William's description. He rolled up his sleeves.

William felt young and four-dimensional. He was high, and his heart was supplying drumbeats. Myra waved her blue fingernails for him to join her on the dance floor. When she screamed, her words came out broken between pulses of light, and she told him she was Chilean and had been above the equator for five days. She told him it was winter in Chile, which did not account for her tan.

Two hours and twenty minutes later he left Kaos with Jesse and Myra and two of her girlfriends who spoke even less English (although they insisted on trying) but no Ed. They took a cab six blocks to another club called Bad Engine, where a drag queen chugged a bottle of Jameson on stage and the audience whistled. The drag queen stared down the crowd like she was waiting for an apocalyptic horse to gallop through the room as an excuse to pull out a machine gun and blow everyone away. Jesse waved them into the VIP room, and William drank two vodkas served by a former gay porn star who asked him about breaking into more legitimate films. He sniffed something chalky out of a folded piece of tin foil from Myra's purse and danced with her blond friend to a Stone Roses remix.

They took a cab to a bar in Chinatown, and Jesse rolled down the window, dry heaving along Seventh Avenue to the shrieks of a Pakistani driver with a cell phone clipped to his ear.

"Just get there," Jesse said. "We have to get somewhere else, you know, before the air starts turning blue. Somewhere without windows. And please, everyone, place your watches in your pockets. Under no circumstances are you to tell me what time it is."

William's heart was racing as he leaned against Myra, who grabbed his hand and guided it between her legs. His fingertips were numb, but he forced them under the elastic of her underwear, and she closed her thighs to keep his hand from traveling any farther or from withdrawing it entirely. All of the nerves down his spine were firing. He wanted to stand up or lie down or play a never-ending game of chess. He wanted to move to Chile with Myra. He had seen pictures of Santiago in a magazine, the gorgeous dark eyes of teenagers in bright brandless sweatshirts under a mountain covered in smog.

They walked into a Chinese restaurant that held no customers but was filled with tuxedoed waiters holding trays, through a kitchen canopied with washed silver pots, and into a large back room with a bar and torn vinyl couches. Myra bought him a vodka with nine one-dollar coins, and they sat around a coffee table, the three women speaking quickly as if each thought was an urgent message that would cure the future if only it were articulated *right now*. Myra's teeth chattered even when he kissed her.

"I am in New York for only a short time," she told him.

"Me too," he replied. She bit into an Adderall and put half on his tongue.

At four thirty, they turned down an alley and entered an apartment building where a party was in its slow dissolve in a sixth-floor walk up. Even though there were only nine college students in the railroad living room, trying to build enough enthusiasm to finish a box of Michelob on the floor, the guy in a tank top at the door said he'd only let in guests without penises.

Myra's two friends went inside, and the remaining three, heads bent down from the lightening sky, walked seven blocks in silence through the Lower East Side to an after-hours club that required a secret knock and a piece of red paper flashed over the peephole.

"The bar is 'free' with 'suggested donation,'" Jesse said with fingering quotation marks. "So if the cops bust, they aren't technically selling."

"Who runs this place?" William asked. He held on to Myra's waist.

"It's technically abandoned, so technically there is no 'they' to arrest. A guilty building with innocent people inside. We all wound up here by accident."

A black bedspread covered the single window. Porcelain lamps lined the perimeter of the room. Men who looked like members of a British punk band in their popular decline jumped around the makeshift card-table bar. Myra and William finished off what was left of the powder in her purse, and he briefly thought about putting one of the lampshades on his head as a joke, but considering the morose crowd and the possibility that the lampshade cliché had perhaps not yet traveled below the equator, he tangled his legs with Myra's on top of a dresser by the bathroom. Kisses held currency in Chile. Kisses were what made the night slow down.

Ed suddenly appeared with a scratch on his cheek and sat down next to him.

"It's five thirty," he informed them despairingly. "Want a beer?"

William felt too awake, and he wondered how deep into the next day this place stayed open, protecting them from the wrecking ball of sunlight on the other side of the door. Negotiating a pocket of cab receipts, ripped paper bracelets, and one-dollar bills seemed far more difficult than what Ed was rambling on about—wars and American casualties and the dissemination of nuclear bombs. William looked at the crowd, the young half-exhausted bodies squatting in semicircles on the floor. Night was New York's great conspiracy, he thought. Everyone had come here for money and success but in the end they also came to get lost, become anonymous, disappear into the traffic of nine million people. The night hid the embarrassment of what they were during the day.

"It can't go on," Ed kept saying. "How much longer can we go on like this? How much longer can we pretend we're safe and nothing more will happen?"

"We can go on," Myra said softly, not quite following the thread. "They don't know where we are."

"Maybe it will just go on," William offered in an attempt to join the conversation. "On and on. Maybe the idea that there are all of these terrorists dying to blow us up is just an effort to make us hate the enemy. I mean, do they really care that much?"

"Of course they hate us," Ed hissed. "Jesus, why do most Americans have such a hard time believing that anyone can possibly not like them? They hate us and they hate us more every day. We have problems our parents never dreamed of."

"No one in New York has parents," William replied. "Or families for that matter. We're all pretty much immigrants taking shelter here." Myra and Ed stared at him blankly. "I mean, we don't even *know* our parents."

"I know my parents," Myra said.

"I call my father every Tuesday," Ed admitted.

"But you don't know them. You've deserted. Gone AWOL. There are no more mom-and-pop businesses because there aren't any more children to take over the register. That's why this city never supports the military. We don't know what it means to serve. But I mean that in a good way. We're liberators, activists. We've made an army of . . . " He was channeling Quinn.

"I live with my mother," Myra said, pushing his legs off of her. "My brother's in the army."

"William, you're fucked up. That's not it at all. Casting us as a bunch of infidels just gives the government more excuses to ignore what we're saying, while it's doing pretty fucking little to keep this island protected. I'm telling you, the worst will come. And when it does, I dare anyone to act surprised."

"I was born under a dictatorship," Myra said. "You are with your family or you have nothing."

"You aren't following," William stammered, wiping his nose anxiously with his wrist. "We're an army that refuses to fight, which is like fighting. We fight with our backs." His mind was warped from the drugs, he regretted that last sentence, and he could no longer even remember his original point. He went to the bathroom and when he returned, stumbling over a Japanese girl in a transparent dress who found his loafers insulting enough to ash her cigarette on, Myra and Ed were nowhere to be found. They had left together. Or just left. It didn't matter. They had abandoned him.

William opened the metal door and walked into the morning light up Stanton Street and west on to Houston. He laughed at the fleeting impression he left on bakery glass windows and on the car windows parked along the curb. He didn't mind losing Myra. He didn't care about Ed or the spread of uranium plants or even bombs being delivered by UPS to uptown embassies. He felt all of his jealousies and regrets disappearing the way the sun burned up the smog over the city he imagined living in. Not Santiago. Los Angeles. You can't keep stepping in place, he was learning. By the time he found an off duty cab willing to take him uptown for his last twenty, his feelings about Jennifer had faded. Burned out in a sudden flare like it was all another year with its own set of problems.

As the stock market opened, he was just a man going to bed.

CHAPTER SEVEN

SOMEWHERE IN THE filing cabinets and hard drives of the INS department, there must be classified interrogation reports on how closely immigrants married to U.S. citizens approximated a legitimate union. Did they hold hands during their INS interview or exchange well-timed adoring glances, talk of pregnancies like impending vacations, wince when the subject turned to the first time they met each other's parents? If the INS really wanted to judge the authenticity of love, they could do no better than to catch a couple trying to sleep during a summer heat wave. That's what Del figured when she rolled onto her side and kicked the sheet off her body, while Joseph reached his arm over her waist and flattened his hand against her stomach.

Tonight in their bedroom, the heat was merciless. The few drops of rain that clanged on the air conditioner outside the window had threatened a cooling reprieve but even those drops had gone dry. She and Joseph had both taken showers, bringing the cold water with them to bed, and after an hour of tossing, had sex to waste excess energy. But still the sleep didn't come. Del felt the sweat build in the crevices of her armpits and tick along her thighs. Just moving out of Joseph's reaches would have helped, but she liked the tight grip on her body and the way she could hear every inflection of his voice travel up her spine.

Joseph always fell asleep first. He could switch off in the middle of the loudest argument echoing through their windows from the street, but he was also the kind of sleeper plagued with constant nightmares. Sometimes in the night she'd wake to find him caught in the inner logic of a dream, sitting up or reaching over to grab her hand, mumbling, "It's gone now. It won't wait any longer. I can't keep it off," or "a trick, they plotted for it to look like an accident, but the numbers are off." She'd calm him by pushing him down on the mattress and saying, "I've got it. Don't worry. I'll take care of it now." He never remembered those incidents in the morning and laughed when she recited his dream messages back to him. Tonight, though, Joseph tapped his fingers on her stomach and wiped the sweat of his mouth against her shoulder. She felt the small divot of his lip, always badly shaved, which she often suctioned as the last of a kiss. He whispered, "Did you call the lawyer?"

"I'm going to," she replied. "Madi says he's the best. All of her Indian friends used him. They got their green cards within a year and could finally quit their jobs or file for divorce."

"Don't divorce me," he said. "You should wait until I make more money."

She slapped his arm and then held on to his knuckles.

"I'm sorry you have to deal with this. The whole process is revolting. It's like the love gestapo. You go in for an interview and are forced to answer all these personal questions just to prove we're legitimate."

He clenched her stomach. "How much more legitimate can we be?"

"I'm not worried," she said defensively. But she was worried. What kept her awake wasn't just the summer heat but the mistake of visiting Raj in his studio two days earlier. It had initially seemed like a way of closing the door on the past for good, but instead it induced a resurgence of old memories and hesitations. *The quakes of love are different.* She had said that to herself when she left Raj that evening, and she said it to herself now as she wrapped her fingers around Joseph's hand. The room once shook violently for Raj, and it now shook for Joseph. Why did she feel any need to compare them?

She slid deeper against Joseph's chest and felt his muscles rise and fall with his breathing. She felt the tick of his heart against the fragile cage of his ribs. She could hardly understand that version of herself who had fought so hard to stay with Raj against all of his aloofness. How can you compare a person who barely fulfilled the fundamental requirements of a relationship against someone who let you in so easily? She had trusted Joseph enough early on that she wasn't afraid to tell him about the heartbreak of losing Dash. They had sat on the roof of this very building bundled in thick winter coats under the freezing February moonlight, while she stabbed cigarette after cigarette to pulp on the tarred brick. She told him how the car crash that killed him hit her so forcefully she could still feel the impact travel through her body eleven years later. Joseph's eyes flinched as he grabbed her by the wrists, almost too tightly for reassurance, and said, "the pain will never go away. You shouldn't blame yourself for not being able to get beyond it." Raj would have taken that confession as proof that he couldn't compete with her past and let the quiet fall between them.

Joseph ran his fingers up her body, and she turned over to face him. His eyes were closed, but even in the darkness she could see them moving under his lids.

"I'm sorry," she whispered. "I'm sorry that we have to go down there and prove we're a couple. I'm sorry we have to prove that for anyone but ourselves." She meant it. The idea of government agents tracking through their personal lives did not sound appealing no matter how you rationalized it. But she knew that Joseph could be trusted to concede to the agreement, play up the devoted husband, and even memorize the items she routinely bought at the drug store if an INS agent asked such a question for proof of domestic partnership.

"I'll do whatever you need," he whispered. "You don't have to ask."

"I know you will," she said. "At the end of the day it just comes down to luck. We'll be alright. We *are* alright."

He didn't respond, and she took his silence for sleep. She lifted his hand from her stomach and checked the clock on the nightstand. Her mind habitually calculated the difference in time zones whenever she looked at the hour hand. She climbed quietly out of bed and tiptoed into the living room, grabbing her cell phone from her purse before dialing sixteen digits to ring her east into a kitchen filled with morning.

"*Mitera*," she said to her mother's voice. "*Kalinishta. Kalimera.*"

MADI TAPPED HER platinum ring against the porcelain handle. Two cups of tea sat on a teak tray between two former college roommates. Two cups of tea and fifteen years, in the span of which, it occurred to Del, they had traded lives.

Del had made a point before coming over to Madi's apartment not to mention freshman year of college. There was nothing worse than a friendship that can never let go of its genesis. She loved seeing Madi, and the promise they had made in their dorm room to one day serve as each other's maids of honor would have held if Del had planned that kind of wedding. But lately she was disturbed by the fact that the silences between them were filled mostly with memories of dorm room antics that were only rehashed in each other's presence. The first week of classes, half the staff at Columbia had gone on strike— not the professors preaching deconstruction and Marxist revisionism but the building custodians and the women in hairnets who drew up the multicultural dinner menus and the secretaries who fielded calls for the dean. The strikers had created a human, sign-waving barricade around the Morningside Heights campus, and classes were rerouted into conference rooms at the nearby sister school of Barnard. Del had refused to attend in support of the workers, and Madi delayed her first week of course requirements in the conviction that she had applied to Columbia College, the co-ed Ivy, not Barnard, the vaguely lesbian all-women's version separated by Broadway and its own wrought-iron gates. It took two weeks for Columbia to settle with the strikers, and in that time, two strangers, cooped up together in a dorm room barely big enough to fit a bunk bed and a wood desk, forged a friendship that would lead to four years of marathon drinking, hangover breakfasts, bisexual rumors, bad dye jobs, positive acid trips, and the unwanted name-splitting nickname around campus as "Mad Fiend."

In those early days, Madi had been the romantic, the one to lose her heart to the New England stoners passing bubble machines coated in latex as senior art projects. Del had been slower on the draw, the less likely of the duo to be dragged from a poetry reading to a bed on Riverside Drive, the less likely to remove her bra in front of two hash-smoking NYU students and toss it out of the window where it hung for months in the branches. It was, as it usually went, the literature and not the biology major more prone to oral sex with teaching assistants and remarks such as "When you let a little twerp eat you out in the archive room of Avery Library, you at least expect some leniency on the metaphor of flowers in Virginia Woolf." But over the course of that first year, their styles began to merge. Madi took on some of Del's darker European accents and Del some of her roommate's glossy Florida highlights. "They put us together because we both sound like foreigners," Madi had said that first day. "Thing is, you are and I'm not."

Watching Madi sip her tea in a linen caftan and clasp Del's ankle affectionately, she had trouble finding any trace of those old finger-prints on her friend. Madi had widened, gaining weight in her face and hips, and, although she still had long slender legs that looked primed for a bikini, the dark tanner applied to her cheeks and neck made her appear as Indian as her outfit. If anyone happened to walk in today on Mad Fiend, they would assume Madi to be the foreigner. Del once joked that she looked like she had just been spit out of immigration and was surprised by the smile that leaked across her face.

Madi's apartment also possessed the same sense of reinvented identity, partitioned with elaborate embroidered screens, ginger tapestries, and a gold peacock holding up the coffee table glass by its head. She had bought the apartment two years ago. Walked into an abandoned sweatshop in Chinatown and bargained the price down to two million. The place smelled of old fabrics, fresh paint, the rotten fish of Chinatown stalls, and too much sandalwood incense.

"You know what's been really bothering me lately?" Del confessed. "There was a time when we all seemed on the same level. And suddenly you and everyone else shot forward, and I'm still where I was, where I've always been. How did that happen?"

"Raj says I think about money too much." Madi laughed and shook away the complaint. "Of course I think about money too much. That's what I do for a living. He says it like it's a revelation, like he only just realized I work in finance and maybe *I* don't even know what I do all day. But I tell you, what stopped all those kids we knew who refused to go to Wall Street because they were afraid to sell out and instead just sat there, fucked out of their heads and shaking about paying rent each month, was the inability to see what good you can do by playing the game. I tell Raj, you think I'm not helping the poor in India. Go take a look at what's being built there. Watch how the economy is developing. See the opportunity. Who do you think did that, artists and Peace Corp volunteers? Not a chance. It was those of us staying up at 3 AM in our cubicles so we could conference-call Bangalore. That's who."

"No one's accusing you."

"I know." Madi tried to lighten her tone with a laugh. "I just wonder when I'll stop buying dinners for people who sit there, order whatever they want, and go to great lengths to tell me how they refuse to fold to the corporate mammon and never even pretend to reach for their wallets when the check arrives. One day you have to wake up and see this city as more than a playground for bad decisions and never-ending hangovers. Well, don't you?" Del tried to come to her own defense, raising an index finger over the tray. But Madi anticipated her reaction, smiling as she grabbed Del's hand to smother the critique. "I'm not talking about you. You work hard, and I respect that. But don't you ever find it odd that you and I pull down nine-to-fives and all the men around us snap photographs of blank walls or audition for the opportunity to act like an irrelevant page in a bad Elizabethan romance? I'm beginning to believe that art is the black hole of ambition. If you want to know where the most useless, self-indulgent complainers are, try going to an art opening."

Del punched her friend's leg, which was kind considering that she wanted to apply a few sobering slaps to the face. Where was old

Madi, the bleached blonde who quoted poetry when you asked for practical advice?

"There was a time you would have busted the lip of anyone who said that."

Madi shrugged innocently.

"Things change. Or I did. I sound completely awful, I'm aware of that, and you know I wouldn't say any of this to Raj. If taking photographs of nothing makes him happy, then go for it. But don't tell me you're living *la vie boheme* when you're decorating the walls of dens in Ft. Worth." Madi's tan cheeks reddened with the embarrassment of conservatism, but her tongue kept on stoking her point. "I'm just seeing the larger picture. A few weeks ago, Raj took me to art galleries after lunch. First we go into a room full of children's Huffy bikes that have been dipped in mounds of plaster. Raj got all thoughtful. I think he even put a finger to his chin. He said the artist was subversively removing the market purpose of the bikes. I said, 'Raj, the market doesn't care if you ride the damn things. They just want you to buy them. This artist bought seven.' In the next gallery, we walk down a narrow hallway, completely black, to the sounds of barking dogs. At the end of a hallway, a cocktail napkin was taped to the wall with the word 'good-bye' written across it in Sharpie marker. Raj said the installation was reminiscent of Soviet Gulags—like this artist had ever been in one. Like someone who failed out of Cooper Union needs to remind me of Cold War atrocities. What am I, eight? The thing had already sold for twenty grand, but let's not even explore that."

"Madi."

"Don't 'Madi' me. A cocktail napkin worth twenty thousand dollars. That's what we call a market with bloated asset values."

"Well, I've really appreciated attending this lecture. What is it called?" Del pushed herself into the soft cushions and fought the urge to roll a cigarette. "When Will America Stop Loving Art and Start Respecting Money? You've grown disgustingly practical lately. You do get that this is all about Raj. You're just a jilted sibling trying to beat up your brother because he won't go to India with you or say you won the race to the top. Or whatever it is your pissed at him for."

Madi sucked her teeth, darting her eyes to the side in fair consideration.

"Maybe so. You always treat us Singhs so cruelly. Did I tell you he called me the other day at work to say how hurt he was about your getting married? I guess that doesn't surprise you."

Del looked down at her chipped fingernails. The flashback to her visit to Raj's studio last week stung too deeply to repeat the scenario now.

"He's just lonely," she finally said.

"Oh yes, my brother is big on loneliness. The deeper the ditch, the better for his mind to sink. You think I would have broken that news to him? It's better that you didn't have a big wedding, or there would have been trouble. I don't mean a scene or anything. Can you imagine Raj barging into the ceremony? He's just like our mother. He takes all of the small problems as proof that life is awful. Okay, life's awful. But why add to it? Why make an art out of suffering? You know he refuses to talk to our own father. They never got along, but you'd think a phone call every few months wouldn't kill him. The poor thing can barely find the strength to dial a phone number."

"If your brother is so terrible, I'd like to know why you set me up with him in the first place."

Madi whistled, shoving her chin in the air to let her eyes ponder the ceiling rafters.

"Because, you ingrate, I wanted to hold on to you. It was purely selfish. I'd get you tangled up in the Singh psychosis until you'd be the fly stuck with us spiders. Plus he's attractive. And for all of your social consciousness, you're a complete sucker for a pretty face. Otherwise, explain the husband."

It was not always hard to love Madeline Singh. Del leaned over the teak tray and wrapped her arms around her friend's waist, resting her head against the scratchy linen that bound her thighs.

"And what about you?" Del asked. "When are you going to start loving someone so we can stop talking about Raj all the time?"

"Groan," Madi said, scooping up Del's hair and running her violet fingernails softly over the nape of her neck. "Do we have to do that?"

"Do what?"

"That awful cliché of asking each other about who we're dating or not dating, giggling about love and sex and vibrators. We aren't those women, are we?"

Del lifted herself up, almost knocking over the teacups, and examined Madi's face. Her muscles tightened along the jaw, which made her look momentarily weaker, gripping in defense.

"I just want to see you happy." Like Del had to explain that. When was the last time Madi had lent her heart out for a night? When had she woken up naked in another person's bed, called in sick to fester in that bad after-sex smell of used tissues and unwashed armpits, felt the whole world constrict temporarily to the size of someone else's bed? Madi was right, there really was a Singh psychosis—pushing away those who tried to interfere, assessing the risk and finding the costs too great. Del sensed that Madi was reading her thoughts, because her eyes went wet, and she pinched them closed with her finger and thumb.

"Sorry," Del said.

"No, you're right. I don't know how couples do it. I see two people kissing in the street and wonder how they could have possibly worked themselves into such a state that they can't stop hanging all over each other. I can't imagine it anymore. How do people get together and stay that way?"

"By trying, I guess."

"You can't try. It happens or it doesn't. Half the time I really do see it as this infantile utopia of thinking that you're a better, more complete person if you aren't by yourself. It's a sick fascination. Totally anti-individualistic. I think some people are born with Velcro for skin. They can't stop sticking. Others of us, well . . . " she looked down at her chest, "steel plates."

"It happens by putting yourself out there. Why don't we go out one night? Why don't we get drunk anymore?"

"We have gone out. You do get drunk." Madi cleared her throat, pressed her bare feet onto the floor, and walked over to a set of oak drawers. "I have something for you," she said, returning with a small envelope. "A wedding present. I know it's tacky to give money, but . . . "

"Please don't," Del said with a dismissive wave of her hand. "Put that away." But Madi grabbed her wrist and pressed the envelope into her palm.

"Take it, Fiend. I don't know what you need, and I don't know Joseph well enough to get something he'd hate and you'd love. It isn't much. I was going to buy you a tablecloth or a colander, but what fun is that? Just get something ridiculous you'll only wear once."

Del opened the envelope and found a check for two thousand dollars written out in her name.

"That's too much. It's more than we spent on the wedding."

"Now that's just embarrassing. Take the damn money, will you? Try to enjoy it."

"Then promise you'll come shopping with me." Del felt like she was always begging for this, for time, and Madi scanned some mental calendar for a rivulet of white between meetings.

"In this heat?" Madi bunched her long black hair in a fist and swept it behind her shoulder. "Fine. Next week. Or when I'm back from my trip. I have all this space and I never use it. We can make dinner. There's something empty about rooms no one has sex in, don't you think?"

Del put the check in her billfold among the crumbled twenties, and they stood smiling at each other in silence. She got the sense Madi was waiting for her to leave, like she was one appointment that was breaking in on another, so she slid her hand around Madi's arm and steered her toward the elevator that opened directly into the apartment.

"So we won't go see art. That's decided."

"I didn't mean to say all of that. I'm just overworked. Be honest with me. Have I started looking like a middle-aged man? Take me out of this dress. Could I be selling incense sticks on a foldout table in Curry Hill?"

Madi lifted her chin as if posing for an imperial portrait.

"Not a bit."

Madi wrestled her arm free when the doors split open, and, with a surprisingly hard push, sent Del sailing into the metal tank. "Go home to your movie star. I'll call you tomorrow."

The summer when Del moved back to New York and she and Madi had lived in that railroad-style apartment in Alphabet City, they had a system for looking out for each other. It was when dope was still sold on the corner and every shadow looked like a rapist and cuatro music played all morning from every other apartment tuned to the same Puerto Rican station. It was a summer where white women, even dark, street-minded ones like Mad Fiend, were indications that the neighborhood was changing hands, reshuffling its race cards. Their system: When one of them was coming home late at night, she would call the apartment to announce her imminent arrival from the pay phone on the corner. The one at home would climb out onto the fire escape and watch as the other sprinted down the center of the street, making as much noise as possible, waving arms wildly, screaming "del del del del" or "madi madi," until she got to the front door of the building, unraped and unmugged.

They had both moved out by winter. But this had been their way of keeping each other safe. This had been their way of loving each other when no one else did.

CHAPTER EIGHT

ON THE CORKBOARD behind her desk, Post-its—red and pink and yellow and toxic orange—were tacked like butterflies, each luminous wing addressing a new concern. "Lunch with the Indian embassy press attaché, 12:30, Raol's." "Intel Corp conference on satellite hookup, 4:15, Friday." "New World Foreign Policy Briefing, Marriott Marquis, 8/28." Underneath the Post-its, glimpsed by the occasional rapid rise of air-conditioning from the vent, the photograph of a man could be seen. A man with a mustache rolled across his reddened face and tucked into a powder-blue turban. A man carrying the weight of old age in his cheeks and a Bud Light in his left hand. A photograph taken on a long dock in the Florida Keys three summers ago. Her father. Her bloodline to the continent whose economic development had been her mission to nurture for the past six years. The continent that was making her rich.

"My daughter. You make me proud. You have not forgotten," her father had told her on that trip to Florida and, several times since, on their weekly Sunday phone calls. "Your brother may not want to believe. But you believe. You are still Sikh."

Six years ago, you couldn't talk an Indian-made watch onto the wrists of an American venture capitalist. When Marcus Villareal, a freckled Swiss banker with a five o'clock shadow creeping over his chin around noon, had opened two management consultant offices, one in New Delhi and the other in the very office where she sat as vice president today, he had taken a chance on hiring a second-in-command with little business experience other than a part-time job reading investment strategies on Latin America for a big-name brokerage. But it didn't hurt to have an attractive half-Indian with an Ivy League pedigree on a team selling the third world to the first.

"Data sweatshops," the grunt against Indian tech centers went. Their fledging consultancy was called Eval-ution. "White-collar saris, I'm sorry, but no stockholder would risk a dime on that," the market had grumbled. But six years ago, Madi dressed herself in silks from a tailor in Curry Hill to sell a country she had not yet stepped foot in to corporate heads who didn't want to hear it. "Firing members of your own demographic and shipping the jobs overseas isn't very popular, you'll find," one man had said to her as he slid a presentation packet into his briefcase.

She didn't stop, though, building her case in front of long tables littered with paper cups, pencils, and investment strategies. "Send your customer-service jobs offshore and you'll be delivering them to a population of men and women with pitch-perfect English and advanced degrees. Do it at salaries one-third what you are paying some high-school dropout in the Midwest who wants health care and paid vacations. I'm asking you to do the math. Outsourcing your calling centers, your computer tech help desks, your frequent flier programs, you debt collection agencies, fill in the proverbial blank. Folks, this all has the potential to double profits within a matter of two years." Madi spent every square on the calendar selling desk jobs out of America, advertising Bangalore as a global back office to the richest conglomerates under the Western sun. She discovered right away what India meant to the ladies and gentlemen of the business class. They worried about inferior service. They imagined phone lines that crackled and went dead in the night to due to flash floods, one power strip to light an entire warehouse, low-caste workers who couldn't relate to flag-waving patriots pissed about a broken laptop.

"I've been to India. I've seen the buses those people take," a young executive said raising her hand against the rhythm of Madi's sales pitch. "When the motor breaks, they are stuck for hours. How can we be sure they'll even get to work?" Madi had to explain in reductive outline the history of a British colony, a top-notch educational system liberated into a new democracy, a nucleus of PhDs simply waiting to be put to use.

Then, four years ago, lightning struck.

By one and two and then twenty, companies began to shut their home centers in Seattle and San Antonio and St. Paul and relocate East, following her numbers, watching her six arms dribble zeroes like basketballs across a global court and shoot them into open hoops. The details had a way of hitting her with unexpected emotion—not just the money but the stories. She cried when she accompanied a delegation of future prospects to Bangalore, each loaded with green and saffron-colored caps and cocktail stirrers, and found that managers were trying desperately to sell their stock of old sewing machines for telephone headsets. The latest reports showed that India could soon see a growth of double its gross domestic product. Eight billion. That was how much money had already been lost overseas. Lost or made.

A year ago the current prime minister of India, a Sikh no less with the last name Singh, had written a commending letter to Evalution. Thanking and encouraging them. It hung framed in their sparse beige lobby, over the mail bins that so often came filled with letters from hate groups telling them they were destroying America, stealing jobs, ruining good, honest American lives. *Evil*-ultion, most of them began.

That was a year ago.

The fact was, India was not a bubble created in shatterproof glass. Problems, four years into the windfall, were growing. Problems that suggested call centers did not simply close in St. Paul and open in Bangalore without a certain gravitational shift.

Those were the problems that brought Madi to work on the Saturday afternoon shortly after she had said good-bye to Del. Her eyes froze on the picture of her father standing in front of that ribbon of blue water, when she heard a knock on her door.

The building doorman craned his neck into her office, holding a vase of flowers.

"I thought they'd die before Monday. Should have guessed you'd be in today."

They were from Marcus Villareal, currently in the New Delhi office, telling her in a short typed note to keep up the good work, that he was dealing with the wrenches. So should she. He was scheduling their meeting in Bangalore on her next trip with the prime minister himself.

At least someone was sending her flowers. Del would appreciate that. Perhaps Madi had given up her most furious years where love roared and boyfriends crept in and departed with the reckless, debilitating speed of winter colds. Perhaps she had sacrificed some part of her life to get to her position and could be considered impertinent for labeling everyone else's obsession with romance as nothing more than elective lobotomies. But Madi was proud, the kind of pride so unaccustomed to her generation that sprung from doing something more substantial, more effective, than building up a string of private excursions through the heart. *Poor Madi*, Del had said with her eyes an hour ago on her sofa. One part of her had thought, *yes, you're right*, while another concluded, *No. Poor Del*. She placed the vase on the windowsill, rotated back to her computer, and caught her reflection on the screen. Was this the face of someone who had gotten into a ditch deeper than she could climb out? She hoped not. She ripped one of the buds from the bouquet and placed it behind her ear.

CHAPTER NINE

No one who lived in New York ever felt inviolable to break-ins. They were as inevitable as earthquakes in Los Angeles or drunk-driving accidents in Boston. Whenever news reached Joseph's ear of a friend being robbed blind via an unlocked window or busted front door, he conceded to the etiquette of mustering an "Oh no, that's awful," but the shock was more an expression of sympathy than a naive response to a disaster endemic to the city. Joseph had always seen sickness as a similar kind of intruder, picking through personal items, rifling for valuables, stealing whole days or weeks, or worse, the entire substance of his life. It would happen, and when it did, no comforting condolences would return what it took.

When he woke in the morning, Del had already left for work. The nausea hit him as he walked toward the bathroom, softly first in a bout of vertigo. Then his stomach lurched, and the pulse of his left temple clamped his eyes closed. By the time he reached the toilet, he managed to wrap his arms around the cold porcelain before vomiting out a stream of yellow liquid. Each heave—four, then five, then six—amplified the beat against his temple, producing tears that mixed with the saliva dripping down his chin. He reached for a towel and pulled it from the shower rod, wiping it over his face as he fell against floor. He pressed his temple against the tiles to steady the pulse, his chest muscles aching from their effort, and he waited, for ten minutes and then twenty, to determine if the sickness had passed.

He had been told since childhood to expect such symptoms. They were the first warning signs of a heart condition, indicators of a far more robbing pain that would chew and swallow until the muscle eventually stopped.

After a half hour, Joseph gathered enough strength to climb from the bathroom floor and run cold water in the shower. His stomach had regained its stronghold, but numbness ran through his arms and legs. He filled his mouth with water from the shower nozzle and spit it down between his feet. Was this the sickness that he hoped would never find him, the sickness he tried to ignore but which always seemed right around the corner, just beyond the next day, traveling like a storm front straight from Ohio to New York?

He roped a towel around his waist and staggered into the living room, where his cell phone blinked red. It was from Janice Eccles. Texting was his agent's preferred method for scheduling auditions that didn't allow for questions. "1:45, Carlyle hotel. Aleksandra Andrews. Asked for you by name." He considered calling in sick, but he was sure the vomiting had subsided and he didn't want to give in to the vacant stalemate of a day lying in bed. He dressed quickly and sipped only enough coffee to allow the caffeine to strengthen his pace.

Joseph caught a cab that sped up Park Avenue, careening on the viaduct around Grand Central Station and through the hollowed-out base of the Helmsley Building until it swept into the clean geometry of uptown, passing Mercedes and BMW dealerships gleaming on the ground floors of corporate skyscrapers. Joseph always imagined driving one of the new cars right through the plate-glass windows and breaking away, gearing it north, waving good-bye to the deodorant stick of the Met Life Building, and breezing over the Queensboro Bridge. But the dealerships must have expected such consumer hallucinations when they parked the latest models there, that impossible pileup where the thing you steal is the very thing that aids your escape. Joseph's fantasies were consistent on one theme since childhood: they always involved the plotline of getting away.

He paid the cabbie a twenty on the corner of East Seventy-Sixth and was directed by a receptionist toward a bank of black elevator doors. He wiped the sweat from his hairline and shook his wrists to startle the blood that was still running cold through his fingers. Joseph dreamed of getting away or disappearing completely. That had been his motivation for moving to New York in the first place, and it also explained why he worked so diligently in his chosen profession. As an actor, he could stand in front of an audience and disappear right in front of them, transform into any given character and tell stories that weren't his own.

This morning hadn't been the first bout of sickness to creep over him and leave him splayed on the bathroom floor, caught in a standoff with his own body to determine whether the sickness would travel deeper or simply fade. Those attacks had struck at least five times in as many months, and he had secretly scheduled appointments with four different doctors, three general practitioners and one heart specialist, for a battery of tests that came back clean. He had purposely not told Del. Even in the middle of the night when he woke up panicking, he muffled his mouth with both hands to prevent from rousing her. If he let that fact into their apartment, he worried it would remain there, moving in like an unwanted relative who would never leave. He had seen how quickly a house became infected with death. How his mother had shut the curtains and locked the doors to keep the paranoia trapped in with them. Joseph felt that if he said it out loud—death, the possibility of it, right ahead of him, one birthday away—it would be like admitting it, agreeing to the pattern, encouraging it along. He inhaled deeply, whipped his fingers through his hair as if to drive away all memories of the morning, and followed the medallion pattern in the carpet to 706. He knocked lightly on the door.

"Come in."

The room was dark, the sheer curtains that scrolled from the rod over the window diffusing the sunlight. He caught the smell of perfume and coffee, as he nearly tripped over a tray of dirty saucers on the floor. As his eyes adjusted to the darkness, he saw a woman sitting in a chair in front of a set of French doors. His hand lifted to wave, but he wasn't sure if she could see him.

"You're Joseph Guiteau?"

She didn't wait for an answer, rising from the chair and walking over to the wall with her arm outstretched, her fingers already forming a grip to turn on the light switch.

Joseph had come here for work but, as she turned on the light, he felt as if he had escaped one sickness only to find another. He recognized the woman, the thin silhouette and soft monotone of her voice reminding him exactly where he first saw her. The prisoners-ofearth meeting.

"What are you doing here?" He took a step back against the door.

"Waiting for you," she replied, forcing a polite smile. "I'm your appointment."

"But I know you . . . " he replied, thinking maybe he shouldn't mention it, maybe she wouldn't recall, "from the meeting."

"Yes." Her fingers still grasped the switch, as if at any moment she might turn the light off and leave them in the darkness to work out how they had found themselves together again in a very different room. "That's where I saw you," she confirmed. "That's why I've asked for you to come. It wasn't easy. Do you usually give out fake names of other actors in your agency?" It took Joseph a second to remember the misinformation he had passed on to poor, confused Rose Cherami at the conspiracy meeting, identifying himself as William. "I asked your friend, what was her name? Well, I thought you two were friends, because you were talking. I guess you shouldn't trust anything you see in those kind of places."

"I thought I was coming here for an audition."

She let go of the switch and walked over to him. The shoulders of her thin, black sweater carried a few blond strands, and her loose white pants clung with static down her legs. She wasn't wearing makeup. He could see the crosshatch of wrinkles around her mouth and eyes and the gray hairs weaving into the blonde at the roots of her scalp. The red birthmark was no longer hidden by a collar and had the intense line of a slash down her neck. She did not look as

calm and collected as she had in that basement meeting more than
a week ago, but she seemed comfortable in this hotel room, as if she
had made it her home for some time. Something about this woman
frightened him, how quickly she was moving toward him or the way
her eyes were scrutinizing the details of his face. People are supposed
to stay where you have left them last, they aren't supposed to crop up
unannounced in other unrelated situations. At the meeting, he had
wanted to follow her, but now that she was standing in front of him,
Joseph's first reaction was to run.

"Yes, it is you," she said, stopping a foot away, still staring up at
his face. "I knew as soon as I saw you that you were right."

"I might be awful," he replied meekly, realizing that he was still
shoving his back against the hotel-room door. "I don't really believe
all those things at prisonersofearth. It's more curiosity, killing free
time. I don't know why I find it calming. But I remember you. I
remember wondering how a woman like you ended up there."

"Maybe we end up finding what we need there. You look exactly
like him."

"Like who?"

"My husband," she said with a slow exhale. "Not when he died.
But when we were young." She shook her head and pressed her
fingers against her eyelids as if she had been in the dark for so long
that the light bothered her. "That must sound crazy. I'm not crazy.
It's just that, without even realizing it, I've been waiting for you."
She noticed his tense posture with his fingers frozen on the doorknob
and again tried to smile.

Joseph wondered what it was about him that was like her dead
husband. For she had reminded him of his mother, so many years
lost now back in Ohio, and the resurrection of that memory arrived
like any homecoming: filled with strange warmth and the fear of
returning to old ground.

CHAPTER TEN

EVERY MORNING DEL woke precisely at seven. She did not choose rock music or the tremolo of St. Patrick's bells or even, as one AM station offered, the deep-ocean blowhole orchestra of bottlenose dolphins; no, Del elected for the honking Long Island accents of 1010WINS announcers to drag her back to consciousness. It seemed as if the last New Yorkers who still possessed that cartoonishly vowel-skidding speech were the ones delivering the city's news and weather. Del had tuned her alarm clock to that station ever since 9/11 as a preventative measure for hearing the terrible fate that might await each day: "The terrorists have poisoned the water supply, don't take a shower." "Try to avoid midtown. The streets are coated in anthrax." Or worse, "All of Manhattan's radioactive. Life as we know it is over." She no longer worried about such probable atrocities, but the dial remained fixed to the station.

On the subway, she watched the morning workforce reading newspapers or staring with zombie eyes at the strip of plastic-surgery advertisements. She wondered what beds these commuters had just left, what crazy sex acts they had just extricated themselves from, what bitter sleeping partners kept their eyes shut until these early risers dressed to catch this exact uptown train. In the subway, it was impossible to tell who was happy and who was miserable. Everyone looked slightly constipated, as if the entire car had ordered from the same Chinese restaurant the night before. It was inhuman to be so human this early, she thought as the doors split open for her stop in the Bronx.

Del climbed the staircase to the sidewalk and performed her junkie move of leaning against the stone wall while she rolled a cigarette, dug for a lighter, and pulled smoke into her tired lungs. At least today she would call the immigration lawyer. Then she remembered the children. Oh, god, the children. Her immediate future was overrun with them.

Two hours later Del stood before an electronic map of the world, speckled in outdated blinking lights to indicate thriving reptilian populations. Collected around her were twenty sixth-graders on a summer class trip, smacking gum, drinking red slush out of plastic elephant heads, and trying to push the weaker members of the group toward the darkened cobra display.

"Welcome to the reptile department," she said in a flat monotone. The teacher with candied metallic hair and gallon-sized breasts frowned at her. This teacher had probably taught for so many years that, in every human interaction, she treated adults like misbehaving twelve-year-olds constantly out to disappoint her. "Today I'm going to talk to you about snakes." The children's eyes widened. Slushy-stained lips grimaced. Two girls turned their backs to her with hands over their mouths as if to vomit. "I am one of the zoologists specializing in snakes here at the zoo, and I hope by the end of this discussion some of you will have changed your minds on how you consider these animals."

"Snakes are disgusting," screamed one of the girls who still couldn't bear the courtesy of turning around to face her. "My brother ate one."

"But what you may not know is that the rattlesnake was originally chosen to be the animal to represent your country." Del caught herself. She still said *your*.

"That's a lie," a boy with spiked blond hair yelled. "It's an eagle."

She stared down at him hard as if to indicate that, in a less democratic country, his impertinence might render him prime beef for the alligator pit. "It is an eagle. But it wasn't always. To continue, the rattlesnake is in a group of venomous pit vipers found only in the New World. Benjamin Franklin picked the rattler for a number of anatomical reasons. As the rattlesnake has no eyelids, Franklin prized it as a symbol of vigilance. Consider the utility of the rattle itself. The fair warning of danger the snake offers its enemies before it strikes. In 1754, before the Declaration of Independence was signed, Franklin drew a political cartoon of the rattlesnake cut into eight parts. He wrote, 'Join or Die' under it. There was a superstition in those days that a snake cut into pieces could come back to life before sunset. He was encouraging the eight colonies—"

"There were thirteen colonies," the teacher corrected.

"That came later. He encouraged the colonies to be united as one body or die alone in the desert of war. Think what a different country you would be living in if the rattlesnake graced the coins in your pockets and was stamped across the president's podium during press briefings. Think of the Middle East waving snakes angrily into news cameras to protest the war your president started."

This speech was not her invention. Okay, "desert of war" onward had been ad-libbed to provide a little menace to her lines. But Abrams had penned this pat introduction to herpetology twenty years ago as a method of drawing the listener in on historical hooks, endearing the reptiles sleeping behind the dense plexiglass to the visitors shielding their eyes as if navigating a house of horrors. Snakes wrapped around proud founding fathers instead of suffocating necks, snakes biting warship enemies in national defense rather than ankles in the garden. Abrams forced every staff member to memorize it and often listened by the door to ensure it was being delivered with the proper inflections. Del did not use the inflections. She waved the school group to follow her to the window of a bull snake coiled under a piece of driftwood. She explained the patterns on its skin as an imitation of the rattlesnake, a visual trick in the wild, a Darwinistic tactic to keep the animal alive by mimicking a far more venomous cousin, like an unloaded gun fending off a police force (she wasn't allowed to use that comparison).

These public tours were her least favorite duty, right above gassing the baby mice with carbon dioxide on feeding day. Her years in the department gave her seniority never to speak to a children's group, but Kip had begged a switch when a Catholic high-school sisterhood had crowded the entrance in skimpy plaid skirts and crisscrossing A-cup trainers a week ago. She forced herself to continue. "Many snakes are strategic actors in making us believe they are dangerous, when really they are anything but."

Del wasn't thinking about the bull snake or the argyle diamonds webbing down its epidermis. She wasn't looking for signs of Abrams listening by the door. She was thinking of the phone call she would make to Frank Warren, Esq. as soon as this tour concluded. Madi said that Warren was the best for climbing the prickly branches of immigration law all the way to a green card. Del imagined green cards blooming on maples, dropping like open leaves, drying into curls in the baked dirt.

"Ma'am, have you ever been bitten by a snake?"

A hush fell over the school group, as if something extraordinary were about to be revealed.

"Dry bites," Del clarified, instinctively rubbing her wrists. "Once or twice. No poison. I've never been struck by any of the venomous here. We are extremely careful. We have procedures that make those possibilities impossible." The image of Francine dropping the diamondback on the floor came into her head, but she did not feel the need to relay this mishap to an audience only now growing accustomed to the display cases. "Snakes don't always inject poison. Sometimes they strike as a warning. It stings, maybe ten minutes."

"Would it kill you if they did?"

Del smiled and the teacher frowned at the fat black girl in skinny black glasses conducting the Q&A.

"Depends on the variety of snake. But we keep antivenom on hand in the lab to be on the safe side. If antivenom is administered into a strike victim in time, say two or three hours, death is usually preventable."

"Which snake is the deadliest?" the girl persisted. Del felt an immediate liking to her, and, of course, it helped that she was the only non-white member of her class and, because of this, must have learned courage faster than the rest. It always amazed her how quickly the subject of death entered these tours—lions, tiger sharks, and honeybees all killed far more efficiently with bigger yearly death tolls, but her specialty was construed as the armless grim reapers, the creeping killers under the porch stairs.

"Diamondbacks, cobras, inland taipans, these are the vipers with the potent juice. This bull snake wouldn't hurt you more than a pinch, although I'm sure he wishes he could."

Bites were the mandatory occupational duty that Del was good at. The roaring Whirlpool refrigerator in the lab held twenty-nine antivenoms for the entire New York county, icy packets ready to be grabbed and thrown in the Honda Civic parked out back with the keys in the ignition for a race to the emergency room. She had taken this course of action only five times in her career. The general polyvalent was marked green on the top shelf for unidentifiable bites. The monovalents, marked in red and labeled by species, were used for those rare victims who knew what variety attacked them— knowledge usually acquired because they owned them illegally as pets. Del stocked the antivenoms. She knew the exact location of each packet in the refrigerator. She knew the different symptoms for each bite. The rattlesnake, for example: swelling, bleeding, nausea, chills, salivation, spasms, tingling of the tongue, fluctuations in blood pressure; this venom was a hemotoxin: a rapid rise in the heart rate, paralysis of the circulatory muscles. She knew the exact serum to neutralize these effects. Twenty minutes ETA from hospital call to emergency desk. She had obsessively run through the symptoms on those five drives out to the hospital and often repeated them to herself on the subway to work: *bleeding, nausea, extreme fluctuations in the blood, heart attack, swelling, dilated pupils, cramping, vomiting . . .*

She did not recite these symptoms to the class. Instead she told them how farmers released snakes into cornfields to kill the vermin that infested the crop. She told them how rattlesnakes burrow together in winter in complex societies, sleeping intertwined through the cold just above the frost line; how recent studies indicated that the rattlesnake was losing its rattle in certain newly developed urban areas in the Southwest where their warning could not be heard over the highway traffic.

When Del had entered the lab that morning, she had taken her notebook up to the nursery to inspect its newest addition. Del had tapped her fingers on Apollo's tank and had watched with relief as his black shovelhead dipped low. He was still alive. His tail rose, and he struck his fangs against the glass. A rattle wouldn't crown Apollo's tail until the first time he shed. The tail was powered like a heart, an involuntary muscle beating out of fear, a little maraca playing on diamond skin.

As the tour ended and the class funneled out of the hall into the yellow heat of the park, the black girl walked up to Del and poked her hip.

"Can I ask you something?"

"Of course." She smiled. "I liked your questions."

"What I want to know is if the rattlesnake loses its rattle, like you said, then basically it will be exactly like a bull snake. Am I right?"

"Physically. But you forget that the rattlesnake still has venom stored in its glands."

The girl nodded anxiously and rushed to her next question. "Won't bull snakes mate with rattlesnakes, then? Could they, I mean?" She grinned in embarrassment, pushing her glasses farther up the bridge of her nose. "If they don't know."

"They know. They know to keep clear of each other."

"But," the girl said impatiently. "Then if rattlesnakes can just lose their rattles because of traffic, why can't the bull snake just grow a rattle? And then, why don't bull snakes make poison too? I mean, why only copy the skin? Why not get what really hurts?"

"These are excellent questions," Del said, lowering herself on her knee and placing a hand on the girl's shoulder. She had never been good with children, but when she met a smart one, usually the oddball outsider, an inexplicable wave of affection swam through her, which she assumed must be the closest thing she ever felt to a maternal instinct. "You should consider a career in biology when you grow up. We need smart researchers like you."

"Oh, no, I could never do that," the girl gasped, backing away from the threat. "I'm going to be an actress. I definitely want to do movies. I want to be a Hollywood star at least by the time I'm your age."

As the girl sprinted off to join her classmates, Del wondered if she were the only person left in America who did not dream of the fame that comes from imitating others. Even the indigenous bull snake pretended to be a rattler. Del had married an actor. Why did fulfilling a dream in this country always mean becoming someone else?

She made her way through the lab door in the exhibition hall, passing Abrams in the long hallway to the break room. He stopped her with an uncharacteristic greeting, which unnerved her before she noticed the visitor behind him, a thin smiling woman with wool-white hair tied unevenly in a bun. "Sarah, this is Delphine Kousavos. She's on staff here. She attended Columbia." The visitor's face brightened, and they shook hands. "Sarah Isely is a visiting researcher at your alma mater. She wanted to see some of our collection." Del was about to ask her what she was researching, but Abrams grabbed the woman's sleeve and led her away, unwilling to waste any more time than necessary in demonstrating his kindness to the subhuman slaves of his department.

The clock in the break room struck noon. Kip cut a tuna sandwich in half and offered her the smaller portion. His red pompadour was slicked above his forehead like an upturned hat brim, but the fluorescent overheads turned his freckles a corrosive green.

"No thanks," she said to the sandwich. "And we're never trading tour groups again."

Kip reached into the Whirlpool refrigerator stocked with the antivenom and pulled out a can of orange soda.

"Were there any lookers?" he asked.

"They were twelve, you asshole." He shrugged, choking on the sandwich hanging from his teeth. "Who was that woman with Abrams, anyway?" she asked.

"Researcher. Something about poisons being used for medical testing." Kip pointed to the morning newspaper spread across the table. "I just read that a couple got married on top of Mount Everest this week. Can you believe that? The first time in history. They took their oxygen masks off for the five-minute ceremony, and the groom started hallucinating, saying he didn't know where he was. They had to keep him from walking over the edge." Kip put his hand to his mouth and mimed an invisible oxygen mask. "You know what he should have said to her at the top?"

"It's all downhill from here," Del replied, predicting the punch line while searching under the newspapers for her notebook with the lawyer's number copied in its pages. When she looked up, Kip was holding his sandwich meaningfully between his fingers with a hurt expression on his face.

"I love you. He should have said I love you and that they were going to be happy together and nothing would ever come between them. God, isn't anything sacred to you? Are you really that cynical? Poor Delbert."

"You really are an asshole," she said. She slipped out the back door, stood in the shade of the department's dumpster, and dialed Frank Warren on her cell phone. After she introduced herself, he broke down the first, necessary steps of proving a marriage to the INS. "You and your husband need to know as much about each other as possible," he told her, as she copied his words down on paper. "They will ask the most intrusive questions in the interview, so try to memorize simple things. The brand of shaving cream he uses. Where you first met. I've done this job for fifteen years, and you'd be surprised what couples don't know about one another. And please, Mrs. Guiteau, keep a photo album. No one likes unsentimental couples. Not even the U.S. government." That was the first time Del had ever been referred to as "Mrs." She repeated it to herself, as if to commit a new taxonomy to memory.

CHAPTER ELEVEN

WILLIAM WALKED THROUGH the midtown Flower District with a slow stagger to reduce the clinking noise in his backpack. He had wrapped the contents in newspaper to avoid chips, but the stoneware vase was knocking against the silver nineteenth-century mantle clock. The dinner set kept jangling at the bottom of the bag. He slowed past the stalls selling birds of paradise, dripping azaleas, and palm fronds, careful not to get his feet caught in the green hoses that lassoed across the sidewalk, suddenly yanked by gardeners into trip wires. One fall and the entire inventory would be worthless, and then what?

The pawning of Jennifer's antiques had begun a month ago. Checking a bank balance that had dipped into three digits, William had promised, rolling an ivory sculpture of the god Orissa into a bath towel, that he would only sell one or two items, the least prominent and most unappreciated in their time together as husband and wife. He had found two Chinese women, black-market dealers, who ran their operation behind a plant store devoted to exotic cacti. These twin sisters, or at least they both had the same lipless mouths underneath their matching red visors, were willing to pay in cash at a hefty discount in lieu of his providing an authenticity certificate. "Very nice," one would say, with eyes that consulted the other, "but hard to sell. We give you three hundred dollars." Once or twice became once or twice each week, and even William had been astounded by how many things looked missing in the apartment, as if they had been burglarized by a picky thief. And maybe, he could swear, it had. Maybe when and if Jennifer returned, divorce papers in hand, he would be long gone to Los Angeles having to perform the minor acting role of crime-wave victim by phone. "Wasn't the alarm set? Did you check the door to the patio? What are you waiting for, call the police!" At first he felt guilty for selling Jennifer's collection, unrolling the goods for the Chinese sisters to inspect before they dropped each piece into a velvet drawstring bag. But with each new extraction, as the amount looted become more obvious to the apartment, his sense of blame diminished. Jennifer must have known what kind of financial trouble he would be in, how desperate life would get. Did she imagine he would sleep surrounded by all of those riches and find work at a restaurant or folding jeans at H&M? He needed money to live.

The cacti that usually guarded the storefront in unwelcoming spikes were gone. The doors didn't budge when William tugged the handle. Caving his hands against the window, he peered into the deserted space. Sunlight spilled across the empty wood floor. He could see all the way to the back room where two sisters should be waiting with their lockbox of cash, but only the bare butcher's table remained.

"Not possible," he wheezed.

The midget shopkeeper next door shook a spray bottle at him. "They gone. Left."

"Have they moved? To another location?"

"They close. Gone. What you looking for? You want plants?"

"Clocks?" William replied, about to unzip his bag to show the items weighing on his back—maybe all flower shops in the West Thirties were black-market fronts, maybe all nurseries doubled as antique dealers. But William thought better of it, kicked the door, and stumbled toward Seventh Avenue. He tried to calculate how

much of the money he had saved. The amount did not seem near
enough. His stomach lurched as he passed through his least favorite
part of town, Herald Square crowded with Macy's shoppers who
always looked enraged even as they swarmed the walkways with
their bulky department store bags. The soles of his shoes stuck on
the concrete in the afternoon heat, and he walked in a daze, only
coming alert as he passed beautiful women stepping into idling
town cars and young men with cheekbones fluted like architectural
eaves and with no doubt dependable erections even after several shots
of tequila. They reawakened him the same way someone lost in
a daydream was snapped back into reality by sharp spoken words.
William used to love New York because of all the forced interactions
on the street, the sordid, disparate occupants of the city meeting each
other without any defenses, stepping together through their after-
noons. Now it seemed as if his eyes were only attuned to those rare
inhabitants whose lives were ruled by luxuries he could no longer
afford. That was the hell of his psychology lately—the editing down
of the world to its most glamorous and irretrievable parts.

When he returned to the apartment, he opened his backpack and
repositioned the objects on their shelves, briefly acknowledging their
fragile beauty as if for the first time. He stood for a while staring into
the silent living room, wondering where Jennifer was and why she
hadn't called to tell him when the papers would be signed. He had
not made communication either, for fear she would remember that
he still took up space in her apartment and would make good on her
threat to kick him out. The quiet of the room with its French sofas
and slender end tables—all of Jennifer's new money attempts at a
WASP pedigree—felt like chaos waiting to break. A joint would
have killed the panic, but he resisted the urge to phone his dealer,
a headphoned NYU student with a toolbox of small ziplock bags
packed with the turbo-hydroponic pot he grew in the neon greenhouse of his closet.

In the evening, when indoor lamps collected their light in faint
halos before night finally settled, he considered the one backup he
had left. Friends. Friends with money. He still had that to depend
on. He dialed Joseph's number.

"It hurts to wait around, so I've decided that I'm going to do it. I'm moving." William mustered enough enthusiasm to make the statement sound optimistic. The result was that he sounded like he was reading the words. "I truly believe it's the most mature decision to make at this juncture."

Joseph responded with a shrill whistle.

"Are you sure? I really don't think you've thought this through. I can't believe things won't get better."

"They will get better. They will when I'm out of town. I don't have much of a choice. I'm getting to a point where I'm out of luck here. Out of options. I sit around all day in my ex-wife's apartment wanting things I no longer have any chance of getting."

"Maybe you should go in and talk to Janice."

"I have talked to Janice," he said furiously. "You don't know how bad it's gotten."

"Then try something else."

"It's too late for that, Joe. I've only done one thing for the past ten years. And if I have to submit myself to a day job, I'd rather do it someplace else, where everyone I know can't watch me fail. It's too embarrassing. Oh, people would just love that, wouldn't they? Nothing would make people happier than finding me waiting on them at some shit restaurant."

"Don't get paranoid. Just calm down. How about we meet for a drink? Hairy Bishop?"

William hadn't meant to say what was running on overdrive through his mind. He wanted to stick to the script of asking Joseph for a loan, but the curiosity got the better of him. "Be honest. Are you getting any work?"

"This isn't a competition," Joseph replied coldly.

That sealed it. He breathed harshly into the receiver. "I know it's not. I'd be happy if you were getting work," he lied. "You can be honest."

"Well, a few commercials maybe. And then there's some kind of project in development. I don't know what will come of it. I'm still deciding."

William's fingers contracted around the phone in a slow strangle, and his top teeth dug into their lower orders. It hadn't occurred to him that Joseph's options were so vast that he could actually decide which roles to take.

"Congratulations," he said. "I don't think I'll get that beer with you."

"Why not?"

"I've got to plan a good-bye party. One last celebration in this awful apartment that I don't even own. But here's the catch. It's a charity event: Help William Asternathy Get to California. Sounds fun, right? It's a hundred dollars a head and if you can't find it in your heart to pay, then fuck you. Beer will be complimentary, of course."

"You can't," Joseph moaned in horror. His friend's innate snobbery always seemed to come alive in moments of William's desperation. "I won't let you. I thought you didn't want to make it clear to everyone how bad off you are. Christ, if you need some money . . . "

But William couldn't ask now. He couldn't take money from another man who was succeeding precisely where he failed. It was one thing to live off of the cash supplies of rich friends who hadn't earned their wealth and quite another to accept a donation from someone who had beaten him at the game he had played with delusional intensity for the span of his adult life.

"I can take care of myself," he said. "You just wait for the invitation. Then I'll be out of here, and the whole town will be yours."

"You're not leaving. You're just upset. This is the only place where you can—" but William hung up before Joseph could finish. It was pure insanity to think that anything would change for him. Insanity was Manhattan at sunrise with barely enough cash to pay the fare home. Insanity was the sunrise beyond that one, and the next, and again one more without a single decision to break the pattern. William walked to the bedroom to go to sleep early. He felt a rush of comfort in realizing that he had at least made a choice.

CHAPTER TWELVE

ALEKSANDRA AND JOSEPH sat on the floor of her hotel room
with the lights off, the curtains closed, and the chain engaged on the
door. Even in this quiet refuge, she seemed on edge, pausing when
she heard footsteps in the hall and periodically turning to stare at the
traces of light that broke underneath the curtains. Joseph watched
a housefly crawl across the thick carpet, a black zigzag along the
knotted threads.

This was their second meeting, arranged again through Janice.
Joseph had wanted to ask his agent exactly what Mrs. Andrews had
to offer him. But involving Janice now seemed like a betrayal of
Aleksandra's trust. When he left the hotel that first afternoon, she
had said, "I will explain more the next time you come back. It's hard
for me to talk about it. But please, promise to come." There had been
a weight to her eyes, sincere and yet filled with urgent worry, which
had forced him to agree.

He waited five days expecting the call, but when it arrived and
Janice gave him the time, his stomach dropped, his throat hardened,
and he almost decided to cancel. Aleksandra Andrews had something horrible in her life, he could feel it. He knew very well what

the face of a person with a terrible secret looked like. It was the face of someone who does not seem invulnerable to the simple negotiations of a day. He had learned over the years to control that face whenever he encountered it in the mirror.

In the elevator up to her room, he had promised himself to make no promises to Aleksandra Andrews. Just to listen. There was no danger in hearing her out. He calmed himself, exhaling three long breaths outside the door to 706. When he entered, he found her sitting on the floor in the darkness, her knees drawn up to her breasts. The rims of her eyes were swollen, and when Aleksandra first looked up at him, a small tremor shot through her tiny frame, bunching her shoulders and arching her neck. The birthmark disappeared against the redness of her skin. She gave a nervous smile that did not entirely reassure him, but he sat down anyway across from her on the floor. Then she stood up and chained the door.

Joseph asked her straight out, "Why were you at that meeting?" Aleksandra had warned him that it was difficult for her to talk, but she began relating the kind of story that perhaps could only be told to a stranger. Her words weren't the product of memorized recitation. They often swam hurriedly as if trying to grasp the next fragment, then suddenly disintegrating as if she were weighing them for accuracy. She often stopped to bite her upper lip mid-sentence, and in those cracks of silences, it was as if her courage might disappear into them, might just dissolve, leaving Joseph to stare into the shadows her eyes made.

"Our dream came to an end in 2001, or my dream really," she began. "Because Ray was having nightmares well before that. We were happy once and doing quite well. You see, we were living on electricity. We were getting rich off power. It never occurred to me there was anything wrong in that."

She stretched the neck of her sweater and rested her fingers on her collarbone. A silver necklace managed to collect some of the scant sunlight and project it into a prism on the ceiling.

"But Ray started waking up in the middle of the night. He'd put his hand over my mouth so tightly I could hardly breathe. He'd say they were out in the bushes. They were coming up the stairs.

I'd ask what he meant, but he'd just start to cry. He said he knew terrible things and no one would let him live with all of these facts in his head. He looked so scared—I mean *scared* like he believed in monsters. Ray was a strong man. You'd never seen anyone so stoic in the twenty-five years we were together. But those nights a little boy woke up who suddenly realized how dark and malicious the world can be. I didn't recognize him. That's when reality hit me. Right there on our bed in Malibu with his hand clamped over my mouth. That's when I knew that Ray was part of it."

She yanked her fingers from her neck and pet the carpet with slow strokes.

"Your husband was part of what? I don't understand." He worried his confusion might stop her cold, but she nodded her head as if in agreement.

"When we first married, Ray was in politics. He wanted to become governor, his goal since Stanford. He served as a junior senate assistant lumped down with bills on the California Energy Commission. He hated the work, but like anything, over time, you start to become fascinated with what you're thrown into. Eventually Ray went over to the private sector. This was maybe fifteen years ago. He became a lobbyist for deregulation. He had so much conviction for doing right to the people of California, I don't think he realized at first what was going on. He believed in free market, he believed in the private sector and the drive of competition to provide the cheapest energy to the state. But somewhere, when I wasn't looking, Ray changed. I often think it's ironic that I only started seeing him in the right light when the blackouts hit the state. By then it was too late."

"Blackouts," Joseph repeated, and again she nodded.

"You remember Enron?" she asked him. He did. For a while, no one could turn on the television or listen to a radio in a cab without hearing about Enron's deregulation scandal, a cautionary tale of price fixing and forced shutoffs. It was a subject that had permeated the basement meetings of prisonersofearth for many months.

"So your husband worked for Enron," he guessed.

Aleksandra bit her upper lip. She could have stopped her story here. She still had the opportunity to derail the narrative and let

Joseph leave the hotel room knowing only the faintest glimmers of the nightmare behind her lips. She struggled to swallow, fighting off the impulse to stop.

"He worked for bigger people than Enron," she said in a tone that almost accused Joseph of naiveté. "The deregulation scandal goes so much deeper than a single pony company in Texas. It amazed me in those months when the Enron story was breaking how cleanly the whole incident was being wrapped up with the trial of a few executives. Ray knew just how far the web spun. You see, he had all of the implications in his head. Not just fraudulent business crooks. I mean the government. Ray had enough information on key politicians in the White House to bring the whole country down if it ever got out."

She rubbed her wrists and gathered her knees against her chest, hugging them so tightly that her bare feet lifted an inch off the floor. It was as if Aleksandra were bundling her body up so that only her mouth and mind mattered. Joseph remembered as a child how his mother sat in her study chair, her entire body erased underneath a wool throw, with only her head and hands visible when she talked about her research on conspiracies and cover-ups. His mother had eventually given up the rest of the world, but her body went first. Even now Joseph could only recall her face and hands in precise detail, blue veins and blue eyes both pulsing.

"Ray started to tell me things, always at night," Aleksandra said. "I asked him to stop talking, but he couldn't. I wonder if he thought telling me all of those secrets felt like he was getting rid of them. He said they'd come for him."

She stopped, and he waited for her to continue. She released her legs from her arms and began twisting a loose thread in the seam of her pants. She let the quiet settle around them for a few minutes. Joseph tried to imagine the beautiful, unguarded woman Aleksandra must have been before she had this story. His mother had once been beautiful as well. Everyone always claimed that their parents had been great beauties in youth. But there had been a time before his father died when her lean frame and long black hair carried a gravity that forced heads to turn toward her like a law of physics.

Aleksandra must have possessed that same kind of magnet. Some of it still remained. In the conspiracy meeting she appeared strong and complete, her tightly closed mouth over a set of agitated teeth the only clue to a crack just under the surface. He wondered how much of that crack had already swallowed her. And how much farther it might open.

"For a while I thought we'd be safe. But I was wrong. When the entire family of one of Ray's chief associates died in their home one night from a carbon-dioxide leak, I finally started to believe him. When we heard the news, Ray pulled our luggage out and demanded we pack, put everything we could in the car, and drive north. That night I had to talk down a man who could run marathons, who ate dinner at the White House as the president's guest, who once told me that as long as we were in California, an earthquake couldn't break us apart. I refused to leave that night, creeping off with what cash and valuables we had like thieves of our own life." Aleksandra exhaled and wiped her eyes with her knuckle. She bit her lip and swallowed. "I sat Ray down and told him he had to go to the papers, even if it meant prison. I assumed the safest route was full disclosure. Ray would be safe if he told everything he knew."

"What did the papers say?"

"There were no papers." Aleksandra stopped talking. Her head tilted to the side as if she were trying to make out a picture that had been hung the wrong way. Joseph instinctually tilted his head to match the line of her eyes.

"Ray was found in the front seat of his Lexus in a parking lot off the Pacific Coast Highway on April 27, 2002. A bullet had been fired into the left temple with a pistol in his left hand. Never mind that he was right-handed. The coroner concluded suicide." Her face was too shadowed to read, but stands of hair floated flame-white around her head. "Now you know why someone like me goes to conspiracy meetings in a city on the other side of the country. Because all I have are Ray's secrets. I've given up going to the papers. They want proof, and I don't have so much as a piece of paper. I'm just a raving wife trying to rationalize her husband's suicide."

Joseph realized now what distinguished Aleksandra from the other members of the basement conspiracy meeting—and what had fascinated him about her that day. Her eyes held a fixed gaze that was not quite focused on the objects in front of her. "We were married for twenty-five years and lived in that house in Malibu for twelve of them. I sold everything a week after Ray's funeral. I got out with a few suitcases. Do you know what it's like to leave a place you've called home in a matter of days, unable to speak to friends you've known since childhood? Do you know what it's like to have your world emptied? You can't even let your memories digest. But I'm going to salvage something. You don't live in Los Angeles for as long as I did and not know some pretty good contacts in the film industry. I don't care if it sounds cheap. It's the only medium people pay attention to anymore."

"So you want to make a movie?" Joseph asked. "About his death. Am I right?"

"I'm not asking you to believe everything I'm telling you. I'm just asking that you play him."

"Because I look like him?"

She lifted herself from the floor, holding onto her knees for support. Then she walked quietly to the window and opened the curtains. Taxis streamed up Madison Avenue in hurried yellow waves. In the sunlight, Joseph noticed a typewriter sitting on the rosewood desk in the corner with typed white papers stacked around its metal shell.

"Not just because you look like him," Aleksandra said, turning around and walking toward him with her bare feet soft and deliberate on the carpet. Her toes were hairless but the nails were chipped and the skin gray with dirt. "Because you were also in a conspiracy meeting in a city on the other side of the country. Because that means you might believe me. Do you think I sound crazy? If you do, you don't need to come back."

As she came closer, he saw her face appearing from the shadows, tearless but strained with jaw muscles swollen from clenching. The slender birthmark on her neck swelled and dimmed as she breathed. Joseph had been in the presence of hundreds of attractive women in his career. His profession brought so many gorgeous specimens in close proximity that their looks began to read as dull and indistinguishable. He loved that Del was beautiful in an unstudied way, which could never be captured on film. But staring up at Aleksandra, Joseph felt a tick of that same attraction, maybe because she had long stopped caring about what she looked like. She gazed down at him, and he scooted backward on the floor to put some distance between them.

"Are you frightened there's still someone looking for you?" he asked. "Is that why you're here in this hotel? You think maybe they haven't blocked up all the leaks?"

"Yes," she said, nodding. "But I'm far worse frightened that I'll never get to say what I know. That terrifies me far worse. That's why I couldn't stop telling you once I started. It's been building inside of me for so long." He could see that she was exhausted, but her shoulders relaxed as if they had lost their heaviness. "Do you know the etymology of the word *conspiracy?*" she asked him. He shook his head. "It comes from Latin. It means to breathe together. So you see, for a conspiracy to exist, there needs to be someone else to share it."

Joseph crawled forward onto his knees. He had been wrong earlier: there was a danger in listening. He should have learned that lesson in all of the years he had spent listening to his mother. Words stay lodged in the ear where they multiply like a virus.

In the loud whirl of the midday traffic, he offered her the only thing he could. He reached out his hand. Aleksandra grabbed his fingers and told him there was more.

CHAPTER THIRTEEN

ENTER THE LIGHT. Every decent party needed a theme. This had always been William's party-throwing ethos. He spent hours of his afternoon at a going-out-of-business lighting store on lower Broadway digging through bins and buying back stock of every imaginable light source ever to have been factoried out of Taiwan: strands of white Christmas bulbs, blinking yellow duck bulbs, chili pepper bulbs, grape-cluster bulbs, bulbs in the shape of Chinese take-out boxes, the Virgin Mary, jumping salmon, disco balls, and novelty incandescent bulbs with *dickface* written across their upside-down foreheads. He also bought a cardboard klieg light and a fiber-optic bouquet that lit up like a sea anemone. He plugged power strips into the outlets of his apartment and wove a black spider web throughout the living room, hooking cords around shelf ledges, doorframes, sprinkler pipes, and sofa legs. That left only pressing the switch, and the entire apartment shone like one great ball of happy fire that would eat through sunglasses and radiate spleens. It was like standing inside the flame of the Statue of Liberty, waving good-bye to the confused, uninvited tourists galvanized around her feet.

At seven, he opened the door to the beer delivery, directing the carts into the kitchen. At eight, he shaved, applied beeswax to his hair and cologne to his neck, and then proceeded in his underwear to empty the medicine cabinet of the prescription pill bottles, hiding them in a pair of boots in the bedroom closet. Even close friends become impenitent thieves in the presence of pill bottles. Jennifer had been prescribed the mostly mellow stuff, although William had already raided the single exception, her long-expired bottle of Ritalin. He now found only a few bitten-off crescent moons at the bottom of the bottle, slipped one remnant into his mouth, and gulped it down with a palm of sink water.

First he dressed in a houndstooth jacket but decided against that bit of cocktail formality. This was his last party in New York. He might as well dress for spills. Anyway, even with the air-conditioning cranked on high, the lights were slowly roasting the rooms. Instead William wore a black T-shirt emblazoned on the front with the demon face of Klaus Kinski in *Nosferatu*. He loved this shirt. Like an uglier friend, it made his own features stand out by comparison.

"I have a Jesse Lowman here for you," the doorman announced over the phone.

"Send him up. Say, Steve, I'm having a little party tonight, so you can let everyone pass and don't make them sign the registry."

"That's not policy."

"Come on. It's a party. You can't expect me to keep answering the phone every six seconds."

"Where's Jennifer?" Steve always asked this question in the tone that sought approval from a higher rank. The doorman knew damn well she hadn't lived there for months.

"Don't worry. She's not invited. I'll give you fifty bucks."

Steve paused. "What president is on the fifty?" he asked, retreating into the condescending demeanor of the building's co-op board, which would never have allowed a character like William to set up a home on the twelfth floor if he hadn't been the unfortunate appendage of a sensible young woman with an advantageous last name.

"Eisenhower. Calvin Coolidge. For fuck's sake, you'll get your money."

Jesse had agreed to guard the door, collecting the one-hundred-dollar admittance fee for a small cut of the revenue. "Sorry I'm late," Jesse said, dashing in like someone ready to do more rigorous labor than simply accepting cash in the hallway. He wore an army-green shirt buttoned up to the collar. His hair was parted down the center. Jesse's left eye was tinted in a lusterless yellow bruise, and he reeked of weed. "Jesus, I can barely squint in here. If I'm going to have permanent retinal damage, maybe you could give me a little extra for the corrective surgery."

"It's beautiful, isn't it?" William said, taking a minute to inspect the lights. "Like we're in the middle of the sun." William threw a beer over to him before retreating into the kitchen to dump ice into a plastic laundry basket that would serve as a cooler.

"You're going to trip the circuits," Jesse, so out of character with this sudden practicality, warned. "And the electricity bill."

William's throat summoned a laugh. At least the bills were in Jennifer's name.

BUT THE PARTY was beautiful, like dancing through an explosion. The strands of bulbs wrapping around the room forced everyone into the center, offering few corners for the less communicative and uptight to isolate themselves. There was Joan and Glenn and his first roommate in New York who was already slow dancing to very fast metal with a handsome Latino kid with a pink plastic comb stuck into his braids. William didn't want to do any drugs. He told himself to hold off, but his old friend, Gibby, a blogger on parties and socialite itineraries for various fashion Web sites, hustled him into the bathroom and guided a pen cap of white powder to his nostril. The offer of free drugs was a New York party ritual bestowed to the host. In any other circumstance, Gibby wouldn't have conceded so much as an empty baggie for William to rub his teeth numb with.

"Things will get better," Gibby said in the mirror, pinching the clefts of his tie.

"I'm not doing this for sympathy," William replied. He wiped his nose with his wrist. "I'm doing this for the money. I'm sure that's something you can understand."

Truth was, things had already gotten better. The front door opened, and in came ten more arrivals, paying customers but also friends, dazed momentarily by the sunburst. They wore cocktail dresses and monogrammed T-shirts under sport coats, hair assembled in loose buns that exposed the dark roots of blonde dye jobs, black fingernails clutching cigarette packs, teeth glowing in the shine.

William had e-mailed his *Enter the Light* invitation to almost forty addresses, but the exponential nature of party invites continuously forwarded to constellations of less familiar hotmail and yahoo and mac suffixes assured that the apartment would reach its capacity by the end of the night. Even though a few purposeless strangers stood by the laundry basket of beer, William, already four vodkas into his celebration, was ecstatic to see so many friends from downtown who had come to the Upper West Side to wish him off. The turnout was impressive. There were the younger syndicate kids who carried their youth in place of any higher status—they were the quickest to fall down drunk or be dragged off into strange beds while their friends still searched for them in the crowd. There were also the older, semi-accomplished writers and editors and managers of esoteric bands who provided conversation to those who pretended to listen. And, as always, William spotted more than a dozen attractive, precisely dressed men and women whose only real profession was the legacy of their last names. These were the city's most endemic partiers. They were all children or grandchildren of somebody. They were actors with no film credits. They were part-time deejays.

One iPod was disconnected from the speakers for another, and now slow songs from the '80s played. The names of the bands were utterly forgotten, but the lyrics were instantaneously memorable and sung loudly with clenched fists. The soundtrack brought everyone onto the living room's makeshift dance floor, because these were the songs from their childhood, the ones that they had listened to on the radio in the backseats of cars as acne-scarred misfits, imagining what their lives would one day be like as adults. William felt certain that they had imagined something very close to this party. The alcohol and speed pumping through his bloodstream made the party feel necessary and profound—as if gathering together in close confines was the raw matter of existence, a human need since time began to fight off the darkness in the company of fellow survivors.

William confessed this belief to Ed, who sat cross-legged on top of the walnut credenza taking great care in smoking a tiny brown tick of a joint.

"I think I kissed my babysitter to this song." He went back to coaxing whatever weed remained with his lungs. "But I guess you can be sentimental since you're leaving. When *are* you leaving?" Ed caught a glass that nearly toppled off the ledge when a girl in a red shift dress, perhaps the first casualty of the free alcohol, knocked into them.

"Very soon. Definitely before summer's over. You'll visit, right?"

"L.A. is a cultural wasteland, a desert of opinion. You go there, you get thirsty for back here. I think it's best to let it be the mirage it is." Ed waited for a response, and, getting nothing, changed subjects. "Where's that old dude? That creepy gay guy you're always throwing on everyone?"

"Quinn? He's not creepy."

"Will, the last time we were forced to interact, he spent the entire evening trying to convince me to let him put his hands in my underwear for sixty seconds, because, if I'm not turned on, what difference does it make? And if I am, we both win."

"I didn't invite him. He doesn't have the money and he doesn't know I'm going. You know, Ed, some people might actually be a little upset about my leaving."

"Everyone here looks pretty exhilarated."

Even Ed's cynicism couldn't spoil the night. For the past hour, William had entered a revolving door of arms gathering around him one after another, lips kissing his cheeks and whispering luck into his ear. Even a few ex-girlfriends from before his marriage had shown up, older and skinnier than they had been in their twenties, each dragging a new boyfriend in tow, and each one—Arden, Byrdie, terrible Carolyn with a neck brace of another self-invented injury— all shelling out money to say good-bye. Joseph had been wrong about the party. Friends could find it in their hearts to donate a small contribution to his cause, because they knew how difficult it was to leave the city. They understood that you could do everything wrong and still go out in victory for just having tried.

The music changed again to harder, more vengeful rock, and William heard a lamp crash on the floor. He was too high on happiness to care about the damage inflicted on the apartment. His friend Diggs, mutantly tall with bleached-white hair tied back in a rubber band, poured a shot of tequila, and William pounded it down in a single swallow. William refused a tiny glass bowl of pot that was being passed around because he already felt like he was floating across the room, where a guitar solo stretched out endlessly like its strummer was flying off a cliff and leading him to follow along. *Good-bye New York, good-bye and thank you, thank you dearly for every moment . . .*

AN HOUR LATER, William found himself trapped in one of those black hole conversations only attempted in the proximity to free alcohol. Ed braced his arm around a redhead with skin the glossy, airbrushed sheen of magazine paper. She let out a series of unprovoked laughs and, despite this symptom, affirmed on three separate occasions that she was getting her master's in media studies at NYU. That should have been a warning siren instead of a point of pride.

"You people don't realize what is going to happen with technology," she said, her palms waving to indicate a massive invisible explosion of technology rising up around them. "We think our parents are prehistoric because they can't figure out how to turn on a laptop. But the *real* reality is that fifty years from now we are going to look back at this time as utterly medieval. This isn't the first of days. It's the last of the old ones. We're on the edge of tomorrow, but we're on the wrong side." She was the kind of person whose entire impression of the future was based solely on the most recent inventions.

Ed kissed her on the cheek before dismissing her theory outright.

"You're talking about simulated realities, right? I don't think actual experience is ever going to disappear. Yeah, maybe one day our children's children will remember the comforting bygone smell of their grandparents nuking up processed chicken in their kitchen microwaves . . . "

"The nostalgic odor of fresh plastic . . . " William offered.

"Yeah, the old-fashioned feel of silicone implants. But come off it. We're never going to live full-time inside of a microchip. The way I see it, experience will always win out because there's always a real chance of dying. No one does anything if there isn't that slight tinge of risk."

William glanced around his party for a sign of Joseph. He still hadn't seen his friend come through the door. He sipped his drink, only faintly listening to the conversation.

"You're wrong," the redhead whined in growing grad-student distemper, irate that her own private seminar had been hijacked for a free exchange of ideas. "Real experience will be swapped for virtual. There will be no need to fly all over the earth, to witness any event first hand, to even touch the cheek of the person you love. All living will be done in virtual zones, where we will exist as avatars and then, finally, all of our desires and dreams will be fulfilled. That's what really separates the past from the future. It will be the fulfillment of all human wishes, all the time, as fast as a click of the button. And honestly, Ed, the beauty of this inevitability is that it supplies the answer to all of these land wars in the Middle East or the fallen condition of the environment. The only way we can keep living on this planet is if we stop ransacking it and make a new world that exists in the ether, one in which we never have to move a muscle to experience. You might not believe me now, but look me up when you get there. I'll be the avatar with ten breasts and the head of Helen of Troy."

"I'm not going home with you," Ed huffed, before making good on his threat by removing his arm from her shoulder. "Don't you see that's the problem with kids growing up right now? They don't understand the concept of boredom or frustration or wanting what you can't have. Everything has gotten too easy. William, remember when you'd rip out a page of a porn magazine at a store and sneak it back to your bedroom and you'd concentrate on a single picture, maybe the size of a postage stamp, and from that you'd spend whole weeks imagining everything about those bodies, just from one little photograph the size of your fingernail? That's what got me to leave Montpelier, my boredom and desperation. And no kid today is going to have any chance of being happy because they no longer need to go out and find what they want in the world. They don't have to imagine anything. How can you be excited by all of those nude bodies being thrown at you on the Internet twenty-four hours a day? William, back me up here?"

He nodded distractedly and let the conversation continue without him as it dissolved into the mind-numbing questions of whether or not we were already living in a simulated reality, and if so, why on faux-earth would the programmer controlling this universe pack it with so many boring phone calls and soulless day jobs. William was sure Ed would go home with the grad student no matter what she said, and he left them midway through their techno-existential trip. He had too much to say on the topic of boredom and desperation. Instead, William concentrated on walking without staggering. He kept his head raised. He danced as stupidly as he could in the center of the living room with a blonde he had once met at an audition, and no one laughed at his slow, clomping feet or writhing arms. All evaluations were in his favor tonight. He was the reason for all of the light. The future didn't frighten him. It was the past that had put a hole in his heart.

AT ONE IN the morning, the party had reached its maximum capacity, and the effects of William's drinking were starting to pay dividends. He couldn't fix the blur in his vision. His T-shirt was soaked in sweat, and his skin almost hurt from the heat. He licked his lips and tasted the iron of his skin.

"The bathroom line is too long," Jesse said, breaking from a circle of young women who were dancing to the latest pop song. Their dresses cut out down their backs, and their spines beaded like strands of pearls. They were wasting all of their excess energy before they drifted off to Amagansett or the Catskills or Shelter Island to wait out the rest of the months until autumn brought the first chill to the city. A bearded skater in a gas-attendant's jumpsuit strung the duck bulbs around his body, and he fell over as his legs got lassoed in the cord. "That guy's so wasted, he's going to start a fire."

"Aren't you supposed to be guarding the door?"

Jesse slapped a large roll of bills inside a handshake that William couldn't bother to count. He put the money in his pocket, satisfied with the bulge.

"It's already too crowded, and the beer's gone. I think you've made enough."

William looked past Jesse and noticed Del worming her way through a huddle of smokers by the door. She wore an emerald green dress that made her skin look pale, and a smudge of eyeliner muddied her cheek. He waved to her. She lifted a bottle of champagne wrapped in silver foil.

"Thanks for coming," he said.

"It's a million degrees in here."

She offered him the bottle, and he popped the cork. It sailed beyond his vision, and he gathered the exploding foam in his lips.

"Where's Joseph? You guys are a little late."

Del hadn't heard him, distracted by Jesse who was eagerly reaching out his hand, half handshake, half frantic wave. The heat from the lights was destroying everyone's sense of self-restraint.

"This is Joseph's wife. Del, Jesse," he said.

"Oh," his friend sighed, realizing his chances with her were already hopeless. "I don't think you paid."

Del went for the purse hanging at her hip, but William stopped her.

"Don't worry about it."

Jesse tried to whisper something into Del's ear, but he overshot his balance. Her hands caught him by the shoulders before he fell into her. William grabbed her arm and led her into the hallway where it was quieter.

"Charming guy, your friend."

"Never mind him," he said. He tried to kiss her cheek, but she pulled away, leaving him to swerve back awkwardly, going through the unnecessary act of pretending that he had tripped. He noticed how her eyeliner amplified her deep brown eyes. Wolf eyes with specks of yellow like fall leaves. He knew, standing there with her in the corridor, that she was the kind of woman who looked down on him. As they stood in silence, he could sense that she was judging him, picking out his slobbering speech and sweaty face, restyling, critiquing, but it didn't matter tonight. He felt like a huge open field upon which all had been planted and had so many seeds already growing inside of him. He didn't want or need this woman to like him.

"So where's Joseph?"

"He's in the bedroom," she said, nodding down the hall. "He's helping one of your stoned-beyond-cognition friends find the second bathroom."

William took a gulp of champagne. "Can you tell him to tone down the miracles tonight? It is my party after all. How do you live with someone like that, Del? Isn't it hard to sleep at night in the light of that halo? It would give me a headache."

"Maybe you should stop drinking," she replied, squinting her eyes at him.

He took another long guzzle. The anger he had felt for Del was suddenly spreading over onto Joseph, both of them trying to ruin his own good-bye party by arriving late and then judging him for the effects of the happiness that had occurred in their absence. He wished they hadn't bothered to come.

"Why is that?" he asked her. "Because you think I'm drunk?"

"Because the police are here."

He turned to catch sight of two officers in squat mailbox leg stances standing at the front door. Silver nametags, black leather holsters, plastic zip-tie handcuffs hooked around belt loops. The music instantly lowered, the conversations turned into nervous whispers, which only called attention to their panicked tone, and a bullet, William could swear, passed into his pancreas. But just as he was prepared to pull the plug and apologize to his neighbors, he spotted Ed heading straight toward the door like the cardinal of sanity ascending a pulpit. William could always count on Ed for calming words that satisfied cops. In a minute, both parties were nodding their heads in concession, as if they were agreeing on the accidental nature of a roadside collision. Still, William felt too wasted to go near the door until the police were safely escorted out of the building. He didn't have Ed's talent for talking down authorities.

"Let's go find your husband," he said, steering Del down the hallway toward the bedroom. As they approached the door, Joseph opened it. The two men stood for a second, as if trying to recognize each other, before Joseph reached his arm out and gathered William's neck in his hand. "Congratulations," he said so sincerely that William instantly suspected its authenticity.

William pulled his friend into the bedroom, sweeping him along in the arm that held the champagne. He wanted a break from the noise and the sweltering lights and the dangers of law enforcement. He dug into his pocket to release the stash of rolled-up twenties, waving the money momentarily in front of Joseph's face to show him how wrong he had been, and then tossed it on Jennifer's vanity table. William's eyes ascended from the table to the oval mirror framed in gold. He caught his own reflection and froze at what he saw. A razor rash of puss-white bumps rose around his chin. The sweat on his face made his skin sallow, patchworked with red lashes across his cheeks. The pupils of his eyes were so constricted that he worried they would disappear entirely into the quicksand of brown. Dried blood caked the edge of his left nostril, although he didn't remember a nosebleed. He began to pick off the blood and, embarrassed, forced his fingers up to his hair to straighten the part.

"I look like shit," he said. "I guess everyone out there was too polite to tell me."

"You look fine," Joseph said with a smile. William stared at Joseph's reflection in the mirror—sober and clean with those brilliant white teeth that landed commercial jobs. It was the smile of someone purposely lying to him when the truth covered his face. William couldn't place exactly why he felt a sudden rage tearing through him at the reflection of his friend over his shoulder. It must have started in the hallway with Del, who now leaned against the bedroom window rolling a cigarette like she was waiting for the right moment to leave. Sudden bouts of anger had always been a hazard of drinking and drugs for William, and so too was the irrepressible feeling that he had been slighted, wronged, treated for less than he was. William could usually keep that anger in check, but here Joseph was smiling at him in the mirror, and the disparity between their faces had the neutralizing effect of gasoline.

"No, I don't look fine," William yelled. "You don't have to lie to me. I look terrible." He looked down at the pile of money on the vanity table and that fact embarrassed him too.

"Maybe you should lay off," Del said.

"Lay off what?"

"Whatever it is you're on."

"Are you going to let her talk to me that way?" William swerved around. Joseph sat quietly on the bed with his legs crossed and his eyebrows furrowed in a cheap show of concern.

"We just want to make sure you're okay," Joseph replied, trying to smooth the hostility. Those words, however, carried a condescending undertone that brought William to take a step back in defense. Then Joseph tried to change the subject. "How much money did you make?"

"I made enough," he replied. "But that really wasn't the point of the party tonight." He wished he hadn't waved the money around a minute ago. "The point was to bring friends together—the people who *love* me—to say good-bye. It might be the last time you see me before I rent a car and pack all my stuff in. I could fly but I thought it might be nice to drive across and see the country." William felt a need to sound reflective, but he also knew he could steer the conversation into a faint attack on Joseph. He took a sip from the champagne bottle. The spillover leaked down his wrist. "Maybe on the way I can even crash at your folks' place. Ohio's right on the way, isn't it?"

Joseph's smile tightened. His teeth disappeared.

"I'm afraid my mom's not much for visitors. And you wouldn't find Ohio exciting enough, anyway."

William laughed, slamming his left hand down on Joseph's shoulder.

"That's too bad," he said, squeezing his collarbone roughly. "I was hoping to see what kind of family produced you. I feel like I should thank them."

"I haven't even met his mother," Del said quietly. She was staring out the window, blowing a small cloud of smoke against the glass. "So I doubt that's going to happen."

"You haven't brought Del home to Ohio?" William faked shock. "My god, they must be dying to meet your wife. Del, you must at least have talked to his mother on the phone."

She turned and shook her head without any trace of resentment, but her eyes were focused on her husband. Joseph placed his hand over William's knuckles to pry them loose and gazed up at him.

"You know I don't talk to my family," he said, increasing the severity in his eyes. "You know that."

"It's none of my business. But, come on, they must be so proud of you. We all are. Aren't we?" He turned to Del for confirmation, nearly tripping as his foot dragged on the floor. "So successful, this guy. You know, I used to hang out with Joseph all the time before you two got together. We used to be really close. Well, as close as you can be to someone who never really says anything. Now I never see him. It's like he disintegrated and there's just a faint trace left. Something called Joseph that you can't really locate but know is still there. Congratulations, Del. You must be making him so happy."

Del inhaled on the cigarette and, uninterested in corroborating William's insinuation, bent her head forward to let her hair fall over her cheeks.

"But at least, Joseph, you must have met *her* family. No?" William shook his head in disappointment. "You don't talk about families? Is that off limits? I mean, I always knew the topic of Joseph's family was barred for me, but certainly not for you, Del? You *are* married, aren't you?"

"You were right before," Del said in the shadows of her hair. "It's none of your business."

"We're here for you," Joseph said with a strained voice. "Why are you acting like this?"

"Well, I'm not acting much these days at all, am I?" William couldn't stop himself now. He had already sped past the warning flags and he was headed straight for the detonation. What difference did it make? He was leaving town. He could be honest with Joseph, and who cared if it was the last time they would ever share a room together? He didn't need to hold on to him anymore, and the pity that filled Joseph's face as he looked up at him increased the magnitude of every old grudge and quiet offense swallowed down with backslaps and beers. The music in the outer room was vibrating the bedroom walls, and that potent seed of jealousy deep inside of him, which too many drinks nurtured, began to vibrate as if looking to erupt. William was mistaking his rage for self-dignity, some part of him knew this, but adrenaline was racing through his blood. He wanted to get the deceitful nature of their friendship out on the table, so at least they both knew where they stood. "I want to know what jobs you're getting. Then you and your wife can leave."

"Let's go," Joseph said as he rose from the bed. For a second they stood facing each other, the cold spray of Joseph's breath blowing on his skin. Their lips were a few inches from touching, their eyes so close that the vision of each other blurred from lack of distance. William bunched his fists, but he considered throwing a punch for too long to reclaim the spontaneous courage it required. "Call me tomorrow when you sober up," Joseph said. "You should go back to your party."

"You know what the problem with you is? You lack character." William nodded his head to rev the thought, to sail it right through Joseph's dignified departure when he was just getting started on the duplicitous nature of friendship. "You're so sweet and quiet and, just look at you, helpful. My god, is there even a man inside that body?" He tried to grab Joseph's ear, but his friend's head whipped back and in another minute he had gathered Del's hand and they were walking toward the door. "I'm sorry to tell you that," he screamed after them. "But you make it too difficult to like you. You don't try, and that's not fair to the rest of us."

William found himself yelling at a slammed door.

In the emptiness of his bedroom, his head spun, and the first flutter of guilt was extinguishing the anger that had caused him to destroy all of the promise of the night. Already an apology was forming on his lips. His balance knocked sideways as he tried to run for the door and he fell backward into the dressing room, crashing through the hangers and into the empty arms of blouses and coats and whatever else Jennifer had decided not to wear into her new life. He pulled himself up, bringing half of her wardrobe down as he climbed the clothes, and sprinted out of his bedroom to catch up to them. He hurried through the hallway, preparing his first words for forgiveness, but when he reached the front door, Joseph and Del were already gone.

AN HOUR LATER, after a failed attempt to reclaim his earlier triumph on the dance floor, William squatted against the cold tiles of the shower while Diggs shoveled coke up his nose. Sweat poured down his cheeks, and his eyelids were creating film dissolves. Someone started kicking the door, as if at any second, those feet would be replaced with fire axes.

William staggered into the kitchen and filled a glass with water. He listened to a rant about American politics between two British guys he didn't recognize while bringing the glass to his lips. William could feel hives swelling around his Adam's apple and resisted the urge to scratch. A chill ran through him, and the glass dropped in the sink where it cracked against the faucet. He wobbled back into the party. It had grown smaller in the last half hour, subtracting into couples that leaned against the walls. He wanted to kick everyone out, but it was already late and the end would come soon. The music was blasting in and out like someone was toying with the knob. Jesse punched him in the shoulder and said good-bye.

"Stay, just for a bit longer," William pleaded with his eyes shut. He steadied himself against Jesse's arm. "I don't feel well. Something's not right. Something hasn't been right for a while."

"You're wasted. It's two thirty. Roll with it. We're all assholes after a certain hour. The trick is to think about something else. Think of a story, the first thing that comes in your head."

William tried to erase the shame he felt for the fight with Joseph. Tomorrow he would call him and apologize. He would beg forgiveness, he would send Del flowers—not because there was no truth in what he had said, but because there was no reason to leave a bruised memory of himself behind. He focused his thoughts on the first image that came into his brain, a sunken family room with a television set blaring through the Illinois sunlight.

"Okay. A story."

"That's right. Tell me." Jesse coaxed. "I'm listening. Don't worry about anything else."

"Did I ever tell you when I was a kid, all I did one summer was watch HBO?" He could hear people pushing around him quietly and knew they must think him far too gone to bother with a good-bye. He didn't care. "I'd sit in our dark basement on the warmest days while every other kid was outside, enjoying the weather, making guns out of the lawn sprinklers, and throwing rocks at the cheapest cars. I'd be ten inches from the TV screen shivering in central air and watching any movie that came on. Really, the shittiest teen flicks and romantic comedies. They'd eventually repeat, and I'd sit there, memorizing the dialogue of all the parts until I got them perfect, and then, when my parents called me up for dinner, I'd try to use those lines on them." William didn't open his eyes. He was afraid his vision would scramble. He wanted to be the man he was three hours earlier.

"That's it," Jesse encouraged kindly, holding on to his shoulders. "How did your parents react?"

"I didn't really care what my parents were talking about. I'd put in a 'I don't think love is going to save you from getting out of this amusement park alive' or 'How can you watch every man walk out on you and not wonder if maybe you're the problem?' The weird thing was, my parents would just nod and go quiet for a minute over their plates, like they were really considering what I said, weighing it for some insight to their failed paving company or the neighbor's escalating divorce battle. Once I told my mother, 'If you don't see that the whole town wants you dead and try to do something about it, tomorrow you'll wake up next to a vampire who only wants to rip your heart out.'" Telling the story was helping him. It was keeping him from passing out. It was cutting through the clouded thoughts.

"How did she take that?"

"She began to cry." Spit burst from his lips. He started laughing hard, involuntarily snorting, even though he didn't find what he was saying to be the least bit funny. His knees buckled, and suddenly the pressure of the lights stopped beating against his eyelids. The music skidded to a silence. William opened his eyes, and the living room was black. A long collective "ahhh" passed through the mouths of the few guests that remained.

"We blew a fuse," Jesse said, lifting William's chin. But already he could hear other voices saying "brownout," then "no, look out the window. The whole city's gone."

William took Jesse's hand and kept going with the story. He wanted to get out an apology before he lost consciousness. Electrical failures would have to wait. Manhattan would have to remain in the dark until he uttered one proper apology—one honest appeal for forgiveness that would stand in for all of the others.

"Okay, story time's over," Jesse replied with a nervous voice. "We have an emergency. Seriously, man, get it together. Where are the stairs?"

Matches and lighters began to crack the blackness. Bodies fumbled over chairs to locate jackets and purses, and the windows were opened to let in sirens and screams coming from the street.

"Sometimes I think about calling them and saying that none of what I said was meant for them. It had nothing to do with their lives. They were headed to divorce court no matter what. I mean, my poor mother. Did she start thinking all of Breeze Falls, Illinois, really wanted her dead? Even her own husband?" His laughing returned in harder waves, exploding up his windpipe from his stomach and out through his nostrils, and he bent over, wheezing out laughter uncontrollably, gasping for air as his entire body shook with painful joy. He clenched his hands around his stomach like he might throw up. "Wait. It gets worse."

No one had seen her enter the apartment, and if they had, most would not have been able to identify her. They would have taken her for a late arrival stuck on the twelfth floor of a party in its death throes. She wore a silver charm bracelet that caught the match light and dirty canvas sneakers that tracked beer across the rug. She held the receipt from the cab that had dropped her off in front of the building. She did not need to grope through the dark. She knew the layout of the apartment. Her hand slid along an empty shelf of missing curios as she passed.

William slowly regained his composure. He tried to tuck his T-shirt into his pants, breathing evenly through his nose. He was all right. He wasn't going to lose consciousness. He could resolve whatever catastrophe he had caused with a simple apology in the morning. Nothing could ever get so broken that it couldn't be fixed. Then he turned and saw the face of a woman unspeakably familiar to him.

Her eyes were wet as they stared into his. He wiped his mouth with the back of his fist, and it took him half of a second to connect this comforting face with her name, and in that half second, which felt like a piece of eternity breaking off its rock face, the impulse of his body moved to embrace her as his brain caught up and stopped him from reaching out.

She stared at him, as he turned pale, the sweat shining on his blistered face and his lips dotted in white spit. He could hear a fire door opening in the outer hallway and the echoes of feet descending the first of twelve flights down. She said a word so softly it sounded less like an insult than a matter of classification.

"Animal," Jennifer whispered, almost as if she had said *don't worry* or *I love you* or *you're safe*.

CHAPTER FOURTEEN

JOSEPH ROLLED OVER on the couch, opened his eyes and closed them, and opened them again when he felt the moisture of rain coming from the window. Candles pulsed in the fireplace. Del stood with her back to him in white underwear and the frayed tank top she usually wore to clean the apartment. The inside of his head felt jagged. His stomach lurched, and his fingers were numb on the coarse wool cushion. He shook his wrists to try to circulate the blood.

"No electricity," Del said, sensing him stirring behind her. "I can turn the radio on if you want. Most of the island's out."

"All of Manhattan?" His mouth was dry.

"Almost." She propped her cigarette in an ashtray and stretched her arm out the window. "I think a storm is coming too."

"What time is it?"

"A little after four. You passed out, and then the lights blew. If you think about it, William did us a favor by sending us home early. Otherwise we'd be stuck up there, nothing but us and miles of road flares."

Joseph tried to picture William's party, a hundred people mashed together in a room that had suddenly gone black as if all of their enthusiasm couldn't save the city from a shut down.

"I hope William's okay," he said.

"I doubt he's too concerned about us."

"He was drunk."

"You give him too much credit," Del said without turning around to face him. "You're naive about William."

Joseph expected the anger, weighed and redoubled in the hour that he slept. Del hadn't wanted to go to the party in the first place and didn't appreciate the outcome. No one liked to be the sacrificial victim of somebody else's drunken disorderly. On the cab ride home she leaned against the window, following the fast fragments of sidewalks in the late-night resolution that talking could too easily journey over into an argument. But still, as she stood staring into the blackness of Twenty-Second Street, he couldn't help feeling sorry for William. "You can't attack failing," he said. "You can't ask people to fail more quietly. That's what failure is: loud."

"Shhh. Do you hear that? Listen." They both concentrated on their ears. Joseph heard crowds screaming far off, like echoes of a stadium from across a highway. "They're partying in Union Square," she said. "The whole city's out getting wasted, dancing in the park to the disco of police lights. The radio says people are stuck in the subways and in god knows how many elevators. That's always frightened me. Being trapped somewhere way down while the world adjusts above your head. You don't realize how truly helpless you are until something massive happens. Helpless and unable to do a single thing about it."

"Come here," he said, reaching out to her. "Don't be scared."

"I'm not scared," she laughed. Joseph wondered whether she was laughing at the notion that the blackout scared her or that he might be able to protect her from it. "Actually, I kind of like it." She pressed her index finger into one of the candles and let the wax harden around her nail. "Disasters have a cheap thrill, don't they, before the real costs set in. There's nervousness to them like nothing's going to be the same. Only it always is."

Del climbed over him on the couch, her knees fumbling between his legs and her elbows pitting the cushions by his ears. She lowered her lips to his neck, and he pulled her waist against his own to prevent her from kissing him because he still felt nauseous. She wrestled onto her side and placed her hand on his chest.

"You feel like an earthquake," she said.

"That happens sometimes in the middle of the night. It'll stop."

Her breath smelled of tobacco, and shadows roped her face until only her eyes and cheekbones held the shape of her skull. She leaned in for a kiss, gliding her tongue over his own, and for a few seconds he tried to force out the dizziness and concentrate on her mouth, the eraser gap between her front teeth, the rutted plain of her palate, the lips that lost muscle against his own. Del kissed without having to breathe, as if she packed away oxygen for the long duration the way a climber packs air tanks before footing a mountain. But her knees clamped over his thighs, and her hand slid under the elastic of his underwear. He could no longer fight off the sickness. He pushed her away with his arm and rolled over on the couch to catch his breath.

Del sat up, reaching for her rolling papers on the armrest. She pinched the tobacco along the groove in the paper and inhaled with deep purpose, as if setting up a chess move in her mind. He knew her sighs so well he could document her every mood by the intake of her breath. She lit her cigarette and held it out with her forearm resting on her knee.

"Can I ask you something?" she said. He tried to get a glimpse of her face to gauge her expression, but the cigarette focused her features to the work of smoking. "Have you told your mother that we're married?"

"I told you before. I don't talk to her."

"But it is strange. It is. Strange you never talk to me about your family. Strange I've never even heard her voice."

"It isn't strange." He climbed onto the floor and sat hunched over his crossed legs so that the candles wouldn't shine on his face. The candlelight polished Del's skin the color of honey and elongated the shadows of her eyes until they mixed with the darkness of her hair. He should have expected this sort of fallout. Sex would have been one way of repairing the break, confrontation the obvious other. He searched his brain for words that would fix the damage that William had done. "I moved here fifteen years ago," he said. "Fifteen years now. So long ago I doubt anyone back there remembers me. You're my family. Can't we keep it at that?"

"It's just that I don't know anything about her. I know you two don't talk, but I have no idea why. If someone asked me the details of your family, all I could do is shrug. I've got nothing to say. *Nothing*," she repeated worriedly. "Do you know how that makes me feel?"

"Please don't do this," he begged.

"Don't do what?" She shook her head and took a hard drag on her cigarette to gather her resolve. "I'm your wife, remember? Last I checked I'm allowed to ask that kind of question. Jesus, is it so bad that you can't even tell *me*?"

Yes, it is so bad I cannot tell even you, he thought. *It is so bad you're the only person I can't tell.* Through their first months of dating, Joseph was thankful to find a partner who didn't pry into every corner and question every silence, never demanding entry into the infinitesimal details of his life that he wasn't willing to supply. She didn't treat love like weigh stations on the highway, constantly measuring the load between distances for something out of check. But tonight William had managed to put a crack in that trust. He knew Del had suddenly understood the liability in not knowing her husband inside and out, that such ignorance showed an embarrassing lack of romantic detective work, that she had, in a sense, missed something necessary. And now Joseph couldn't find the words to set her at ease.

She stared down at him from the couch, waiting for him to reply, and he kept his mouth shut, letting the silence pool around them.

"I'm not asking for every single detail," she said.

"Then what are you asking?" he replied, burying his eyes into his fists.

"I'm asking you not to go mute when I ask you a question. I stood there while your friend asked me about your family tonight, and I had nothing to say. I felt like an idiot. Like I don't even know you."

"If you feel that way, then why did you marry me?" he said in defense, gazing straight at her. He regretted the sentence as soon as it left his mouth. Del's hands balled into fists, and her feet scrambled toward the floor.

"You think I only married you for the papers, is that it?" she screamed, pushing herself from the couch with a fast momentum. "You think that's what all of this is, just an arrangement?" But Joseph was already jumping to salvage whatever he could, grabbing her wrists and pressing her down on the cushions to keep her from running into the bedroom and slamming the door. She didn't fight him. She fell easily, her eyes staring up at him like she was daring him to agree with her.

"The truth? You really want to hear it? My mom's *not there*," he said. "Not anywhere. Do you hear what I'm saying? There is no Katherine Guiteau to talk to. There will be no flowers. No congratulations. No nothing. She's lost her mind."

Del's face crumpled, and thin strands of saliva roped her teeth. She knocked her head back and squinted her eyes. Her feet kicked against the armrest, but when he removed his hands from her wrists she kept them frozen in place.

"I'm sorry," she said curtly, the apology still tainted with bitterness. "Why didn't you ever tell me that? God, Joe, it's things like that, no matter how much they hurt, that I need to hear."

"There are reasons I don't talk about my family," he replied. Shame hit him even as he felt the returning peace of their lives together. Shame, because he had only told her enough to derail her questions. Not the full truth. Not the extent of the story. Here were the first small cracks, he thought, still so faint they might go unnoticed, but they were there, deepening and splintering in the air between them. He had seen in other married couples how silence turned in on itself, how it spoke of old provocations and broken pacts. For the second time since their wedding, a wave of doubt came over him. Maybe marrying her had been a mistake because he couldn't give her all the answers. And it was stupid of him to think those questions would never come.

He waited for Del to walk into the bedroom or to crawl over to him and rest her forehead against his shoulder. She did neither. They remained alone on their separate corners of the couch for several minutes, until pale traces of fireworks flashed across the windows. Roman candles were being set off on a rooftop a few blocks north. Some small incendiary pocket of joy would always rise up in this city even in its darkest hours, disturbing the sense that anything serious had occurred.

"I'm sorry," she finally said, reaching her palm toward him in reconciliation.

"Please, Del. Just let it go."

AFTER DEL WENT to bed and turned against the wall, Joseph left the apartment and climbed up to the rooftop. The roof was sticky with tar and covered in brittle wet leaves from previous autumns. Cables snaked across the cement, and a plastic bag scraped back and forth, caught on a cord that tied down broken patio chairs. Two helicopters circled high over the island, darting their spotlights into the gulfs of the avenues. Their rotor blades ticked like locusts in the faint, hot wind. Joseph stabbed his heel on a spent nitrous-oxide cartridge. One section of the roof was littered with rusted metal shells, left by teenagers who must have shot whippets and watched the apartment towers cave around them as they laughed themselves unconscious. The fireworks were over. Besides the beams from the helicopters, the only light pouring through the city came from idling police cars and tiny bonfire flares marking lanes up and down the roads.

This is how the island must have appeared to early explorers, a quiet, peaceable drift of dirt cut off from the mainland, as if the first settlers had wanted to get away from where they had started but were not entirely committed to the destiny of the huge new continent beyond it. Broadway cut the island down the middle, once an animal trail, retread by Indians, bricked and then paved and then lined in store chains by European colonists. In the darkness, one city—alive, adrenaline-pumped, unrelenting to any force of weather or hour, colored by every shade of idiosyncrasy—drifted into shadow, and another city emerged, heaps of steel and concrete jutting upward, dreaming arrogantly of value in height, no matter now if those owners of penthouses and balconies were marooned in their own sky hubs. The spikes and domes and jerry-rigged rooftop terraces chopped across the skyline in sporadic waves, and, below them, dark scaffolding braided together, home to the infrastructure of a billion dead switches and outlets. The sound the city made was of its residents screaming in the streets, as if celebrating their own sudden obsolescence.

What if it never came back on? Joseph wondered as he stepped closer to the edge. *What if the power was unplugged permanently?* Within a week the city would be emptied, the richest refugees the world has ever known clambering across the bridges in despair, a mass exodus moving on and out like seeds blown across a country that had grown inhospitable to them. Within a week, seven days, this entire island—with all of its dreams and industries—would be deserted.

It occurred to Joseph as he stepped closer, just a foot from the ledge, that New Yorkers had a reputation for being hard-skinned survivalists but were perhaps the least equipped with survival instincts of any lot in human history. Del said earlier that disasters carried the sense that nothing would ever be the same, only they always were, but she had been wrong.

In 2001, Joseph had been living in a small studio on East Third Street, the downstairs neighbor to an elderly Polish woman whose husband had died of renal failure three years prior. She had redirected her love onto a fat, blue-coated greyhound who, frightened by the alien booms and smoke of the Word Trade Center collapsing, disappeared into the alleys of the East Village on the morning of September 11. For weeks, Joseph could hear his neighbor calling in the street for her dog. When Joseph tried to comfort her on the front steps, she shook her head and cried in anguish, "I never put a name tag on her. Even if she's found, they won't be able to contact me." He had lost sight of this neighbor, although he heard her nightly rounds across his ceiling until the day she died eight months later. The firefighters broke down her door and discovered every item in her slovenly one-bedroom was pinned with a tag that read, IF FOUND, PLEASE CALL EILEEN KOWALSKI AT (212) 969-8704. HAVE A WONDERFUL DAY. Pots, fedora hats, a set of her husband's dumbbells, weathered photo albums, even unwrapped bars of soap carried their own emergency contact label. And on the body of his poor upstairs neighbor, they found the same tag dangling from her St. Anthony necklace. Joseph had not thought Eileen Kowalski's manic attempt to hold on to whatever she had an unusual response in the months after September 2001. Everyone in New York had been holding on, desperately, emphatically, because they had never before learned the valuable lesson of letting go. Now it seemed as if everyone—even Joseph—waited for some new horror to wake them, until then living out the last of their dreams. No one bothered to wonder whether those old dreams still applied in the aftermath.

Joseph swerved back from the ledge and gave a final look at the darkened sea of buildings. To the west, a band of low, black clouds gathered, silent and sharp with rain.

CHAPTER FIFTEEN

WILLIAM SHIVERED IN his blue parka as he rang the buzzer, trying to wipe the rain from his face with his wet hands. He had walked all the way from the motel on Fifty-Eighth Street that he had checked into at 4 AM, the hospitality desk lit with candles and the bald, horse-faced proprietor, with his beleaguered cross-eyes, shaking his head to payment by credit card. "Machine not working. Nothing working. You got to pay in cash. And don't complain about no light. That's city problem." William noticed two framed newspaper articles on the wall behind the desk proudly calling attention to the fact that the drummer for a popular '90s rock band had chosen this particular motel to empty thirteen glassine envelopes of heroin into his veins and die in the bathtub; such was the establishment's foothold in local folklore. William had handed over three hundred dollars to unlock a black pool table-sized room, which smelled of disinfectant.

"You lucky we still use keys," the clerk had sniggered. "These fancy hotel with their swipe cards, guess what, don't work with no power." William threw down the bag of clothes he had managed to collect from the bedroom while Jennifer had patrolled behind him in the dark, demanding he "get the fuck out" before she called the police.

He had frantically searched for the cash collected from the party and found only 400 dollars on the floor by the bureau, a mercilessly small portion of the funds, which had, at some point, been stolen by one of the guests during the blackout. William had been on his knees, cursing god and blindly grabbing at the carpet for money, while his ex-wife stood over him screaming about the apartment and her rightful ownership over it, cursing herself for her foolish generosity. William had passed out on the motel bedspread without bothering to take off his shoes and was almost thankful the lights were still not working when he woke up the next morning at noon. At least it saved him from having to see his own face. He caught his reflection in storefront windows on his route to the West Village. Purple blisters crusted his cheeks, and a green hangover swelled his eyes and lips.

Rain broke as he crossed Twenty-Third Street, intensifying into thick squalls that pounded his shoulders and laked sidewalks a few blocks later. Just as he made the turn onto West Twelfth Street, he heard cheers from the residents camped inside their million-dollar brownstones. Light flooded windows, alarm systems competed for emergency attention, a neon bar sign twitched on.

As if by miracle, the power returned.

"My god, what happened to you?" Quinn groaned as he opened the door. He was dressed in a midnight-blue robe and a pair of black rubber boots. "Were you beaten up by a street gang? Get in here this instant."

William accepted Quinn's soft nurturing hands, guided through the backyard of decaying oaks, into the cottage, and onto the batik-covered couch to the chorus of his old friend's sympathy moans. In a minute, he had tea warming his fingers and a patchwork throw shelled around his neck. Quinn pulled off his sopping shoes, and William almost cried at the gentleness of the action. Someone, he thought, still cared for him enough to warm his feet.

"Jennifer finally kicked me out." William decided not to mention the particulars of the disaster, not so much to cheat Quinn from the real story as to leave it dead and buried behind him, taking instruction from the series of bolts and chains that clamored across the door after Jennifer had slammed it shut. "I have nowhere to go."

"That bitch kicked you out in the middle of a blackout?" Quinn whistled as if impressed. "It figures. Never underestimate the cruelty of someone you once slept next to. They're all vultures once you show them your weak spots. That's why I never take all my clothes off when I have sex. It's too vulnerable. They know just where to gouge you. Relax. Close your eyes. Did she have to attack you? I can see her nail marks. We'll need to treat them."

William let his friend apply salve to his blisters, thanking him repeatedly as he tried to come up with the most delicate way of asking if he could crash in the cottage for the next few days. The downpour was beating on the roof, and a metronomic leak from the skylight made a puddle on the floor. Quinn pushed a houseplant over with his foot to catch the drip.

"Can you believe that blackout," Quinn said, dipping a Q-tip into the ointment. "They blamed it on a transmission failure. Some over-worked breakers. This city's falling back into the slump it was in during the '70s, without all of the crazy people that made living in a disaster area so much fun."

"I have nowhere to go," William repeated.

"You're lucky I'm even here. I was about to take the car upstate. I thought this power outage might go on for days, and best just to get the hell out, you know? Let the condo brats jam the Con Edison phone boards until they figured a way out of the mess. Do you want me to get you a mirror?"

"I can't stand looking at my face right now."

"Don't worry. It's still a good one."

"She wouldn't even let me pack all my stuff. She just ran around, yelling about how she deserved to be happy. Do you know what she said when I asked her what would make her happy? She said, 'You gone.' She said, 'This is where we end it. It's time someone else paid for your messes.'"

Quinn swiveled back to inspect his nursing efforts, then with a slow smile, squinted his eyes.

"Then let it be the end of Jennifer too," he said, clasping William's hands. "You can stay with me for a few days. Until you get on your feet and find your own place. I'll give you the extra key. You always have me. Remember the ones who love you, William. Then nothing's ever really lost."

Thunder shook the walls of the cottage, and harder rain slapped the roof. Rivulets of water ran across the ceiling's chipped wood beams. It seemed miraculous that this structure had managed to survive nearly a century without caving in on itself, reduced to a pile of mold and debris. Quinn filled the room with opera music, as he went to work clearing a corner of magazines and photo albums to make space for William's bags. It occurred to William that he had always visited Quinn like he was performing a favor, a young man calling on an older, sicker one with the patronizing devotion of charity work. But Quinn, with his hairy white knuckles appearing from the sleeves of his blue robe and his bloated knees, now stooping to gather ingredients out of his mini fridge for the preparation of two hot meals, was not some ailing charity case. He had learned to stomach so many crushing blows and laugh right in the face of it. The cottage remained standing as if by Quinn's insistence and would only collapse after its loudest, last resident collapsed first. *So this is how you make it*, William thought, too tired to help his friend boil water. *Ugly, merrily, not demanding too much.* Quinn quickly brought his fist down on a cockroach that crawled across the counter. William turned away and shivered under the blanket, not wanting to see the remains.

CHAPTER SIXTEEN

A FEW DAYS before the blackout, Del had retrieved her old Nikon camera from the bedroom closet and loaded a roll of film. She had intended to start taking pictures like her lawyer advised. In the morning, when the electricity had not yet come on, Del picked up the camera from the kitchen table. She drew it to her eye and focused the lens on her husband who stood quietly against the window. She began to wonder what kind of photographs would make their lives together look meaningful and intertwined. She didn't press the button.

"Did you get me?" he asked while freezing with closed lips and hardened eyes.

"No."

A call came in on Joseph's phone. She kept the camera over her eye and considered dressing for work to find another means of getting to the Bronx as the subways still weren't running. She wanted to take the day off. After their argument the night before, perhaps she and Joseph needed a day alone to repair the break.

"Okay. Yes, I'll be there," he said into the receiver. He snapped the phone shut and watched her for a minute, as she continued to play with the zoom without pressing the button.

"Take it or don't," he said.

"I'm waiting for the right light."

"Otherwise you'll have to wait until tonight."

"Why?" Del brought the camera down to rest on her hip. He was just a shadow against the bright rain pouring across the windowpanes.

"A commercial in Brooklyn," he said. "I guess the actor they hired couldn't fly in last night. It's a three-day job, so I'll be back late."

"Do you have to?" she asked. "I'd rather you stayed here with me."

"This isn't volunteer work. I have to take it. You're still angry at me, aren't you?"

"I'm not angry," she said, lifting the camera and taking a shot blindly without bothering to check the focus. "I never was. I just wish—"

"What?"

"Nothing," she replied. "Go."

Del managed to flag an off-duty cab that was willing to take her all the way to the Bronx for a special blackout fare of seventy dollars, which she figured, as they sped through Harlem, was roughly equivalent to her day's pay after taxes. She tried not to worry about Joseph. What right did she have to demand facts and dates anyway, like her own worst INS case worker coming alive inside of their home? "Just let it go," she said against the window, repeating Joseph's own words. *Bleeding, nausea, heart attack, cramping, vomiting . . .*

The Bronx had not lost power. Abrams shook his head at her late arrival, as if the story of a Manhattan power failure was merely an elaborate excuse to hide ingrained irresponsibility. Del changed into her uniform and took the stairs to the nursery, notebook in hand, to check on Apollo. She found him lying in his tank and assessed his skin, the elaborate brocade of diamond marks that flared down his spine, the dorsal imprint that defined him as a member of his subspecies and which he would carry for his entire life. The top layer of skin would shed for a brighter palette underneath, but he would never lose that particular patterning like his own unique fingerprint. A gassed white mouse had been placed by another zookeeper in the cage. She tapped her fingernail against the glass, hoping he would be driven to eat. Then she opened the terrarium and reached her hand a few inches above him, watching carefully for a reaction. His small spade-shaped head slid under her palm with his tongue whipping into the air to take in the molecules of her scent. This act was dangerous, a clear violation of zoo procedure, but she knew the first indicators of a strike posture, and her muscles moved with his own.

Apollo was as venomous as any viper. Even a decapitated rattlesnake could still bite after its neck had been severed, fangs entering a toe and injecting the poison stored in its glands, a final payback in death. The only safe snake was one stiff with rigor mortis. It occurred to her that Leto had not stiffened when she performed the C-section. Del imagined the mother biting into Francine's shoe, the way a woman in labor bites down on a pillow, while she removed the embryos from the fetal membrane. But, of course, Del had been the one to crush Leto's head and shatter her teeth on the floor.

She began to draw Apollo's diamond pattern in her notebook, crosshatching the scales underneath the humming fluorescent light. She had not heard the door to the nursery open and almost jumped as two hands pried the notebook from her grip and began flipping through its pages.

"What is this?" Abrams asked, as Del quickly put the lid on the tank. He didn't wait for an answer, tucking the book under his arm. "And why are you up here alone? You know you aren't allowed to be opening cages without the assistance of another keeper."

Del suppressed the rage firing inside of her. She fought the words crowding her tongue. *If I hadn't acted, this animal wouldn't be alive.*

Abrams pointed to the door.

"My office. Right now," he ordered and retreated with the fast confidence of knowing she'd follow close behind.

She walked slowly down the steps and through the dark hallway. She passed through the break room, ignoring the staff that silently followed her with their eyes. Abrams stood, hand on doorknob, to let her pass before slamming it shut and closing the metal window blinds.

He petted his tie as he sat deep in his chair. The wheels wheezed with his weight against the floor.

"This notebook isn't authorized paperwork."

"It's my own," she said, her voice flickering between insolence and remorse. "I still fill out the dailies in the binder. I just wanted to be a little more thorough in my observations. I know we aren't technically supposed to keep our own records, but it's not exactly a violation, Dr. Abrams, is it?"

She considered the ridiculousness of this moment, of having to fight to keep a job she had imagined quitting so many times, sitting in this very seat across from his desk to deliver the long-awaited good-bye. She would have been happy to tear a page from the notebook and write out her resignation letter, but that would not have been quitting on her own terms. What she had before her, as Abrams twisted in his seat and brought one leg over the other, was the possibility of being fired, as if she hadn't devoted the last decade of her life to this department.

"That's exactly what it is, Ms. Kousavos. A violation. I'm not sure if you understand, but what we are responsible for at this institution is a curatorial program that involves a dangerous, poisonous, rare, and priceless collection." He overarticulated each word. "We follow a strict policy set up over an eighty-year history to ensure the safety and well-being of these species. We cannot, we will not, allow staff to make their own rules and set their own conditions. You are not a visiting professor. Understand?"

Behind him hung a poster of a loggerhead tortoise swimming unhurriedly through green, sun-mottled water. As always, Del noticed the likeness between the tortoise and her superior—the same lipless grimace, beaked nose, and flattened, bald head.

"Of course I understand," she replied. "I've been here the longest of anyone out there. Dr. Abrams, I believe I'm owed a little consideration. If you want an apology for opening the cage alone, I'm happy to provide one. But this is just a notebook. No more."

"An apology." He laughed with irritable glee. "No, I'm afraid that's not enough. I am aware that you have a specific interest in rattlesnakes and for the past months I have allowed you to take a little extra time with the rattlers while compromising your other duties. That's going to end. This notebook looks to me like a personal research project."

"It's not a personal project," she lied. To his credit, Abrams had a good mind for assessing situations. It was so often the least compassionate people who gauged human behavior so succinctly.

"It looks like an outside study. We have researchers here already, tenured professors, experts who have waited years for an opportunity to observe these animals. It is a breach of contract for you to do research on the department clock. I've been too lenient."

Del reached for the notebook on the desk and expected Abrams to keep it locked under his fist, but he let her take it. *That was too easy*, she thought nervously. Like it was the last thing he was going to let her do.

"I have let you name it. I'm afraid you've confused naming with owning," he said. "It is not uncommon for a young staff member to mix these emotions. But you're a zoo employee, not a pet owner. You don't have a personal relationship with these animals."

She stiffened in her seat. From a certain angle, the tortoise looked like it was balancing on top of Abrams's head.

"Ten years. I've been here ten years," she repeated. "When have I ever thought I owned anything?"

"I don't dislike you, Del." He cracked a smile and studied her face as if he were looking at a photograph, free to roam the contours of her cheeks, eyes, and lips. "I know that you're with us on a work visa and I want you to understand that I wouldn't jeopardize your status in this country without serious reason." She looked down at the wedding band on her finger, but decided it was best to use that last weapon on her own terms, when she was ready. "I'm giving you a warning. Strike two and maybe we will have to reassess your situation. I'd hate for that to happen."

Photographs hung around his office, group shots that mostly looked like faded portraits of colonizers on safari, sidling up to a jeep or standing in front of a giant turtle shell with proud, arrogant smiles. Del only appeared in one picture, taken in front of the building with a more multicultural congregation of employees, less tall and rigid and neatly arranged. It had been taken seven years ago to commemorate the zoo's centennial anniversary, and out of those twenty faces only three staff members remained.

"I have always tried," she replied with careful restraint, "to be professional."

Abrams breathed with satisfaction.

"Good. Then I think it's best if you spend some time away from the animals. A little vacation from the nursery just to get your bearings. And, so you know, we are donating the baby rattler to a research project. I don't want to hear a word of protest from you."

"What project?" she asked, so flustered she didn't bother to disguise the shock.

"The professor I introduced you to a few weeks ago. She's studying the effects of venom."

"What effects?"

"That isn't important, is it?" Abrams swiveled back in his chair and ducked under his desk. He reappeared with a stack of brochures printed in yellow lettering. WELCOME TO THE REPTILE HOUSE. COLD BLOODS WILL WARM YOU. He might as well have been pointing a gun. "You'll be passing these out at the entrance for the next few days," he said with a smile. "Face time with the public. A good way of remembering one of our chief responsibilities is educating more than ourselves."

The brochures had been Francine Choi's punishment for killing a rattlesnake. And now they were Del's punishment for saving one. Yes, she should have taken the day off. Soon, hopefully, she would have every day off. Del made a silent promise right in Abrams's office to quit the day that Apollo was donated to animal testing.

CHAPTER SEVENTEEN

MADI TRIED TO look her brother in the eye as she sat frozen on a stool in his studio. This attempt was frustrated not only because of the two blinding towers of tungsten lights trained on her but because Raj's eyes were mostly hidden behind his camera.

"Do you remember Raphael?" she asked, rubbing her neck.

"Raphael? The guy you thought you loved, what was it, eight years ago?"

"Six. And the R sounds like an H. *Haf-ael*. Brazilian. Portuguese."

"Don't move so much. I'm trying to get you, not your blur." Hunched forward in the position of a defensive linesman, Raj held his camera an inch from his eyes, waiting for his sister to stop moving. She fixed her hair to make sure the part cut evenly down the center of her scalp.

"Well, the point is, when we broke up, I always harbored a particular animosity for Brazilians. I didn't allow bossa nova to be played on cab radios. I refused to eat at those restaurants where you turn a card over when you want more meat. I'd meet someone from Rio and go cold. I wouldn't even put out my hand."

Defeated, Raj balanced his camera on his shoulder as a sign that

Madi was being an uncooperative subject. Even when she wasn't speaking, her eyes blinked, her feet fidgeted, and her lips expanded into an exaggerated smile when he had specifically asked for no smile. No fidgeting. No blinking.

"Stop it." He reached forward and pried her hand from her hair. "Film is expensive. This isn't digital. Do me a favor. Close your eyes. Relax your face. And then open them again. It isn't about how you think you should look. Let me judge that."

"How can I not squint from all the light you've got on me?" she said incredulously. "It's like I'm under deep interrogation."

"When you see the pictures, it'll look natural. Put your arm back on your lap. That's it." Raj snapped a few more shots, leaning from left to right to capture off angles, hoping to cleave the angularity in her face. For a good thirty seconds, Madi managed the blank, saturnine expression of the mildly brain-dead (admittedly biting the insides of her cheeks just enough so Raj wouldn't notice). But self-consciousness got the better of her. She erupted into a laugh and then collapsed on the stool, rocking against her knees.

"I'm sorry," she gasped. "I can't help it. I'm not good at this."

Raj put the camera down on his desk, returning to face her with crossed arms impatient at the fingers. "Now you know why I don't shoot people anymore. There's no use. Would music help you relax?"

"Help me relax?" she mocked. "You sound like you're pressuring a teenage model into removing her bra. How can I relax when I know you're going to use these for some future exhibition with my face blown up so huge that everyone can study my wrinkles? And if you don't mind, can you please manage the illusion of high cheekbones?"

Raj had shot portraits of his sister for the past five years, nodding through her protests as he positioned her on the stool each time and told her not to move. She'd always complain, but secretly Madi was flattered. The shoot had become something of a yearly ritual, and afterward Raj would buy her dinner and they could finally talk without the interference of the camera. The truth was that Madi liked to have her picture taken by him, even sitting in front of the white scrim in the blazing heat, because it proved that they still factored in each other's worlds. Only occasionally did Madi worry that the results of all these photo shoots would one day manifest in some exploitative series framed on gallery walls.

Raj cranked the small fan in the corner a notch higher, although the increased current merely ruffled his curly hair. Sweat the shape of an arrowhead stained the front of his V-neck T-shirt, and thin black hairs stuck against his collarbone.

"Staring in direct light only increases the lines on my face. I'm squinting. Am I squinting?"

Raj waited for his sister to reclaim her expressionless mouth and eyes. Then he picked up the camera for another round of shots.

"The reason I brought up Raphael," she continued.

"Yeah, Rapha. Didn't we call him that?"

"What I mean is, even when the Brazilian economy refused to keep tanking and started going global a few years ago, I was secretly pissed. Stupid President Lula and his Labor Party making economic trade deals all over the northern hemisphere. All this anger. All this venom spit toward a corrupt South American democracy. A whole population cursed a zillion times in my head to endless poverty simply because I had some unfinished issues with that prick from Ipanema who, let's face it, never had any real potential. Can any man have a serious stake in love if he sing-songs English like he's molesting you?"

"Why don't you stand?" Raj suggested, taking a second to exchange a spent film cartridge for a fresh one.

"Mind if I keep sitting? So my point . . . "

"Always a point. Yes, you're squinting."

"It's exactly like your not coming to India with me, your absolute refusal to consider the option. You hate Dad. But Dad's not India. So come with me because you don't know shit about the country and maybe you'll end up finding inspiration there."

"That's not why I'm not going."

"I know what you say," she moaned. "Anyone who spends ten minutes with you knows what you say, and we're all pretty sick of hearing it. You don't want to do work for corporate interests, blah, blah, blah. That artist nonconformist act is so tiring. But I have a new proposition. You'll come to India as my companion. I don't even expect you to shoot anything. I'll pay for your trip myself. No company commitment. No pictures of call centers. Just me funding some forced experience on my older brother. It's my present. We leave in ten days. That's as simple and uncompromising as it gets."

Raj turned off one of the light towers, changing the angles on Madi's face and throwing her shadow against the wall.

"Thank god," she said, leaning down to grab a towel on the floor. She dabbed her forehead lightly, trying not to smear her makeup. "We can spend a week together sightseeing. We can go to the Taj Mahal if you want or the Gothic church in Goa. Whatever you want. Like old times."

Raj read the light meter that hung around his neck and adjusted the aperture.

"What old times?" he asked without looking up. "We never took a vacation together. We never once went anywhere. We lived in Florida, in a house sprinkled in seashells. Dad never took us—"

"He took us to Tampa," she interrupted with a noting finger. "You threw up. You came to visit me my sophomore year, and look what that did. You moved here after that, didn't you? Okay, we haven't traveled much together. But wouldn't it be fun, the two of us?"

"Tons," he said and then lifted the camera to his face, where he appreciated the excuse of not having to look directly at her. There was nothing so damaging as staring into his sister's eyes and rejecting her advances. Because in those eyes he could find what they did share—the attempt to force the other over to their side by their own stubborn will. "No, Madi," he said calmly. "I can't go. Too much work to do right now."

"What work? What work is worth forfeiting a free trip halfway around the world?" She preformed a frantic gesticulation of her hands, while managing to remain perfectly still from the neck up, fearing Raj's lens would catch her in some hysterical fit.

He shot through the roll and then turned to his desk to rifle through papers and contact sheets. He pulled out a small square of white paper and held it in front of her. It was the announcement card to his first solo show.

"No!" she screamed proudly. "At a real gallery? Raj, when did this happen?"

"About a month ago," he said, unable to control his smile. "So you see, I need time to get it all together. I need to make my selections, do the print order, frame the damn things. I can't be riding off to India with you. I've only got a few weeks."

"Are my pictures going in the show?"

"Of course," he said, stumbling backward as his cheeks flushed in embarrassment. Raj had never been able to accept compliments from his family. Whenever one of his parents had stumbled on one of his magazine editorials and begun the predictable chorus of praise, he'd instantly cut them short, complaining that the printing had been muddy or that he'd never been paid. He picked up a cigarette from his desk and blew the dust off of it. "Don't get all congratulatory. It could be a complete disaster."

"When did you start smoking?"

"I don't. I just like to hold it between my teeth when I work. It smells good. And my fingernails don't get bloody from biting them." Madi recognized the rolled cigarette as the shape of Del's handwork. A piece of tape held the cigarette together at the center, and she wanted to comment on it but knew any remark about Del would send her brother back into the black hole of his thoughts. There was so much wounded pride in Raj that she could hardly believe that they both had come out of the same womb.

"Put on some music then," she said instead. "If I'm going to be hanging on walls, I want to *relax*."

Raj turned on his stereo, filling the room with a piano concerto. When he walked back to his desk, still unable to look Madi in the face, she slipped up behind him and rested her chin on his shoulder.

"What are those?" she asked, gliding her arms over his ribs and pointing to the contact sheets.

"I did these last week at an apartment uptown. It was built in the 1950s. I stood there for three hours, just watching the condensation build and dissipate on the glass. The woman who owned the place kept running in and out of the room like she was hoping to catch me stuffing my bag with her china. Offering me tea every five seconds was her way of making sure I wasn't stealing. But I got what I went for."

"They must be pretty rich to have a greenhouse in Manhattan."

He wondered if Madi could pick out the difference in the photographs—the crease of shadows, the fractures of bending light, the clarity of the white walls that abutted the wet glass. His sister was a head-trip to photograph, but he lied when he said that shooting people was difficult. It was easier to get the living down than it was to capture a place. The main part of his work—the part that didn't involve Madi—was taking these studies of modernist architecture, those mammoth spare interiors built on sublime mathematical principles and the purity of form and line. They weren't cold shells or unfeeling unions of steel and glass. He often said he could see walls breathing, whole atmospheres moving in and out to fill voids. That's what he wanted his camera to pick up. He had spent hours in that apartment, refocusing the lens, pressing the button, staring straight ahead, listening to his own heartbeat. He had been so patient, and somewhere in those contact sheets, there would be a single frame that revealed how the breath of the greenhouse flowers frosted the glass, how the bare walls opened their pores to take the air in, how the light bled in puddles across the glossed wood. He had to find it, his eye straining through the glass loop, the momentary sense of something human in the sea of raw materials.

"They're beautiful," she said. "But you aren't going to show them along with me, right?"

"Yep."

"So I'm competing with architecture? Oh, Christ, which is colder? I get it."

"I was thinking, which is more humane?"

"Asshole." She walked over to the window, staring out at the skyline of New Jersey and its watery reflection in the Hudson River. Her eyes moved over the lines of the buildings set against the black sky.

"Remember when we were kids and we'd go to the beach on summer nights and dare each other to dive in?"

"Yes," Raj said, returning the cigarette to the desk. "We never did. We just watched the hookers walk a few feet in front of the men who came down from the hotels. Our beaches contained either shells or prostitutes, and the tourists collected both. That's what I remember."

"We never did jump in, did we? What were we afraid of?"

"Sharks. Riptides. Mom beating our asses for going out without permission."

A yellow light trailing in the river reminded Madi of the swollen lemons at a market stall in Lisbon, near the bleak Moorish ruins of Castelo de São Jorge. She and Rapha had climbed up to that castle on their only excursion out of the hotel room on their trip to Portugal six years ago. It had been November, and they both had come down with the flu on the plane ride—sickness being what they had been trying to escape by leaving New York in autumn. They had spent four days watching CNN with the trashcan and the remote between their bodies on the coverlet, each taking turns vomiting and changing channels. By the fifth day, they had gathered enough energy to ascend the hill above the city and stood silently under the low, gray clouds that shot out into the Atlantic. She remembered Rapha kindly for once, as he fought with the pharmacist in thick Portuguese to fill a prescription, his hairy, naked body quivering as he ran towels under cold water to place on her forehead. He had taken care of her, and, being the first to feel health return (a fact that later convinced her that she had contracted the flu from him), nursed her with lobster bisque and squeezed lemon juice. Madi's only solid memory of that vacation, the only value she had found in a week of fever and chills and indifferent maids rubbing their cigarettes in the room's ashtrays while vacuuming around her bed, was the rare, indescribable light that drained through the cloud cover over Castelo de São Jorge. It was as soft as the underside of lemon rinds, as frosted as chilled tap water.

It was something to remember.

She wondered if Rapha, six years later wherever he had gone, ever thought of that light.

"Do you think either of us will have children?" she asked, turning to look at her brother.

"Get back on the stool. We'll do one more roll, and then I've had it." He kicked an extension cord and turned on the light tower. "I'm hungry. And I'm not eating curry tonight. It's bad to let you get your way too often."

"I'm serious."

He knew she was. Her voice had lost its sarcastic guard, and she had the look of someone who had woken up in the middle of the afternoon confused as to how much time had passed.

"Why the hell would you want children?" he snapped.

"We would do a better job than our parents did."

"That wouldn't be difficult." Raj grabbed her hand and led her back to the stool. He repositioned her chin with his thumb, pressing the divot in her chin.

"We're not monsters," she said. "It could happen. You're pretty loving when you want to be."

"Sit still and think about what you just said. You think about how people like us could get into a situation like that and be glad we're the monsters we are."

"People like us," she repeated somberly. "So you do think we're monsters, that there's something wrong with us. I guess we can fight over which parent caused us to turn out like we did. The bad Singhs. Never married. Too screwed up for love."

Her eyes were a different color than his, chestnut brown instead of blue. Her nose trumpeted at the end where his caught a bump midway down the bridge and slid straight to the tip.

"Monsters don't cut their losses like we did. Monsters, like the ones in the movies, keep coming back, meaner and more hateful, seeing nothing good in knowing when to quit. I'd say we're not the monsters. Other people are."

"I suppose I should thank you for the honesty," she said ungraciously.

He smiled at her. "Don't mention it."

They left the studio and walked east in silence. They passed the art gallery where Raj would soon show his work, but he didn't point it out to his sister, afraid of another spree of compliments and overblown expectations. Maybe it was because Madi had moved to New York first or simply the fact that she made more money, but he could never shake the sense that she was the older one, not he. She encouraged instead of admired, defended instead of looked for reassurance.

Madi shook her purse on the corner and said, "Since we have something to celebrate, I'm buying tonight." He tried to object, and she rolled her eyes irritably before stepping into the street. Her hair caught the wind of passing taxis. "Can I at least tell Dad about your show?" she asked him. "It would make him happy."

He was five inches taller than she was, and yet they probably weighed the same. When they were kids—before puberty redirected their ambitions—they were both obsessed with the scale in the bathroom. They competed to see who weighed more, squeezing every muscle to force the scale to deliver a higher reading. Who took up more space in the world? Who was more massive and essential? That was the last time Raj could remember beating her at anything.

As they crossed the street, she slowed her pace to remain next to him. The sweat from the studio lights chilled their skin even in the hot night air, and Madi wrapped her arm around his. Raj made a mental note to tell his gallerist not to let anyone named Madeline Singh buy a single piece of his artwork—not even anonymously. He suspected she might try such a tactic to give him the illusion of success, and she'd never understand the deep humiliation that would result in that kind of sisterly meddling.

Still, when Madi's palm grazed his wrist, he opened his fingers, and they walked two blocks together squeezing each other's hand.

CHAPTER EIGHTEEN

JOSEPH SAT ON the edge of the hotel bed, while Aleksandra dug
through a white dress box on the floor. Inside the box were letters
and newspaper clippings. Pages of the script she had been working
on drifted around her bare feet, a few pages crumpled into Ohio
snowballs, others smoothed back out and clipped together with red
ink slashed through lines. "They're here somewhere," she swore. "No
wonder I can't seem to get Ray's story down in any order." Defeated,
she brought the entire box over to the bed and sat down next to him,
searching though the papers until she found a stack of photographs.

Joseph had not gotten a job in Brooklyn like he told his wife. In
the late afternoon he took the subway to the Upper East Side, making
certain to turn his cell phone off to avoid Del in case she called. He
didn't want to gild the lie of a fictitious last-minute commercial
any more than he needed to. And, anyway, it was only a lie of three
days—a break from tripping over each other, some needed distance
from the sweltering Gramercy apartment and all the unbearable
questions he knew were circling in her head. He'd return at night so
late that Del would already be lost to sleep.

Aleksandra pressed her knees together on the edge of the bed, the skin corrugated from kneeling on the carpet. Her pale eyes gently traced his features, and she held the photographs tightly against her chest. Now that she had found them, it was as if she were afraid of letting them go. Her arms were covered in faded freckles, and blue veins cabled along her wrists and fingers. She had used those fingers to wipe his damp hair across his forehead an hour ago when she opened the door. "Thank you for coming," she had said, blushing awkwardly in the door frame as she brought her hand back down to her side, embarrassed by the intimacy of the gesture. "I thought you might decide not to in the rain."

The instant he saw Aleksandra standing at the door—her hair tied back in a loose bun, the faint birthmark trailing down her neck, her small, precise lips opening in gratitude, even the gentleness of her fingers pushing the hair from his eyes—he knew why he didn't have the heart to turn her down when she called. He could have said, *I hardly know you, and all you've given me is an outrageous, paranoid story that even the police concluded was a suicide. I'm sorry but I have no time for you. Good-bye, Aleksandra. I wish you luck.* But a person turning around and walking away could never measure the damage they left behind. And one day, he might ask for a similar concession—*believe what I tell you, follow along, don't doubt what is so easy to disbelieve, this is what happened. I swear it's all true.*

"I was worried I'd lost these," Aleksandra said, staring intently at the snapshots in her hands. "I've moved around so often, from one hotel to another, I can't keep track of everything I had."

"How long have you been at the Carlyle?" he asked.

"About a year," she said, and then paused, as if to track some jumbled hotel-starred cartography in her mind. "But I moved around a lot at first. A few nights here and there, first in a number of gritty motels on the edge of Times Square and then in some drab, efficient business lodges in the Financial District. At first I always asked for the smallest room they had. I'd unplug the phone and cover the window with the bedspread. I wouldn't even let the maid in. I just wanted to be alone. Some people want to be surrounded by others when they're grieving. I didn't. No one could reach me, and I couldn't reach them. That was as close as I could find to being nowhere."

Joseph heard a phone ringing in the room next door. Inexplicably, they both waited in silence until the caller gave up. Aleksandra shifted on the mattress, and her hip nudged against him.

"I'd think places like that would make you feel worse," he said.

"Worse, better. I wasn't trying to get better. I was trying to think. I just stopped trying to pay attention to Aleksandra Andrews, the poor useless widow who had lost her world. I even stopped looking at myself in the mirror every morning. Isn't it interesting how you stare at the same face every day for your entire life? I often think about how each person I pass on the street must have spent months of their lives when you add it up studying their face in the mirror, getting to know every bone, every line, specialists of such a small circle of skin. You keep looking at your face like it's going to tell you something about yourself, reveal some fact about who you are that your brain hasn't managed to figure out. I think when you live so long with another person, you don't really know who you are anymore without them. It's not just you minus them. It's as if they've cancelled a whole other part out, a part you assumed was yours but wasn't. I figured those dark, tiny hotel rooms two-thousand miles from Los Angeles were as good a place as any to avoid looking at myself."

She placed the photographs in Joseph's hand, and any doubts as to why she had first asked him to come were erased. He flipped through the stack slowly, careful not to crease the paper. In one picture Aleksandra had her arms around her husband's neck, both of them smiling with wind-burnt cheeks on a dark California beach. In another they stood blazed by the candles of a birthday cake in a dining room. In another, Ray wore a black suit at a banquet table surrounded by other businessmen. Joseph stared at the face of her husband, his light brown hair peppered with gray, his sagging chin dipping from a strong jawline, his thin, almost effeminate nose webbed in blood vessels. He was a handsome man slightly ravaged by the first fissures of old age, while his wife, younger and healthier in the gold softness of western light, skirted around him with her eyes on the camera, as if she understood the instant these shots were taken that each captured moment would later be memorized and missed.

Joseph tried to remember his own father, a man whom he also

looked so much like. Joseph had seen pictures of him in his twenties and early thirties, bounding through forests and rooms in dirty workman's clothes wearing a blameless, easy grin. At thirty-three, Joseph had turned into the man arrested in those Guiteau family photographs. But his father had never passed through his thirties to allow age to invade his face. Joseph couldn't picture what the years would have done to him. If his father had grown old, maybe Joseph could also have imagined how he himself would age, how his features would be recast into the hard, brittle circuitry of his forties and fifties. He couldn't, and perhaps that was because he wasn't sure he would live to see those years. There would only be Joseph Guiteau, suspended forever in his early thirties, brushing his teeth in a toothpaste commercial, the mile marker before the explosion just beyond.

Joseph let out a sigh, which Aleksandra mistook for sympathy. She nodded her head and placed her hand on his shoulder, sliding her palm down his spine.

"He's much older than you are here, by twenty years I'd say. But he could have passed for you when he was young. He probably looks more like your father when these were taken."

"My father died of a heart attack at thirty-four," he said quickly. "It runs in the family." That was already more than he had ever told Del and it surprised him how easily this information left his mouth. Aleksandra rubbed his back in consolation. Her fingers softened to the tips of her nails, as if she were afraid to upset him with any more than the faintest point of contact. He and Aleksandra were mourning for different men but staring at the same picture. He dropped the stack of photos in her lap, and she returned them to the dress box.

IN THE GRAY evening light of the bedroom, Aleksandra told him about survival tactics.

She told him about knives hidden in mattresses or under pillows of hotel rooms. She told him that when she first moved to Los Angeles at twenty, she had slept next to a kitchen knife for the first two months, unaccustomed to the city and its nocturnal sounds. The knife had been for protection against break-ins, freak rapists, and whatever chance monsters crawled up into bedrooms of single young women in a town that wasn't yet their own. She told him that when she fled to New York five years ago, she again slept with a knife by her side, but this time she knew precisely who might be coming for her.

Aleksandra told him that, after Ray's funeral, she returned to the house in Malibu and found their study turned upside down. Not ransacked, there hadn't been a mess, no valuables stolen, but the papers had been rummaged through, the drawers of the desk searched, the books in the library shaken. Datebooks going back ten years had disappeared. The police couldn't find any evidence of forced entry, presuming Aleksandra in her grief had invented the burglary. She left Los Angeles five days later. She told Joseph that, when she landed at JFK, she checked into an airport motel and in the middle of the night the phone rang. A man's voice asked for Mrs. Andrews. She said wrong number, and then the voice asked for Aleksandra Andrews. She packed in fifteen minutes. She took a cab to the Pierre on Sixty-First Street, the very hotel that she and Ray always stayed in on their trips to New York. When she went to check in, the receptionist told her that two men had come by earlier that evening asking for her. The Pierre had appeared in a number of those missing datebooks. She left the hotel, walked west, and took the smallest room the Penn Station Hyatt offered under a fake name. She told Joseph that she paid in cash for an entire year. She used names that never appeared in any datebook or photo album. She called friends and family from pay phones, and once or twice, they told her that someone had phoned asking if they knew of her whereabouts. She said she didn't know if the fact that these men couldn't locate her only encouraged their suspicion that she knew something. That maybe her disappearance persuaded them to search harder. But by that point she had stopped going by Aleksandra Andrews. It was only a year ago that she began using her real name.

"Do you still think they're looking for you?" he asked. Aleksandra wiped her forehead to consider a reasonable answer to a question that had nothing reasonable about it.

"I don't know," she finally replied. "But I can tell you that I've learned to pack in five minutes. I've rented this room for a year, but I could be gone by a single wrong number in the middle of the night."

She looked at him with fear in her eyes. He wanted to tell her that he understood that fear, how impossible it was to swim out of it, that he kept a gun in a metal box under his own bed and that it also wasn't for random break-ins. But Aleksandra stood up, shaking her arms to compose herself, and he felt it was time for him to leave.

"I'll come back tomorrow," he said. "If you want me to." She said yes, she'd like that. She pressed her fingers against the closet door and slid it open.

"Before you leave I want to show you something," she whispered. She said it lovingly, as if inviting him to glimpse a precious artifact. Inside the closet, he found suit coats spaced evenly on wood hangers with pant legs folded in between the soft silk linings. The suits were navy, charcoal, black, tattersall, houndstooth, and pinstripe, the lapels curled like flower petals. "These were Ray's," she said, touching their collars with her fingertips reverently. "I brought them with me, packed in one of his old suitcases." She grabbed the shoulder of a blue double-breasted jacket, which slipped off its hanger and into her hand. "He wasn't a vain man," she said, shaking the wrinkles out with gentle strokes. "He was nearly colorblind when it came to most things. When I first met him, he wore cheap suits that looked like leftovers from a yard sale. I had to teach him what a real suit meant, how it shapes the body and makes a man look like a thing to watch." She opened the jacket and waved it like a matador's cape. "Try it on. See if it fits."

"I don't feel right about wearing that," he said nervously, stepping back from the closet, afraid he'd defile some vital memory she had managed to preserve. "It was *his* suit. I don't want to try it on."

"He didn't die in this jacket," she said, smiling. "It isn't haunted."

Joseph turned and let his arms fall slack, the limp position costumers preferred while dressing him for an acting job. It occurred to him that he had built a career wearing other men's clothes. This time was no different. Aleksandra threaded his arms through the sleeves and guided the jacket onto his shoulders. Then she sat down on the bed and took him in.

"You're a little smaller and leaner," she said. "But it's almost right."

"You two must have been very happy." He watched her expression carefully in the mirror as he buttoned the coat.

"Yes, we were," she replied. "Aren't you with your wife?" Joseph had never told Aleksandra that he was married. He turned around in surprise. "I noticed the ring on your finger the first time I met you. I imagine she must be very beautiful. You're happy, aren't you? You're a better person for marrying her?"

"Sure," he said, more flippantly than he expected. The intensity of Aleksandra's love for her husband, the photos of them happily floating through the decades of their marriage, the pages of his death typed and revised on the floor, suddenly made his relationship with Del seem embarrassingly deficient. If Aleksandra knew he had a wife waiting for him at home, he wondered what she thought about him visiting her in this hotel room so late in the evening.

"You don't sound so convinced," she said with her eyebrows pinched.

"Oh, I am," he sighed. "It's not easy, but of course I'm happy."

"I'm glad to hear it," she said with fingers wrenching in the space between her knees. "I hope she's not mad you come to see me."

He exhaled deeply and gathered his composure with a smile.

"I can take some of the pages you've written home to read if you want," he said to change the subject.

Aleksandra shook her head, indicating that she wasn't going to let them out of her sight. He could see a question forming on her lips. She held on to the first word before finally letting it go.

"Can I ask you something?" she said. "Why were you at that conspiracy meeting? You seem like you have your whole life going for you, like the world as it's turning right now would be enough."

His fingers trembled as he slipped them into the jacket's inner pocket and felt the edge of a matchbook. He removed it and read the word HILLCREST written in green cursive across the flap. He decided not to show it to her, having no way of gauging what painful connotations it might evoke. Some remnants of the dead were better left lost to linings, to coats, to hotel rooms, to other shores. He wondered at what point Aleksandra would stop thinking that there was anyone out in the world still trying to track her down, and, when that realization came, would it bring her comfort or emptiness? When you get to the point where running defines your character, there might be nothing so destructive as turning around and finding no one there.

"It's not something I'm able to talk about," he said, taking off the jacket and placing it back on its hanger.

"I'm a great believer in the unbelievable," she said, lying back on the mattress with her eyes fixed on the ceiling. Her bare feet rubbed against the carpet. "You can always try me. It's been a long time since I've had the comfort of doubt."

"Maybe sometime," he said, imagining what those first words might be and how unbelievable, even to him, they would sound.

CHAPTER NINETEEN

"WELCOME," DEL SAID to stroller-pushers, to fat children, to angry hand-holding Puerto Rican teens. "Welcome," she said to families of eight, to skinny mustachioed single men, to gorgeous Swedish nannies who didn't understand her. "Welcome to the Reptile House," she said outside of its smoked glass doors, waving a wet color brochure to anyone who passed by her in the rain. "Care for some information on our exhibitions?"

Mostly they didn't, and she couldn't blame them. The categorical descriptions listed on the brochure were indecipherable, as much by the smudged print from the rain as by the fact that no eye could discern the words in the darkness of the exhibition hall. After two hours of intermittent showers while sheathed in one of the park's hooded blue rainproof slickers, she finally gave in to the urge to light a cigarette.

Del had pointedly not gone up that morning to check in on Apollo. She had performed her checklist duties with loud, slow intent. But by noon, she could no longer stave off the inevitable fact that a stack of brochures sat on the break-room table decorated with a Post-it from Abrams that read, "For Del, to remember the reason we are here."

A fierce torrent of rain created a lapse in foot traffic, and, underneath her hood, she jammed a cigarette into her mouth and lit a match. Her cuticles were bloated. Her thighs were wet.

From the crest of the hood, she glimpsed two waterproof boots walking toward her and she lifted a brochure, hiding the cigarette inside the sleeve of the raincoat.

"Del?" a voice broke from under a competing hood. The man swept it back to make the recognition easier. "Is that you?"

"William," she said very coolly, impressing them both with her indifference, although his sudden presence outside the Reptile House made her heart beat in panic. Her first instinct was to turn and run. He gave a warm smile, an erratic homeless man's smile, she thought, because his face was bruised and scabbed. She had not seen him since the night of his party and only now considered taking a more outraged tone. He grabbed the brochure from her hands and studied it for a minute, as if the black cobra on the cover made sense of some bigger problem enveloping his mind.

"What are you doing outside in this weather?" he finally asked.

The idea of being forced to explain made her cheeks go red, and she searched for a dignified response. One of the chief comforts of working at the zoo was that none of her personal acquaintances ever made their way into the park unless they phoned first at the gate, usually for free entry, and that gave her the needed minutes to cut a more professional pose.

"I'm working." As if to prove it, she thrust a brochure into the chest of a passing grandmother, who in turn grumbled a complaint about visitor treatment. "The real question is, why are you here?"

"I was looking for you," he said after a long, anxious laugh. "But it's a good question for me in general lately, isn't it? I've been asking myself why I'm here for a month. Shouldn't you be inside where it's dry?"

"Well, when you have a real job, you sometimes have to do unpleasant work along with all of the glamorous stuff. Educating the masses is a responsibility we don't take lightly." She wanted to vomit for regressing into Abrams speak. "If none of my colleagues can stand outside in a little downpour, I'll have to do it."

William waved his palms as if to show no offense, although his mind must be busy recalibrating whatever esteem he held for her career. Suddenly her fingers started to burn, and she cursed as she let go of the cigarette and slapped the sleeve at any smoldering embers. William stomped the butt out with the heel of his boot.

"Are you okay?"

"I'm fine," she said curtly, sucking her fingertips.

"I tried to have the ticket desk call you, but they couldn't get through. I told them I was a friend of yours, so they let me in for free."

"That's nice," she said, pretending to look at something more important over his shoulder. Anything was more important than William Asternathy. The bagel-shaped hotdog vendor slumped over his metal cart was more important than this man. She decided to put a stop to the pleasantries. "Why are you here, William?"

"I went to the bat cave along the way. Have you ever been in there? It's called the World of Darkness. Don't you love that? All you see is this constant flutter in the dark. When I finally got a turn to push my nose against the glass, I saw one. It was just hanging there upside down. Weirdly, the bat looked peaceful. And why shouldn't it be? All of these animals have homes. They've got everything taken care of for them. The way I see it, they're at the top of the evolutionary ladder—no starvation, no predators, no cold nights. All they have to do is walk three feet and the whole audience claps like they've just witnessed a miracle."

Del considered the possibility that William might be stoned. His pupils were dilated and his smile was constant. Teenagers often came in droves to the zoo reeking of marijuana. She could find them standing in front of the lion exhibition for hours, occasionally muttering a distant, protracted "wow" to no one in particular.

"I'm afraid I don't have time to give you a private tour," she said impatiently. "But you're welcome to go inside and see the snakes."

"Do you have a minute to get a coffee?" William looked around as if he were worried someone was listening. She knew she couldn't leave her post. Not with Abrams lingering around waiting for her to slip up, and especially not for a friend of her husband's who had gone out of his way to make her feel unwelcome in his own home a few days earlier. She almost laughed at the invitation of wasting a work break sitting across from him in the cafeteria.

"I really don't have time," she said, placing a hand on his forearm. "I'm sorry. I have to work."

"You see, I tried calling Joseph all morning."

"He's in Brooklyn shooting."

"Shooting what?" For the first time, William seemed to concentrate on her words.

"I don't know. A commercial. Some last-minute booking. I really can't talk now."

"Good for him." William ducked his head down reverently. "He gets everything, doesn't he? As long as I've known him he's never had an ounce of bad luck. The guy's a fucking golden—"

"He's on the job for another day or two," she interrupted. "I suggest you keep trying his cell."

William chewed on his bottom lip.

"Thing is, it's an emergency," he mumbled. "I need to borrow some money."

She sighed. It was the sigh of both recognition and disappointment, the sigh a lover might give in the first moment of understanding that a conversation was moving irrevocably toward a split and everything said before it was merely empty words to get to this point.

"I'm sure Joe will be happy to help you. He always is. As I said, he'll be free in a day or two."

"I need to borrow money *now*. Today. A thousand or two. That sounds like a lot, doesn't it? But like I said, it is an emergency. I'll pay it back. I hate asking. But I have to get out of town. That sounds crazy, I know. But people have emergencies, don't they? You saw what happened at the party."

"All I remember is you screaming at us." She appreciated that he had brought up the night of his party and hoped that memory stung him a bit.

"I'm sorry about that," he said. "I was drunk. I meant to call you both the next day and apologize. But everything that's gone on, inside and out, all of the bad luck thrown my way, is the reason I'm getting out. I'm making good on L.A. It's always been my plan and I'm beginning to think it's the growing consensus."

"I know."

"So I need to borrow some money until I get out there."

"You have a lot of friends, William. That party was filled with them. Why don't you ask those people?"

He sucked his cheeks in frustration and cleared his throat.

"I tried. They all said the same thing. 'Oh, I'd really like to help but I'm low on cash right now.' There are really only a certain number of times you can ask people to lend a hand. But I'm asking you. I'm asking you to help me."

Del shook her head and stared at him, at this man who repulsed her with his convenient kindness and his dumb, dark eyes opening wide to appear vulnerable and wounded. She could never understand the friendship of Joseph and William, how someone as sure-footed and temperate as her husband made acquaintance with such a messy, unstable person. But she couldn't just let him suffer any more than she would let an animal suffer. He was Joseph's friend.

"Look. I can't leave this spot. I can't get to an ATM until I'm done with work." She wiped the rain collecting on her eyelids.

"I could wait for you," he exclaimed, jumping at the offer before it was snatched away. "I'll walk around the park. I'll look at the snakes."

She checked her wristwatch. She turned around and opened the door to the exhibition hall. Abrams stood just inside and nodded to her. She shut the door and took a breath, the whole while William's eyes widened with more wounded hope. Instinctively, she grabbed for the wallet in her back pocket—more for show because there was no way she would trust him with her bank card and password—and found four twenties in the bill flap.

"This is all I have right now," she said almost pleadingly. But then she noticed Madi's wedding check for two thousand dollars. Del hadn't cashed it yet because she and Madi hadn't gone shopping together. She could sign it over to him and that would be enough to get rid of him once and for all. It was an investment, she figured, in seeing William out of town. Madi would no doubt scream at her for re-gifting a present that had already lacked intimate value in the first place. Del and William stared at each other for what felt like too long, and she worried Abrams would catch her in the middle of a personal conversation during her forced exile from the lab.

"Do you have a pen?"

William dug through his raincoat, pulling out a ballpoint. She steadied the check on the stack of brochures, signing her name and adding "I hereby sign this over to . . . "

"It's Asternathy," he said, watching her penmanship.

"I know your name," she grunted. It only now occurred to her that William might not know her own last name, might not know anything beyond Del Guiteau.

"Thank you. I can't tell you what this does." He examined the amount and opened his mouth in relief. "Who is Madeline Singh?"

"A friend," she said. "It was her wedding present to me."

Before Del left for the day, she wandered over to the World of Darkness, which exhibited the Rodriques fruit bats. She had hoped to see them flying in the dark, a furious, black army of beating wings. Animals could still hold up their feral mysteries to her, make her feel like there was a rhythm to the world bigger than the one she knew. A cleaning woman with gray cornrows vacuumed the carpet in her custodian jumpsuit, one shade darker than Del's to identify staff rank. The keepers had already turned on the interior lights to coerce the nocturnal animals into sleep. Del stepped over the extension cord anyway and peered through the glass, her nose fluted against the invisible divider, where hundreds of bats made black icicles in the gnarled plastic branches.

She tried calling Joseph on his cell phone, but it went straight to voicemail.

CHAPTER TWENTY

WILLIAM FELT THE fat of two thousand dollars in his back pocket, along with the $759.61 remaining in his bank account. Thanks to Joseph, thanks to Del, thanks to some phantom money-lender named Madeline Singh, his future was finally looking up. So what if he had stuffed his pride down his throat and begged the last woman in New York who owed him even a second of her time? So what if it he had to prey on the pity of Joseph's wife? He'd be gone in twenty-four hours, driving west, and every state crossing would ease the shame of his last days here. They could devour his memory, dance on his ghost for all he cared, put up warning posters on every construction site with his face crossed out in red. He'd be gone.

When Del gave him the check and he started off through the park, still slightly stoned from the joint he had bought that morning on Christopher Street, he turned around to catch one last look at her. She stood in the pouring rain, watching him go, and he felt sorry for her. She looked more caged than any of the animals. She could leave; technically nothing was barring her way. But Del just stood there, drenched and unsmiling, like a dog left out in a storm. And a thought swam through William like a warm ocean current: no matter what deceitful things he had to perform to get out of town, he was free, a moving force with no restrictions, and that single thought filled him with tremendous hope.

He unlocked the door off the street to Quinn's place, drifted down the dark tunnel of the apartment building, pried open the steel second door that accessed the garden, and saw the lit windows of the cottage between the dripping trees. Inside he heard the shower running, and, as he closed the door, he nearly barreled into a slim gawky kid, who couldn't be more than eighteen, getting dressed in the living room. The boy was pulling a polo shirt over his hairless torso, his white-blond hair mohawked in sweat, and his invisible white eyebrows lifted in frightened surprise.

"Hey, sorry," William said. The kid grumbled, quickly reaching to claim a backpack on the floor. A patch sewn on the front flap suggested that MAYBE PARTYING WILL HELP. "Are you guys busy? I can come back."

The kid shook his head robotically, hugging the bag to his chest as he slid his bare feet into scuffed yellow sneakers. His skin was translucent blue where it wasn't rubbed red, and his jeans bundled together at the waist by a nylon belt to keep them from sliding off his hips.

"You a friend of Quinn's?" William asked, trying to ease the awkwardness, because already he noticed a nest of balled tissues on the sofa. "I can come back."

"No. I'm leaving."

The shower turned off. The whip of a towel yanked from the curtain rod competed with Quinn's tuneful humming.

"He's a good guy, you know," William said.

"Why should I care?"

"Okay. You live around here?"

"Yeah," the kid sputtered sarcastically. "I own the brownstone across the street."

William couldn't spot an accent. The words were teenage lazy but they weren't uneducated—not Southern backwater poor or Eastern European desperate. His lack of eyelashes made his eyes appear too big for his face, every glance an uneasy jolt, like a farm animal used to being around humans but not enough to trust them at close range. William got the sense that this guy didn't like being looked at, which was unfortunate because it was clearly his chief means of earning money. So William tried not to look at him at all. He stepped out of the cottage and into the gray night, leaning against one of the oaks.

In a few minutes, the teenager bolted from the cottage with his backpack straddled on his shoulders, walking fast, focused on turning the first corner. William said good-bye and lifted his hand, but the kid didn't turn around, kicking the steel door open and leaving it to squeal as he disappeared into the tunnel. Quinn stepped out of the cottage in a pair of madras shorts with an orange towel wrapped around his neck. His fat, red belly hung over his buttoned waist.

"Christ, Quinn. That guy was young. Too young."

"He's legal, so please no guilt routine," Quinn said with squinting eyes. "It was perfectly soft-core, if you really must know. I didn't even take my clothes off. I'm sure I was the most innocuous valetudinarian he's screwed around with all week." It was Quinn's habit to disguise his vices in a rich vocabulary.

"But he's a kid."

"He's an escort who's got to make money. At least that's what his ad said." Quinn tugged William's sleeve in exasperation, leading him back inside. "Forgive me if I don't want to air-condition all of the West Village. And stop giving me that look. When did you get so prudish about the necessities of sex?"

"I just feel bad for the guy."

"Thanks a lot."

"You know what I mean," William sighed. He was glad to see the tissues on the sofa had been cleared. William took off his jacket and hung it on the wooden coatrack in the corner. Quinn was perhaps the last human on earth who still owned a coatrack. But he was also the first human on earth William knew who was so open and nonchalant about his sexual indulgences. That kind of freedom impressed him. No secrets were concealed behind silent pauses or heated refutations. Quinn was that rare being who did not meet the world halfway with his head lowered. So liberated, so blameless, nothing he did could come back to haunt him.

"What I meant," William said, "is that it's just bad to be used so young."

"Then we all might as well quit right now," Quinn replied more seriously than William expected. "Because that's the way it's eventually going to run. *For everyone.* You want innocence, you're not going to find it here. The only people who talk about the innocence of teenagers are the ones who have forgotten what it's like to be a teenager. Personally, I find innocence overrated—creepy, really, because it shows a deplorable lack of curiosity in the world."

"I'm sure it wasn't curiosity that brought him to place that ad."

Now it was Quinn's turn to sigh, placing both hands on William's shoulders. He gazed lovingly at him. His white whiskers bristled over his tiny upper lip like a flag tattered by rough weather. The wrinkles deepened under his eyes. "There are no perfect situations. You're not going to be absolutely happy." Quinn spoke in his most flagrant proverbial voice. "You never will. Enjoy what you can scrounge out of it. We're all mistreated. We just have to appreciate the seconds that we aren't. Now I've rented movies. You better not have plans."

Quinn went to work rewiring the back of his antique television set to plug in his equally antique VCR. William watched the old man bending down with crackling joints, excitedly shoving wires and cables here and there in preparation for a quiet evening of lewd comments and cheap food delivery. It was a joy for Quinn to have someone to share his evenings with—much more so than the hour with the escort in a silent, loveless transaction of one-way pleasure. William understood what his being here meant to his friend.

"Quinn." William's voice broke, just as it broke a zillion times in his mind as he imagined this worst-of-all-that-had-ever-come-before deceit. "Would you care if I borrowed your car for a little while?"

"The Cressida? I guess I don't need it. Why? Where are you going?" He arched his head over the dusty television screen.

"Upstate. I have some friends who invited me to their cabin. Thought I'd get out of town for a bit."

"The keys are in the desk drawer," he replied, jamming cables haphazardly into the back of the set. "Just please be careful. I could only afford to insure myself, and I have all of those unfinished costumes in the trunk. So promise no accidents. Now which plug . . . I hate modern technology. They can't make it easy. They want to frustrate you into believing it's an actual science."

"It's not modern technology if it's twenty years old." William tried not to think of driving the Cressida west tomorrow. It killed him to imagine the moment it dawned on Quinn that he had been cheated by his own adopted son, the one young man he had shown the most kindness to, the one he had not treated as a transaction but had selflessly taken in. "Let me do that," William said. "You're half blind, and you'll never get it working. What movies are we watching anyway?"

"Family fantasy adventures," Quinn replied sarcastically, slitting his neck with a quick finger. "Horror. The pernicious destruction of goodly innocence. Maniacs with their chainsaws. The food menus are in the cabinet."

IT WAS NOON before William packed his suitcases into the Cressida's trunk, shoved on top of period costumes draped in clear cellophane. William had hoped to return the costumes to the apartment after Quinn left, but his friend had unexpectedly asked a favor: "Drop me at the theater before you go. Forty-Third Street. It will give me a chance to make sure you can actually drive this thing." The thing in question was a 1992 dinosaur, if dinosaurs had been shaped like bars of soap, painted electric blue and emblazoned with a sticker that had long faded white on the right bumper. The Cressida's cramped interior was a cockpit of ripped pleather upholstery and cracked knobs. An alpine forest of deodorizers hung from the rearview mirror, and the air-conditioning vents made a hissing sound that produced no more than a faint breath. William tried to clean the windshield with the automatic wipers, but the twin blades smeared pigeon droppings and dirt across the glass. Quinn stuffed himself into the passenger seat, jacked forward some years ago and jammed permanently into place. They drove in silence through the afternoon traffic up Eighth Avenue. When Quinn pointed to a corner in Times Square, he leaned over and kissed William on the cheek. William did not return the favor, staring straight ahead.

"See you in a couple days, gorgeous," Quinn said, climbing out. "Remember to refill her before you're back. *Yet hold I off. Women are angels, wooing: Things won are done; joy's soul lies in the doing.*" Quinn waited expectantly for a reaction in the sliver of the unrolled window, and when he got none, howled, "*Troilus and Cressida*, you idiot. The make of this car. I have to teach you everything."

A light rain flecked the windshield, washing away some of the grime, as William took the first corner to steer back into the downtown traffic. It hurt not to say good-bye to Quinn, a final farewell to a beautiful, dying man. William kept his eyes not so much on the road but on the buildings and mile-high billboards and the crowded gridlock of bodies that flowed along the sidewalk. He wanted to see it, to talk to it all, one last time before he descended into the Holland Tunnel.

He sped south into the West Thirties, glad to be free of deep midtown, into the diamond, plant, and garment districts that intersected in a chaotic game of rock, paper, scissors. He fell behind a U-Haul with its cargo hull open, rumbling Oriental rugs over the potholes. The rain slowed, and William slapped the console blindly to stop the wipers from scraping the glass.

He entered Herald Square with its department store madness and crosswalks overrun with extended New Jersey families cushioned in layers of I ♥ NY bags. He nearly hit two female backpackers who stopped in the wake of the Cressida to scream German insults as horns herded them back to the curb. He raced down Ninth Avenue into Chelsea.

The city had always scared the shit out of him. He never felt completely safe here, like he had been thrown around in a tornado and managed to grab on to whatever happened to be flying by. In all of his nights here, it was the feeling of dread that accompanied him the most. And what had come of it? William could have given bus tours on all the different apartments around New York where he had hung out, fought, stayed up speed-talking until dawn, or had one-night clumsy affairs in. He could have gone on that way forever, finding someone new to try it with again, like it was still an experiment worth conducting, only the same results each time.

New York was beautiful too. He could say that.

He broke across Twenty-Third Street, sidling up to a taxi driver in the curb lane who sucked on a drumstick to light Jamaican jazz. Wine glasses and slicked hair glistened under bistro canopies, endless lunches, as the sun lit the windshield, brightening the grime into yolk stains.

William gunned through the West Village, red bricks and black wrought iron, flowers withering against windows in the heat. He cut through a yellow light, taking the engine up to thirty to increase the sidewalk blur. Liquor store, Starbucks, too many magazine shops with too many magazines in their splattered windows, the faces of celebrities faded to the bland beige of porn stars, dogs to adopt, bikes for rent, shuttered nightclubs with ripped colored awnings, a children's hair salon. He saw Houston Street ahead. Two cop cars blocked it with their lights flashing, forcing traffic to turn. He rolled down his window and heard the echo of a rally somewhere farther downtown. A few teenagers in army fatigues drifted along the sidewalk carrying banners about oil and Iraq. Another anti-war rally, another demonstration primed for the media—signs pointing up to the news cameras in helicopters instead of to each other in the street—just to prove that New York was superior, a more outstanding, outraged example of what already looked to him like an indulgent, well-orchestrated lie. Thank god he was leaving, because eventually—William was convinced of this point—more terrorists would come to finish the demolition job. They were probably already here, strapping explosives to rats to burrow deep into the cracks and sewers. Once William had said that if the whole world blew up, he would like to be in the center of Manhattan, riding the last skyscraper into the dust. No longer.

He tried to turn down Seventh Avenue, which would have linked him directly to the Holland Tunnel, but it too was blocked, cordoned by blue sawhorses. He drove east, turning south and weaving through the tinier labyrinthine streets of Tribeca, as his wheels ground the debris of a recently dissolved parade route. A group of protestors on the corner yelled something about "gas is murder" to passing cars. One held the head of a George W. Bush piñata, already bashed by sticks and empty of its spilled candy. William maneuvered a middle finger out the window to add his opinion to the debate. He peeled the wrong way down an empty cobblestone street. Abandoned construction sites were wrapped in plastic sheets and tied down with yellow police tape. *What gifts*, he thought, *more condos*.

William wasn't complaining. He didn't feel pathetic or even sad. His entire windshield glowed white like an overdeveloped photograph. He could barely see out of it. William tried to make amends with Joseph, to love Jennifer again, to laugh with Quinn, but they were already behind him. The sun warmed his hands on the steering wheel, and he squinted to make out the color of the traffic light already high up over the car's hood. He couldn't see, and his knee accidentally triggered the wipers, which whisked over the glass. William couldn't see a damn thing. Like this city was trying to screw him one last time, he could almost believe that, blinding him the very moment he finally wanted to look at it clearly.

He struggled to glance out the back window to check what street he had just passed, and he caught his reflection in the rearview mirror: a young man, not old at all, some would say handsome, minus a few bruises and scabs. Those would heal. If someone like Quinn, who carried his own death in his blood, could open his eyes every morning and shove that damaged body into the day, so could he. Instead of adjusting the rearview mirror, he watched his own smile creep across his face.

Of all the moves that defined his recent history, William believed this one, right here, was done all on his own. He floored the gas, laughing into the blinding haze of glass.

CHAPTER TWENTY-ONE

MADI WOKE LATE, finding a text on her cell phone that had been sent from her boss, Marcus, at some point in the night. "Emergency meeting. The colonels are here from Bang. Not going to be pretty. Advise a straight face."

Bang. They had come to complain, the Indian men in immaculate gray suits with lavender handkerchiefs folded in their breast pockets. Marcus called them the "colonels" because they were the managers of the company's remote support headquarters in Bangalore. She and Marcus were the brains of Eval-ution and they were the hands. The hands had come to attack the brain.

Their suits fit perfectly, tailored in the British style, not the bulky loose-crotched American standard. They didn't look like colonels. Small bellies bulged from their shirts, and their skin was smooth and hairless with the dew of aftershave. One thing Madi knew for certain: they didn't trust her, didn't like her, didn't want her telling them how to conduct operations. While their business was made in the utility of phone calls, Madi tried as much as possible to keep her conversations with them to e-mail.

She took the elevator to the twelfth floor, rushed through the

sparse beige lobby, and entered the conference room. Three men—
Narayanan, Hinduja, and Spohr—sat side by side across from
Marcus with three glasses of water in front of them. The windows
were open, and the room was insufferably hot. The colonels didn't
like air-conditioning, even in a late New York summer. They said
central air made them sick, and, deferring to cultural bias, Marcus
kept it turned off. Just open windows and tap water and Marcus with
his sleeves bunched to his elbows.

"Sorry I'm late," she said, bowing her head as she took the chair
next to her partner. The colonels stared at her, at her scarlet silk sari
extending over a pair of tan trousers, with detectable disgust. She
had to remind herself that the colonels worked for her and Marcus
and not the other way around. "I trust we can see eye to eye and come
to an agreement on the minor problems rearing their heads."

There were no minor problems. And there was no trust. Spohr
raged for an hour through a litany of dilemmas hitting Bangalore, all
of which she had known for some time, known them so intimately
she could have supplied the details to back them up.

Bangalore was on the brink of collapse; the city had ground to
a halt, choking on its own successes. Spohr named erratic power
supplies, the narrow roads studded with potholes, the inadequate
water systems and faulty sewers that were blocked and seeping
over. Bangalore, beautiful exotic Bangalore, with its lush toppling
gardens and mild springtime climate, had experienced a population
explosion unprecedented in the nation's history. The rapid boom of
the information-technology industry had created an urban hub out
of dust, and now that industry was paralyzing the very city that had
flowered it. The money that flowed into the streets jammed traffic,
all the new-model SUVs, all the French boutiques and shipments
of imported computers and young college graduates migrating in
waves, demanding New York–style loft apartments. Yet foreign
companies like Eval-ution were opening new service centers each week,
expanding their prospects, overstaffing, bringing in more workers,
making new billionaires who bought motorcycles and opened nightclubs and extended the congestion into the late-night hours. The
infrastructure of the Karnataka town was breaking under the weight.

Calmly, Madi nodded her head through Spohr's list of antago-
nisms. Spohr did not need to school her on the growing pains of capi-
talism, and she resented how he dogged her replies—had dogged
them in e-mails and phone messages and now flew for an entire day
to dog her in person. She softly explained that they had expected
oversaturation in the city center and that they needed to put pressure on the local government for support—a government, she noted,
whose coffers had been filled by Eval-ution's growth.

But the three men balked at her response as if they'd said they were
starving and Madi had merely described the menu of an expensive
restaurant. "Easy for you to say," Spohr stammered. "You aren't being
vilified in your own home." They informed her that the government
had already turned against them. The chief minister believed too
much had been given to the elites of the city and was now actively
taking measures to check the progress. Farmers in the rural sector had
been struck by failed monsoons and had taken to killing themselves
in the Bangalore streets while all around them Chanel boutiques and
minimalist Western lounges popped up by the dozen. "It all looks
too indulgent," Spohr huffed miserably. "The local government has
not appreciated the foreign market's disinterest in the city's politics
and now its sitting back and watching us sink."

"Then they are idiots," Madi said abruptly. She found three
faces staring at her with their jaws locked and their eyes open in
horror. Marcus braced his hand over her own as if to tell her to be
quiet. "Well, it's true," she yelled. "The job growth in technology is
unlimited. What India cannot return to is cheap labor."

Spohr wrenched his head back like he was on the worst roller
coaster of his life.

"You don't know India, Ms. Singh," he snapped. "You are an
American woman who says what's good and bad for us? You know
nothing. We live in dust and you grow fat? Is that the idea? India
needs to be given more than jobs answering phones. It needs the
respect you bestow so easily on your workforce in America. We must
to protect the people of Bangalore. You can dress however you want,
in your sari—"

"Mr. Spohr, there is no need for insults," Marcus warned. "Ms. Singh is your employer as much as I am. These problems are affecting all of us."

"Here you are wrong," he yelled. "You don't live in Bangalore. Maybe you own it. But it is not your home."

"I am here to determine what this company needs to run efficiently," Madi said in the softest voice her anger would allow. "And, since you asked, I do care what happens in India. Very, *very* much. My family is from India. I didn't pick out this sari to flatter you this morning, Mr. Spohr. I have as much claim as anyone to it as a homeland—"

"I will not work with her," he shouted as his fist pounded against the table. "We come to tell you we need help, and all you ask us to do is expand. We cannot grow just because you sit in an office in New York and will it. Who told you that you were one of us, Ms. Singh? I'd like to know the name of this man."

"I am—" she said and stopped.

"You *are* a greedy, ignorant American. You are a tourist to us, that is all."

At first she thought Spohr's voice had caused the water in the glasses to ripple, but slowly the sound of chanting protestors funneled through the open windows. They screamed a child's rhyme about money, greed, and thieves—*colonize, monopolize, despotize*—and no one in the conference room spoke as the chant grew louder. Spohr folded his arms over his stomach and nodded to Narayanan and Hinduja, as if some truth had finally slipped into their ears this morning from the refrains of the street. Something happened as Madi sat there waiting for the parade to pass. She knew she had spoken too broadly about India, had written the colonels off as narrow-minded complainers who couldn't grasp the larger picture, one she had worked so hard for so many years to shade in. She felt her lips go cold and her eyes sting, a tremor of doubt slipping up into her brain like a splinter. What was the larger picture? What was this money doing for the people of Bangalore? Who did she think she had been helping? What is a remote outsource service doing in India in the first place?

"We are not politicians," she said to break the silence, her voice shaking at the truth of her own words. "We are not responsible for the burdens of the poor. We have to look at the numbers. That's what our investors ask of us."

"Gentlemen," Marcus interceded. "I will be in Bangalore next week. Madi will remain here to work on the problems from this end. The temperature is rising fast, but we can keep it from boiling over on all of us." Madi nodded her head compliantly, as she realized that Marcus had just cut her from partaking in the larger picture, her trip to meet the prime minister, the glorious moment she had envisioned as a crowning achievement for a lifetime of brilliant work.

THE MEETING ENDED ten minutes later, and Madi did not speak another word. As Marcus shook hands with the three colonels, she fled to her office. Marcus followed her a minute later, his head shaking in reproach.

"You were out of line," he said coldly, and she forced herself to stare at him because she knew if she were being watched she wouldn't cry. "Emotions don't help the situation. While I'm gone on this trip, I want you to think about your role in this company. It shouldn't be personal. If it's personal, then you're going to be of no future assistance in keeping this project grounded." He turned and walked out, slamming the door behind him.

Standing alone in the hush of her office, she avoided the photo-graph of her father. *Project* and *company* and *situation*. What empty distant words these were to describe a whole country of people whom she thought she had been helping by delivering jobs from overseas. Of course it was personal, just as the hate letters she received daily on her desk from angry Americans were filled with personal slurs. Madi stood frozen at the side of her desk, unable to sit down in her chair. What was she then, dressed half in a sari, half in trousers, not here and not there?

She looked around her office as if inspecting it for the first time. The walls, the carpet, even the files arranged neatly in a rack, were all beige. *The color of nothing*, she thought. *Of nowhere*. The yellow tulips Marcus had sent her were dead and withered on the windowsill. She fought a shiver and tried to breathe, but there was only beige air in a beige room that floated like an obscenely bland bubble twelve flights above the ground. She suddenly felt like her fingers had been touching nothing for the last six years: not a billion people, not even a single one. Impulsively she grabbed the vase of dead flowers and carried it with her as she careened through the lobby, desperate for the wet, fresh air of the street. She took the elevator down and exited through the revolving doors, thankful for the last drops of rain that fell on her face and hands.

The protest march had vanished as quickly as it had materialized. The sunlight guttered through the nearby construction sites and filled her face and eyes. Madi searched through her purse for her sunglasses while holding the vase at her hip. Maybe she wasn't one of them. Maybe she was just what they said, an American getting rich while farmers killed themselves in front of nightclubs in some country she had only imagined she could call her own.

She tried to think where Raj might be at this hour on a Friday. Raj would talk sense to her. Her older brother would remind her of a place she inhabited beyond the terminal beige of an office tacked in foreign investment strategies. "Do I have to remind you that we're from Florida and we're Sikh not Hindu and you used to swim for a high school team called the Bald Eagles?" Raj had once asked her. *Yes*, she should have answered. Yes, she needed to be reminded of that. She pictured the long docks in the Keys with her father standing on the wood planks drinking a Budweiser with his powder-blue turban wrapped across his forehead.

Madi took tired steps toward the street corner. Maybe next week she would fly back home for a day or two and force Raj to come, because he would have to go with her, she would need him with her to see their family.

She breathed deeply, as she watched the crosswalk light change.

Yes, she wanted Florida, the yellow palms and the morning surf that brought in the reef air and her father in his tiny apartment praying the Guru Granth Sahib and maybe even her mom, sucking on Newports in the house they had grown up in. Raj would come. They could stop fighting for a weekend. They would be good kids again. India could be fixed when she got back.

She stepped into the street, slipping the sunglasses over her nose, and heard tires gunning over the cobblestones. One look, a dirty sparkling windshield framed in blue, going the wrong way. Madi only had time to straighten her back, her hands dropping the glass vase and reaching out as if to pull someone back who was walking away.

The car struck her, tossing her out of her shoes and slamming her against its hood. Her limp body slid over the left bumper as the car lurched to a stop. She was dead two minutes after she landed on the wet cement of the street.

PART
TWO

CHAPTER TWENTY-TWO

THIS IS HOW William was supposed to go: flying across the map of America, one blue cell traveling the arteries of the Eisenhower Interstate System, first south and then west. He was supposed to be a man living one page of the atlas at a time, gunning the motor, memorizing the number of the next off-ramp. He accelerates, stays in the far left lane, and sets the cruise control to seventy. At fill-up stations, he chooses self-service, grabs a bathroom key attached to a piece of particle board from the attendant, and, in a buzzing Dairy Farmers outside of Farragut, Tennessee, buys a discount cassette tape of Princess Stephanie singing "Live Your Life."

He was supposed to follow the West Express to I-78 and then merge onto I-40 South, passing Knoxville rodeos and strip mall water parks. He flows down I-75, the Mississippi of highways, and threads through Chattanooga on the straight shot to Birmingham. From there, it's a slingshot right, fighting the western sun until darkness races past the blue Cressida. Baton Rouge foams in the distance like a fallen meteor. The gulf sparkles. Dust halos ragweed. The moon glows the exit signs all the way through the suburbs of Houston.

He was supposed to be building a rhythm, becoming a loose blur, burning fuel without leaving tracks. The flat pink boom of Texas skies. The Cressida devours the blacktop as he sings "Live Your Life" until he knows it by heart and tosses the cassette into a trashcan near the Salado Junction. He creeps through a surprise border check on the outskirts of El Paso and disappears into Tucson. Phoenix is a mirage of locked liquor stores and hitchhikers who have given up on their thumbs. He shoots through the desert at dawn, blasts the radio into coyote country, does eighty through Twentynine Palms, catches I-10 for a few more miles, before he steers the car into the baked, stalled traffic of Los Angeles and, just beyond it, the sea. Four days on the road, and he would have been out there. He would be crashing in Laurel Canyon with friends who went out years ago to rent pool houses with sofa beds that open up for him. He would have been guilty of nothing worse than car theft, for which he knew in his heart Quinn would never file charges. Four days flashed through his mind in four minutes.

William never got out of New Jersey.

He checked into a motel off the West Express, parking the Cressida in the back lot between two dumpsters. He tried not to look at the damage as he struggled out of the driver's seat, but he could see the fat dent in the hood, the broken blinker, a warp in the front bumper with pieces of red fabric caught in its splintered plastic. His hands shook as he signed the motel registry under the name Joseph Guiteau.

"Do you have ID?" the scrawny teenage girl asked, her mouth gumming a piece of banana, her eyes freezing on him. In the room behind her, a television flashed the five o'clock news.

"What? No," he groused. "I don't. I'm only staying a night or two."

She managed a hard swallow and gave a flirtatious grin.

"That's fine. I trust you. Just pay up front. We got a fun '80s night at the bar next door. You should come if you got nothing else to do."

He tried to smile as he took the key, but he just made it out into the parking lot before he vomited, twisting down on one knee with a hand pressed against the cement as his stomach unloaded yellow acid. William didn't wait for more convulsions. He sprinted down the walkway to room six, unlocked the door, bolted it behind him, shut the curtains, and collapsed across the bed.

William pushed his fingers into his closed eyes, producing a constellation of red stars, but he still saw her, he still felt the impact with his entire body. Suddenly, a dark-skinned woman in red silk and black hair appeared just beyond the windshield in all of that blinding Manhattan sunlight. He had slammed the brakes and watched as her body slid off the hood. He wished he had stopped, wished he had jammed the emergency brake, jumped from the car, called 911, made sure her eyes still focused and her wrist held a pulse, but he hadn't. Some instinct had taken control of his right leg and applied the gas, slowly at first, like he was trying to find a place to park, and then, as he looked back in the rearview mirror and saw no one on the street crowding around her, sped faster, his foot more attentive to the movement of the car, turning right at the next inter- section. Seeing the green light on the corner, he went through it, and then through the next one, green, and then the Holland Tunnel, a big black exit hole in the earth, with two black policewomen in yellow reflector vests waving him underground.

William jerked over onto his back, but he couldn't slow the panic. His right leg kicked wildly like it was caught in a rope. *"FUCK,"* he screamed into the fingers that covered his mouth. He tried to take account of his crimes. He hadn't stolen a car, because he hadn't gotten out of the East Coast. He had driven the wrong way down a Tribeca street. An accident. He had hit some woman who had run out of nowhere just to collapse on his hood. An accident. One minute earlier or one minute later and it wouldn't have happened. An accident. Driving off was an accident too, fight or flight, which seemed to him now like the same exact thing. He lurched forward off the mattress and sat on the edge of the bed. The room was purring in the white noise of an air-conditioning unit on low. Trucks rumbled the light fixture on the ceiling. He stared at his reflection in the blackened television set bolted to its stand, and he tried not to think of her in the emergency room, tried not to think of the broken legs or the fractured arm or the split tongue that could barely articulate the description of the car and/or driver to a bedside of police detectives.

If he sat still, maybe he could think clearly. But his muscles were tweaking, his shoulders bunching up and then his arms flailing uncontrollably. He moved to the window and pushed the curtain aside. The sun was setting. Cars drove by so quickly. The sky was pink over the abandoned gas station across the street.

"Hi, Quinn," he said after the beep. "Just wanted to let you know I got upstate okay. I'll see you in a couple of days. It's beautiful up here."

CHAPTER TWENTY-THREE

JOSEPH TURNED ON his cell phone as he left Aleksandra's hotel room. In the elevator down, he listened to a message five hours old. "Madi's gone," Del said. Her voice sounded so distracted and uncertain, so lost in the air space, he knew immediately to read her words for their worst meaning. "I'm going to see Raj," she told him. "I don't know what to say." He tried to call her but got no answer. He tried three more times but she didn't pick up.

He took a cab to their apartment, asking the driver to hurry. Night lit up midtown, and they sat in its stalled traffic. When he reached home it was after ten. He opened the door to find the apartment dark. Joseph ran through the rooms turning on the lights, but he already knew he wouldn't find her there. Her purse was open on the kitchen table with its makeup spilled on the floor. The faucet in the bathroom was running. A record skipped on the record player. The clues to panic were everywhere, and now, Joseph was here, too, ready to console her. But Del didn't come home that night.

CHAPTER TWENTY-FOUR

THE POLICE HAD called him to identify the body. Madi stored his number twice on her phone, once under his name and a second time under "emergency contact." Raj stood in the cold hospital basement and when he looked, her skin was wiped white, as if her whole body had been scrubbed, and her lips were blue. But he had already known by the shape of the body under the sheet. He had already known because she was the only person on the planet who stored his number under "emergency contact."

"It's her."

"Do you need to sit down, sir?" the supervisor asked, lifting a hand over Raj's shoulder and leaving it to levitate there, as if knowing that a touch can either encourage or shatter whatever strength remained.

"No."

He called his mother from the hospital. She screamed into the receiver, her voice pleading with him to take back the news. She wouldn't get off the phone, not until he promised to take it all back. After fifteen minutes of his mother weeping into his ear, he asked if she would phone his father. He couldn't tell him, he couldn't say "Madi's dead" again to another parent.

As Raj walked outside and drifted down the wheelchair ramp to the sidewalk, his whole body stiffened as he imagined, at that very moment, his father finding out that his favorite child was gone. He wished it had been him instead of her, and it occurred to him suddenly like absolute logic that he could be the dead child for his father and Madi could be the one lost for his mom: splitting the burden, sharing the responsibility, sparing each parent the loss of their favorite. That was the kind of ludicrous proposition that only he and Madi would think up. But there was no Madi. There had been Madi up until an hour ago, and now there wasn't. There was only Raj.

The thought of leaving her on that table in the hospital basement barreled through him, and he swerved on the sidewalk to lean against a brick wall surrounded by outdoor tables. He careened around two couples eating plates of spaghetti and pressed his head against the wall of the restaurant. Raj expected tears to come, but they didn't. He returned to the sidewalk, knocking against one of the tables, and started up the street.

An hour later he found himself standing at his own doorstep, not remembering a single second of the walk home. He called Del. "Madi was killed by a car this afternoon. The driver didn't stop. She was gone by the time the ambulance arrived. No way of knowing . . . " He meant "no way of knowing if she had suffered any pain." Or maybe he meant "no way of knowing what to do now." Or "no way of knowing anything."

Del didn't wait for clarification. She said she was on her way.

She met him on his doorstep after running down the sidewalk with her eyes swollen, her teeth gritted, her arms out at her sides like her muscles had frozen, unwilling to touch anything, even herself, until she first touched him. Del hugged him so tightly that her fingers yanked his hair, a shot of pain that he hoped would wake him up. To anyone else on the street, they could have passed for two lovers reuniting after a long separation. They went up to his apartment not touching again for a while. Del sat on the couch, crying against her knees, while Raj stood by the window, then by the desk holding his stomach, and then in the hallway biting his nails.

"No," Del murmured, her face crumpled in pain. "This wouldn't have happened to her. She's too careful. That's one of the things I can never stand about her. She looks both ways. She'd never let anything hit her." She rubbed her left eye with her palm and gulped on mucus. "The driver didn't even stop? If he'd stopped, maybe he could have—"

"He didn't stop," Raj said quietly, unsure if she even heard him from the other end of the hall. He waited for Del to ask what Madi's injuries were, the shattered pelvis, the broken breastbone, the damage to the internal organs, the horizontal gash on her left cheek, but she didn't, and he was thankful.

"What did the police say?" she asked instead. "Do they have any leads? I can't believe there isn't a video camera, or an eyewitness, someone who wrote down a license plate. I mean, what kind of city is this?"

He walked over and sat on the arm of the couch. He placed his hand on her shoulder to steady her shaking.

"Please, Del. I don't care about the driver right now. What's important is I can't get her back."

She made tea at midnight, dragging the leaves through the hot water, and spooned honey into two cups. She placed the cups on his desk, but neither of them touched the tea. Del turned off the lamp, and the blue floodlight of a boat turning on the Hudson River trailed across the walls, coloring their faces and then leaving them in the dark. Raj could hear her phone vibrating in her pocket, but she didn't reach to answer it. They crawled into bed together in their clothes and shoes, and Del wept into the pillow.

He was glad she was there, glad she was crying, shaking on the bed next to him, because for the first time in all of the years he had lived in the studio he was terrified of being alone.

They pressed their hands together in the darkness.

"I don't want this day to be over," she said, gripping his knuckles. "I don't want to leave her here. If she's gone, I want it to have just happened, not yesterday, not far away from now. I don't want to lose her like that."

"I want one more day," he said.

DEL SPENT THE next day with him. She wrote down the names of friends, acquaintances, and distant cousins in Orlando who called to offer their condolences. She answered the phone when his father called. He pleaded with her to put Raj on and then screamed at her before curtly asking for the hospital number. She waited on hold for twenty minutes to be connected to the case detective, who told her that one person had finally come forward. "Not a suspect. A bystander. She took a cell phone picture," Detective Tasser said through a sip of coffee. "It's too blurry to read the license plate, but we've got our computer team on it. Otherwise, we're doing the rounds, asking questions." Del only left the studio to buy the newspaper and folded a page of the metro section down to a small manageable square, which detailed the hit-and-run. The paper wrongly identified the victim as Madhavi Singh, of Ft. Lauderdale, Florida, Junior Vice President of Eval-ution, age thirty-three.

In the afternoon, she finally phoned Joseph. He asked her where she was, and she told him.

"I came back right away," he said. "I waited up for you. I thought you might need me."

"Raj needs me more," she replied.

"What do you need?" Joseph asked.

"Nothing. I'll be home. Probably tomorrow."

"Do you want me to come over?" he persisted. "I can bring you a change of clothes. I'll just stop by and give you a hug. I won't stay." She looked over at Raj, who sat on the corner of the bed in grainy white underwear and a sagging T-shirt. His hands were wedged between his hairy thighs.

"I'll be home tomorrow."

"I came back to be with you," he repeated, this time pleadingly, a whine in the wire.

"Please, Joe. I'll be back soon. I have to go," she said and hung up.

There was no room for outsiders. Del wanted to be alone with Raj in the cramped studio by the water. It was the only way to keep Madi in there with them.

SHE RESTED HER head on Raj's chest and wrapped her arm around his stomach. Raj talked in broken sentences about how he wished he had agreed to go to India and how Madi wouldn't take no for an answer, like India was going to disappear by winter and he'd missed his chance for good. Like it only existed for a few more weeks, a whole country of one billion, about to vanish like it was built on balloons. Raj kept bringing up this trip, as if his agreeing to go would have prevented Madi from crossing the street in Tribeca, as if she would still be with them if only he had relented. Del tried to change the subject. She reminded him of the time he first showed up at their college dorm room all of those years ago, and Madi kept making excuses to leave so they'd be alone together.

"She always wanted us to be a couple," Del said, squeezing his hipbone and letting her fingers trail across his waist.

"That wasn't it," he laughed. "She just found my presence so irritating in her brand-new Manhattan life, she figured it would be easier if you adopted me."

Raj grew more animated the next morning. He smiled when she talked about Madi as if he were mining every memory about his sister for its maximum worth. Del read this animation as a good sign. Time moved so quickly, punctuated only by phone calls and sleep. She smoked cigarettes out the window and cried when he took a shower.

The only call Raj actually made that day was to his mother, drilling through the funeral arrangements. Madi would be buried in Florida. The family would have a small ceremony over the grave— nonreligious to prevent a parental altercation over divine rights. The body would fly out tomorrow, his father had arranged it, and Raj would be on that plane, too.

"I'll buy my ticket," Del said. "What flight is it?"

But Raj didn't want her to come. He said it was family only, not the kind of ceremony to involve anyone else. "Please, don't argue," he begged. They could do a proper memorial back in New York later, something extravagant and ludicrously expensive that she would have liked.

"It's not right, her being buried in Florida," Del said, collecting three days worth of glasses that had been filled but never used. "New York was her home. She never wanted to go back. I guess that's what happens when you don't have your own children. You get shipped back to the place you were born, to the people who hardly know you anymore."

"Family will always take you back," Raj said. "It's the least they can do."

In bed that night he kissed her. He pressed his lips against hers, and she didn't refuse. It wasn't sexual. They kissed for the love of someone whom they couldn't have anymore.

But Raj heard Madi in his head, wagging a finger at him, only a year ago. "You screwed up big time. How the hell did you let that girl get out of your sight for a minute? Well, I tried. That was my part in the Raj Happiness Project. Now what?"

Now what?

CHAPTER TWENTY-FIVE

AMAZING WHAT A DAY CAN DO. Del had seen that toothpaste advertisement on the side of buses all summer, with bright white teeth flashing over its busy font. But only on her walk back to the apartment did that message register. *Amazing what a day can do.* She kept repeating the phrase as she walked east to Gramercy, as if her inner ear had suddenly transformed into an open echo chamber, receptive to any lyric or jingle that carried a perverse lesson she had somehow previously managed to deflect. "I owe you my life," blasted a pop refrain from the speakers of the deli where she bought a pouch of tobacco. "Do you want change, miss?" *I owe you my life. Amazing what a day can do. Do you want change, miss?* It had been so much easier to deal with Madi's death locked in the studio with Raj. How much more agonizing it was to be alone with that fact. She put Raj in a taxi for the airport not fifteen minutes ago, and already she wanted him back. She wanted to remain in that studio with only their memories and each other's arms for support. Death pulled people together, at first, and then it left each person terribly alone.

As soon as Del returned to the apartment, she frantically began to clean, trying to tire her body down to match the dim wiring of her mind. She poured a bucket of water and mopped the floors. She rubbed years of grime off the windows, killed spiders between her fingers, and wiped away their webs in the rafters. Through all of this manic cleaning, Joseph stood staring at her from the bedroom doorway. He placed a record on the stereo, but Del screamed before he engaged the needle. "I don't want to hear any music." She scoured the toilet, swept dust into a pile the size of a sweater, and ignored Joseph as she carried the broom into the kitchen. He followed behind and grabbed her arm. Del yanked it away and then proceeded to slap his bare feet with the bristles of the broom. She didn't allow herself to look at his face.

"I'm here," Joseph said, vulnerable in a pair of navy boxer shorts, which exaggerated his pale legs and rutted rib cage. "I'd like to talk about it, make sure you're okay."

"There's nothing to say," she grumbled, closing her eyes while adjusting the purple handkerchief across her forehead. "Can you get out of my way? I'm trying to clean this place."

"Please," Joseph said quietly. "I know that you're suffering. I know you loved Madi very much."

You don't know anything about Madi, she almost shot back. Del took a step backward to calm down. Without meaning to, she was blaming Joseph—not for Madi's death but for trying to help her recover from it. *Why are you blaming your husband, when he's only trying to be here for you?* She didn't know the answer. Maybe if Joseph had rushed to her side the instant she first heard the news, maybe if he had been the one to hold her for the last two days, she could fall against him now and let her muscles relax and the pain spill out. But he hadn't been there. Raj had been there, and Raj understood Madi better than anyone else. Joseph hadn't known Madi at all. Del would have drowned without Madi. She had been the one to comfort her through the loss of Dash. Madi had stayed with her until Del had been strong enough to gather her senses. It was only after she watched Raj drive away in a cab that she realized that Madi was the second person in her life to be killed in a car accident. Two people she loved so much and never expected to be taken from her died suddenly and senselessly in the ordinary rush of traffic. For all the years she had been living in New York, Del hardly paid attention while crossing the street. But on that walk home, she felt like every person around her was a fragile piece of cargo managing by complete miracle to cross the avenues without breaking into a million pieces.

It occurred to her that when someone died they didn't vanish. They left a hole in the world so big that even time couldn't close it. *Time didn't heal wounds*, she thought. *It only made more of them*. First Dash, a hole blown so huge she fled to Greece to get away from it. And now, so much worse, so much later, so much the same. All that was left of the dead were holes, and those holes held even more dimensions than their bodies possessed in life.

Del didn't want to talk to Joseph about Madi. She didn't want to take those meaningless steps toward acceptance. It occurred to her that if she began the process of healing, Raj wouldn't have anyone to help him do the same when he returned from the funeral. She would do that for him, they would be strong for each other, they would remember Madi and lose her together. She couldn't leave him alone like that.

Joseph reached for the broom and plied it from her grip. He rested it against the refrigerator and stared at her.

"I don't want to force you if you're not ready," he said. "But I'm here for you. I just want you to know that."

"I'm sorry," she whispered, roping her arms over her stomach. "I don't feel like talking. I just want to keep busy. Please, let me have that. Okay?"

She cried in the bathroom with the shower running, taking long drags from a cigarette on the toilet seat. When she went to sleep that night, her head splitting, her hands reeking of ammonia and a shot of whiskey burning her throat, she stopped at the doorway to the bedroom. Joseph lay with the white sheet open on her side of the bed, his face slack against the pillow. She knew he was trying. But it felt wrong to lie next to him while two Singhs were lying somewhere in Florida, preparing for a funeral she wasn't allowed to attend. It felt too much like getting back to normal. Maybe the way to keep the dead with her was never to go back to normal. She curled up on the couch, listening to the billion isolated sounds that made up the night with her cell phone next to her ear in case Raj called.

TWO DAYS LATER, while dressing for work, Del received a call. It was Frank Warren. "Your meeting is set with the INS," he yelped with the lawyer's pride of earning his salary by scheduling an appointment. "December 1. Write that down on your calendar and circle it in red. How's the photo album coming? I hope you're preparing like we said. It's essential to stay positive."

For the first time in her life, Del preferred the dark staccato underworld of the subway to the gleaming, window-washer's glass of summer above ground. The bleak rhythm of the crowded platform prevented her from unnecessary distractions. Even when a gruff deliveryman bumped into her on the staircase carrying a chandelier by the hook, its crystals chiming like rain and throwing rainbows on the concrete, she turned away from its music and light. She sat on the steel bench of the car, picking her cuticles distractedly. She had been staring at a page of the *Post* for a good three minutes before its headline crystallized. A businessman held the folded newspaper in front of him, with its second page facing her. MEAN STREETS, ran the headline, and underneath it, a fuzzy pixilated photo showed a Manhattan street with a blue square in the distance and a small red oval lying against a curb. Del's eyes tried and failed to focus. That oval was Madi. That blue square was presumably the car that had killed her. Del bolted up, leaving her purse unattended on the bench. Her fingers reached for the pole, while her other hand lurched toward the page. Tears filled her eyes. The brakes squealed. The businessman threw the paper down next to him and got off. A group of teenagers toting a ghetto blaster entered the car and started doing a breakdance routine next to her. She grabbed the *Post* from the bench, collected her purse, and fled through the door into the connecting car. She ran through two more cars, until she could go no farther. She stopped at the window in the front of the train and watched the tracks disappear as the subway shot through the winding tunnels into the Bronx.

She held the newspaper against her stomach like it was a rare treasure, like there weren't 700,000 copies circulating on newsstands in the city that very morning.

CHAPTER TWENTY-SIX

JOSEPH KNOCKED ON the hotel room door. He could hear
Aleksandra on the other side, pressing her eye against the peephole.

"Are you alone?" she asked.

Joseph had waited around the apartment for three days in hopes of
consoling his wife, to no avail. Sudden loss turned even the strongest
into a dazed survivor, unskilled and scared. Joseph had only met
Madi a few times and remembered her mostly by her arrogant voice
and lightning-quick jabs, but he saw how Del came loose and alive
in her presence. She had already lost one person she loved to a car
crash. That second blow would resurrect the first, sorrow always
reconnecting to the pain of past tragedies. For a second, Joseph
wondered if Del noticed the similarity, compared those two deaths
until they fit a pattern, as if fate called and echoed through her years,
ripping her one by one from the people she loved.

"It's just me," he said against the door. "You can open it."

The chain fumbled, and the bolt snapped.

Aleksandra opened the door with two eyes streaked red. She
allowed just enough space for him to enter before slamming it shut.
Her hands quickly reengaged the lock. In her frantic movement, her

white bathroom robe fell to reveal two skeletal breasts and a stomach sagging with folds of skin in a testament to healthier days. Joseph looked away to prevent her any embarrassment, but Aleksandra was past such concerns. A far greater anxiety sent her sprinting across the room to a pile of clothes and papers scattered on the floor. The curtains were bundled. Gray afternoon light flooded across the carpet, reflecting every metal surface and shrinking the room to its sterile proportions. Joseph realized that he had only talked to Aleksandra in darkness. She looked much smaller, older, and more desperate with the daylight shining in. The gray overtook the blonde at the roots, and her upper lip was a fissure of wrinkles. He wanted to draw the curtains shut.

Aleksandra kneeled before three suitcases and began packing up the papers, then froze, dropping her hands to her thighs in fatigue: packing meant carrying, carrying meant walking, walking meant running, finding a new place to hide, and then unpacking to sit in a room not so unlike this one—its only benefit being somewhere else.

"What's wrong?" he asked, stung by the evidence that she had decided to move out in his absence. He didn't want her to leave. He didn't know if he'd ever find her again. It occurred to him that no matter what impossible circumstances had been discussed between these walls, the hotel room had become a refuge, a quiet place resistant to the city just outside the windows. He suddenly understood how quickly Aleksandra and the silent drone of the air-conditioning could be taken away.

"Yesterday I went to check my post-office box," she said, reaching toward the empty rosewood desk that had once held her typewriter. Her hand slid blindly across the top, her fingers searching for an object. "I use the box to keep in touch with old friends. I've only given the address out to a few people, the ones I could trust. Yesterday, inside, I found this."

She grabbed an envelope off the desk. Joseph took it and unfolded the thin, white paper stored inside. A series of black letters cut from newspapers and magazines were glued crookedly into an ominous, almost infantile formation: LET THE DEAD STAY DEAD.

Joseph flipped the envelope. No return address. It had been post-marked in New York. "Is this real?" he asked.

"How else can they get in touch? E-mails, text messages, phone calls. Those can be traced."

He stepped toward her and stopped out of instinct. He stared in doubt at the letter with its convenient threat arriving in his absence of five days. Aleksandra crouched on the floor below him. Her hands yanked at the zipper to seal the suitcase. The muscles of her neck contracted as she jerked her arm. He couldn't help but wonder if she were telling him the truth.

"You don't believe me," she said flatly, not even accusatively, as she tilted her head up to catch his eyes. "You don't have to. I'm sure whoever sent it knew no one would."

"It just doesn't make any sense," he replied. "Why now? Why after all of these years when you've been so quiet?"

"I don't know," she replied wearily as if she had been asking herself those very same questions for an entire day. The lids of her eyes twitched, swollen and sore with the work of keeping them open. "When you came into the picture, when we finally started talking and I felt the words return in my head, I called a few people I know back in Los Angeles. I told them I was continuing with the script, that I would see it through this time. Maybe they caught wind of it."

Joseph couldn't shake the sense that Aleksandra was testing him, determining how much he trusted her story of a gunman creeping through Pacific scrub brush to shoot a hole in her husband's head and then trying to do the same to her. Before, all of her fears could be written off as symptoms of excessive grief, but this letter was either solid evidence that everything she imagined was true or a desperate act by a woman who had lost her mind. Joseph studied the letter more closely. The words had been cut and glued with meticulous precision. Perhaps he had misjudged the childishness of the threat— or rather the childishness *was* the threat. Aleksandra was right. Intimidation didn't work by e-mail. Terror needed a personal touch. Aleksandra turned back to the clutter on the floor and began shoving the pages in another suitcase. She wiped her nose with her forearm and closed the lid. He didn't want her to go. He didn't want this doubt to be the last memory she had of him. He knew some stories were impossible to get your hands around; they slipped when you tried to hold them steady.

"What are you going to do?" he asked.

"I don't know," she said. "I feel like I need to get out of here but I don't know where to go. I tried to sleep last night, and all I could do was stare at the door like every sound in the hallway was headed straight toward me."

"Maybe they don't know that you're staying here."

"Maybe," she replied.

"I'm sorry I didn't visit the last few days. Someone I know died. A friend of my wife's was killed crossing the street."

"That's terrible," she said, lowering her head. "I forget that accidents still happen." The thought seemed to send her into a memory of an easier time. "Really, I should thank them for sending that letter. For a while, I wondered if maybe I was going crazy. That maybe Ray had killed himself after all. There's been nothing worse these last few years than doubting what you know is true, even if no one else believes you."

"I believe you," he said. He watched those words smooth some of the anxiety from her face.

"It's very nice of you to come up here to check on me, but I'm not your responsibility." She raised her arm to shield his view of her. Aleksandra's eyes and cheeks were wrinkled from every hour she hadn't slept, but she was trying to superimpose a sense of calm. "It sounds like you have a wife who needs you. There's no reason for you to get mixed up in my problems. I appreciate your coming up here like you have, Joseph. It meant something, but now it's best if we just say good-bye." She waited with her arm raised for him to unbolt the door and walk out.

He stood in the center of the room, pressing the letter against his palm. Joseph realized why he felt so drawn to a woman who refused to let her husband go. He needed someone else who believed in impossible circumstances. Tobias from prisonersofearth had once broken out of his own manic paranoia to deliver one bit of haunting poetry: "Conspiracy theorists are midnight astronomers to a world that only sees by day. They describe a constellation of stars that slide over the skies, which the rest of the population can't even imagine." Who else did he have to tell his own secrets to? Who else who would listen to the unbelievability of those words? He knew if he waited any longer Aleksandra would be gone.

"I don't want you to go," he said. He resisted kneeling down to put his arms around her shoulders. Instead he walked over to the windows, grabbed the curtains, and drew them closed. The darkness swept over the room and opened it up again, increasing it, making it safe and vast. "I need to tell you something. If you're willing to stay here. If you won't leave."

He did not want to die with this story inside of him. The story itself was a wish not to die. All stories were, he supposed.

"Will you stay and listen?" He squatted down on the floor next to her. He opened his hands, white and smooth with no scars or calluses. White and smooth but trembling with the work of holding them open. "Please?" He waited for the answer. He had never come this close to telling anyone this secret, and if she said no, he might never be able to tell anyone again.

Aleksandra took a deep breath and dropped her arms on her lap.

"Yes," she said slowly. "If that's what you need."

And just like that, where air met the voice box and applied its simple chords, he told her the story of a family.

THE ONLY REMINDER that Joseph kept of his father was his teeth. They remained in a padded ring box that sat in a metal case under Joseph's bed—two incisors and a canine held together on a piece of wire along with a cheap plastic bridge. They split from his father's jaw in a fall from the roof right before he met Joseph's mother.

"Your father had blanks in his smile," she used to tell Joseph. "They didn't care about dentistry where he came from. They were poor—straight out of god's country—and didn't think teeth would help feed the cows. At least he had blue eyes, which they couldn't figure out how to ruin." These insults were an attempt to ingratiate Joseph to her side of the family, which in the end, was all she had. She didn't know that her son kept the evidence of his dental defect in his bedroom, where he often closed his eyes as a child and envisioned his father high in the sky, staring down with missing teeth that would have otherwise kept him looking a handsome thirty-four forever.

Eventually, all other physical signs of his life were destroyed. Joseph's mother made a fire on the hill behind their house in Cincinnati, where, years before, his father burnt the leaves he raked from the sludge grass in autumn. She carried out her husband's suits and sweat socks, the blankets that covered their bed, his entire underwear drawer, photographs from their honeymoon in Acapulco, and even his toiletries and torn leather wallet. She lit the pile with the matches he once used and tossed the matchbook into the fire. The smoke rose behind the roof of the house, while she stood before the blaze in a flannel nightgown peaking under a black fur coat. The wind swept the ashes into the woods and beat the flames. That was how his mother began to sign off on the world. She burnt it up.

When she was fired from her post as a tenured professor of American history, she shut all the windows of the house and covered them with wool curtains. His mother lost the keys to the Cadillac parked in the garage, although she never looked for them. She should have known that shutting herself off from the world made her more prone to her memories. She never looked for those either, but they were always around her, never lost and never recovered. Countries survive the histories of their massacres by forgetting. Families are not so lucky, the personal always harder to retreat from than the political. Joseph possessed no physical evidence that any of the Guiteau tragedy took place other than three teeth in a padded ring box stored alongside a gun in a metal box under his bed. But that doesn't mean every detail in the Guiteau story didn't happen just the way he remembered it. And whether he was the product of some mutant genes or something worse or perhaps nothing at all, the Guiteau history was all he had left to tell. They all lived, every member of that family. Some part of them still did in the one they left behind.

For a long time Joseph believed he could escape these terrible predictions and ludicrous curses passed through a bloodline. Even the doctors admitted that inherited diseases were as much nurture as nature. Change the environment, break the pattern. He left Ohio at eighteen. He stocked the refrigerator, said his good-byes, and bolted the front door behind him. He went where anyone looking to escape their trapped beginnings went—that loophole in American identity, that city of reinventions. In New York, Joseph thought he had really performed the ultimate vanishing trick. Until now.

Right before Del moved in, Joseph started having trouble with the stairs. After two flights, the air knocked out of him and a river of ice ran through his hands, turning to water at the elbows. At night, his chest raced like it was trying to reach the ceiling, and in the morning his feet swelled to the point that he struggled to fit them into his shoes. Instead of telling Del, Joseph told a doctor. The cardiologist found nothing wrong—they never did. He suggested his problems were induced by stress. "So many of these symptoms are self-willed, Joseph. Your heart is fine. You have nothing to worry about."

But the evidence was there: His great-grandfather, grandfather, and father all lost and buried five hundred miles away in different Ohio cemeteries. All dead at age thirty-four.

If Joseph Guiteau lived through the year, he would be the oldest man in the history of his family. He might be the last person of his generation, and certainly of his chosen profession, to see the gift of growing old.

CHAPTER TWENTY-SEVEN

RAJ WANTED TO watch the casket lift into the cargo hold but couldn't see it from the windows of the airport lounge. He had to trust it was on the flight, buried somewhere in the container below his economy seat on the starboard side of the plane. When he and Madi were kids, the family owned a tan Oldsmobile Toronado, and the car's seating chart never once changed when they piled in for Saturday pizza night or a trip to the mall. His father drove. His mother sat in the front passenger seat, pressing her hand against the glove compartment whenever his father hit the breaks or made a sharp turn, as if to illustrate how little she trusted him with her life. Raj filled the seat behind her, and Madi always ruled the back left. Already their alliances had formed in that car, as if their love could move horizontally and vertically but never diagonally across the center console. He couldn't remember if the arrangement had been planned or if it had happened instinctually, that they just piled in and stuck that way for life.

He watched the flight attendants perform their safety demo in the aisles. No passenger believed opening a door or strapping a seat cushion to their chest would save them from a failing aircraft.

But most watched respectfully anyway, smiling as the stewardesses continued their emergency directions, and everyone was complicit in the charade. Raj put his earphones in to listen to the jazz on the airplane radio, but the music twittered like the cheap atmosphere of a gift shop. His mother had worked at a gift shop in the mall for a few months. That was after the divorce, when the stores staffed temporary employees during the holiday rush. She brought home embezzled angels, elves, and snowflakes, covering every inch of the living room in a New Hampshire Christmas decor. He hadn't seen real snow until he visited Madi in college, not more than a few flurries. Snow created blackened ice ridges along Broadway, covered in gnarled fragments of fresh graffiti. It was on his second visit to New York that he decided to stay for an entire month. He couldn't remember at what point his return ticket expired and the two-year lease had been signed. Madi had been insistent about his staying in the city. He had been living at home with their mother, wasting his days after four years at Gainesville. "You're going to become one of those men," she had warned him, "the ones married to their mothers who have to sneak out on dates." By then, his sister had already gone through what was known around the house as the Manhattan Butterfly Effect. Every Christmas when she came home, her hair was a different color; first she had a lip ring, then a predilection for black leather pants worn with obscenely high heels, and in the last year of college she kept arguing about Blur versus Oasis like the bands were warring nuclear states that must be resolved before the Singhs opened their presents. "I never know *who* I'm going to pick up," Raj said once on Christmas Eve leaning against a duty-free marquee. "I thought you were that Elvisy looking man in the wheelchair before you came strutting down the gangplank." "It's so easy for you," Madi had replied, slapping his shoulder in lieu of a hug. She had on a thrift-store mink and lime-green eyeliner, both looking greasy and disheveled after the three-hour flight. "You love cameras. I love . . . everything." He hadn't brought his camera down with him. It hadn't even occurred to him until now that a photograph of Madi to place on her casket might be the one thing he could have brought.

Raj woke as the pilot announced that they were ten minutes away from landing. His mother would be waiting in temporary parking to take him back to the house where he'd sit on her chintz couch. The plane taxied to the gate, while a stewardess listed connecting flights to foreign capitals he had once visited years ago as a freelance photographer. He couldn't remember anything about Bogotá or Caracas except for what he had caught in his lens. He grabbed his carry-on, shuffled through first class, and began the slow pilgrimage through the terminal to baggage claim. He stiffened at the thought of his mother bending across the seat to unlock the passenger-side door, staring silently at him with a look in those contracted blue eyes that demanded answers. She would expect an explanation for why Madi had died, because he had been there, in that awful city, not a mile from the accident, not looking out for his little sister. What good was an older brother if he couldn't even protect her from traffic?

He descended the stairs, swerving out of the way of running husbands and shrieking grandmothers. A green outline of palm trees decorated the wall next to the escalators, but the neon reminder of the tropics was unnecessary. Already he could see real palms exploding in the hot Florida sun just beyond the automatic doors. A row of suited Cuban men stood holding car-service signs at the bottom of the stairs.

One man edged behind the drivers, chewing on a piece of black licorice. Raj hadn't seen him in his loose white linen pants and brown leather sandals exposing tan impatient toes. But as Raj searched for the baggage carousel, he suddenly saw his father walking slowly toward him. His turban scrolled neatly around his temples, and his wiry beard parted at the cleft in his upper lip, framing a puckered expression that didn't express joy or sorrow, fear or love, only a determination not unlike the Cuban chauffeurs to pick up a passenger on the flight from New York.

Raj froze, watching his father approach. This was the man he would become. This was his future walking toward him at the Miami International Airport. He hadn't seen his father in years. Time had not worn him down but swelled him up until he was a soft fleshy bear of a man, almost sexless, like a benign cartoon chef on an Indian soup can who didn't look capable of strict religious discipline or a loud broken marriage. He didn't look capable of once setting eyes on his son, fresh from his first haircut, and opening his palm to strike that son across the face.

Actually, Raj was wrong. He was nothing like him, not outside or in. It wasn't his father's presence over the years that turned Raj into the man he was. It was his absence. And no one gets credit for what their absence makes.

"I have waited a long time for you," the old man said somberly, standing a foot in front of him and extending a chubby hand blotted in black licorice. "Let's find your bags and bring you home." Those words must have been rehearsed for patriarchal strength, because once they were out his father stumbled forward and fell into him.

Passengers departing flight 361 from New York that Wednesday afternoon were witness to the strange sight of an obese, elderly Sikh wrapped in a powder-blue turban sobbing into the white V-neck T-shirt of a slim, young man. After five minutes, Raj crossed the street with his father who carried his two suitcases, and they left the airport headed north in a dented Oldsmobile Cutlass. If anyone could listen through the windows they would have heard sacred verses being read over the car speakers while the father and son sat staring forward in silence.

The hymns of the Guru Granth Sahib played on the car radio from the audiobook Sikh Scriptures Series: "Ye fear lions, jackals, and snakes; but they shall make their dwellings in your graves. Oxen shall root up your graves, and even your enemies' hatred of you shall cool. The sinners who have committed transgressions are bound and led away. Their luggage of sins is so heavy they cannot lift it."

CHAPTER TWENTY-EIGHT

WILLIAM FOUND AN open spot on West Twelfth Street. He parallel-parked in front of a silver Lexus, which unleashed an electronic pit bull of sirens and honks when the blue Cressida accidentally tapped its bumper. The owner, leaning from a second-floor window, drew his keychain out and silenced the emergency. William waited until the quiet pooled around him again. Then he opened the door, climbed out with his bags strapped around his neck, and delicately pressed the door shut. He tried to act casual, a loose pace, hands in pockets, but he glanced anxiously at the hood, assessing the work that a garage in New Jersey had performed on hammering out the dent and touching up the scratches for three hundred dollars in cash. In the sunlight, the area of impact looked cleaner and bluer than the rest of the hood.

Now the future came down to gestures: he'd walk in, hope Quinn wasn't home, write a quick thank-you note, and get as far away from the Cressida as possible. It had been five days since the accident, and, sick with desperation, William figured it was best to return the car to its owner, disappear into the normal routine of New York as if he had never left, and try for a second escape plan as soon as he found more money. The thought of pouring gasoline over the car and letting it bonfire in an abandoned lot had flashed through William's mind more than once, but cars on fire in New Jersey were about as suspicious as guns wrapped in towels in the East River. Anyway, how would he explain no car to Quinn? One thing had been certain: waiting around in a motel room in the far shadows of the city wasn't helping. *Whatever comes, come now.* There was no more waiting to be done.

He used the spare keys to unlock the doors to the garden. Finding no light trailing through the cottage windows, he entered cautiously. Fruit flies buzzed over unwashed dishes in the sink, dirty clothes covered the floor, and ripped envelopes littered the desk. Quinn might not have been devout in his cleanliness, but he was neat, the way anyone who lives in a tiny tinderbox learns to be, so the state of the apartment set off a nervous jolt of panic. William threw his bags on the sofa and walked into the bathroom where more gnats floated dead in the yellow toilet water. He opened the medicine cabinet and flipped through the prescription bottles—multivitamins, herbal immune system boosters, iron and zinc tablets, Emtriva and Viread (both marked experimental), Valtrex, Viagra, Xenical, drugs with names like undiscovered planets that once sounded like the future but now reeked of terminal illness. He finally found the Klonopin stashed behind an ancient bottle of Brut, shook out two pills in his palm, popped them in his mouth, and scooped water from the faucet to push them down. He breathed hard as he waited for the medication to take its effect, carrying him over into a lighter, fragile world.

William stood so long staring at his reflection in the bathroom mirror that when he heard Quinn open the front door, he wasn't sure if minutes or an hour had passed. The door hinges squealed out of tune, and house keys clattered on the desk. Then he heard *William?*—uncertain, distrustful, like the name of someone who wasn't supposed to be there. William practiced an easy smile in the mirror before he fixed his hair, slicking it back with wet hands, and walked out into the living room.

The pills were supposed to make all movement easier, but they only worked properly when situations were already easy, and instead

William felt like he was walking too slowly, so he jerked his legs forward to overcompensate. Quinn, zipped in a red nylon windbreaker, spun around and stiffened at the sight of him. His hands darted into his windbreaker pockets, and his fingers pinched their inner linings.

"Ah, Quinn, my man," William said, stepping forward in the first movements of a hug, but he only got a foot before he noticed Quinn's sleepless eyes and the deep wrinkles across his forehead. "Who'd you think it was?"

"You're back." Flat as pavement.

"Yeah," he laughed. "I hope I'm not interrupting. You don't have a young guy outside, do you?" The mention of a hustler should have sent Quinn into a spree of winks and complicit sexual innuendos, but he remained frozen, glaring at him. William wiped his mouth and continued laughing. He could laugh for days. He'd laugh until Quinn would start laughing along with him and then he'd know he was safe.

But Quinn didn't so much as breathe, and William stopped laughing. He hadn't spoken to anyone he knew in five days and had hardly eaten, preferring the numbness of weed to food and water. Suddenly William missed the quiet indecision of the motel room.

"Guess I had to come back sometime."

"I guess," Quinn snorted.

"What's wrong?" He turned his eyes to the attention of the mail fanned out on the counter.

"You know what's wrong."

"You saw the car outside." William refused to look at him, slipping his finger across a Verizon bill on its third and final payment notice, hoping one last second for the leniency of a world that would work in his favor. Don't admit anything. Play dumb. Don't say a word.

"Yeah, I saw it," Quinn replied.

"Then you know I'm back," he sighed softly. "The Catskills were perfect. Did you know—"

"Cut it out," Quinn said roughly, groping his nylon pockets before yanking his hands free to point one in his direction. "You know what I mean."

"No. I don't."

Quinn rummaged through the contents on his desk and pulled a newspaper from under a blanket of envelopes. Quinn turned the front page over and wiped it flat with his palm. Then he thrust it out in front of him, rattling the paper as if it would come alive and speak. It did. MEAN STREETS, ran the headline. In an instant, William read the aftermath of the freak accident in Tribeca and what price had been paid while he had kept driving away from the scene. He took a step back and grabbed the counter. He smiled, but the verdict was already swimming through his eyes. Dead. The woman had died right there on the street as she vanished in the rearview mirror. He had done that, or at least the car had. The victim hadn't just suffered broken bones or been knocked unconscious like William had imagined for all of those days hiding in the motel room. She had been killed, her whole life wiped out as he continued to speed away. He looked up at Quinn, hoping for him to contradict the report, because he couldn't accept what a split second of carelessness now made him. But Quinn's face didn't ease. He was not a murderer. Even with the fact spelled out right in front of him, William hated Quinn for suggesting that he was one. He filled his cheeks with air and blew.

Quinn brought the paper closer, shoving it against his face. "See that car," he yelled. "That blue shape in the picture. Do you see it? That's my car. I can see the fucking bumper sticker, that little tab right there!" His finger jabbed the blur. "I noticed the paint job outside. You had it fixed. You hit her. You hit her, and you drove away in *my* car."

Now that Quinn had gotten his accusation out, he backed away sheepishly, clenching the paper over his belly like it was in danger of being ripped to shreds. William shook his head, vowels muscling their way through his teeth, and he reached his arm out, but his balance was failing. He held himself against the counter. His knees gripped the cheap wood paneling of the sink. His fingernails dug into the cold metal basin. He had killed that woman. In one second she had been alive, and in the next she was dead. The realization kept returning, like he'd shielded the information off and it found another way of penetrating. He had no way of dealing with that kind of news, and his whole body was struggling to adjust. If he didn't submit to it, if he didn't let it sink in, it still didn't need to be true.

"Don't lie to me. I don't know where the hell you've been for the last few days, but it wasn't upstate with friends."

"You're wrong."

"You stupid son of a bitch," Quinn hissed. In their years of friendship, William had never seen Quinn angry, and he almost didn't recognize the tattered, swollen face now cracking in blood vessels. "How the hell could you just keep going? In *my* car." Quinn mentioned his car again like that was the most gruesome detail in the entire situation.

William let go of the counter. His shoulders jerked as he let out a cry that had been building in his stomach since he had watched the city drift out of view on the turnpike. He took a step toward his friend's fat, rigid body, but Quinn lifted his arm to shield whatever he thought was coming for him, an embrace or a punch. William pushed past him and collapsed on the couch, snaking his fingers into the limp bundled fabric. For another second he clung to the lie, he even improvised a deer dazed by headlights on the highway, but Quinn was shaking his head right through it, staring pathetically down at him.

"Don't even try it."

William dropped his head. He could grab his bags, race out the door, run north toward Fourteenth Street, and keep running. But Quinn would still be there, holding the newspaper, holding keys to a car dented and repaired.

"Okay," William whimpered. "Fine. Yes." Quinn moaned. He banged his fist on the top of the bureau, which sent a picture frame that was leaning against the wall to crash face down. Quinn carefully picked up the frame and then shook it at him—a photograph of his former self, young and blond, laughing with a muscular chest and a flat stomach on a beach in Fire Island, like that loss was William's fault too.

"It's sick. You hear me? Sick."

"What do you think, that I meant to hit her?" William could

scream as loud as he wanted in the cottage. There were no next door neighbors, no eavesdroppers frozen just behind the walls with satellites for ears like there were everywhere else in New York. The strain of William's voice shouting his own defense strengthened him. "I didn't know what was happening. All of a sudden I was driving away. I drove like I wasn't even in the car. And then suddenly I was in the Holland Tunnel, and by the time I reached the other side it was too late to go back. You know I didn't mean to. Quinn, it was an accident."

"It doesn't matter what you meant. That poor woman was killed, and you didn't bother to stop. Don't you feel an ounce of anything?"

William stared up, waiting for a sign of compassion to ease the corners of Quinn's eyes and mouth. William pumped all of the pleading and vulnerability he could into his face, hoping to catch any splinter of love that Quinn had felt in the years William had visited him. He waited as a minute went by, his eyes begging and insisting, *come on, find me in your heart*, but the coarse geography of Quinn's face refused to weaken. Quinn gazed down in disgust. That expression woke William up. Quinn wasn't going to forgive him.

"I didn't know she was dead. I figured a few broken bones. I'm not a murderer. It was an accident. I didn't even mean to drive away. How are you supposed to know what to do in a moment like that? How can you blame someone for an instinct?"

Quinn's jaw worked at grinding up his words before he spit them out. "How long do think it's going to be before the cops figure out what kind of make that car is? And how many blue Cressidas are registered in the city? And how many have a white bumper sticker, and how many of those just happen to have undergone a nice little patch-up job on the hood?" Quinn was shaking too. Suddenly William realized, with some degree of hope, that his friend also felt complicit, like his own innocence had been pulled out from under him. Quinn slumped down on the couch next to him, slapping away William's arm for the comfort of his own hands. "You really did it. You really did," he repeated. "I was hoping it was a mistake, that I was embarrassing myself by even accusing you, that you'd come back and tell me I was crazy."

"I'll fix it," he whispered. He tried for a second time to put his arm around Quinn, who was staring in a daze out the window. "Quinn," he begged. "I'm sorry. Please. It's still me. I'm like your son, and I'm in trouble. I'm asking you to help me."

Quinn took those words with a dismissive hiss, but he accepted the arm that collected around his shoulder, and in another second William's mouth burrowed deep into his chest. He cried into the red windbreaker, releasing all of the guilt and fear that had wracked him for so many days in the motel room. He reached for Quinn's hand, brought it to his lips, and kissed the hairy knuckles, hoping those hands would help share the burden of saving him.

"You did a terrible thing."

"I know."

"But I'm going to help you. I told you I'd always be here for you and I won't break that promise now."

"Thank you." He pressed his face into Quinn's neck, smelling the chemical flowers of laundry detergent mixed with expired cologne. Quinn would save him. He was older and stronger and lived with death every day. He would protect him. William's eyes closed in relief. He could have fallen asleep in that tight embrace.

"Here's what we do," Quinn said finally. "We go down to the station, find the detective, and explain. We don't even need to mention the repair to the car right now. We just say you were scared. That's enough, I think. I'll be with you at every step."

William lifted his head in shock as he stared at the meaningful clench of Quinn's pale lips waiting for it to ignite into an altogether different proposal.

"What?"

"That's how we fix it. We walk right down there, and you turn yourself in. That way, they'll go easier."

"No," he choked. "No. I'm not doing that. They'll put me in jail."

"William," he whispered tenderly, the kissed knuckles still pressed in William's hand. "You have to. It's your responsibility. You have to accept what you did. It's the only way you'll be able to live with yourself."

Quinn stared so solemnly, he could easily be mistaken for a man who had weathered high moral roads all his life. He looked utterly unlike the reckless prankster that William had come to love, the man who told stories of harassing cops and throwing used condoms at patrol cars. His fat, bloodshot face with its brittle dent for cheekbones and its burdensome drape of jowls showed every year of living outrageously on his own appetites—his loud indecencies and the even louder declaration of his rights to perform them, which always fought against the order of the law. William couldn't believe that same man was telling him to turn himself in when it wouldn't change a single thing. The woman was dead. She wasn't coming back, no matter how long William sat in jail. He realized he had misjudged Quinn, his entire nature, all along.

"No fucking way," he screamed, jumping off the sofa and trying to reach under Quinn's legs to gather his bags. "You can't ask me to do that."

Quinn pushed William back, and in a second he was off the sofa too, collecting his wallet and house keys from the desk.

"It's for your own good," Quinn snapped. "I was wrong about you. I expected more."

"Where are you going?" William asked in panic.

"Where do you think? Down to the station. I'm going to tell them whether you come along or not."

William could feel his own heart racing so hard his fingers bunched as if to collect the blood. So few seconds were left to bring Quinn back to his side. "What good will it do?" he screamed. "I told you it was an accident. Please, Quinn."

Quinn wasn't listening. He tossed his keys into the pocket of his windbreaker and shouldered past William's halting arms. He stood at the door, trying to release his hands from the jacket pockets and said one last thing without turning around.

"You have to behave like you share this world. You should learn this. We aren't all just decorations for you, William. It isn't right to treat a person like that. Like roadkill. Like they aren't even human."

Every muscle was firing down William's spine as he whipped his arm around Quinn's neck, and his body fell on top of him before he could open the door. At first William held him almost like he was hugging him, like they were both staring out of the door's small portal window at the weaving branches that hid the black lace of a fire escape. William only meant to stop him, to bring him down to the ground and make him listen, force him to understand. But Quinn's hands quickly jerked to wrestle William's arm from his throat. His hands were caught inside the pockets of the red windbreaker so they only lifted up like two oven mitts performing a boxer's pantomime. Then Quinn jabbed an elbow into William's stomach, gutting his air, and tried to wiggle free. Quinn started to scream, no longer in argument but shrieking as if he were under attack. His elbow struck William again, and to stop the screaming, William squeezed his arm tighter around Quinn's neck, until the cry dissipated into a gurgle that exploded from his nose and lips.

William closed his eyes, pinning his forearm against Quinn's throat as hard as he could, all of his panic concentrated on that arm. If William let go, if he softened his hold, Quinn would scream, and if William looked into those eyes he would find them so engulfed in hatred that no pleading would ever be able to stop that hatred from spreading. Two feet frantically kicked against the base of the door. William kept his eyes shut and breathed into Quinn's ear, the one action his friend could no longer perform. He constricted every muscle in his body, tightened every vein. William squeezed so hard it was as if his own brain contracted into the smallest pinprick, with no room for thought, no room for guilt or even understanding of what he was doing, just squeezing until the tightness blotted out any other message in his head. He felt Quinn's legs buckle, and they both dropped quietly to the ground.

When all thought was the size of a pinprick there was no room for consequences. But now the pinprick grew and with it came the realization of where he was and what he was doing. William wrenched his arm away. Quinn stared absently at the tiny black gap under the refrigerator. His face was purple, and his mouth hung open. William slid back frantically on the wood and grabbed the first thing his fingers found, a T-shirt balled on the floor. It was Quinn's tie-dye rainbow shirt, his errand-day favorite. William wound it over his own face, stuffing the fabric in his mouth, and screamed with every

ounce of strength into the sweet, dank body odor of the wonderful
man who lay in front of him, gone.

SUICIDES TELL LIFE backward. They start with death—the how,
with what weapon—and the entire biography becomes a scavenger
hunt for what went wrong. It hurt to acknowledge how easily the
facts of Quinn's life would make sense of such an end. The cottage
was a museum wholly devoted to lost glories and leftover vices. And
so was Quinn's own body, disintegrating like everyone else's, only at
a faster rate.

He pulled Quinn's heavy body into the bathroom and finally
released his hands from the windbreaker's twisted pockets. He took
the house keys out, threw them in the sink, and tied the end of a bed
sheet around Quinn's neck. Then with all of his remaining strength,
he lifted the body on one shoulder while lassoing the other end of
the sheet around the steel shower pipe. William pulled until only a
few inches hung between the nozzle and Quinn's neck. He made a
tight knot and then let the body drop. The pipe bent at the weight
but held. Quinn's black Converse sneakers, a ridiculous but touching
testament to youth, swayed an inch above the basin of the tub.

William grabbed a towel from the closet and began wiping the
tub under Quinn's feet, the sink, the medicine cabinet, the pill
bottles. He scrubbed the bathroom floor, backing out on hands and
knees until no trace of his prints remained.

The living room glowed in the evening sunset, all orange and
cobalt reflected across the glossy plaster walls. He grabbed his duffle
bags, shoved the dirty towel into its pocket, and placed them by
the door. He knew his fingerprints were all over the room—why
wouldn't they be, they were friends?—but he was afraid that any
further cleaning would look suspicious. Who cleans before they kill
themselves? Suicides tell life backwards because they beg for answers
close at hand. The calm disorder of clothes and furniture strewn in
the eccentric effects of poverty, with magnets and LGBA pamphlets
announcing Quinn's condition before an autopsy would, were proof
enough. Who would look further for answers into a life so strangled
in old age and disappointment?

William picked up his bags and locked the door behind him, ducked across the garden, through the tunnel, and out onto West Twelfth Street, moving in the opposite direction of the car, which was still parked five feet from the entrance.

He walked toward the Hudson River, drenched in sweat, pressing his palm through his hair to keep an appearance of sanity, as his lips trembled at the flash of Quinn hanging in his shower like the loneliest man on earth. The path along the river was full of baby strollers and spandexed bikers whirling by on ten-speeds. William leaned over the railing, pretending to watch the sun dissolve into New Jersey, and tossed the dirty towel wrapped around the set of car keys into the water. He tried to catch his breath and, shivering, waited only long enough to see it sink.

PART
THREE

CHAPTER TWENTY-NINE

IT STARTS THIS *way, with Joseph's great grandmother, Aurelia Guiteau, pacing at the bedside of her dying husband. It is 1928 turning 1929, three hours left before the calendar becomes a useless piece of scrap paper. Chintz curtains are pinned closed, and the sounds of joy and fistfights stream through the open window.*

Aurelia clenches her auburn hair, cursing god, as the house is riddled with specialists. The doctor at the foot of the bed shakes his head, and the Catholic priest hides in the downstairs pantry. Their boys sit on the staircase, biting and pinching and staring dazed the way children do when they are suddenly thrown into the wilds of adult panic.

Aurelia bends over, registering her husband's eyes, small, black orbs reflecting the room like mirror balls, and she sees a word coming across his lips. He's trying to say something, but it just won't come. Aurelia has the jittery streak known in redheads, clamping a wet washcloth to her own cheeks and then to those of her husband. He's still breathing, but there's no flash of recognition, no light that so often settled on her, that psychopathic look of violence, which she always mistook for love. She realizes this New Year's Eve that she won't feel his hands root across her back again. She realizes she is losing something forever that she had always counted on. Tyson Guiteau is a large man, just like his father, with bloated, hairy feet that hang over the edge of the mattress. Just like his father, she has been told, dying of heart failure at thirty-four.

On the bed, Joseph's great-grandfather, Tyson Guiteau, is somewhere else. Tyson's last memory is also his first. It appears drained of color like an X-ray held up to the sun. He is six years old and trailing through a crowd of overdressed giants. He is not in Ohio but in New York—Buffalo to be exact, courtesy of an overnight train and two breakfasts packed in banded cigar boxes. His father, donning his best black suit, doesn't trust the locals with their illiterate smiles and jacked-up prices and ruthless bargaining tactics. But he wants his only son to see this, as much as he wants to see this. It is the future. It is a thousand watt bulb.

Tyson wouldn't be able to remember the hour or the day of his first memory if it weren't later marked in history books. Four in the afternoon with the heat firing down on the creamy, pastel-colored domes. So many people alive and curious on a three-hundred-acre stretch of parkland. Camel rides, bands playing rag on rickety stages, African emperors dressed in leopard-fur togas, a demonstration by the Life-Saving Service held at the lake on the latest advancements of shipwreck rescue. Everywhere the exhibition ground explodes with the strains of exotic flowers: pansies, delphiniums, cannas, rambler roses, cacti. But Tyson's father pulls his son across the dirt by the arm, indifferent to the horticulture or the pretty girls under massive pompadours or the roar of distance organs.

Sweat drips down his father's chin, as much a sign of the dizzying heat as his growing irritation. As they walk, the music of one band drifts into another—a mournful pioneer folk song answered by a swinging set of banjos. His father explains that, as the sun sets, the lights will turn on. The Electric Tower is wired with thousands of colored bulbs, coming alive at night to liquefy the world.

September 6, 1901. The Pan-American Exhibition. Not bad as far as first memories go. Tyson remembers peanut shells crunching like cockroaches under his feet. He remembers the Dutch chocolate that his father bought to keep him quiet and little boys sitting on gigantic stalks of cauliflower. But he won't ever get to see the wonder of the Electric Tower. Nor will he visit Edison's X-ray machine that his father is determined to find (foolishly thinking he can find the owner and put money down to help finance it). In a world exhibition, everything is a spectacle. But some acts are better attended. President McKinley, guarded by his Secret Service soldiers, shakes hands for ten minutes, as the crowds gather in line under the afternoon sun to touch the man who opened trade routes and conquered the Philippines. The future has arrived.

Which catches fire first, a heart or a handkerchief? Not Tyson's father suddenly going slack, letting go of his son's sticky fingers and keeling off the path into a bed of pink geraniums. That must have happened second, because Tyson, stunned, frozen next to the invisible column of air where his father just stood, looks around for help from strangers, and already news is breaking over faces and men are running in one direction. Already Leon Czolgosz has blown two holes in President McKinley through a handkerchief that conceals a .32-caliber Iver Johnson revolver decorated on the handle with an owl's head. The President falls in front of the Temple of Music to the soundtrack of organ pipes. The handkerchief catches on fire. One bullet ricochets off the president's breastbone and another plows through his stomach, pancreas, and kidney. Tyson runs, zigzagging and pointing, but no one pays attention to a little boy waving furiously toward the marvel of exotic vegetation, where, if a passerby examined more closely, two brown leather shoes in a desperate need of a polish stick out from miraculous pink petals.

"Ma'am, ma'am," he finally manages, as he grabs at the folds of the nearest skirt. The woman turns and dusts him off her dress.

"Run for cover," she screams at him. "They are killing people."

Frantic, he returns to his father, digging his knees in the damp soil, crying on top of him, panicking, trying to push his father's body into public view with his scrawny arms. Two more women appear so close to Tyson, he could reach over and untie their bootlaces. Their mouths are gaping. "It's a blessing," one cries. "The president isn't dead."

Neither is Tyson's father. His eyes re-attain their hold on the sky, and he pushes his son roughly from his arm. He coughs, spits, and rubs his chest, while sliding to his knees in the dirt.

"Jesus, Mother Mary. Like a stone passing. Like glass." His father's face is drained of blood, with terrified eyes lined in soft pink pollen. He can't calm his fear, not even in front of his son. The fear of dying right there, in a city that isn't his, in imported flowers, at thirty-four and a half.

This is the future.

They take the train back to Cincinnati that very afternoon, spending part of his X-ray investment money on seats in a first-class berth. Tyson's father doesn't talk. In fact, he doesn't talk for the entire week after Buffalo, until early one morning, he collapses while stumbling out on the front porch on his way to buy a newspaper. A second strain rips through his heart and kills him outright, not bit by bit like the gangrenous blood that consumes McKinley one day later. This memory in mind, it's no surprise Tyson developed a life-long distrust in the wonders of technology only matched by his deep hatred of flowers.

That first memory is the reason why the dueling bouquets of peonies (signs of health) and lilies (acceptance of death) that have been delivered to the house never travel up into the bedroom to decorate Tyson's sickbed. Tyson's first and last memory is the scene of not one man's death but two: a president and a father. His eyes have lost their practical use, as his wife stands over him rubbing his forehead with a wet towel. But in place of her face, he sees African nobles with gleaming black nipples, enormous vegetables, and camels kicking up sand clouds. He feels his father dragging him through the tents and the music. Of course, there are no ticket stubs or park maps to document that the Guiteaus were anywhere near Buffalo in the summer of 1901. But they were because Tyson remembers it.

That day hangs in his mind right now. Tyson has suffered far worse. Months of agony on this tiny rosewood bed as the tendons of his heart wrench in two across his chest. He shred the linens with his writhing fingers as he screamed, so much so that Aurelia ordered the bed fitted with quilts and army blankets, industrial strength, to make them last longer. Tyson punched holes in the wall, bloodying his knuckles, while Aurelia prayed at his side, first for a miraculous recovery and then, secretly, shamefully, for a kind of spiritual passing. She can't be a widow. Not with two young boys. He refused to go to the hospital, no X-rays, none of those machines strapped all over him. Instead he relied on daily visits from a doctor who could do little more than drug him up in the evening and touch his stethoscope to his heart, saying, "Family condition. His father died the same way."

Tyson twisted and turned on the second-floor bedroom for months like a tornado that couldn't find a farmhouse to crash into. The neighbors started to complain about his screaming at night. Aurelia went every morning to St. Mary's, keeping up appearances. She wore her emerald clip earrings, two inset diamonds sparkling on her ring finger, and a mink stole that wrapped snugly around her shoulders. She sat in the first pew of morning mass and waited for her turn in the confession box. "Father," she whispered tiredly through the iron grating, allowing the poise she carried on her long walks to the church to deflate in the safety of the dark closet. "How could this happen?"

A good question, but arguably Aurelia knew the risks when she married Tyson Guiteau. God may not roll dice but her husband did, running the single casino and prohibition bar in downtown Cincinnati, buried in the basement of the St. Regis Arms hotel. Everyone knew that Tyson made a small fortune on the sins of the community, and they blamed Aurelia, who never once stepped foot in the casino, for it. She heard the rumors leaking from the porches on her way to church that her husband had women on the side, that every stickpin or pearl necklace he bought for her indicated another knocked-up debutante in the Northern Kentucky hills. Every shred of gossip that reached her clipped, sparkling ears made her love Tyson with more insistence, as if it were a test of her loyalty, her faith.

Aurelia stands over the bed. Tyson can barely squeeze the tweed blanket in his grip. He's vomited up everything he's eaten in the last week. His eyes stare at the ceiling, exposing the soft creases of his bristled neck.

"Ty, Ty, can you hear me?"

The doctor at the foot of the bed shakes his head.

It is time.

She collects her skirt in her hands and runs down the hallway, the folds of her dress slapping the faces of her two sons as she descends the stairs. The youngest sobs, blocking out the noise with his knees against his ears, but Aurelia pays no attention, dashing down the oak staircase and into the kitchen where Verda, the cook, sleeps standing up next to the stove.

Inside the pantry, crammed between the canned vegetables and the tangled spice branches that hang from overhead rafters, hides Father Murphy dressed in his most saturine attire. Murphy is the lean, tinsel-haired prefect of the St. Mary parish. He holds a gilded Bible over his heart and gives an expression that is simultaneously concerned and irritated by his confinement in the kitchen closet. She had forced him into the pantry that evening in the blinding fear that her husband, even unconscious, would magically sense his presence.

Aurelia, with Father Murphy trailing closely behind her, races up the stairs, passing the two boys now collected around the cook who hugs them dreamily like she's using their little bodies for pillows, and into the bedroom, as the clock on the wall strikes eleven. Laughter and cheers from neighboring houses fill the room in anticipation.

Aurelia, who never cheated on Tyson once in their marriage, now betrays him for the first and last time. Tyson threatened to kill any priest who entered his house and warned her that if he were accidentally forgiven of his sins, he'd manage to crawl out of bed and commit new ones before his heart gave out. But Aurelia is now placing her own bet on the table. She stretches her hand an inch from Tyson's broken nose to check that he's still breathing. She then retrieves a crystal rosary from her jewelry box. Father Murphy begins the Prayer of Last Rites, assuring Tyson's ascension into Aurelia's one-shot constellation of everlasting life.

"You think I'd let you go just like that?" she had replied quietly to Tyson's repeated threats. She pinches the rosary beads, resting her thumb and forefinger momentarily on each crystal as Father Murphy drills through the Latin prayer.

Tyson mumbles, his cracked lips moving through a word.

Aurelia bends her head down to hear him, with her eyes flashing over to Father Murphy to speed up his verses.

The doctor, standing by the window, cranes his neck to catch the dying man's words.

"Lia," Tyson Guiteau utters before his last breath. A touch of romance, the name of his wife on the closing stroke of his tongue. Then this. "Leon," he says. Not Aurelia. As clear as the ding of glass.

Leon.

Aurelia drops her rosary on the floor. Father Murphy closes his Bible. The doctor advances to measure the stillness of the wrist.

The sound of death is ugly. Who knows what army of letters elbows its way through the cranium and marshals out of the mouth before the blood evacuates the brain? Aurelia avoids Father Murphy's consoling arm and walks blindly down the hall. It is her turn to be the victim of the house.

She opens the front door to the porch, where the Victorian houses around her glitter with lights through which shadows sway and dance, waiting to be thrown into the midnight of another uncertain year. Aurelia has entered the darkness an hour before they do.

Leon.

Leon Czolgosz. Twenty-eight-year-old assassin of William McKinley, twenty-fifth president of the United States. A self-styled anarchist and fifty-cent attendee at the 1901 Pan-American Exhibition with his own business interests. Doomed to a short life of American alienation due to a hard-to-pronounce last name. Tyson's first and last memory is of his father keeling into a grove of cultivated geraniums while a bigger man's gutting took center stage. His father on the ground, and people crying into their hands for somebody else. They buried Tyson's father while the entire country mourned, and even though the same funeral songs were playing and the same color adorned the banisters of the staircase at home and the downtown courthouse, he recognized the distinction in the deaths.

Ghosts blame the men who take their places. The final name on Tyson's lips is not Aurelia. It's a change of heart that Aurelia now sees as a final betrayal, or maybe an indication of all of them.

He left her empty, that's all she knows. Tell me you love me. He never did. Tell me one last time so I can hold on to you. He chose someone else.

When they take Tyson's body from the room, Aurelia lies down in the sag in the mattress that the body has left. She wears the black silk dress she bought for his funeral. She refuses to move until her mother steps into the room.

AT THE CEMETERY, *Tyson's mother walks up to her, grasping her by the arm and kissing her cheek coldly. For a moment, the old woman seems to be searching for a word just beyond her reach. Aurelia waits for it, frames all of her vision on those lips, cracked like the edge of a glass, like they might explain what was wrong with her husband, and then realizes that her mother-in-law is simply struggling to free her heel from a divot in the grass.*

The hay-brick Victorian draws more guests than the mass did, which is expected considering Tyson's hatred of the church. But Aurelia doesn't return to the house. She doesn't go back for coffee and condolences. Aurelia goes to the one house that isn't haunted by Tyson. She reenters the freezing vestibule of St. Mary and takes a seat in the last pew, breathing in the incense. She doesn't kneel with her hands clenched toward the cross that hangs above the altar. She slouches, crossing her legs at the ankle and leaning her elbow against the armrest so she can chew on her fingernails. Finally, she gets the message. No amount of praying could have saved that man. His soul was weighing her down, and all she had done was fall in love with a liar who deceived her at every turn. You left me here without one last look. You didn't even bother to say good-bye. *"Leon," she mutters out loud in the darkness of the church.*

JOSEPH WOKE IN his bed, gasping for air. The pillow and sheets were soaked in water, and he flailed his arms as if trying to swim to the surface. But the water was his own sweat, dripping down his back and legs. His heart pounded, and he couldn't get air. His lungs were filled with fluid. A whistle blew in his chest when he tried to breathe. Clenching the damp mattress, he pushed himself up, slamming his shoulders against the wall.

The last fragments of the dream drained through his ears and eyes, loud and jumbled against the darkness of the bedroom. He had told Aleksandra the story of his family, he had told her of every sad and perfect death. Maybe somewhere in saying it out loud, he had encouraged it along, resuscitated those starved facts with ferocious life. Joseph had waited for the sickness for so long, expecting it to burst like a seed deep in his body, and, now two weeks short of his thirty-fourth birthday, he couldn't help but wonder if these symptoms were the first signs of that disease digging its roots in. A dull pain pulsed through his chest, and he pushed his palm over it to ease its beat.

"Del," he cried, reaching over to her side of the bed to find it empty.

She came in with a confused stagger, rubbing her eyes sleepily. It took her a second in the darkness to understand that something was wrong, and her face lost its defensive guard. She covered his forehead with her hand.

"You have a fever," she said. "Oh, sweetheart. You're sick." He had not heard that loving tone in her voice for so long and missed it. He could live inside that voice. "Do you want me to call the doctor?"

"No," he said, catching more air sitting upright. His tongue was sandpaper. Del gently lifted his head and placed a pillow behind his neck. "No, I'll go tomorrow."

"Must be the flu."

"No," he said. "It's not that."

Del sat on the edge of the bed, holding his hand and staring at his tongue as it fought to wet his lips. A long blue T-shirt dipped between her legs, and her newt-white skin collected the street light along her thighs. He had shared the apartment with her for almost ten months, but suddenly her body seemed so far way from him, as if placing his fingers against those thighs might be met with an instinctive jolt of resistance. Joseph wondered when their instincts had betrayed them, their immediate reaction being to drive each other away.

"Do you want some aspirin or a sleeping pill?" she asked him.

"I'm a little better now."

"You don't look it."

"Just sit here a minute," he said, not wanting her to leave. He was afraid that if he let her go, he would lose her again, lose her to rooms, to other people, to wringing hands and phone calls far away. There were a million forces competing to come between them, and some already had. He realized what effort it took to preserve this simple gesture of Del holding his hand on the bed. "Talk to me," he said.

"Don't you think you should sleep?"

"Just for a minute."

"Okay," she said, wiping her teeth with her tongue. She told him that she had finally come to a decision about her job. There was no point staying on any longer at the zoo, and she planned to give her resignation as soon as possible. "I should have done it a long time ago," she said. "I'll stay until they find someone to replace me."

"I'm glad," he replied. "I always said you should."

"Just so you know, that means I'm officially just your wife."

"Officially?" he repeated.

"I mean, on my visa. I'm the wife of a citizen."

"Now I know why you're being so good to me," he said, squeezing her fingers. He didn't mention that she still wasn't sleeping next to him in bed or that they had barely spoken in more than a week. He tried to smile. Then his eyes closed, and he fell asleep, bringing Del, as if by hand, into the current of his dreams.

CHAPTER THIRTY

RAJ HAD NOT meant to become his father's son so late in life. It had been Madi's wish for a reunion and it had been her funeral that had delivered Raj to his portly, towel-headed father who quietly placed sandwiches and glasses of milk on the kitchen counter, as if leaving offerings to an invisible deity. Raj slept in his father's cramped guest bedroom on a sofa foldout that dug its springs into his shoulder blades. After the funeral, he laid there for two days in his black suit, refusing to change, as two rounds of sunlight burned through the closed metal blinds. He hadn't meant to stay at his father's apartment. It was his mom he thought he was returning home to, but she had long since renovated his bedroom into an office for her monthly church newsletter (titled, in black authoritarian capitals, GET WITH WORSHIP!). That left the option of Madi's old room—still decorated with posters of forgotten boy bands and pirouetting ballet slippers. It might seem odd that his mother had chosen to scrap Raj's room, the child she was closest to, and keep Madi's, the prodigal, intact. Maybe she had hoped the daughter who once slept there would one day return to her, stripping off the Indian wardrobe to embrace the cold, dusty prom dresses that still hung on pillowed silk hangers in the closet. The one other sleeping option at his mother's house was the couch, where four half-feral cats arranged themselves like ailing fashion models, each named after a Beatle (the cats were all female and Ringo was missing a left eye). "If you stay with him, you must promise to visit each day," she had demanded. "You must help me go through her *room*. I can't just let it be." Raj chose the silence of his father's green-wallpapered Miami condo, where he could administer his own pain in his own slow doses. "You watch out he doesn't hurt you," his mother whispered, even though it was just the two of them in her kitchen. "He's not civilized. That man still carries a knife!"

The knife was the snaggle-pointed kirpan, and, along with a wood comb, a silver bracelet, and saggy cotton underwear, it hung somewhere in the bulk of his father's body as a testament to his faith—as if to unwrap a slovenly businessman was to find one of god's armored foot soldiers. His father hadn't cried at the funeral. He stood behind Raj, staring in concentration, as if he were trying to tighten every internal organ simultaneously. Raj had waited for one word, one sigh, one cough, one break of the larynx, but the old man stayed silent.

His words came later, at the ambrosial hour before dawn when his father sat on the floor of the living room.

What Raj heard that first morning after the funeral, still dressed in his black suit on the bare foldout, were words of scripture chanted through the wall.

"True here and now. O Nanak, forever and ever true. By thinking he cannot be reduced to thought, even by thinking hundreds and thousands of times. By remaining silent, inner silence is not obtained, even by remaining lovingly absorbed deep within . . . "

Raj let the chanting go on for several minutes before rolling off the mattress to pound his fist against the wall.

Quietly then, but no less devout: "The hunger of the hungry is not appeased, even by piling up loads of worldly goods. Hundreds and thousands of clever tricks, but not even one of them will go along with you in the end . . ."

After two days of prophetic psalms creeping through the wall into his ear, Raj had had enough. At least his mother mourned in the local vernacular. Wiping the crust from his eyelids—strange to return to his hometown to discover he'd grown allergic to the air—Raj pulled himself from bed and decided a cheap motel room, even with its drunk, horny vacationers, would be a more benevolent way to greet the morning. He opened the guest bedroom door, stumbled into the living room, and found his father sitting before a low table strung in velvet, head bent toward the pages of the Guru Granth Sahib.

"Dad, please," he wailed, hand judgmentally braced on his hip. "Do you know what hour it is?"

The smile cracked through his father's beard, and under blue tinted reading glasses his eyes gleamed.

"Rajveer, I am only performing my duty."

"So I've heard. You've been at it for days. Can't you at least go to the gurudwara and let the soulless get some sleep?"

"You have been sleeping for days," his father replied solemnly, as if the observation sprang from the text in front of him. "When will you wake up?"

Raj shook his head and leaned against the doorframe, plotting packed bags and a room key at the motel a block from the beach. He knew what duty his father was performing, the Sikh sacrament of Saptahik Path, a less lunatic marathon variant of the Akhand Path, which involved reciting the entire Guru Granth Sahib from page 1 to page 1,430 in a concentrated amount of time—often performed after, say, the loss of a favorite daughter. Raj looked down at his father, at the curled conch-shelled turban, as the man read on: "In that pool, people have made their homes, but the water there is as hot as fire. In the swamp of emotional attachment, their feet cannot move. I have seen them drowning there." Here was a lone believer so far from his Punjabi home, holding on to a custom in the last place that cared about celestial paradise when the sun licked the Atlantic waves and teens tied on their floss bikini tops. Raj knew that his father had stopped attending the only gurudwara within miles, electing instead to celebrate his own slightly irreverent version of the religion at home. He no longer, for example, read the scripture in the native Gurmukhi, preferring the tainted English translation in paperback form. What other Sikh concessions had he made? Oh, yeah, he married a Christian, his son chopped off his hair, and he drank Budweisers while eating his dinner over the kitchen sink at night. In other words, his father spoke Sikh with an American accent, and maybe the orthodox believers who attended the boxy, stucco gurudwara wouldn't have let him through its sacred doors. Raj sat down on the floor.

"I will not stop reading, son, until I finish. Two hours every morning. I do this to commemorate your sister."

"I'm listening," he sighed. "Go ahead."

"If you insist on remaining while I read, you must cover that offensive head of yours."

Raj pulled a lace doily off a side table and placed it squarely on his head. He expected his father to slam the book shut or banish him back to the guest room—the doily, after all, had been a childish jab of rebellion—but the gesture seemed to pacify the old man, as he slid his finger under the words and read aloud.

For the next week, it became their morning ritual, the first they had shared since the divorce. The white doily remained affixed on Raj's head until seven thirty each morning, even as the black suit was traded for a white T-shirt, yellow swim trunks, and black dress socks. Raj listened to the Guru's hymns and praises and atrocities, passing in and out of attention as his father plodded away at the verses with his resolute tongue. There were words and names he did not recognize, passages that made little sense, others too conveniently contemporary ("To the addict, there is nothing like the drug; to the fish, there is nothing else like water"). But also, there were familiar verses that fluttered mental photo albums, bringing back the Turbinator in less tormented times.

After the morning observance, he and his father walked along the beach. They didn't speak or touch. They stared at the blondes on towels with their tops untied, and Raj jumped through the ocean waves and dove under small crests, while his father held his shirt, shoes, and socks at the tide line. They sat at a booth in the local diner, eating eggs, and his father ordered small cups of chocolate pudding for dessert. Raj wondered if this was another concession— he remembered a sacred pudding was served after scriptural readings at the gurudwara—but he never commented on it, not wanting to break the peaceful silence of their mornings together.

The afternoon Raj showed up on his mother's doorstep, she took one look at him head to toe, and spat, "This is the way you treat the woman who gave birth to you? I lose one child, and the other one can't find it in his busy vacation schedule to visit me. My you look tan. Have you been at the beach? I've been on my knees crying, and you've been out getting sun."

He did not tell her about the pre-dawn recitations, but he did say that he and his father had taken time to be together. "Get to know each other again" was exactly how Raj phrased it. She walked into the kitchen to slam a few cabinet doors.

"Honestly, Raj, I thought you had more sense. That man and his charms—pure brainwash." Raj followed her across the candy-speckled linoleum, surprised that Vicki Birch still thought that the man she divorced twenty years ago still possessed any charm. "I suppose he'll have you back in a turban by Friday."

"Do you want me to hate him?" he asked. "I think Madi would have liked the fact that I spent some time with our father." His mother spun around, too incensed to busy her hand with another cabinet door.

"Don't you tell me what your sister would or would not have liked," she screamed. "If she had the good sense not to get wrapped up in that India fixation, we wouldn't be visiting her grave later this afternoon. Ohhh," she moaned, liquid brimming her eyelids. "I've been lonely too. I lost a child as much as he did."

He sat with melted ice and lemonade in his mother's backyard, while bees threaded the clump of Spanish daisies growing from under the house. Vicki Birch cried until dusk. Raj didn't want to admit it, he couldn't put his finger on why, but he found his father's stoic silence more honest, more pure, in its mourning than his mother's stomach-wrenching sobbing at any mention of a topic that might lead her back to the subject of her daughter.

"She's gone, Mom," he finally said a week later. "She's gone, and we're alive. I want to think of Madi as I knew her. Not as she was in this house when we were kids, but just last year, last month, last week in New York." His mother recoiled, grabbing a sponge and lobbing it into his stomach. Perhaps she heard the influence of the Guru Granth Sahib in her own son's words—to look forward and not backward, to accept death as part of life. On page 1,429: "Says Nanak, nothing lasts forever; the world is like a dream. People become anxious when something unexpected happens. This is the way of the world." He and his father had turned the page on 1,430 that very morning.

"You make me sick," she said, before burying her face in his chest.

The Oldsmobile was idling at the curb to take him to the airport. His bags were in the trunk, and his father was sitting behind the wheel, pretending not to search for his ex-wife's silhouette in the window.

"You can call me whenever you want," he said, hugging her.

"I guess that's all I have left. That's all parents get, the sound of their children already drowned out in other places. Raj, promise me you'll be careful up there. It's not safe. And promise you'll come down for Christmas. I'll put your room back just the way it used to be. You'll stay with me this time, and I won't bother you."

On the way to the airport, his father finally broke the silence that had enwrapped them for the past week. As a baseball game drifted into extra innings on the radio, his father suddenly gunned the motor and spoke quickly to match the acceleration of the car.

"Rajveer, there is still one thing we must discuss."

"What?"

"The man who killed your sister. He has not been apprehended."

Raj continued to look forward, rattled by the sudden turn of his father's attention to the specifics of Madi's death. These were not the words of a sacred book.

"It was a hit-and-run," he replied. "An accident."

"I have called your police in New York many times. I have asked the detective if they have found the party responsible. But they throw me off. They don't care what an old man in Florida thinks about their negligence. But we care. Your sister must have justice, Rajveer. The driver must be punished."

The Oldsmobile wove into the far left lane, where air gutted through the half-open windows. He could hear cicadas beating in the median grass.

"I didn't think you cared about such things," Raj replied. "She's gone. Let it be."

"We are Sikh and we do believe in avenging injustice. When one's life and dignity are violated, the guilty must face her bodyguards." This mention was as close as his father got to the subject of Indira Gandhi's 1984 assassination by her two Sikh bodyguards, after she ordered the storming of the Golden Temple in Amritsar to suppress rebel activity. But Raj picked up on the reference immediately; he remembered how his father had advocated the shooting, had used forks and knives at the breakfast table to illustrate the atrocities of Indira's army, and had cried against the anti-Sikh violence it fueled in the days after her death, when Raj was only a child watching the foreign carnage on the television set.

"I'm not a bodyguard," Raj said. "I'm her brother."

"I ask only that you encourage the police to continue their investigation. You must go and speak to them directly. That sin cannot be forgiven without a fight."

Raj stared into the dead center of a palm tree whose dried fronds skirted the departure lane at MIA. His father placed a hand on his knee.

"Do you know I'm not even allowed to board a flight with my karpin," he said incredulously. "They want me to check it in my luggage."

Raj pulled his black leather jacket around his shoulders and waited until his row was called. He tried to remember random verses of the holy book, while flipping through magazines by the cash register. In three hours he would be home.

CHAPTER THIRTY-ONE

THE TRUTH WAS Del couldn't get back to normal even if she tried. Madi's death was like a laser, slicing right through the center of her life. Like a ringing phone in the middle of night, where a stranger's voice on the other end whispers *you're running out of time.*

In the evenings she spoke to Raj quietly on the phone from Florida, mostly listening to the silences filling the gaps between his sentences. He talked about the funeral (quick, without a single family conflict, his mom so dazed that she walked with her arm stretched out to keep her standing straight) and about the progress on Madi's case. Raj asked if he could see her when he returned, and she let more silence, a thousand miles of it, drift between them before she answered yes.

She climbed into bed with Joseph. He had come home late, breathing heavily from the short flight of stairs, his eyes blackened like two used ashtrays, nodding at her as she sat in the kitchen, and undressed for bed. He was still damp and feverish, fighting the residue of a late summer cold. He looked sick and yellow, but so did everyone, so did she, barely able to eat and smoking through a pouch of tobacco every two days. Only after Joseph fell asleep did she return to the

couch where she curled in a ball, scratching old nail polish off her
toes. She felt close to that moment when the silence between them
would finally lift and they could continue on together, but for now
she preferred to remain locked in her own arms on the couch listening
to the laughter and the screaming that made up the night.

She listened to young women who passed under the window on
the street, girls going out, girls getting ready in dresses tighter and
shorter each year, hair longer and blonder, going to the clubs, going
to meet men, going to live the way they pictured living in New York
should be—that fast live wire current circulating through the city,
which was only felt by those who hadn't yet lived here long enough
to be inured to its charge. Then she thought about Raj lying in bed
at his father's house, an overgrown child returning to his care after so
many years out of his reach. She imagined Madi fluttering through
the window, the edges of her red silk sari licked by the wind and her
black hair streaming in tendrils. Del knew the hallucination was
of her own making, but she waited for this phantom Madi to say
something to her, some answer that would make sense of the world
erupting all around her without her best friend. The dream never
got that far. Del woke to hear Joseph stumbling into the bathroom.

She dressed for work quickly and said good-bye to him while standing
on the other side of the bathroom door. For once on the subway to
the Bronx, she didn't run though the list of snakebite symptoms in her
head.

If Madi's death was like a laser, its first target was the mud-brown
building of the Reptile House. Death was capable of producing
amazing life. Leto's death had produced little Apollo, the miraculous baby, an inch of cord with lidless eyes, moving on ripples of
muscle, creeping through the white sand of his crib. If that death
had brought life, perhaps Madi's death could do the same.

That morning, she slipped a sheet of department letterhead in
the lab's electronic typewriter and typed her resignation letter to the
Bronx Zoo Herpetology Department c/o Dr. Abrams. Whipping it
from the machine, she carried the letter through the break room and
knocked on Abrams's office door. He sat in front of an open book,
a concave chest bolstered by twin elbows, and his eyes glanced up

distractedly. She closed the door, placed the letter on his desk, and anchored it under a crystal paperweight with a black winged beetle frozen in its core.

"What is this?" Abrams wheezed, as if calling her bluff before he even bothered to read it. "If you aren't happy here, you could have come to me. This is very irresponsible so late in the summer. We've already done the fall budget. I'm afraid if it's a raise you are looking for . . . "

"You're right, I haven't been happy," she said as she took the seat across from him. "Not for some time. But that doesn't matter now. I'm giving you my notice."

He eyed her with irritation, pulled the paper from under the glass weight, and then threw it back on the desk as if it were an exorbitant electricity bill.

"You know what this means, don't you?" The corners of his mouth pitched upward in satisfaction. "It means we can't sponsor your work visa anymore. I don't see how you will remain in this country, Del, if you decide to leave us. I didn't realize you were thinking of moving back to Greece."

"I'm not," she replied, matching smile for heartless smile. She could hardly contain the warmth spreading through her chest, tremendous warmth filling her like a helium balloon. She rolled her shoulders back to capture more of it. She almost felt sorry for poor Abrams, forced to patrol the endless halls of caged reptiles until he confused the employees with the animals locked inside. "I don't need to be sponsored, Dr. Abrams. The visa hasn't been valid for some months. Although I do appreciate your concern."

Abrams's cheeks flushed. He busied his fingers with a pencil, dashing a gratuitous checkmark into the top right corner of the paper.

"It's still irresponsible," he complained while straightening his neck. "So late in summer. After we've been your family for nearly ten years."

"I'm willing to stay on for the next two weeks, or at least until you find my replacement," she replied, appreciating the dignity of the offer but also a little disappointed that the moment she had imagined for so long was now concluding without a bottle thrown or some hysterical chase through the exhibition hall.

"You're damned right you will," he muttered coldly.

She stood up to leave, already picturing a future free of cages, checklists, and tours, when Abrams shot up from his desk, sending his chair orbiting into the corner.

"One thing," he said. She should have known Abrams was not the sort of man to go down without trying to strike one last blow in return. "That Crotalus atrox, what's it called, Apollo. I need it driven to the research lab at Columbia. It's being donated to testing. You don't mind doing the department a favor, do you?"

ON THE DRIVE into Manhattan, Del continually glanced over at the carrier in the passenger seat, the ratted seatbelt buckled over its plastic basin. Inside Apollo nested in a corner, no doubt frightened by the vibration of the car motor and the sudden jerks of southbound traffic. Tears filled her eyes. She didn't want to hand the infant— *her* infant—over to a research lab of needles and dissections. All of that effort to save him had resulted in a few months' survival before being probed and tortured simply to study how badly he suffered and what could be learned from his pain. Which philosopher said that every day for animals was a holocaust? The way they're worked until their knees break, their eyes sprayed with household cleaner, their fur stripped for glove liners, their bones ground up for soup stalk, their tits milked, and their babies eaten. What would animals say if they could speak: *You beasts without hearts, for sharing the planet with us, fuck you forever.*

It occurred to her as she drove through the wasteland sprawl of dollar shops and bullet-scarred liquor stores that she could simply keep driving south: she could pass right by Columbia and keep accelerating until she brought Apollo home to Gramercy. There she could keep him alive in her tub, build a desert of sand and plastic branches, and feed him mice from the pet store until she organized some way to send him out west where he could be released in the wild. The fantasy carried such joyous momentum, she pressed her foot more firmly on the gas, excited to get home and begin frantic phone calls to rattlesnake preservation groups. For a few stoplights, Del almost believed she would do this. She would save Apollo, right the wrong, and sacrifice herself to prevent this beautiful creature from the hell of human treatment. What difference did one snake matter to the rest of the world, which shot and skinned rattlesnakes every day by the bucketload in the west? Of course, there was no crime in killing a snake. There was only a crime in saving one. One life mattered so little. That obvious, terrifying fact—perhaps the first fact a child learns to acclimate them to the realities of the world— drove through her with an overwhelming punch as she searched for a parking space on 114th Street. She shook her head to vanquish the fantasy, because, in reality, there was no way to save Apollo. She would be arrested, deported, and never allowed to return because she had cared for this single, insignificant entity as small and thin as a crack in the sidewalk.

She parked the department's Honda Civic next to the campus. More tears clouded her eyes now, because this campus had been the place that she had met Madi what seemed like ten lifetimes ago. Maybe the tears had been for Madi all along.

Del grabbed the carrier and walked through the wrought-iron entrance gates on Broadway, holding Apollo gently in her arms. She waited for the memories to crash down around her, four years coming back into her mind with the swiftness of an old classmate tapping her on the shoulder. But so much had changed at Columbia since she had graduated. The crumbling brick buildings of her student years had undergone clumsy techno-club renovations, steel and glass promising a learning curve at a faster, sexier rate. Madi would have approved. She had probably doubled her alumni donations to expedite the process. Madi always loved torching the old to make way for the new. As Del climbed the steps of Low Library, which she once sledded down in winter wasted out of her mind on red wine, she was thankful for the transformations. The less to remind her of those years the better.

She followed the brick path lined with curving box hedges around the library rotunda. Three shirtless young men in skimpy blue shorts jogged toward her. They must have been eighteen, but their hairless bodies, taut with stomach muscles ribbed like the smooth dorsal shells of beetles, made them seem much younger. Or maybe Del had finally reached the age that no longer found similarities in youth. She tried to remember Dash's body or even her own from those years of college but came up with blank outlines, a pink nipple or a feather of red stomach hair, but no definitive teenage anatomy. Maybe that failure to remember was the brain's consolation, a mental trip wire to protect itself from time.

Del passed through the science building's automatic doors, entered the chilly cargo elevator, and took the nine flights down, deep into the core of Manhattan. Navigating a maze of antiseptic white hallways that reached so far back into the building they must have overshot the campus above ground, she finally found the name Sarah T. Isely, PhD and the sign CAUTION: LIVE LAB. She rang the buzzer and pushed her shoulder into the door, careful not to shake the box.

Del waited ten minutes in a white bowl chair after giving her name to the grad student at the reception desk. She opened the top of the carrier and looked in at Apollo, slithering against the darkness with his wet forked tongue drilling in the air, the first bead of a rattle starting to hatch on his tail. *He's just a snake*, she said to herself, *whose brain is merely a reception center of heat and impulses.* If so, then why did she feel like she was betraying him?

She scanned the office for some clue to the research conducted by Isely and her team, but the waiting room merely doubled as storage. Filing cabinets were jammed with outdated paperwork and crowned with plastic ferns. A buzzing sound signaled the opening of an interior door, and the same white-yarn-haired woman who had accompanied Abrams through the Reptile House appeared, smiling in a tan lab coat. She extended a hand, which Del shook, while her other hand dug for a ballpoint pen in her breast pocket.

"Are you alright?" Sarah Isely asked, staring at her sympathetically. "You look like you've been crying."

"Oh, I haven't," Del said, quickly wiping her nose with her wrist.

"Abrams," she concluded. "Most of the researchers think he's a ruthless bureaucrat. I find that *twat* describes him more succinctly. At least that's what I limit it to behind closed doors."

Del liked her. Of course she liked her. The woman was a senior professor of herpetology, a wizard of biology, some long lost vision Del once had of her future self, the walking talking paradigm of the idea that you could spend a day with Squamata Serpentes and leave looking like a normal human being at night. Normal in this case meant two silver earrings cast over drooping lobes, a fresh application of peach lipstick, a bun tied loosely over silver streaming eyebrows, and a habit of drawing her chin close to her neck when she spoke. Her skin smelled of hand sanitizer.

"Where do I sign?" Sarah asked, eyeing the shipment. Del searched her pockets and pulled out the release documents, pointing to the appropriate line.

"Do you mind if I ask you something? Are you going to dissect him?"

The older woman smiled.

"Ah, that's always what it comes down to, isn't it?" She rocked back on her heels and let go of the tightness of her chin, lifting it to the ceiling. "Don't worry. This little one isn't destined for the knife."

"Then what are you going to use him for?" Del asked, unable to relinquish Apollo until she understood the full scope of his imminent extinction.

"We need his venom." Sarah said matter-of-factly. "A lot of facilities have their venom shipped in from private suppliers, but there have been too many tainted samples, blood and puss and a whole saturation of I'm not sure what. I prefer the extractions performed on-site. Fresh and cold, less chance of outside spoilers. Sorry. I have a tendency to go on."

"No, I'm interested," Del entreated. "You know, I studied here. Undergraduate. I was a biology major. I never got this far down in the building. Dr. Isely, I hope you don't mind if I ask. Why do you want rattlesnake venom?"

Sarah opened the box and peered in at Apollo, inspecting her latest venom-maker. Then she glanced back up at Del, whose eyes were still holding the question out for her.

"Do you know anything about the Furcifer labordi chameleon?" Sarah asked.

"Green little lizard. Lives in Madagascar. About the size of my hand."

"That's right," Sarah said, clearly impressed. "You know, then, that its entire life cycle is a little under one year from conception to death. It's the shortest living tetrapod on earth. You figure out Furcifer's genetic makeup, determine what molecules are responsible for shoving it out of existence so quickly, find those analogues in human cells, wipe them out, and you've got the recipe for the fountain of youth. Or at least you turn eighty-year-olds into the new middle-agers. Of course, then you get into the problems of delayed mortality, but with STD rates among the elderly spiking the way they are, I guess humans always manage to figure out new ways to kill themselves early." Sarah clasped Del's arm affectionately and then closed the carrier, lifting it to rest against her hip.

"But what's that have to do with rattlesnakes?" Del persisted.

"It's the same principle. What does venom do when it hits the bloodstream?"

"Bleeding, nausea, dilated pupils, cramping, vomiting, heart attack . . . " Del had repeated this list so many times, she was proud of how quickly it poured from her lips.

"Those are outward symptoms. And they're the same symptoms as heart failure, aren't they? But I'm asking what the venom does inside. It drops blood pressure. It clots the blood and causes paralysis, allowing time for more toxic poisons to take effect. Now imagine what those isolated molecules could potentially do for congestive heart failure. Essentially, they could relax the heart muscle and allow blood to flow in and out of its passageways. Voila. Rattlesnakes, the answer to the biggest grim reaper in America."

"That's brilliant," Del said in astonishment. She had read some journal findings on this subject but had never been so close to an actual scientist working the case. Del's self-appointed rattlesnake study seemed so limited, so superficial—a book on mothers? Cross-hatching diamond patterns in a notebook?—while women like Sarah Isely were digging deeper, turning the holy terror of teeth into real scientific possibilities.

"It's all research for now," Sarah said, smiling. "You stare at cells all day under a microscope, you start thinking that all of life's problems can be discovered in a petri dish. But we've made some strides. We've already begun testing, but we have miles to go yet." Sarah consulted her watch and drew a conclusive breath, indicating she had somewhere more pressing to be.

"Thank you for your time," Del said, folding up the release papers in her pocket and again offering her hand. "I'm glad you'll put Apollo to good use."

"Apollo?"

"His name," she said, blushing. "That's what I called him."

When Del returned to the zoo, she spent the afternoon wandering around the grounds. As the last visitors funneled out into the dusk, she sat on a bench and listened to the animals. Their cries in the darkness were slow and piercing, a birdcall answered by a chorus of primates. They weren't crying from hunger or thirst, as those needs no longer concerned them. The cries rose from somewhere deep in their blood, and Del made no attempt to speculate on their causes or origins. For a few hours after closing time, she simply listened to the noises that saturated the park, drifting through the bars and cages in an acoustic collision of continents and ecosystems. By day, the institution exaggerated comforting connections between animals and humans. A mural outside the Monkey House depicted Darwin's familiar evolutionary chain of progress from slumped ape to straight-backed Homo sapien, with one last slot empty where visitors stood for photographs, demonstrating in their nylon running jackets and baggy Levi's that they were inheritors of an unfinished project that would surely, at some future date, even render them obsolete drafts. But at night, there were only these invisible, lone cries, spilling into each other like some mirror city where no human brain could outthink the real connections: desperation and survival, the noise of night no matter where anyone stood on that long chain of progress.

On the way home, she checked her messages to see if Raj had called. He hadn't. "Are you home yet?" she wrote in the electric halo of her phone. She rechecked her phone an hour later as she exited the subway. Raj still hadn't responded.

THE APARTMENT WAS dark when she returned. She found Joseph in bed, murmuring through a fit of sleep-talking delirium. "Tyson first, then Thomas," he whispered against the pillow. She changed into a T-shirt, brushed her teeth, and sat on the edge of the bed to place her hand on his shoulder. His skin was wet with sweat and coarse from a chill. He woke when she lifted the blanket over him.

"I tried to wait up for you," he said.

"Sleep," she replied, leaning over to kiss him on the cheek. "You're still sick."

"Don't go yet," he pleaded. "Stay and talk to me."

She began to tell him of her visit to Columbia, her transfer of Apollo, and the scientific discovery of rattlesnake venom to cure heart attacks, but Joseph's eyelids had already closed. He looked like a child when he slept. When she cancelled out the nervous blue jabs of his eyes, the beams that lit his features with purpose, his face rounded and softened in innocence. He seemed too young to be married to her when he was asleep, too much like a Midwestern boy sleeping under a galaxy of fluorescent green stars that he once told her he affixed to his bedroom ceiling as a child. She gently patted his chest.

"I'll get you some water."

Del walked through the living room raked in streetlight and down the hallway. She couldn't be sure whether the knocking had just started or she had only now come across it. The wood floorboards creaked under her bare feet, which brought more knocking on the front door. She froze. Her heart twisted as it always did late at night with anything involving a stranger. She leaned into the kitchen to consult the microwave clock. 12:17 AM. She thought it might be Raj, back today from Florida, but he never would have barged in uninvited. Raj would have called her first.

She shook her hair to bring some life to it, pressed her hands quietly against the door, and failed to make out the dark silhouette on the other side of the eyehole. She paused, waiting, but the stranger continued to knock. She pulled her thin, white T-shirt over her thighs, unbolted the lock, and cautiously opened the door.

William's hands straddled the sides of the door frame. His lips opened. He was all mouth.

CHAPTER THIRTY-TWO

"I'm SORRY IF I woke you."

William's lips, chapped and chewed, struggled with the words and offered the kind of insincere smile that must creep across the face of a drug smuggler when placing a suitcase in front of a custom's agent. He watched Del cover her breasts with her arm and her legs close together from the draft of the outer hallway.

"You did," she replied. "We were sleeping."

"Is Joseph here?" he asked, peering over her shoulder as if expecting to see him materialize out of the darkness.

"Of course he's here. He's in bed. This isn't a good time, William. Joe's sick."

"Well," he stammered. He pinched the back of his neck and then shook his hand through his tangled hair, greased into an accidental mohawk. "I was hoping, if it isn't too much of a problem, if I could crash here for the night."

"He's really sick."

"I don't have many other options right now."

"Aren't you supposed to be out in California?"

He winced and nodded his head to indicate the million wrenches thrown into that plan. His eyes suddenly dipped down to her thighs, and, in a pang of embarrassment, she clamped the white T-shirt lower down her legs.

"Okay," she said, letting go of the door. She ran into the bathroom and returned a minute later with a towel tied around her waist. By then, William had already piled his bags underneath the windowsill. He was standing in the door frame of the bedroom, staring in at Joseph.

"What's wrong with him?"

"Be quiet," she whispered. "He's got the flu or something."

"He looks twelve, doesn't he?" he laughed. "Like it's all money and palm trees blowing through that head. Some people are always lucky like that. For some, the world makes sure there are a million arms ready in case of a fall. Other people just keep hitting rock."

The tone of William's voice was sharp and slow. He stared at the bed with a weird intensity, and Del grabbed his arm to lead him away from the door. William whipped his neck around when she touched him, as if startled, taking a long second to readjust his eyes on her.

"Why are you out of options?" she asked.

"I'm low on cash. And on friends. I don't have the strength to be subtle anymore."

"What happened to the money, William?"

"What money?"

"The check I gave you," she said, clearly irritated that he had forgotten the loan. "Two thousand dollars. Did you cash it?"

He grunted, and she let go of his arm.

"Why? Do you need it back already? Christ, I told you I'd repay you. You'd think Joseph could help me out a little bit. You know, I helped him out a lot when we were younger. I introduced him to his agent. He has balls to forget a thing like that."

"I'm not trying to fight with you," she replied. "I was just asking if you cashed that check."

"Yes, I cashed it," he said quietly, only now realizing the roughness of his voice. "I'm sorry. I'm just tired. I need to sleep."

"I only asked because if you hadn't cashed the check yet, it wouldn't be any good," she said, taking a step back.

"Why is that?" William sat down on the couch and kicked off his shoes. He placed the blanket over his lap and punched the pillow against the armrest. He was too exhausted to bother wondering why the living-room sofa was already doubling as a bed. Del walked to the bedroom door, took a breath, and exhaled slowly as she leaned against the wall.

"Because the account is closed," she said. "My friend who wrote that check died. She was hit by a car in Tribeca over a week ago. So you can forgive me if I'm not a very good host right now."

William's head jerked toward her with his mouth in an open lock. His eyes widened, and she couldn't help but compare those eyes to the white mice in the zoo lab on feeding day, scurrying into corners when she opened the cage like they somehow knew that the slowest would be caught and never brought back.

"What?" he rasped. "What was her name?"

"Madi Singh," she said. As soon as she spoke her friend's name, grief exploded in her throat. "It was a hit-and-run."

"No."

"Yes. It's terrible."

William buried his face in his hands. Then he lifted himself slowly from the couch and swerved blindly through the room. His hip slammed into the dresser, but the blow didn't slow him. He rushed into the bathroom, where he spit saliva in the sink and brought his head up to examine himself in the medicine cabinet mirror.

"Not possible, it's not possible," he whispered to his reflection. He tried to decipher the sequence of events that connected Del and Joseph to the hit-and-run all the way to Quinn, but the synapses of his brain were failing to create a bridge. All he could say was, "it's not possible" over and over to his swollen face. When he turned, as if searching for help to put these pieces together and make sense of what he just heard, he saw Del disappear into the bedroom and shut the door behind her.

HE WANTED TO lie down and sleep, to disappear into the blackest pit of no-thought anywhere, to be unaccountable for eight hours, to leave Quinn and his death far behind him. But when he tried to shut his eyes, he felt a mosquito skim his temple. He slammed his palm against the side of his head and then grabbed at it as it flew over his shoulder, clapping around in his blind spot. In a minute, its wings swam across his neck, and he jumped from the couch, yelling "piece of shit" as he tried to smack it between his hands. The insect was out for blood. When he lay back down on the couch, it flitted over his ear, blaring its hard battle whine, and again he bolted up, grabbed a magazine off the coffee table and swatted it through the air, chasing it into a corner, where he thought he finally crushed it against the wall. Out the window, dozens of moths were fluttering around the bulb of the streetlamp like pieces of satellite junk caught in orbit. Standing by the window frame, William waited for the mosquito to dance around his ear again. It did, buzzing like a radio frequency, and he went on the attack, slapping his face and neck. Finally, he caught it in his fist and squeezed his knuckles until a small drop of blood and black insect wire were smeared on his fingers. Probably Joseph's blood. Or Del's. Or maybe his own or someone else's in another part of town. There was a whole fleet of microscopic blood vials, samples of the population, drifting through the city air tonight.

William wiped his hand on the cushion and dug his head into the pillow to block out the image of Quinn's body hanging in the bathroom. But when one body disappeared, another took its place. Madi Singh, dead and buried, but right now still on the hood of the car, a flash of black hair and white fingernails tangled together in wet sunlight. William glanced at the door of the bedroom, behind which Joseph and Del slept unconscious to the mosquitoes waiting on the ceiling for their turn with them. He stared into that column of darkness, waiting for it to open and for Del to walk out in her white T-shirt pointing her finger—*You did it. You were the one.* How many days could he go on waiting? Waiting for Quinn to be discovered, waiting for the connections like barrels in a combination lock to click, waiting for the traces of him to be added up until Del and Joseph pointed their fingers. *You did it. You, who slept under our roof, you with the blood of our friend on your hands, you who we took in when no one else would.*

He pulled his hair until loose strands stuck to his fingers. He tasted the bile in the back of his throat.

What had he done? He had been asking himself that question all night as if he didn't know the answer. He had only tried to save himself. Wasn't that the essence of survival? Keep moving, keep fighting, buy time, and, with time, a way out. His head hurt and he desperately needed sleep, but the single fact returned, so real it made little difference what excuses he could offer: Quinn's body hanging from a shower pipe.

Earlier that night, William had already tried to turn his brain off. He had gone to his dealer at NYU, a nineteen-year-old sophomore with trademark acne and a felony-conviction's worth of speed and hallucinogens. William had met him around the corner from his dorm and bought a bag of pot for fifty bucks. The kid kindly threw in a small baggie of cocaine as a present for being such a good customer. William was thankful for the gift. His mind was raw three hours after leaving the cottage, a garbage dump picked by birds for the last sustaining meat. He needed the fuel and the fracture to see him through the next few hours. He smoked a joint and snorted a few bumps of the chalky white powder from the slug of his fingernail while he sat on a park bench in Union Square trying to figure out what options he had left. Soon, the marijuana and speed were competing motor engines, one on warp and the other on propulsion, but neither drug was succeeding in erasing him into his own shadow. Panicked, William kept turning around to find a woman walking her dog or the grating whizz of skateboarders flipping their decks on the concrete. The entire park was loud with panic, repeating his own anxiety back to him, mirroring his heartbeat in screaming teenagers and police sirens. Union Square had once been nicknamed "Death Park" for all of the shootings that occurred there, until the mayor cut down most of the trees and manicured its grass into a safe, Broadway harbor. But, for William, sitting huddled on a bench with his chest against his knees, Death Park had not succeeded in its conversion. The glare of streetlights against the metal storefront grates made the whole city look like a prison yard. How, in all of his years living in New York, had he not seen it for what it really was? He had nowhere to go, not a single place to hole himself up for the night, and he jumped from the bench in panic and began walking north. Then he remembered that Joseph lived five blocks away.

Now he stood at the window of Joseph's apartment, safe, he supposed, if being inside counted as safe. His brain was still rocketing on the drugs' cheap gasoline, mowing through his exhaustion. Outside, Twenty-Second Street hummed in silence, so calm he wished for a car crash or a mugging to call his attention away from the quiet of the apartment. The silence offered too much room to think. Joseph, on the other side of the wall, was sweating out his sickness in sleep. Tomorrow he would wake in the safety of his bed, the fever broken and that opium sense of health returning to his body with his wife beside him. He'd wake to the careless, blind comfort that only the innocent own. The thought disgusted him, and William wrenched his ears as if still battling mosquitoes.

Joseph was the last person in the city he had wanted to ask for help. But he had come to him and what he got was Madi Singh. He had come to Joseph to escape—a few hours, one night of blessed unconsciousness—and instead he found her waiting here for him. It had been so much easier when he didn't know who she was, no connections, no life before death. In William's distorted 2 AM logic, he saw very clearly one key piece to his own situation that had eluded him in the bathroom: every bad event met at a point that was Joseph. Never mind the fact that Joseph had beaten him at his own career. It had been Joseph who ripped down all the promise of his good-bye party. It had been Joseph who had refused to call him back with an offer of support, forcing William to grovel for a loan from his wife. And what had she given him? A check that was now in Madi Singh's bank file, with his own name written and signed on the back like the answer to the intractable question of blame. And now it was Joseph who brought her death back to touch him, leaving him alone in the darkness, while he slept guiltlessly in the next room. If Joseph had stopped for one second to help him, to treat him as a friend, to lift his arm out in rescue, none of it would have happened.

William thought of the loaded gun underneath Joseph's bed but knew he wouldn't use it. He just wanted to look at him for a second, to look at them both, to stand at the foot of their bed and stare down at them, to see just how blameless they were, how beautiful with their skinny legs wrapped around each other and their eyelids as smooth as shells. He walked to the bedroom door and pressed his ear against the wood. He listened for voices on the other side. Hearing only the metronome of slow breathing, he turned the knob to enter. The door was locked.

CHAPTER THIRTY-THREE

THE FIRST PRECINCT building in Tribeca was the color of a faded dollar bill, with windows covered in beige aluminum blinds and green office air-conditioners leaking antifreeze. Unlike the glory of its Renaissance Revival facade, the precinct's chipped linoleum and faux-oak metal desks suggested not money but a lack of it. Raj stepped up to the desk and met the incurious eyes of a saturnine Latina officer crumbling a burger wrapper on top of arrest warrants.

"I'd like to speak to Detective Tasser, please."

"You got an appointment?"

Raj shook his head and proceeded to dig through his wallet for his driver's license.

"You see, he's working a case that involves the hit-and-run of my sister. She was killed over a week ago coming out of . . . "

"Alright, alright. I don't need your life story." She was already reaching for the phone with extensions penciled on speed dial. "Tasser, got a young man down here, says he wants words on his case. His name—" She lifted her chin over the receiver. "What did you say your name was?"

"Rajveer Singh."

Her eyes quickly scanned him waist to forehead. "Second floor. Turn left at the staircase."

Raj had been putting off the detective for two days since returning from Florida. A pestilence of fruit flies had taken root in his kitchen, conducting traffic by air on a small beltway of miniature cockroaches that always sprang from the cracks in August. For two days he battled bugs, and he battled calls from gallery assistants who were demanding answers on when his prints would be ready for the framer. It took twenty-four hours to reach his dealer, back with a bout of heat exhaustion from her house in the Hamptons, and she greeted the news that he didn't know if he could *do* a show anymore with a victimized sigh. "If you give me the photographs I'll do the installation myself. All *you* have to do is come to the opening. Don't do this to me, Raj. Please. The market is already awful right now. I can't go through a cancellation. Please don't make me wish I hadn't taken a chance on you." He wanted to tell Mirabelle Petz that he didn't give a damn what she was going though, didn't care about the work or the art-world repercussions. Instead he agreed and hung up before she could thank him.

The truth was Raj needed something to occupy his attention, and it wasn't the messages from the gallery on his answering machine that left him staring for hours into the corners of his studio, disgusted at the uselessness of his own hands. It was the messages left by his father, five of them, the first recorded when he was still in midair on the flight back from Miami: "Rajveer, now remember. You must go to the police. You must insist they keep looking. That is what you owe your sister." Madi's lawyer had sent a copy of her will, its envelope leaning in his mailbox when he pushed his luggage through the entryway. A typed note on law-firm stationery explained in three short sentences that Raj was the sole beneficiary of her estate. If he could schedule an appointment, they could start processing the paperwork on the transfer of funds and sign over the deed to her apartment.

Raj stretched his hand across the detective's desk littered with paper coffee cups. Tasser, bearded with brown saddlebags under his eyes from years of squinting at accident reports, followed the hand to the arm and up to Raj's face. He smiled in exhaustion. The beard did little to hide the sharpness of the detective's jaw, and his coffee-stained burgundy tie was knotted so low that the top tier of collar buttons looked oddly fragile and boyish against his neck.

"We've spoken on the phone," Raj said, taking the seat across from him. "But I wanted to come down in person to see if there were any leads in the case. I know you've been hearing from my father."

Tasser nodded, perhaps understanding how the grief of a parent inevitably brought a younger family member before him to plead for a resolution. He dutifully dug through his files and flipped open the paperwork on the Singh hit-and-run, pretending an answer might suddenly materialize on the page if his audience willed it enough.

"Your father is like my ex-wife," Tasser laughed. "He calls every day just to tell me how inadequate I am. Thankfully, I don't owe him child support."

Raj coughed, thinking that was precisely what Tasser did owe him. "I'm sorry if he's troubling you."

"No, I understand. We all want the same thing here. But I'm afraid at this point we're still in the dark."

Raj grimaced. "So it's gone cold?"

"Cold as February. We've interviewed every person in the vicinity who might have seen anything. We even went over traffic violations in a ten-block radius, speed cameras, 911 calls, security street video, you name it. Usually if we don't catch the driver in the first twenty-four hours—and mind you half turn themselves in out of guilt—the chances . . . well, they aren't too good."

Raj crossed his legs and controlled his impulse to reach across the desk and grab the file from the detective.

"You said you conducted interviews. Would you mind if I read the transcripts?"

"They aren't *Playboy* interviews, Mr. Singh. They aren't transcribed. You'd read a lot of yeses and nos. People either saw something or they didn't."

"But it was the middle of the day in downtown Manhattan," Raj replied, trying not to sound like he was accusing the entire police force of negligence. "Surely there were people around. Christ, there was a protest march earlier that morning, and there were cops swarming all over the place. How can you be surrounded by NYPD and a mob of people and no one sees a woman struck by a car?"

Tasser leaned back, yanked his necktie lower on his belly and scrounged for a ballpoint pen to weave through his fingers.

"Do you know how many crimes go unsolved in this city in the middle of the day? It's worse than at night because no one thinks to notice. Crimes in broad daylight are the hardest to solve. We love crimes at night. Shit, we pray for them, because everyone's on the lookout."

"What about the cell phone picture? You got that from a witness, didn't you?"

Tasser rubbed his beard and pulled out a copy of the pixilated image that had circulated in the newspapers.

"It was taken by a young woman about a half a block away. We sent it to the geek department but they couldn't get a read on the plates. It's a blue car all right, an older model, probably late '80s or early '90s, but we can't even decipher the make. You do a DMV search on blue cars, you get about half the traffic choking up the bridges. And that's just local registries."

"It said in the paper your team could blow it up."

Tasser snorted and shook his head. He tried to balance the pen on its clicker and watched it fall on the blotter pad.

"A lot of wishful PR. Technology isn't as advanced as you think. When you put the microscope to it, it's just a bunch of colored dots. We placed that on the news, hoping the driver would get scared and turn himself in. Sometimes you've got to frighten these guys into confessing. Truth is, the closer you get the less you see."

Raj uncrossed his legs, uncertain what more he could ask but terrified that he would leave the precinct as empty as he came. He feared returning home to find another message from his father waiting for him, his voice filled with so much reborn belief in his only son.

"Please, there must be something. I could go through the evidence with you . . ."

"Mr. Singh, I'm sorry to say it, but it was an accident. It was homicide, but it wasn't premeditated murder. We've got no suspects.

Without suspects we've got nowhere to turn. I know your family is hoping for answers, but when you're dealing with accidents, it's near to impossible. Unless someone else comes forward, I'm afraid it was a matter of someone reckless getting away with something bad."

Raj wondered how many of the case files on his desk were kept as decoration for families whose couldn't accept open endings. He realized that his presence here wasn't one step toward discovery, it was a step toward the Singhs coming to terms with inexplicable loss. Tasser closed the file, placed it on top of the stack, and netted his fingers together on his desk.

"The woman who took the cell phone picture, do you think I could have her number? I'd like to talk to her."

Tasser shook his head. "We can't give out that information. It's important witnesses remain anonymous."

"I'd just like to thank her. It would mean something to me. I'm asking as a favor. Please, detective. I need something . . . " He wanted to say "something to bring back, the smallest piece of paper to carry out of this precinct," but Raj didn't have to say any of it. Tasser licked his teeth, his eyes offering what sympathy a hardened detective had left to give, and swatted the file back down in front of him.

"I'll tell you what. I'll call her and give her your information. If she wants to call you, she will. Her decision." He copied down Raj's cell number on a Post-it and affixed it to his phone. "But Mr. Singh, do me one favor in return." Raj already knew what he was going to ask. "Tell your father to please stop calling me. It's been every day like this. I can't hear him yell at me anymore."

RAJ WALKED NORTH, following the sidewalks through Tribeca and the West Village. The summer heat drenched his pant legs into roping cuffs. On block after block, pristine, color-coded couples herded loud cabals of pretty, attention-starved children into SUVs and BMWs to escape to their country homes in the Catskills or to the beach fronts of Amagansett, the annual August migration to leave the city to the residents who could least afford it. In a month the weather would turn cooler, the sun would lose its brutal beat, and the days wouldn't flare like matchsticks burning down to the fingers.

It surprised Raj how much he had learned to rely on each new season to extinguish the past and return a sense of purpose to his hours. In Florida, they had one season for his entire childhood, endless summer like an endless hangover, and he thought how much easier he had it than his mother and father because they would not see the colors turn and the clothes change and the daily routine rerouted by weather, all merciful tactics to help Raj think of all that happened as casualties of a previous season.

He had planned to phone Del as soon as he landed. But even in the taxi home from the airport, he had resisted calling her; as he fell asleep, he had resisted sending a text. Walking back to his apartment now, he still resisted, stopping himself as his fingers gripped his phone. A part of him desperately wanted to see Del again, to bring her back to the darkened studio that smelled of gasoline and to feel her body take up space in his arms. But what had stopped Raj in the cab home from the airport stopped him now, ducking out of the sun underneath imbricating café awnings. A year had gone by and they were no longer a couple. No matter whom they had lost or what grief momentarily pushed them together as tightly as a fist, they weren't limitless for each other anymore.

The sky was turning dark too early, and the first pulses of lightning struck deep over midtown. Raj sprinted down his block for the shelter of his doorway. A bike messenger blocked the entrance, holding a wrapped parcel over his dreadlocks as if expecting torrential rain, and when Raj reached for his keys, the messenger leaned over his handlebars and asked, "Singh?"

"Yes."

"Sign here please." Raj printed his name on the messenger's clipboard and carried the package up to his studio, which actually smelled of insecticide and bleach. At his desk, he ripped open the brown paper and lifted the mustard box lid. Inside were contact sheets from the lab. He held his breath to beat back the expectation of pain. On the glossy paper, row after row of Madeline Singh appeared, her face staring straight into the lens, smiling, sucking in her cheekbones, puckering her lips for a look of serious desirability, straining her jaw muscles in irritation at her inability to hold a proper pose. Dropping onto his stool, Raj studied each image, trying to make eye contact with his sister, to stare right back into her and catch something in her pupils, some flash of knowing what was ahead.

He sat there as lightning blazed across the Hudson River chop, trying to select the best photo, the one that described her most succinctly, most explicitly, the one she would have liked. But he couldn't choose. None of them were Madi. Or they all were, each shot capturing a different creature battling insecurities and trying to bring her most striking features to the surface—indications of the beauty that lay deeper if only one would bother to explore. *Do you think we're monsters, that there's something wrong with us?* she had asked the night these shots were taken, only two weeks ago. He couldn't remember his answer.

In near darkness, he spread the contact sheets on the desk, but none of the shots seemed sufficient. Suddenly Raj felt that his camera had just been a machine that floated between him and his sister to prevent them from looking each other in the eye. These were the last photos ever taken of her, and he had failed to get her down. *Useless,* he thought as he pushed the contact sheets aside. Except now, as his eyes scanned the West Side Highway spidered in the glow of head-lights, it occurred to him that these were not the last photos of his sister. There was one more taken later, taken last, on the corner where she had died.

AN HOUR LATER, Raj's phone rang. It was an unidentified number, which he immediately answered. A woman's voice hesitated over his foreign name. "Detective Tasser told me to call you," she said. "I don't know what more I can say."

"You don't have to say anything," he responded quickly. "I'm the one who needs to talk." He wrote down her name and address. At least it was something, the work of a good son.

CHAPTER THIRTY-FOUR

THEY DON'T SPEAK, *the sons of Tyson.*

After the youngest, Thomas, returned home from serving in the war, he found the hay-brick Victorian house in terrible condition and his older brother, Vincent, already engaged. Her name was Christine Garfield, a rake-bodied blonde with a teenager's infatuation with dances at Cincinnati's Coney Island Moonlite Gardens, and with a father in the insurance business. Was it the viciousness of world war that turned these two brothers into hostile entities or was it the secret in their blood: a message conducted through the heart that told each one what little time was left. Thomas came back pudgy and a victim of both a premature receding hairline and a urinary disorder that released a small stream unexpectedly into his underwear (the product of seeing his first dead bodies on the battlefield). He returned to Cincinnati after the war to find Vincent tall and handsome with a talent for the latest dance moves and a harem of girlfriends unknown to Christine. The betrayal of one brother against the other was no negligible act, especially in a town where so many Cincinnati sons had returned home in body bags. All Thomas did was edge Christine toward the discovery of her fiancé's sexual adventures, and, in the weakness of her grief, swoop in to take his brother's place. One year after Thomas returned home from serving in the war, he married Christine

Garfield in St. Mary's Cathedral in front of an audience absent of his only sibling.

Thomas refuses to hear any mention of Vincent's name. The brothers avoid all chance meetings and arrange their visits to Aurelia with the precision of a calendar. The narcoleptic cook, Verda, loses sleep assuring each that the other is safely out of the vicinity. She promises not to pass on any news—travel plans, fender benders, blood test results—and doesn't, until the day she falls asleep one afternoon on the horsehair sofa and doesn't wake when Aurelia comes down to turn off the lights. Neither man attends her funeral.

But letters come from Vincent. They are addressed to Christine using her maiden name. On clean white stationery sent to their new house up the hill from Aurelia's home—its walls sticky from coats of fresh paint, its ranch-style layout smelling of raw cedar—Vincent scribbles, I hope you're happy. You won't be with him. *And* Don't you see he stole you? And worse, you went willingly. *And* He is hell. Burn there.

*These hate-fueled dispatches, arriving every few months after the wedding, are obviously meant to infuriate her. But Christine sits at the kitchen table and opens them slowly, thinking of the tongue that licked them shut. She smoothes the creases and smiles down at the slurs written across the paper. Christine has not entirely let go of the man she once loved who danced with her at Moonlite Gardens through the colored lights in the shape of crescent moons and starfish. She hides these letters in a box of old childhood photographs, tying them together with a ribbon. The last one—*If it's his, there's a monster inside*—arrives three weeks before she gives birth to her only child. After that, the small white envelopes never again appear in the mail slot. But Christine never stops looking for them until the day she finds out that Vincent is dead.*

Christine tracks Vincent's life through local gossip, mostly over lunches at the Clearwater Country Club. She never asks outright, but her friends know she will listen intently to any rumor or chance sighting of her former fiancé. Over soups and salads, between discussions of Republican fundraisers or hospital charity balls, she learns that Vincent married a Presbyterian music teacher and built a small house twenty minutes north of the city. He also works in insurance. He flies small single-engine planes on the weekend at Lunken Airport and is once spotted carrying three loaves of bread and a dead houseplant across Fountain Square during a Sunday thunderstorm. "Don't *worry, Christine," her friend confides, digging her straw into a glass of iced tea. "He doesn't look like he used to. You probably wouldn't even recognize him. Not so handsome anymore, and nowhere near the money Tom makes." In a distorted deference to their communication by post, Christine sends Vincent birthday and Christmas cards, addressing them secretly in the morning after Thomas leaves for work.*

Vincent dies at age thirty-four of heart failure. Thomas says nothing. He doesn't even close his eyes when his wife tells him the news over dinner. He asks for more broccoli. Christine slips into the back pew at the funeral, out of curiosity, out of whatever lasted, and she watches a thin, olive-skinned woman in a cheap, black dress cry at the casket alongside Aurelia. The woman wears black orthopedic sandals that expose her ankles and fallen arches. Christine can't move her eyes off those shoes, the idea of trying to be comfortable even while bawling her eyes out seems so excruciatingly vulnerable, but she is careful to leave before the mass ends without being noticed. A year later, when she finds out that Vincent's wife has died unexpectedly from breast cancer, she has no one to send a sympathy card to. She drives out to Coney Island, where she turns off the car motor and cries. The parking lot is crowded with concertgoers, teenagers in tight shirts and jeans, screaming as they slam car doors. Christine squeezes the steering wheel. She weeps for this woman who died alone, for those breasts she saw a year ago that must have already been ravaged with lumps. Christine's daughter sits belted in the back seat, little arms shaking with plastic bracelets, crying loudly while throwing a cardboard book against the driver's side headrest.

That's Katherine. Even at three, she is not one to stomach other people's heartaches.

KATHERINE GUITEAU, BORN *weighing eight pounds two ounces, the miracle girl in a bloodline known for its broken men. Katherine's sex is the cause of great celebration. Thomas can't believe the luck of a girl. Thomas drives her home and sleeps with her next to him, afraid to keep his hands off of her for a single second. You will live, he says. You're the one true gift that all mirrors wait to hold, and you'll live. The death rate for Guiteau women is not like its men. Tyson had two sisters, his father one, and their hearts never gave out. Thomas is sure that Katherine's heart won't stop either. He presses his ear to her chest and listens to the beat. He will die but this baby will live, her eyelids scabbed from the raw air and pinched closed in the exhaustion of growing. Pink balloons bob on the mailbox. Pink announcement cards sit inside waiting for the mailman to spread them around the world.*

When Christine tells Thomas the news of his older brother's death, he doesn't even blink. But as he finishes dinner and pours a glass of bourbon at the side bar, his head booms with fear like an orchestra practicing in an empty concert hall. Heart failure. A wrestling match with fate that will come sooner or later and pin him to the ground. Thomas says nothing to Christine, but the next day at the office he makes a series of urgent appointments with any and all specialists listed in the Cincinnati Yellow Pages: cardiologists, general practitioners, blood doctors with their trays of long needles, nutritionists. He spends hours getting his pulse taken, his eyes examined with flashlights, his heart monitored while a nurse counts with her wristwatch. Each time he returns for the test results, the doctor takes him into the office, opens the chart, and breathes hard through the nostrils. And they all say the very same thing. "I can find nothing wrong with your heart. No aberrations. No signs of disease. Basically, Mr. Guiteau, no reason to assume it will in any way malfunction. You're completely healthy, sir. Get out of here and enjoy the sun."

Thomas shakes his head and explains his family history. "Help me. Please, you must. I don't want to die."

Thomas is also prone to fits of crying with his fingers wrapped around a steering wheel. All day long at his father-in-law's offices, he talks customers into taking out insurance on the chance nature of unforeseeable acts: a house on fire; a fall down the stairs; a car accident on the corner; an unlocked back window in the middle of the night with the children sleeping upstairs. He is an expert at terrorizing his audience into signing with him, at making them believe that at any moment the worst will happen, instantly reducing life to smoke. "We like to think nothing awful will strike us," he says, moving around his desk, his eyes trained into the distance like a stoic philosopher. "But what if it does? What if it doesn't just happen to other people? What protection will you have against the slings and arrows that are around the next corner?" Thomas sells more insurance packages on those abstract questions than he ever does listing the number of break-ins, electrical fires, and car accidents that occur within the city limits each year. When he speaks, he makes the wildest nightmares sound as inevitable as dinner. But here he is, age thirty-one, with his own tragedy just around the calendar, and he can do nothing to avoid it. Driving home, tears kaleidoscoping his eyes, all he can do is keep going forward until his heart decides to stop.

He cries so hard he can't catch his breath, kicking his feet into the car's maroon carpeting, using his left turn signal and checking his speed as a police car whizzes by, late for a bigger emergency. He pulls into the driveway, all wood beams and marigolds blooming under the hot streaks of bay windows. Here is the life he has built. Katherine runs across the front lawn, sprinting toward his door in her yellow cords and black barrettes. He pretends to gather papers in the backseat while wiping his face. She races to attack him, her legs winding around his knee and her fingers holding on to his belt loops, already too old and heavy for this ritual ride.

He shuffles up the walkway with his daughter strapped to his leg. He is thirty-one and healthy.

THOMAS DIES AT *Christ Hospital four days before a snowy Thanksgiving in 1958. He was admitted a week earlier, complaining of chest pains and numbness in his fingers. When his heart finally bursts, the night nurses on duty say that he made no noise, no twist of the face or groan heard all the way to the station desk. But Thomas knows he is going. He knows this like he knows a train is coming down the tracks. The amount of money that Christine receives from his multiple life insurance policies astounds even a protection expert like her father. She feels guilty when she accepts the reduced widow-clause membership at the country club.*

Their marriage was imperfect. There was little worry when Katherine ran into their bedroom in the middle of the night that they would be having sex or even sharing the same bed. They fought, usually about stupid grievances, a tactless comment at a cocktail party or his lending money to the wrong sort. If Christine ever suspected that Thomas betrayed his own brother to marry her, she couldn't understand where that kind of passion went. She buries him in the same cemetery that holds his father and brother, although a hundred feet away, near a row of leafless oaks. She loved him but not romantically. She misses him nonetheless. Her response is to keep moving. She runs for president of the Neighborhood Watch and secretary for the Woman's Catholic Association. She attends luncheons, arranges golfing lessons, organizes fund drives, plays marathon bridge, and visits Aurelia, now Clorox white from hair tip to toenail, once a week out of obligation, sitting in the quiet kitchen with all of the lights off. When John F. Kennedy runs for office, Christine switches parties and registers as a Catholic Democrat.

Somewhere a teenager with acne and crooked teeth hides in a bedroom painted yellow, smoking cigarettes that turn her nails the color of the walls. There is no heaven above the speckled canopy of her four poster bed, of this she is sure, but when it's late and her eyes won't close, or it's Sunday and the radio counts songs up the chart, she talks to her father.

You left so quickly. I remember so much about you that I'm worried I'll forget. I can remember your smell—greasy coins in laundered pant pockets— but I haven't smelled it in so long I'm not sure I'd recognize it. We still keep your chair at the dinner table. It sits there between us while Mom continues on with her perfect-family trip by making every recipe she clips from her perfect-family magazines. It's weird without you, like one of us is missing. I had a dream last night that power lines fell on the house, and Mom and I could only walk through the rooms trying not to touch anything metal— not the doorknobs or the drawer handles or even the telephone because the electricity would climb through the wires and electrocute us. We had to stay locked in here forever, looking like any other house on the street except one wrong touch and we'd be fried. At the end of the dream, I just couldn't stand it anymore and I finally went to open the door. Mom pleaded, "Please, honey, don't touch. Please, you can't, Katherine." The worst part of the dream was when I put my fingers on the knob for the first time in all the months that we had been trapped inside. Nothing happened. The door opened. Maybe that's what it felt like when you left.

JOSEPH WOKE TO the sunlight. It poured through the window grates and created a diamond pattern across his bed. He woke with a jolt like he was diving forward, and now his body fell back with the heaviness of a fever. He fought the quick convulsions of his stomach. His fingers shook as he pulled the sheet off his legs, and his feet shot over the mattress, numb when they met the floor. Soon Joseph was on his back shivering again. He heard water running in the bathroom and called for Del, but the answering footsteps were too heavy to belong to his wife. It was William who walked into the bedroom freshly shaven and dressed in one of Joseph's polo shirts still creased from the folds of the laundry.

Joseph wished, as he closed his eyes, for a full pardon from having to deal with William. His friend had never been especially adept at sticking to the background, and he knew too much precious energy would have to be spared to keep him at a distance. *Why did William have to show up now?* he thought. But when he opened his eyes, there William was, even with his washed, uncharacteristic cleanliness, looking rough and obstinate as furniture. The tight, wide smile and, above it, two brown eyes staring in a farsighted squint, barely hid the exhaustion swelling underneath. William was trying to appear easy and light, *trying and failing*—that was what amplified the uneasiness, hard and dark. He held a glass of water and jerked it forward, as if he could not establish the proper rhythm of a gentle offering.

"Surprised to see me?" he asked, too light, too easy. Joseph reached for the glass.

"Yeah, I am. What are you doing here?" He drank the water down, feeling the liquid mix with the acid in his gut. "Aren't you supposed to be in California?"

William shook his head, as if that provided enough of an answer, and slapped his palm over Joseph's forehead in the task of amateur temperature reading.

"You shouldn't worry about me right now, you should worry about yourself. We need to get you to a doctor."

"Get me a bucket."

William returned with the trashcan from the bathroom, placing it under Joseph's chin in time for him to puke up pulpy, yellow fluid in four convulsive heaves. When his stomach settled, Joseph turned over on his side and rested his cheek on the pillow. But then he pushed himself up to make another attempt at getting out of bed.

"Maybe you should stay put," William advised. "Del snuck out at dawn. But I'm here. I'll nurse you back." William's eyes tried to engage Joseph in a show of concern, but Joseph couldn't shake the sense that a threat lay under that promise of nursing duties. To be honest, he couldn't imagine a worse fate for an ailing patient. Perhaps his reaction was simply the residue of the last time he had seen William, spitting drunken insults at his party. "Do you want me to run to the pharmacy to get you something? You can't take these kinds of illnesses too lightly. Trying to burn yourself out is going to put you in the hospital."

"What are you doing here?" he repeated, sitting on the edge of the bed as he gritted his teeth in preparation for standing. "I thought you were gone."

"Not yet," William laughed, bending down to cup Joseph's chin. "I changed my plans. While you were asleep, Del invited me to stay on your couch for a few days. Is that all right with you?"

Joseph refused to believe Del had offered that hospitality on her own free will. William walked over to the dresser to toy with the lid of Del's cedar jewelry box. He picked up a silver locket and inspected it before chucking it back into the box. If William was trying to demonstrate his ease in their apartment, he was doing so at the risk of uninvited familiarity. Sometimes it was difficult not to take intimacy as a threat. Joseph searched for the proper response to get William out of their apartment while still preserving some semblance of kindness. The truth was, Joseph hated the fact that William had set up camp in their home. He had hoped for time alone with Del. Only in the last few nights had they begun speaking to each other with the same warmth they had shared before Madi's death.

"It's just bad timing because of what's happened," he started to explain. "And now Del quit her job, and I'm really sick. Maybe you'd be happier in a hotel."

William crossed his arms and glared at him.

"You know I figured you'd say something like that. Actually I thought you'd find a more eloquent way of putting it. Maybe ask Del to get rid of me while you were a few blocks away having lunch."

Joseph saw the hostility forming on William's lips, and he waved his hands to clear the air.

"That's not it," he said with a sigh, exhausted from the need to provide an explanation. "This place is just tiny, that's all. Del and I already trip over each other when we're here alone. I just thought you'd be more comfortable—"

"I *am* comfortable," William yelled. "I don't take up much space.

Look, I only need a few days, just to get everything sorted. Then I'll be out of your hair, and you and Del can fuck and hold hands and try on each other's clothes all you want to. Is this really how you treat a friend who's taken so many bad bullets the last couple weeks?"

"William, you're *always* taking bad bullets," he replied. He gathered his strength and began to ascend on shaky legs.

He steadied his hand against the doorframe and stumbled into the living room. William followed behind, watching the skinny body shuffle in front of him with skin as pale as crane paper. Joseph headed down the hallway to the front door without another word, expecting his friend to be right behind him. But when he turned, he found William standing in the living room with his tongue digging into his cheek. William jerked his head back, his eyes searching for something underneath the bed. Joseph knew William was the kind of person who would take liberties to search through other people's possessions, and it frightened him to think what William might find under that bed. He pictured the metal box wrapped in a towel that was shoved under there. That fact almost convinced Joseph to open the door and to wave him out. But he turned into the kitchen, rifled through a drawer, and reappeared with a set of keys hooked around his finger.

"Here's our spare," he said. "I'm not walking too well. If you aren't doing anything for the next hour, will you help me get somewhere?"

William hesitated in the living room, as if he anticipated that the offer might suddenly be withdrawn.

"You want to go to the doctor?" he guessed.

"No, I've already been to doctors." Joseph weighed whether a confession could be trusted on William. If he felt a single degree healthier, he wouldn't have risked it, but already his muscles ached, his lungs burned with air, and he wanted to go back to bed and pull the covers over him. "I have to go to the Carlyle. Only you've got to promise you won't tell Del."

William stepped forward and took the keys from Joseph's finger.

"I'd be happy to help," he said, cracking his lips in the sweetest smile that his training as an actor provided. "Your secret's safe with me."

It took an hour to get out of the apartment. William helped Joseph out of the shower, wrapping a towel around his hips, and held on to him as he stepped into a pair of pants and slid a sweater over his head. The sweater was too thick for the mercury of August but warm enough to control his shivering. "Come on," William said encouragingly, as he steadied his friend by the waist and led him down the stairs to the sidewalk.

"I can walk on my own." Joseph pushed away William's hands. He stopped for a minute to lean against a neighboring rail post. "I'm just dizzy."

"Of course you are," William agreed, refusing orders and returning his hands to his friend's waist to keep him moving. "You'll be okay in a few days."

Joseph didn't respond, he just nodded and continued down the sidewalk toward Park Avenue. They were walking so slowly, people stepped into the street to bypass them. William waved his arm on the corner and caught the first cab. He ushered Joseph into the back seat so gently, even racing around to the other side of the car so he didn't have to climb across the seat, that Joseph was glad he hadn't disappointed him by asking him to leave. They were still friends. Their love for each other still mattered.

"Carlyle," William yelled through the glass divider. "You want me to wait for you outside? I don't mind."

"No, don't wait," Joseph whispered. "You have the keys."

"Why are you going to the Carlyle? Is it for an acting job?" William kept his tone light to prevent any trace of anger that could be detected in his voice.

"No. I have to meet a friend up there."

"A woman?" William asked.

"A friend," Joseph repeated. "I don't want Del to know because she doesn't need to be bothered right now." Joseph cleared his throat to change the subject. His eyes widened to punctuate the sincerity of his next words.

"William, I want you to know that you can still ask me for help if you need it. I mean that. I realize things have been tough for you lately. If there's anything I can do . . . "

William ignored the hand unclenching on the seat between them, opening like a vulnerable offering. He turned his head to look out the window as the cab accelerated through midtown.

"Too late for that," he replied.

ON THE SEVENTH floor hallway of the Carlyle, the pain in his stomach was already receding, and his chest eased its tight grip. Health, some last warm jet of it, was returning to him now. He had kept tears from his eyes the entire cab ride up to the hotel, but now they were quickly spilling out. Aleksandra opened the door wearing a cream silk dress that amplified the birthmark on her neck. Her dry, washed hair waved down her cheeks, and she pierced her lips at the sight of him as if forming a contracted W—*what, who, why.*

Joseph threw his arms around her. He pushed his chin across her collarbone, and a whine exploded from his mouth so sharp it might have cut through any part of him had it not found a way up his throat.

"I told you once that the pain would come," he said into the darkened room behind her, where a single floor lamp with a green shade burned, filling the air with a soft tortoise glow. "I told you it would happen. And now I'm afraid it has."

HE SAT ON THE SOFA. Aleksandra knelt on the floor in front of him, pulling off his shoes and pressing her thumbs into his arches. He threw his head back to follow the curling leaf molding on ceiling. "I could just be sick. It might have nothing to do with my heart. But what if it is my heart?"

Aleksandra stared up at him, nodding her head like she agreed with each opposing claim.

"It's okay," she whispered softly. "Do you want to go to a doctor?"

"I've been to doctors. I've been all my life, and they don't find anything. I've been to five this year." Joseph's body was shivering.

"Are you cold?" she asked. He nodded his head. She rose from the floor and disappeared into the bedroom to return with one of her husband's suit coats. He slid it around him and bundled the thick lapels at his throat. The smell of jasmine and mothballs and old newspapers drifted around them.

"Sometimes," Aleksandra said calmly, "I sit in on those meetings and listen to all of the conspiracies hatched over 9/11, all because two buildings can't collapse in perfect verticality. Just like Kennedy and the time required to fire two consecutive bullets. That's what all of those theories are based on—the impossibility of their occurrence. Like if you restaged them there's no possible way they could happen like they did." She cupped his hand, her voice strangely soothing like a mother telling a child a comforting story. "But one day it occurred to me that despite all of the slicing and dicing that conspiracists do just to demonstrate the details don't add up, if you did repeat those events, they *wouldn't* happen again as they did. But the conspiracists have it wrong. That only proves that they did happen just the way we've been told. I realized that their very impossibility is what makes them real. They aren't exceptions to reality. No, they're perfect examples of it. If you take any event and isolate it, blow it up huge so you can study its slightest grain, there'd be a million tiny impossibilities worming every which way across the landscape, all the unlikely variables, all of the unaccounted-for seconds, all of the chance collisions falling too perfectly into place. That's what life is. Even you and I, sitting in this hotel room together right now. It's impossible that we're here together, and that's why it's real." She stopped talking and placed her hand on his chest while she studied his face. "You want me to tell you that you're crazy to think what happened to your family will happen to you. But I can't."

Joseph reached his arm around her and rested his fingers against her shoulder.

"Then what am I supposed to do?" he asked.

Aleksandra smiled and wiped her nose slowly with her knuckle. "I think you should tell your wife," she said. She didn't look at him when she said this, perhaps understanding that such advice would render her less necessary to him. "You should tell her the truth."

"I can't," he replied, dropping his hand in his lap. He tried to hold the air in his lungs in an attempt to calm his nerves. "It would destroy what we have. It would ruin everything."

Aleksandra leaned back with a sigh and wove her fingers through her hair. The pale green light softened her skin.

"You sound like Ray," she said. "I don't think he ever wanted to tell me. He thought I'd be disappointed in him. Like if home were kept free from the trouble he had gotten himself into, then there might still be a place to breathe."

Aleksandra shook her head as if to wrench herself from the memory of her house in California. She stood up and walked slowly across the carpet like she was carrying what remained of Ray's memory in arms that crossed at her waist. Aleksandra's back was to him, and she swayed from side to side as if a song had come unleashed in her head. *The work of mourning never gets finished*, Joseph thought. *There is always more to be done.* She crossed the room and stopped at the lamp, collecting the chain in her fingers.

"It's ugly, isn't it?" she said before turning the light off. "All that humming gets to you. Most people can't hear it. They can't hear the current moving in the walls. That's the reason I go to those conspiracy meetings. They can hear it too. I went back this morning to prisonersofearth." In the darkness, the curtained windows lit up white like the underbelly of a fish. Aleksandra was a dark column in the center of the room. Her silhouette was black and smooth. The only sound was the constant whirr of the air-conditioning, breakers of an ocean heard from far away. Joseph could almost imagine that he was swimming underwater, moving through soft, cool currents even as he sat on the edge of the sofa. He seemed so far from that crowded apartment in Gramercy that awaited his return.

"Why did you go back to the meeting?" he asked.

"I guess I missed hearing the connections. I missed the adrenaline of those kinds of questions. It doesn't matter if it's about electricity or satellites beaming your every move into a microchip or even 9/11. I'm just glad not to be the only person who hears the current in the walls." She looked over at him with two wet black eyes. "Your friend was there. Rose Cherami. She asked me about you. She still thinks your name is William."

"Does she?" he laughed.

"I told her I found you. But I didn't tell her your real name."

"Aleksandra," he started and then let a second travel between them while he phrased his question carefully. It was a question that had as much to do with him as it did with her. Their stories were invading each other, overlapping, braiding together by a common thread, as if the death of Ray Andrews, so long dead, were relevant to both of their lives. "Do you ever think it might have been easier for you if Ray never told you the truth?"

She walked noiselessly toward him across the carpet. In the darkness, she looked vague and watery like a gathering of particles, a million atoms coming in and out of focus, teeth and bones and soft palms, almost there but on the verge of vanishing. He could walk through her, swim into her, he could drift.

"Maybe," she said. "Maybe it would have been easier to believe that he just shot himself. It would have been harder at first, but it wouldn't have destroyed me too."

"Then you see why I can't tell Del. "

She leaned down and placed her knuckles against his cheek. The ice of her skin woke him. "Have you ever thought that in the great evolution of Homo sapiens, we're still only inefficient early drafts? We've adapted to the planet, but we still haven't developed the proper equipment to deal with loss."

The work of mourning is never finished. There's always more to be done. Aleksandra curled her fingers around the collar of her husband's coat, titled her chin, and kissed him on the lips. The kiss wasn't sexual. There was no ransack of hands to lead it beyond what it was. It was an acknowledgment of the life left in each of them, the small fragment that wanted to go on.

CHAPTER THIRTY-FIVE

DEL USUALLY TRANSFERRED to the N train at Times Square after work. That was the train that took her back home. But she continued on the 9, trying to picture Raj in his most familiar position, lying in bed with a pillow shoved over his face. It would now be her duty to bring him back to life, to force him into a pair of shoes and walk him to a restaurant, ordering food that could be shared. There she would press him lightly on what had happened in Florida to shut him off so entirely that he hadn't even responded to her calls. That was as far as the reverie went. Or as far as Del allowed it to go, because the thought came to her that perhaps she had misconstrued their brief reunion, holding each other on his bare mattress, for something more. The side effect of her recent estrangement from Joseph was this: she missed Raj, the curly black hair and the clench of his teeth before his guard faded and someone more fragile and awkward appeared, a man who had been alone too long to remember the value of someone else's hands. With Madi gone, who else would lead him back into the world?

Twenty-Eighth Street whizzed by and now Twenty-Third Street. Del bolted out of the car and bound up the stairs to Seventh Avenue.

Here again was the long walk west toward Raj's highway studio. She had already made this pilgrimage two times in as many months, and how different her pace had been on both occasions—the first time reticent and the second crazed with grief. She wondered how many more times she would walk in the opposite direction of home before the date of the INS interview on December 1. "How do you spend your evenings, Mrs. Guiteau?" she imagined the agent asking her. At that appointment, she would have Joseph beside her, nodding through the sanctity of a marriage being fact-checked by professional love readers, and the thought stopped her in her tracks, right on Twenty-Third Street, as tourists with their wheeling suitcases funneled around her into the grungy cavern of the Chelsea Hotel. She should turn around and head back to him. She had left Joseph with a fever in bed, too sick to respond when she checked on him that morning before work. But she envisioned other bodies in the apartment where she had last seen them: William on the couch, sleeping on his stomach with his torn, checkered boxers barely covering his hairy ass, the contents of his bags spilled out on the rug, and her bottle of scotch open on the coffee table. She couldn't return to the apartment, not when it was still daylight with too many hours left to consume with the physically sick and the psychologically deranged. But most importantly, the compulsion to check her phone and smile through the mystery of no news from Raj was too disabling to make it through another night.

She kept heading west, faster now as she broke into a light jog, then running across Eighth Avenue against a DON'T WALK light, dodging an uptown bus that whistled with its brakes. Her lungs were burning from a lifetime addiction to nicotine, but the pump of her heart revitalized her. She zigzagged, she bolted, she galloped the bike lane, hurrying like she was late for her own court verdict. She was already at Tenth Avenue, already rounding the corner on a Citibank that was once an art gallery that was once a pizzeria that was once a savings and loan, and soon his street was in her sight. There was the car wash with its prismatic suds pouring into the sewer and, on the other side, the glass prism of a photo agency with its invisible furniture and alien-thin inhabitants. She ran straight toward Twenty-Fourth Street, crisscrossing between cars, clipping bumpers, flashing her palm to halt oncoming traffic. Her breathing had become loud and shallow, but she didn't slow down, flying across the sidewalk as she culled the last of her strength, bit down on the hot afternoon wind, and sprinted past the frosted glass of art galleries as empty as white vaults. She saw the rusted green dumpster, *his* dumpster, the one that had always guarded his front door and reeked of vomit, and finally, crossing the littered pizza boxes of a finishing line, let herself go slack.

She grabbed the dumpster handle for support and bent over, collecting all of the air she could, which blew out faster than she could swallow. She tried to wipe the sweat from her forehead, suddenly alert to how she must look. She searched for a car window to gauge her reflection. But even before Del could run her fingers under her eyes to mop up the smeared eyeliner, the metal door of Raj's building opened and there he was: Raj in laced loafers, peering past her into the street for a cab. He was not rolling around in dirty sheets cursing the sunlight. He was wearing a crisp, gray shirt buttoned at the wrists, its tails tucked into the waist of a pair of belted khakis. His hair was long and parted down with gel.

"Del?" he said with a startled exclamation, blown back a few inches on his heels. "What are you doing here?"

She pitched herself up, wiping the residue of the dumpster handle on her thigh.

"Raj," she breathed. "I was coming. To see you."

"Were you running to see me?"

"No. I mean, yes, I was running. But . . . " She took a step back as his hand shot forward to steady her.

In a flash, her humiliation turned to resentment, and she stiffened up, hands on hips, her head tilted in the conviction that the most accurate way to read someone was sidelong.

"What are *you* doing here?" she asked.

"I live here."

"I mean outside," she charged. Raj's cheeks went flush, and that was all she needed, the biological evidence of guilt, blood vessels more honest than any clumsy rejoinder, because now he knew that she knew and vice versa. He hadn't called, not because he was too doubled-over in grief but because he was actively avoiding her. A sane Raj had gotten those text messages late in the night. She wasn't sure at what moment her pulse passed over from exertion to pain, but her heart had taken on a thicker beat, worms eating at the aorta, timed perfectly to tinge her words. "So you're back. And looking well."

"I got in a few days ago," he managed. "I've had to deal with some family obligations. I wanted to get that all done before I called you."

"I thought you got in yesterday."

"No," he said uncertainly. "The day before."

"I see." Imagining him still in Ft. Lauderdale when he had, in fact, been eight avenues away felt like a betrayal to the bond they had formed in his studio only a week ago. She shook her head at her own stupidity, shook it because what was becoming clear to her was already clear to him—he hadn't wanted to see her. "Well, I just wanted to make sure you were okay. I was worried. That's why I ran. I know we were both pretty bad off before you went down for the funeral."

"It's been rough, you know," he mumbled weakly. "I'm as fine as can be expected."

"That's good."

He smiled nervously. They both concentrated on a sign hanging across the street. A commercial jet flew overhead on its descent into JFK.

"I waited . . ." she said but didn't know how to finish that sentence.

"I do want to see you," he replied quietly, those glacial blue eyes fixed on her face in either honesty or pity. "Maybe this week if you have some time. Or next. I know I told you I'd call when I landed—"

"Don't worry about it. It's a bad time for you. I can't expect you to think of me as soon as you touch down. Are you off somewhere now?" She asked this pleadingly, one last gesture, one final attempt at reparation, because the thought of walking east against the sunset on this soulless excuse for a conversation seemed worse than grabbing him by the waist and begging for him to go upstairs, undress, and climb into the recesses of his bed to wait for her knock. They could have that again, it would be so easy, a mere cheat on the last two minutes.

"I'm actually off to meet a woman," he said.

"Oh."

"It's not what it sounds like. It's complicated. I don't know her really."

"Okay. Well, I'll let you go. Give me a call when you find some free time."

"I will, Del. I mean it. I'd like that. It really meant so much . . . "

She spun around and lifted her hand in a half-hearted wave and started moving down the block before she could complete the gesture. She walked down Twenty-Fourth Street, marching straight ahead, measuring her inhales and exhales, as the dirty wind stung her eyes. She wouldn't cry. She'd keep the water frozen behind her eyes until she was far away from his building and then, like slamming an ice-cube tray against the knee, let all of it break loose in one snap.

Del got all the way to the corner before she let herself look back. The block was deserted. Raj had gone in another direction. She lit a cigarette, blew the tobacco into her lungs, and, two minutes later, snuffed it out, all of which was more than enough time for Raj to come to reclaim her, reaching his hands out, apologizing for bad nerves, saying all of the things that she assumed he had wanted to say to her and, of course, so stupid of her, never had, not even when they had been together as a couple the first time. *So it's like that*, she said to herself, *the same as it always was*, and crossed Tenth Avenue with her purse slumped against her stomach. Was there any deeper humiliation than running across Manhattan for someone who was on his way to meet another woman?

A block later, Del found a bar with a neon shamrock blinking palely in the window. She entered and ordered a double scotch, while wiping her face with a cocktail napkin. The bar was filled with older, bloated men keeping eye contact with their liquor, who could no longer remember any reason for running across town. They had already made their peace with the limits of their hearts. Del took the scotch down in a single gulp and ordered another round.

CHAPTER THIRTY-SIX

CECILE DOZOL LIVED in the fourth-floor loft of an old granary building on the Bowery just above Houston Street. BOUWERIE GRANERE read the faded words painted on the dilapidated brick, and a wooden pulley wheel floated in the top window, a testament to an old world that pushed the rental prices up for authentic loft living.

Raj had suggested meeting at a coffee shop in the East Village, but the woman on the phone who had just introduced herself in a sedate British accent moaned in disapproval. "Too many people staring. Why don't you come up to my apartment?"

"Are you sure that's safe?" he had asked, surprised by the intimacy put forward to a complete stranger.

"For you or for me?" she had replied, her accent slipping like the Eurostar train under the English Channel into a lazy French indolence. "*Yee*, just come. It's quieter here, and we can talk." He rang her buzzer and climbed four flights of stairs with railings overgrown in locked bicycles. When he got to her floor, pressing his hand along the splintered banister, the only door on the landing creaked open. A young woman stood in the frame wearing a tight yellow dress made out of surgical bandages. Brown-blonde hair was tied loosely back in the day's fashion, artfully unruly so strands fizzed and snarled like a nest of branches. In comparison to her head, her arms and waist were so thin it looked as if her body had withered into a vine to produce this tremendous, ripe face. Cecile was not the kind of innocent bystander that Raj had expected to discuss the death of his sister with. Although she pointed a toothbrush at him threateningly, she offered the kind of demure, chin-lowered glare that she must instinctively bestow upon every member of the opposite sex to indicate that to know Cecile Dozol was to want to sleep with her immediately. She was barefoot, and her legs were sharp and skinny and oiled like African sculptures, only coming into contact with each other at the knees. Raj smiled the irritable smile of a man who did want to sleep with Cecile Dozol but understood he didn't have a chance with her. She returned the favor, her grin surprisingly lopsided and sincere, bearing crooked yellow teeth. She looked like the daughter of someone famous, a more equine, street-smart version of the insurmountable beauty her mother must have been, and Raj mentally scanned through the tear sheets of his twenties when he occasionally shot fashion editorials for magazines.

"I'm sorry to be dressed like this. It is disrespectful," she said, more French than English, though the words sounded wealthy no matter where they hailed from. "I must go to a party in an hour, and they make me wear this." Cecile beckoned him in with a wave of her toothbrush, and soon Raj was standing in a darkened loft with a high, tin ceiling and linen pillows arranged in groupings on the floor like circular crop patterns in Iowa cornfields. The place smelled of marijuana and dried flowers. Mapplethorpe black-and-whites were framed but left leaning against the wall under awaiting brass hooks; owning them was a commitment to taste, hanging them was too much of a commitment to residency. A laptop computer sat on a bookcase with its screensaver cascading smoky rainbows. An acoustic guitar lay on a wooden card table by the kitchenette, the table's legs bound with silver gaffer tape. She kicked a black garment bag that must have once held the dress she wore and extended her arm toward a chair with its cane weaving broken out on the back. Raj was so overtaken with the exotic richness of the world he had suddenly stumbled into he felt embarrassment at the reason for his visit.

"Hervé Léger," Cecile said in the easy rhythm of a native tongue, sucking her stomach in and hiking the top of the dress up over her breasts.

"What does that mean?"

"The designer," she replied. "It's so gruesomely tight. But if you agree to go to these store openings, they demand pictures. Usually, if I want to keep the clothes, I don't mind. But something like this? You stay out too late, you look like a prostitute. *Tch-tch-tch*." She spoke without moving her lips like she was used to having a cigarette rammed in the corner of her mouth, and soon she was on the hunt through a basket of needles and thread for a pack of Parliaments.

"If this isn't a good time," he said, "I can come back tomorrow."

"No, you stay. I'm sorry. You want to talk about your poor sister, and I'm dressed for a party. You see, I forget that I promised. They make me go to these things. They say it is good for my career. Please forgive me." She ran over to clench his hands. Seeing that he wasn't offended, that, in fact, he was thankful for the five minutes she agreed to spend talking about the accident to a total stranger, she exposed her mangled teeth again. Her gums were purple, and no doubt in some other planet ruled on the precepts of dentistry she would have been considered one of the ugliest members of her tribe. In this world, she was one of the most attractive.

"I hope you don't mind my saying, but you look familiar." Raj couldn't shake the sense that he was somehow supposed to know her by sight.

She sat across the table from him on an even more precarious chair. She struck a match and then puffed smoke, much of it escaping around the cigarette.

"Do I?" she replied more in defiance than in doubt. "I came to New York a year ago to get away from that kind of question. I came here to belong to nobody, to work on my music. But New York is not far enough away. There's never getting away from your parents, is there? Not mine anyway. You know who they are and probably see their faces in me. That's why I look familiar to you." Cecile's self-absorption was rather charming in its humility at being bested by the generation before her own. "My mother is Laura Allen." No explanation needed, her mother was the British model, muse, and silent actress in speaking '70s movies, who, when her face turned thirty, moved to Paris to marry the city's notorious French musician. "Sebastian Dozol. That's my father. So now we know who I am. Now we know the reason for this dress and why the guitar lies on the table and no one ever asks me to play it. Who wants to hear a song by the daughter of so and so? It's too bad because I'm quite good." She sighed cigarette fumes. "Now who are you?"

"Raj Singh," he said, appreciating the lack of glamour that followed his name in echoes around the loft. What a prison to have the ghosts of your parents pursuing you around the globe, to have them always a step ahead of you, breezing into rooms just before you entered, the holy cynosures to which you are only the insufficient ambassador. Suddenly, he felt less inadequate in his cheap dress shoes and unironed shirt. How freeing to be Raj Singh of Ft. Lauderdale, Florida, where even Ft. Lauderdale would collectively ask *who?* "I take pictures but not the kind that you're used to."

"You see," she squealed in laughter. "Isn't it nice to have to explain? I don't mean to complain. I think maybe it will be okay for my son. By the time he's older, people won't remember who his grandparents were."

"You have a kid?" Raj asked in genuine surprise. He figured that Cecile couldn't be more than twenty-five.

"Yes, he's four." Cecile reached for the guitar, and immediately Raj worried he would have to sit through a tender ballad devoted to the child. Instead she pulled out a photograph that was woven in the strings. "Seb," she said, holding up a shot of a blank-faced boy with long, girlish hair and breadcrumbs dotting his mouth. "He's with his father in Paris. We are no longer together. *Mon destin est des mauvais hommes.*"

"If you wanted to break him from the family, you shouldn't have named him after your father."

"Very smart," Cecile replied, shaking her fist with her fingers hooked to let the cigarette do the exclamatory pointing. "But even a rebellious girl at eighteen knows to watch out for her son's future."

She paused, digging her fingernail into a skull that was carved into the grain of the table. "I do love my family," she avowed, as if Raj had been the one to suggest otherwise.

"Cecile, I wanted to ask you about the picture you took. The one that you turned in to the police."

"I know." She returned her son to the guitar strings and leaned back in her seat. "I haven't been able to get it out of my mind."

"You saw what happened."

"I was going to talk to my agent that afternoon," she said, shutting her eyes briefly to reveal two painted black lids. "His office is down there. I had just done some shopping. I was looking at magazines in one of those outdoor stalls. I had posed for a spread in a fashion magazine, the kind where they ask you to take off your clothes and then they don't tell you if you will find yourself completely naked two months later in every bookstore."

"You saw the accident?"

"No." She threaded her fingers through her hair and brought her elbows to rest on the table. "I didn't see it. I heard it. It was a sound I cannot describe. Like being in a basement, in the quietest place. And a heavy box is dropped, and the walls are filled with that sound. Like the vibration takes over the entire space, and you can feel it in your fingertips. I remember when I heard it I looked up. I dropped the magazine and stepped back. It had been raining, and it was hard to see clearly because everything was glowing wet. I noticed something lying in the street. I don't know why, but I had my phone in my hand and my first instinct was to take a picture. I don't want you to think I'm one of those people whose first response to something atrocious is to photograph it."

"I don't think that," he said to reassure her.

"Only when I looked at the screen could I see that it was a woman lying in the street and she had been injured. Only on the screen did it make sense that it was a person."

"But you got the car too," he reminded her, speeding up her story so she would no longer retreat into unnecessary incidentals. He wanted her facts, straight and undecorated. His patience was starting to run thin.

"I didn't notice that until I looked up again. It was going the wrong way. A blue car, it was, but far down the block. It slowed and then sped up. I tried to take another picture, because now I understood. This woman had been hit. But by the time I raised my phone the car had rounded the corner. Gone."

"Do you remember anything more about the car? Any details, the make of it, or the license plate?"

"No." She shook her head and closed her eyes as if to return to the scene. "No. *Tout homme est coupable de tout le bien qu'il n'a pas fait.* I told the police everything I saw." She suddenly opened her eyes as if horrified that he didn't believe her, as if she had just realized that this afternoon visit had turned inexplicably into an interrogation. "Please believe me. I would have told them if I knew more. I did not know what it was until it was too late."

He put his hands over her knuckles to convince her that he understood. A tattered, white string wove around a gold Cartier bracelet on her wrist, and her fingernails were a shade of dark ivy.

"And my sister?" he asked. "Did you go to her?"

"Away," she gasped. "Away, away."

"You went away?"

"Yes. As fast as I could. Away." It took Raj a second of mounting anger—you see someone lying in the street and all you do is leave them there?—to realize that she was not saying *away* but *oui* in her French drawl. "I ran to her. I almost slipped on the cobblestones because they were so wet. I ran across the street and bent down."

A chill went through him. He wanted to lift his knees to his chest to protect himself from the rest of her story, but he knew any visible flinch would silence her. He bit the inside of his lip and forced his eyes to stare evenly. She shook her pack of Parliaments and tapped one of the cigarettes upside down on the table.

"I bent down, and I reached to hold the back of her head but then I remembered that to touch someone like that is to do worse damage to them. To hold someone who needs it most is to hurt them beyond repair. I thought I saw her eyes move. Not the eyes but inside the eyes, the black part, moving. There was blood staining her mouth, not blood everywhere, but a red dark stain covering her lips. I leaned my ear over her mouth to hear if she was breathing but nothing came. I looked up, and now there were other people gathering around us and one of them was trying to embrace me, to take me in his arms because he thought I was her friend. He asked if she had had a seizure. I pushed him away and bent down again. I saw that her hips were crooked, broken like a doll. Her eyes were staring up but not at me, fixed somewhere behind my shoulder. I remember I screamed, 'Can you hear me. If you can hear me, hold on to me.' There were flowers everywhere in the glass."

"Flowers?" His eyes were filled with tears. "What do you mean *flowers?*"

"Flowers all around her and broken glass. Pink tulips and yellow daffodils. Maybe she had been carrying them." He could not imagine his sister carrying flowers during a business day, even on a lunch break, not Madi, not tulips and daffodils. But the vision of his sister bringing her own bouquet to the scene of her death caused a small whimper to escape his lips. Cecile quickly caught the grief she was causing and raced her hands over his cheeks. Her fingers were hot and soft, and soon his nose was buried in her collarbone, the thick bandages of her dress so tight he could feel the swell of her skin along its binding. He pushed her back. "I'm okay," he said. "Please keep going."

"The ambulance came and the police. I told them what I saw and took their card. I didn't remember the photo until I got home. I uploaded it on my computer and called the detective. He asked me to e-mail it to him. Did it help?"

"Yes," he said, fighting the sudden need to leave the apartment. He held his nerves as if holding his breath, as if his entire spinal column were a pulley system like the rusted oak wheel that hung in her window and he had to squeeze to keep it from flying into motion. "Thank you," he whispered. "Thank you for doing what you could for her."

"Of course." She leaned over his chair with her eyebrows pinched, waiting for another round of tears. Raj stood up to drive off the pity, her beauty now seeming ugly and artificial, getting in the way of his pain. All of that talk before about her family, all of that polite conversation, disgusted him. Soon she'd be off to her party soaked in flashbulbs, and he'd be left alone in the darkness of his bed. He knocked the chair to the floor and began to race for the door. But Raj stopped four feet into the loft and turned, as she waited by the table hunched over the spot where his chair had been.

"Can I ask you for one more favor?" Cecile nodded willingly, placing her palm on her forehead in concern. "Can you send me the picture, the one you took?"

"Yes." She hurried to the bookcase to reclaim her laptop. "I'll e-mail it to you. What is your address?"

He spelled it for her as she typed it into the address bar and watched as she dragged the file into the attachment box.

"Do you mind if I use the photo?" he asked. "It's yours, after all. You took it."

"It's not mine," she said as if trying to refute any ownership. "You do whatever you want with it." Cecile shifted her attention from the screen to him as if to find some command center in his eyes that would consent to the request or override the hysterical part of him that was still shaking and clenching his teeth. She pressed send, closed the computer, and in two minutes Raj was outside on the Bowery, heading home, where the photograph was already blinking in his inbox.

CHAPTER THIRTY-SEVEN

OF COURSE, WILLIAM could guess the identity of the woman Joseph was meeting at the Carlyle. He had once been up there himself on an audition for her. Aleksandra Andrews, who had told him so succinctly that he wasn't the man she was looking for, the first punch in the stomach that indicated all future treatment in the months that had followed. Evidently she had found her lead in Joseph. And while his former friend swore that his visits had nothing to do with an acting job, William smiled through the lie while he escorted him up to the hotel for the second day in a row. He nodded gratuitously in the cab, promising not to tell Del that her husband was still having trouble walking straight and keeping down water. He even provided a laugh track to Joseph's unfunny joke about their agent, Janice, and her constant pedophilic playground hunt for younger actors to replace them. Then, pressing his hand on Joseph's knee, William asked to borrow two hundred dollars.

Del had come home drunk the night before. She stumbled through the living room without a word to him, even as William shot up from the couch and welcomed her. She collapsed in bed, managing to kick the door closed before she passed out. When he woke this morning, she had already disappeared, but not before stacking all of his clothes and toiletries on the floor by his feet, in what could only be read as a hostile gesture.

After Joseph withdrew the money from an ATM and waved good-bye at the hotel entrance, William raced to the nearest deli to buy *The New York Times, The Daily News,* the *Post,* and *The Wall Street Journal.* In the window booth of a coffee shop on Lexington Avenue, he scanned the metro sections, looking for any report of an elderly man discovered hanging in his West Village bathroom, a victim of suicide or foul play. He found nothing on Brutus Quinn, no trace of him in the ordinary dispatches of homicides, muggings, drug arrests, and child neglect that swept around his cup of coffee. What had made Quinn's cottage such a sympathetic refuge from the city— no neighbors, no shared walls, no well-meaning intruders coming to knock on a door hidden behind the backyard oaks—meant that the terrible actuality of Quinn's body could also go uninterrupted, unnoticed, the sheet creaking under the shower pipe and 180 pounds of Quinn floating perpetually like an astronaut in deep space. William crumbled the newspapers in his fists. Nothing could be decided until Quinn was discovered. William's own life would remain on pause, his future dependent on every anxious look behind him and on the faith in the prying curiosity of residents in the building in front of Quinn's cottage that would lead them to his door. William tried to breathe as he placed two columns of change on the table for a tip and paid the bill at the counter. He pledged to go on with his day avoiding the West Village.

So how did William end up on West Twelfth Street, two hours later, sweatshirt hood unseasonably darkening his face as he walked down the opposite sidewalk? Curiosity had dug its fingers into his cranium. William crept down the block and lingered in the bright sunlight, pretending to inspect a Thai-takeout menu that he found wedged into an apartment buzz box. The blue stucco building that hid Quinn's cottage darkened and lightened in passing shadows. In the top window, a young woman was listening to the radio, dancing as she modeled a bra in her mirror. In the window below this one, yellow curtains fluttered in a crosscurrent breeze. The building's black lacquered door was closed. A dog walker passed with his sniffing ward of Rottweilers and poodles. There wasn't the slightest indication of anything alarming, no murder in the backhouse causing the residents to lock their windows or create a flowery curbside memorial for the neighbor that they had hardly known for thirty years.

William considered crossing the street to peer through the glass panes in the door that held a view of the tunnel, but he resisted, inching his back along the brick of the apartment building across the street. He saw the blue Cressida sitting where he had parked it, two tickets tacked to the windshield and, across the passenger's side window, a Day-Glo green sticker that read: SANITATION: THIS VEHICLE VIOLATES N.Y.C. PARKING REGULATIONS. AS A RESULT, THIS STREET COULD NOT BE PROPERLY CLEANED. A young mother pushing a stroller eyed him as she darted by, and quickly William set off toward the direction of the river. He turned the corner onto Washington Street, stumbled down to Bethune Street, and collapsed in a ball inside the entryway of a veterinary clinic, covering his face with the hood of his sweatshirt. The normalcy of Twelfth Street was setting off a wildfire in his chest.

He walked to Christopher Street and, folding one of the twenties that Joseph had given him, bought a joint off of one of the black teenage vogue queens who he used to buy drugs from in his poorer, less-connected days in New York. He waited until he got to the Hudson River pier to light it. He puffed on the cheap potpourri of marijuana and tobacco, not potent enough to dissolve his senses but enough to release the muscles that cramped down his arms and legs. He leaned against the railing as sailboats buoyed in the water, and beyond them the green silhouette of the Statue of Liberty, and beyond that more glistening water and buildings and the blue sky skidded in clouds. He sucked agilely on the brown crumbling paper.

William didn't know how long he stood staring at the river, but his cell phone was vibrating in his pocket and two cops in black uniforms were mowing across the pier's lawn looking for somebody in particular. His joint had burnt past his fingers, and he flicked the butt in the water. He dug into his pocket and answered the phone.

"William, it's Janice," his agent said curtly. "What are you doing right now?"

"Nothing," he replied. It had been so long since he had heard Janice's wonderful, tyrannical voice on his phone that he grabbed on to the railing to keep himself grounded.

"I have a woman here who wants to talk to you," she said. "She asked for you by name and says it's urgent. Do you want to come up?"

William ran at full speed to the West Side Highway, waving his arms frantically at oncoming cabs.

THE WOMAN WAITING to see William Asternathy wore a wrinkled cream trench coat over a white "I ♥ New York" T-shirt forever popularized by a rock star assassinated in New York. She was not the type of casting agent William had expected to find standing in Janice Eccles's maniacally clean office with sunlight reflecting off every chrome surface. Certainly she wasn't the polished industry insider that he had practiced speaking to with jittery excitement on the cab ride up to Touchpoint. Her skin was covered in red freckles, and her curly brown hair sprouted disobediently in every direction, failing to conceal three bald patches on her scalp. Her shoes were more like slippers, the left moving in nervous circles over the carpet. As William entered the office, he gazed quizzically at Janice. She sat behind her desk and stared back at him with a glued-on grimace, as if the presence of this woman in front of her would soon be blamed on him.

"Janice, you wanted me to come for an audition," William spoke, less as a question, for he was still holding out hope that this woman had nothing to do with his sudden, blessed deliverance into the Touchpoint fold.

"I never said an audition," Janice corrected. William heard her thinly disguised anger. "Rose Cherami, this is William Asternathy, the man you wanted to see."

Rose Cherami glared at him with the same confusion and disappointment that he had shown to her. For a second, they shared the kind of frank disgust for each other that overtook a blind date.

"There must be some mistake," Rose blurted. "This isn't him."
A trip wire in William's mind instantly recalled those very words
spoken by Aleksandra Andrews two months prior, and he grunted
at the insult.

"I'm afraid this is William Asternathy," Janice replied mercilessly.
"I should know. I represent him. Or at least I used to before he began
to waste my time with these little dramas."

Now both William and Rose, in unison, began to lodge their
separate complaints, but Janice's patience snapped. She rose from
her chair.

"Both of you, out. You can use the conference room next door if
you want to, but I will have no more of this in my office. Good-bye.
And William, just so you know, I'm not representing you anymore."

William was too shocked to argue, almost too shocked to do
anything but bow humbly and evacuate the office. He walked
down the hallway as the stunning revelation of being fired quickly
transformed into rage. His fingers balled into fists in search of a
victim. He yanked Rose Cherami by the arm and dragged her into
the conference room. She went unwillingly, slapping the manila
envelope she carried against his chest as he spun her around and
slammed the door behind them.

"What the fuck, lady?" he yelled. He didn't care anymore if Janice
could hear him through the wall. She *should* hear this. Janice should
know that William hadn't asked this pathetic, deranged being to
invite herself here and destroy his last connection to an already coma-
tose career.

Rose's freckles bred exponentially under the fluorescent conference-
room lights. Her face tightened and she looked at William fearfully
before she cupped her hand over her eyes and shook her head.

"It's all a mistake," she mumbled. "I was just trying to help. I was
trying to warn him."

"Warn who?" he cried, wrapping his fingers around her wrist.
The dread in Rose's face scared him as much as her suggestion that
she had something worth warning a person about. He glanced at
the envelope in her hand, trying to figure out what documents it
contained. Through the smog of pot, panic started to grease his

brain. "What are you talking about? You just got me fired. You're not leaving until you explain why you brought me up here."

"But you aren't him," she said. Her hand was red from lack of circulation. She gave another look of bewilderment, which seemed her default expression to offer the world. "You aren't the guy from the conspiracy meetings. I saw a picture of him on that agent's desk. He said his name was William." Rose began to describe the person she was looking for, but William didn't need the inventory of soft blond-brown hair, clean blue eyes, or the skinny Adam's apple that bobbed like a cork when he spoke. He already knew that she was referring to Joseph. He remembered the conspiracy Web sites stored in the history of Joseph's computer. For the first time, William was thankful that the confusion pointed to Joseph instead of him. He let go of her wrist and forced a polite, sympathetic smile to gain her trust.

"His name is Joseph Guiteau," he told her. "He's a friend of mine. What do you want with him?"

"I need to talk to him," she said. "It's something I can only speak about to him."

"He's too sick for that." He was not going to let Rose Cherami leave the room until he knew the full extent of her information. "Look, you can tell me," he said in a calmer tone. "Joseph and I are like brothers. I've been taking care of him."

She stared over her shoulder as if someone might be listening behind the door. "I met your friend at a conspiracy meeting. I'd seen him there a number of times. He's a regular," she clarified. "We both are. Well, until recently, this is. He hasn't come in a couple of months."

"Like I told you, he's been sick."

"At one such meeting, he must have spoken with a woman named Aleksandra Andrews. Does that name mean anything to you?"

Yes, he knew who she was.

"She asked me about your friend. I'm afraid I gave her your name. She was so insistent about finding it out that I couldn't but be suspicious. You see, my parents live in Langley, Virginia, near the CIA headquarters. I knew who she was. You don't specialize in corporate conspiracies without remembering every name that gets thrown around. I looked up the suspects. I even printed their pictures out and tacked them on my kitchen walls. That helps me to remember, living with them, treating them as ordinary as furniture. That's how I remember faces so well. Her husband, Ray, was a minor player in California deregulation a few years back. I'm not talking about skimming a few dollars. I'm talking about billions when you think about reformed energy policy that would undermine any governmental control."

"So?"

"So, anyone could see it if they paid attention. He's a dead ringer."

"A dead ringer? Who is?"

"Your friend. He's a dead ringer for her husband. I knew in my gut that was why she asked about him."

"Rose," he sighed. "I'm not following."

She licked her teeth. The lovers of secrets have ravenous mouths when they're about to reveal impossible facts. They want the moment to slow down perpetually until the announcement is forever a second from leaving their lips. She lifted her eyebrows in pronouncement.

"Ray Andrews was found dead in his car a mile from their house on the Pacific Coast Highway. One shot to the left temple, a revolver in his hand."

"Suicide," he deduced as if she needed the simplification.

"Suicide was the eventual conclusion," she said. "Self-administered gunshot wound. The going theory was that he was complicit in corporate fraud and couldn't live with the humiliation when it got out. But that wasn't always the working theory, and it didn't sit well with most investigators on the case."

"You think the government took him out? Or the energy companies?" Now he understood why Joseph felt obligated to visit Aleksandra. She was a half-crazy recluse trying to come to terms with her husband's death.

"It wasn't a suicide," Rose bulked, chewing on her blistered lips. "It was murder. But most of the investigators didn't think it was any sort of conspiracy, not the kind you're talking about. The CIA got involved for a little while because of Ray's deep connections in Washington. Covertly of course. I have . . . let's say I have family connections. I have evidence." Rose shook the manila envelope in her hand. "The detectives thought Ray Andrews's death wasn't a hit, either." She stopped and let the hush build around them. William arced his neck to encourage her to continue. "They thought Aleksandra Andrews murdered her husband. She shot him in the driver's seat to make it look like a suicide."

"What are you talking about?"

"Ray was going to go public, which would have wiped out all of their money and put them in the center of a very unseemly scandal. It's so simple really. Aleksandra Andrews got rid of her husband before he could talk."

"You're saying she murdered him and made it look like a suicide?"

"The investigation team could never prove it. You can't go after a grieving widow who'd make it very uncomfortable in the press. So eventually they buried it. Do you hear what I'm telling you?" William did. Crystal clear. "It's not a conspiracy," Rose said. "It's just a murder. Why else would that woman leave California so quickly and move all the way across the country where no one knows who she is? She did it. And she didn't get caught."

A smile must have been the last reaction that Rose expected to greet her confession but that's what she received. William tried to hide it in the palm of his hand.

"Your friend is in trouble. That's why I'm here. I wanted to warn him."

"Why?"

The question spooked her. She rocked backward and covered her stomach with her arms. "Because I liked him. Because I don't want anything bad to happen. What do you mean *why?*"

Laughter. Hideous, delicious laughter. He knotted his tongue to hold it down. Joseph, stupid, blind, unlucky, asshole Joseph. "Poor Joseph," he said. Rose nodded her head in agreement.

She handed him the envelope.

"Give this to him. It's police reports and all the public records I could find on the investigation. Anyone can find this information if they dig hard enough. Just make sure he sees it. She's not going to admit anything, but you need to warn him. That's all I'm here for."

Rose left the conference room without saying good-bye. She disappeared down the hallway and into the elevator, where she returned to the street to blur into the anonymity of nine million isolated people, guilty or innocent, who could say? No one could tell by looking at them. That woman he had met briefly so long ago at the Carlyle had killed a man and made it look like a suicide, just as William had done to Quinn. William was no longer laughing as he stared down at the envelope in his hands. Guilty or innocent: those roads wove and braided before departing in opposite directions, and it began to seem like utter chance which route anyone ended up traveling down. He and Joseph had been like brothers once, and some last fragment of that friendship stopped William from throwing the envelope in the trash as he exited Touchpoint for the last time. Maybe he would save Joseph from the sickness that awaited him. Or maybe he would just sit by and watch a man who had been given everything find out for himself how easily it was to fall.

CHAPTER THIRTY-EIGHT

JOSEPH'S PARENTS MEET *the day after John F. Kennedy died. They meet smoking cigarettes in Alms Park beyond a ridge that dips into an awning of trees carpeted in cigarette butts. When the trees are empty of summer, glimpses of the Ohio River sparkle through the branches. The day after the assassination the branches are only half empty. Christine drives downtown to handle her grief in a mourning mass at St. Peter in Chains Cathedral. Her daughter goes to smoke. She goes with her best friend Melinda Nordstrom, a short, lava-haired girl with skin the color of raw bacon from the bitter November winds. They lock arms as they navigate the hard mud and spiked branches, leading them to a stewing circle of teenagers, making efforts not to cry.*

It feels good to be out of the house. In the house, the television never turns off and the phone rings constantly, as news on top of news on top of news creeps its way from Dallas. Katherine is surprised they haven't blown a fuse in the last twenty-four hours—as if the country's newest demonstration of collective mourning is to turn on everything that has a power switch. On the street, people move so slowly it almost looks like they are walking backward, maybe just a few days into the past. The white sky threatens ice but remains blank, like even it is unprepared to release an official statement. That leaves the hands of teenagers, snug under armpits. That leaves teenagers rocking and smoking and glancing at each other distrustfully but still with some quiet knowledge that the world has changed and they are going to be left to make sense of it. They mostly look abandoned, refusing the goading reassurance of their parents, instead choosing to gather together free of supervision, and now lost without their parents' unwanted consolations.

"Give me a cigarette," Katherine says, opening her hand, while Melinda digs through her straw purse for the goods. "And a light," she mumbles between pursed lips.

Katherine knows some of them, the regular smokers who skip out on afternoon classes from other Catholic single-sex schools, as well as a few expats from public high schools whose silent brooding has always been mistaken for toughness, simply because they don't have religion raining down on them all day at school; spirituality must be replaced with knife fights or race riots or whatever goes on in those godless, dress-code-less halls. And there are others here too, an older crowd already out of high school, not bothering with college, returning to the scene of their younger experiments as if unready to let go and become permanent old people. It is one of those who taps Katherine on the shoulder and, when she turns, strikes a match that nearly singes her eyebrows.

His name is Trip Holbly, already a man at twenty, with curly blond-brown hair that takes on a pea-green varnish in direct sunlight. There is no sunlight this afternoon, so his blond-brown hair curls over his ears and pokes from between the chrome snaps of a denim shirt. A trim, blond mustache lifts as he smiles, revealing a hole right in the center of his upper bridge, where two incisors and a canine should be. He cuts a gorgeous figure. To her he is not so unlike one of the marble saints in the church her mother is attending. She nervously sucks the flame he offers through a filter, as she tries not to stare.

"What happened to your teeth?" she asks, unable to resist looking at his face any longer. His eyes are the navy color of her school-uniform skirt. His cheeks are a patchwork of dark freckles over faded ones. Dirt is a prettier makeup than foundation and eyeliner, and that's why men always have the advantage in beauty.

Trip Holbly's laugh only amplifies the hole in his teeth. He takes a step back and lurches forward, swaying on the heels of beat-up brown work boots.

"Knocked them out," he says. "Just yesterday. I was doing a job on a roof, and when I heard that news come over the radio, I slipped. Fell two flights

and landed on a bed of wood beams. When I came to, my teeth were lying next to me. Our president gets killed, I almost followed after him. I spent the day in the hospital getting stitched up."

Katherine nervously rubs her neck, impressed by a man who could speak so casually about losing something as essential as his smile. Her own teeth are chattering, because something frightening is going on with her heart. She giggles and stops, hating the dumb, girlish noise she makes, especially as everyone else around her is staring mutely into the distance. Thank god for the cigarette, which she plugs in her mouth and takes a slow pull, feigning confidence, feigning cool, while her whole body shivers like a door caught in the wind that doesn't want to close.

"So that's it, huh? They couldn't sew them back in?"

He smiles broadly, as if to emphasize the point. "That's it. No more solid food for a while. But don't worry. I'm not going to keep looking like I can only eat applesauce forever. They're making a retainer for me, so I can snap them back in til you won't be able to tell. I don't know why, but it feels kind of fated. Like I'll remember the day always."

Melinda nudges Katherine's shoulder, pointing to a corner where a blanket gathers some of the girls from school, one of them sobbing so hard that she is collapsed in a stretch.

"Come on, Kate," Melinda says anxiously.

Katherine can hear the stories weaving through the trees already, Walter Cronkite breaking into As the World Turns, *Jackie with blood on her suit, the principal's voice bursting in on the classroom through the PA speaker and the teacher turning as white as chalk—all the details of yesterday, which brings a fresh wave of tears to her eyes. But she doesn't want to sit down and cry with the smokers of St. Ursula. She shakes her head at Melinda. "I'll be there in a minute," she says. She turns to Trip Holbly, who is peeling a callous on his thumb.*

"I'm sick of those girls," she says. She has never had to act brave before and is impressed by the credibility of her own performance. "Do you want to take a walk? You can see all the way into Kentucky over the ridge."

Out of his long, gray jacket, Trip Holbly has large biceps and skinny legs. His forearms are covered in cobwebs of fine blond hair. And Katherine, leading him to her favorite view of the river, is already wondering what it must be like to kiss a man with missing teeth.

JOSEPH'S MOTHER FALLS *for Trip Holbly on the spot. She later blames the decision (that's what she called it, a decision) on the vulnerability and confusion of that week in 1963. But to look at pictures of him then— tall and unpretentious, with fresh muscles hatching on his body, with an honest crooked smile that comes from not expecting too much—it's obvious the attraction is physical. To be fair, though, she's right. Katherine Guiteau's generation never fully digested the sorrow of that weekend. It collects in their stomachs and bowels like sediment, flaring up whenever conversations turn to the events surrounding November 22. For Katherine that weekend also carries radically different associations, which haunt and later chisel away at her sense of balance. A bridge connects Kennedy's death to the moment she fell in love, and it is with some degree of shame that she looks at photographs of the First Lady gritting her teeth through her lace veil or the eternal flame bobbing in Arlington and thinks of Trip, slipping his arm around her waist and pointing out boats in the brown slate water that rushes under interstate bridges. She keeps the copy of* Life *with the stills from the Zapruder film, examining the whirl of pinks and silvers locked in nuclear greens, politicians the shape of movie stars, as if the insanity in those images turns into flowers under her eyes. She studies them alone in her bedroom with the door locked. There is an exotic glamour to those pictures, to the center of the world the size of an open convertible. Because her own life has contracted to a single frame as well, the shape of a construction worker raised in the countryside who lives in a factory neighborhood ten-minute's drive from her own. She knows to be ashamed of her thoughts, even as she searches newspapers for photographs of the funeral march, of Oswald's murder outside the police station, or of Jackie waving graciously at Love Field. She hides those thoughts the way she keeps the copy of* Life *hidden under her mattress—the hot pornography of falling in love, the kind that blows her world to pieces, while everyone else stands around not entirely aware that what is happening will have unimaginable consequences.*

Trip picks her up from school in a red mud-splattered truck four days later, the passenger seat cleared of tools and his smile fixed. He opens his mouth wide so she can judge the dental patch-up job for herself. They drive to his apartment in silence.

The three railroaded rooms on the second floor above a hardware store are badly carpeted in thin maroon scraps that fit together unevenly, occasionally revealing brown linoleum where the carpet cuts away at the foot of the oven or the refrigerator. The heat ticks from an organ of old metal pipes, and the windows are lit in white frost. A gritty bar of soap curls like dry leather in the kitchen sink. Katherine notices that it is caked in black resin. He must spend his evenings washing tar from his fingers. There are no pictures hanging in frames, although the walls are punctured like a star map from a previous tenant's attempts at a home. A pencil sketch of a fighter jet hangs on the refrigerator door by a magnet. She wonders if it is an interest in warplanes or in drawing that brought him to trace it.

He pours two glasses of water from the tap; one a chipped coffee mug that he keeps for himself and the other a crystal green glass with no visible set mate in the cupboard. He offers it to her with a surprising lack of embarrassment. In fact, it is Katherine who is suddenly embarrassed, aware that it is the trapping of her privileged background that instantly regards the crudeness of the cup, and too quickly she tries to correct her response. Trip smiles, now guessing the inadequacy of his apartment for a girl like the one in front of him. He follows her into his living room and apologizes for the mess.

She pretends to appreciate the cracked plaster walls with their dust-covered molding, as if inspecting the room for domestic possibility. The place feels lonely, shadowed in slants of late autumn sun, dank with mildew and rotted wood. Crumbled brown leaves drift in the corners.

"Is it your first apartment?"

"I've only been here three months. It still feels new. Are you sure you're okay here?"

"Yes, I'm sure."

"I can drive you back."

He reaches his hand out to comfort her. She unzips her coat with its soft lamb's wool lining and hooks the collar on his open fingers. The heater is failing for all of its effort, but sweat pours from Katherine's neck and she has the sudden urge to dip her head out a window to let the cold wind rinse her face.

This is the first time she's been alone in the apartment of a man; an apartment, not a house with barely concealed parents in her Hyde Park neighborhood; and a man, not a boy from one of the local academies nervously pinching trophies and sports gear as if to confirm that one day, with enough patience, he will grow up to be one. She turns to examine Trip, standing still in the cold, bare light like an organism she can't quite identify in biology books, and it takes all of her courage not to ask him to drive her home. Her stomach cramps and a rush of focus keeps her legs from buckling. Every event in her life before this one has felt controlled, by god or nuns or her own mother or even the government, which until now has always appeared to her as efficient and reliable as god himself. But Trip Holbly is a force outside of those safe lairs.

He leads her to a clear plot of carpet in front of a black television set and unbuttons his flannel coat, flailing as he pulls the coat's arms inside out. She sits on a bed pillow neatly disguised inside of a wool throw and tries to check her appearance in the television's blank screen.

"Do you want me to turn on the TV?" he asks.

"No," she says, turning away from its reflection. She has watched so much television over the last few days, and each time she turns a channel there is new information, new news, new plots overtaking the last ones that have not yet been resolved, new funerals, new deaths; she is terrified to find out what she has missed by spending a day in class. She wants to be terrified by something else, and she is, her heart racing, her fingers fluttering toward her teeth. She sips the tap water slowly, while Trip yanks his sweater over his head, leaving him in a white T-shirt with a gold chain swaying a small crucifix side to side. She thinks of these seconds as if they exist on television, the seconds before everything goes crazy, the possibility that something else might happen, a million things, although only one will. Katherine reaches to put the glass on a wood side table and it slides straight off before she can catch it, knocking against the heater pipes and smashing into pieces on the carpet.

It feels as if everything in the universe is just barely holding together, as if those tiny glass pieces only assembled for a little while to form a cup and decided to break apart again on their own. That's when Katherine starts to cry, not so much for the nation or for Kennedy or even that skinny runt Oswald, but for whatever is holding together in herself.

Trip touches her chin, lifting it with the side of his finger and then takes aim and kisses her.

His hands wrestle open the buttons of her Oxford shirt and start twisting the metal spoke of her bra. She grabs the bottom of his T-shirt, slipping it over his head and feeling the rubbery skin of his back. His fingers touch her left breast, and, with the other hand, he finishes the job of removing his shirt, tossing it to the side, and smiles down at her. She leans back onto the floor and gets a look at his body, the blond hair of his chest descending like a stream over his abdomen. She touches his shoulders, grooved with small scars, as his knees push her legs apart. He is shivering, his arms pocked in goose bumps, his chest puffing in and out. She is terrified if she lets another few seconds of stillness move between them, she'll lose her nerve and stop. So she lifts her hips, pinches the elastic of her underwear beneath her skirt and pulls the white silk material down until it expands between her thighs. Trip swivels back on his knees, pushes the underwear the rest of the way to her ankles, and then, without bothering to unbuckle, snakes out of his pants. Soon his body rests on top of her. He holds his weight with a right arm anchored just above her head, and she can hear his teeth click back and forth as he fills her mouth with his tongue. His penis slips under the pleats of her skirt as she blends her fingers into the curls of his hair, the way hairdressers measure the length before cutting. Only one thing can happen next, and she doesn't cry when it does. Why has it always been described to her as a loss?

Joseph's mother imagined losing her virginity to an artist in Paris or a university professor on a college excursion through Rome. She loses her virginity on the carpeted floor of a weekly rental in the neighborhood where her own cleaning lady goes home every night to cook dinner for her kids. That is as exotic as Cincinnati has to offer a seventeen-year-old, and, anyway, she is deeply, grossly, morosely in love.

Katherine returns to Trip's apartment three evenings each week, strips down to her underwear, and soaks up the filthy stench of poverty, all the nicks and grit staining the walls and dirtying the carpet squares. She washes her hands with the scab of soap in the kitchen sink and then descends upon Trip, whom she likes best when he doesn't shower because he reeks of sweat and lumber, the wilderness of men who build garage additions and third bathrooms, skylights and gazebos, in her part of town. When she isn't with him or about to see him, her body feels as if it wears one of those iron blankets nurses throw over you for dental X-rays. And the only way to shed it is Trip Holbly, who once dreamed of being a pilot although his vision was too poor, who smiles patiently as she quotes feminist theory or prosaic love sonnets, who incuriously never shares her one-way-ticket runaway fantasies to European capitals, and who takes her to dinner when she receives a full scholarship at the University of Cincinnati, which means that she isn't going anywhere. Katherine Guiteau is staying put.

IN THE FALL *of 1964, a rash of tornadoes sweep through the Ohio Valley and rip open the barns in the surrounding countryside like soup cans. Downed power lines inside the city limits kill two and set a mansion on fire. On the last day of the inclement weather, when the noon sky makes a horrific sunrise of purple and black, Katherine Guiteau and Trip Holbly marry in St. Mary's Church to the mood music of warning tornado sirens and steeple bells. Katherine, in a white satin dress buoyed with crinoline and lace, is escorted up the aisle by her maternal grandfather, Dominic Garfield. The couple hosts their wedding reception in the vaulted marble undercroft whose corridors are named after Katherine's grandfather after all of her grandmother's donations. Aurelia, a white ghost in a wheelchair, who gave her granddaughter a pair of freshwater-pearl earrings to wear, is steered through the Tyson Guiteau memorial tunnel. Katherine likes to think of her grandmother's nodding head as a sign of approval, although when she makes her way over to kiss Aurelia on the cheek, her hands and shoulders are also bobbing up and down. "You must always keep those pearls with you," Aurelia tells her, squaring her gulleted eyes on the bride's earlobes. "Some things have to remain in this family, understand?"*

Katherine teaches freshman history at a small Catholic college on the east side of town, while her husband tars driveways into gleaming black pastures for grazing luxury cars. Their own two-floor Queen Anne has the deceptive look of affluence as well, due to Trip's skimming of unused construction supplies from job sites. He is responsible for the greenhouse addition that bubbles from the back and that inadvertently kills birds, sometimes three or four a day, which fly into the polished glass and collect dead on the porch, a mortuary of cardinals and sparrows and brilliant, suicidal blue jays swept into mulch bags on Sunday morning. He also draws a large dirt oval in the backyard, outlining the swimming pool he begins to dig by himself in 1971. Katherine is obsessed with committing the progress of the pool to film, with two years worth of shots of her husband disappearing into a hole in the ground, hands on a shovel, his torso glowing and an orange Cincinnati Bengals T-shirt tied around his forehead to soak the sweat.

Their son crawls into their photos in 1973. Joseph Thomas Guiteau Holbly arrives like an ambassador of peace, bringing all of them together, a fat Buddha baptized at St. Mary with a diaper rash and green socks with crocodile teeth stitched along the toes. He's the solid wrinkled future, the aftermath of astonishing love. Even Aurelia, who takes forty minutes to descend from her attic bedroom to the front porch, hails the child as a blessing.

"He's so little," Trip says, bending over his mother-in-law Christine, who is bathing her grandson in the tub. "How do they make it to adulthood? He's as fragile as an egg."

"Trip," she whispers so her daughter won't overhear. Katherine is upstairs grading exams in her study, covering test sheets with bloodstains from the red Sharpie she uses to correct errors on wars and generals, battles and court justices. "You must watch her. She doesn't spend enough time with him. She shouldn't have gone back to teaching so soon. He needs to be with his mother every second, not with me. He'll come out wrong not having her around all day."

"He'll be fine, Mom," he replies. He calls her Mom—that's how close this family has gathered together around Joseph's arrival. "He's going to turn out perfectly," he assures her. "I won't let anything bad happen to him."

DOES IT HELP to tear the world down before you go? To show what little there was to love in it and what unhappiness you found therein? Does that make the leaving easier? Aleksandra bent over Joseph in her bed. Her cold hands smoothed his cheeks, as atoms of dust swam through the cleft of light that broke from the closed curtains. She asked him—without a trace of sarcasm—an indecent question while he lay dressed in an indecent three-piece suit: if he died, what would he miss most?

"I'm not going to answer that," he said, folding his hands resolutely on his chest. But the macabre game had already started to play in his head so he answered to humor her. "Travel. Going places I never got around to visiting."

"You'll miss places you haven't been? That's a bit of a contradiction, isn't it?" she said. "You'll miss airports, vacuums of time. Is it possible for anyone to love an airport waiting lounge?"

"No, I mean the getting there. I always wanted to see Istanbul. The flood of the Bosporus pouring around the boats. The clamor of markets."

Aleksandra shook her head. "Tourist traps smelling of goat shit and German BO. And that awful whine vibrating out of mosque speakers calling everyone to prayer. It's a constant headache, that city."

"Okay, the Amazon. The Pyramids in Giza. The reefs cutting through the blue waters off Tulum."

"Malaria. Terrorist targets. Overfed tourists bubbling around just to startle the last tropical fish. Is that really the best you can do? You've lived for thirty-four years, Joseph. Give me something with teeth."

Her voice held out the challenge in the same manner that acting coaches used to implore him to deliver a line with more "gut," and Joseph searched for a better impersonal answer. A personal answer would cost him too much.

"Dreaming then," he replied. "I'll miss dreaming. Sleep."

She shook her head again. "Here lies Joseph Guiteau in the position he liked best."

"Alcohol. Getting slowly drunk as the sun dips. Feeling all worry spin away along with your balance."

"An evil drug with diminishing returns," she sermonized, lying down next to him to stare up at the same patch of ceiling. "We all would have been stronger people with less of it. Are you really going to miss being reduced to nonsense?"

"Sex."

"If it were ever really fulfilling, its greatest practitioners wouldn't come off as starved."

"Jesus."

"Is that an answer or just commentary?"

"Revolution, then," he improvised, propping his head on his elbow. "Group dissatisfaction amassing in the street."

"Which one were you ever part of? They're a nasty, nasty business."

"Movies. Books. Poetry. *Bad poetry*. Liking the things you know are junk. Consuming junk and smiling. Junk for junk's sake."

"Commercials?" she suggested. "The ones you starred in? How about those? I'll place them in the time capsule. You really want them remembered?"

The chess game went on this way, each answer immediately and unequivocally devaluated like bad stock, as Joseph offered the smell of rosemary and the first cracks of dawn after a sleepless night, salted steaks, certain nineteenth-century paintings, Gandhi, wildlife documentaries, the ghost of the moon on summer days, even a grating Irish comedian known for vulgar pop shots about the female anatomy. To all of these vague, sacrosanct submissions, he received an instant critique of their non-meaning in the growing whirlpool of abysmal fluff. He went for high roads.

"I guess I should say children. Children. But I didn't get around to having any."

The answer produced a grunt. Aleksandra drove an instinctive arm against her belly and rotated on her side.

"That's the go-to answer. I'm afraid I can't go to it either. Do you think you care more about the future of the planet if you've unleashed your chromosomes onto it? I wonder. Kids are a safe bet, though. Kindness is good. Loving others, it's hard to dispute that."

"How about falling in love?"

Aleksandra laughed. "More nostalgia, the worst, most malicious strain." She stroked his cheek with her knuckles in consoling condescension, and her eyes hardened like she was dispensing some sage advice to the obstinately naive. "You're trying to get back to those first times, chasing after the original high. And the older you get the more you find you're just acting, and the part is a little less dignified and more unbearable each rehearsal. You're an actor. You must know what it's like not to believe your own lines." Joseph was genuinely surprised by Aleksandra's critique. Hadn't it been love that kept her writing the pages of her script, trying to rescue her husband in words after he could no longer be rescued from life? She slipped her fingers under the lapel of the coat. Her fingertips softly followed the curve of his ribs through the wool vest.

"I'm out of answers," he said wearily. "You have such a delicate way of making it all sound so cheap. I didn't realize you hated the world so much."

"Hate the world," she repeated lovingly. She buried her face into his chest and then resurfaced. He could see the plumbing of blue veins traced around her eyes and the corrugated networks of wrinkles on either side of her mouth. They had not kissed again and had not spoken of it, but ever since that brief, inexplicable moment of affection passing between them, Aleksandra had become more solid and substantial. She was no longer the fragile woman who spoke in a quiet monotone as if always on the point of disappearance. Her hands continually rushed to keep hold of him as if to prove that he were still in the room with her, and he could imagine her as the woman she must have once been before her husband had been killed. The fear and paranoia that had clung to her in all of those weeks seemed distant like a bout of sickness. Maybe Aleksandra had just been lonely after all, trapped in a past that wouldn't let her touch it, and she had accepted that loss as a permanent condition. Her need to touch him came like a sudden panic as if she wanted to ensure that she was no longer stuck in this hotel room, or this city, all alone. Joseph had not mentioned the letter she had received and neither had she. Maybe it was possible simply to forget. Maybe forgetting was the only rational way to deal with the past.

Aleksandra blew a scant hair from her eyes and twisted on her side. "But really what is there?" she asked, stretching her neck until the wine-glass birthmark lengthened to a scarlet arrow. "What is so wonderful that makes forty more years of living worthwhile? You should just be happy with what you had. If we've achieved anything over animals, it should be a little comprehension that the triumph of existence isn't simply surviving as long as you can. We'll be forgotten, all of the beauty and difficulties will be wiped out of memory, and the struggle will all have proved . . . what? Food, sex, and vacations? Like our lives are postcards we send off to people who barely bother to read them when we die?" She shook her head and rolled over to let her jaw rest on his shoulder. He knew that she was tearing the world down for his benefit, and maybe Aleksandra was as aware as he was of how unconvincing she was at playing this part. Forgetting wasn't an option. Aleksandra had already made it too clear that she was not the kind of person who could let go easily. Still, he pressed his hand over hers to thank her for trying.

"Okay, my final answer is Ohio." Before she could argue, Joseph heard the hesitant knock of the cleaning women at the door of the outer room, the slide of the card key in its sheath, and the whine of the supply cart as its wheels rolled over the carpet. Their job was to make the place look as uninhabited as possible, to clean up people's messes until even the boarders returned to find a room that wasn't their own. And that, of course, was a hotel room's principle beauty. The Carlyle was limbo, beautiful, antiseptic nowhere, where life could go on not living itself out. It was the space-time equivalent of a hold button, and that's why Joseph had learned to feel so ecstatically not at home here.

"I'll get rid of them," Aleksandra said, crawling across the bed. There was one obvious answer that would have stopped the game with a single word. He could have added Del to the inventory, the one person whom he had rushed out of his life to marry and keep hold of when he could barely keep hold of himself, for a little while at any rate, for long enough to imagine that kicking violently would do any good. That's what love is, he thought, kicking violently, getting off of the world that won't let you go.

"I want to change my answer," he said, when Aleksandra returned.

"Which one?"

"All of them."

She stood over him, the lightness of her face collapsing into worry. Her eyes were as dark as footprints in day-old snow. She pressed her fingers against the shoulders of the wool suit—Ray Andrews's three-piece suit with its gray vest buttoned across his abdomen, the jacket splayed open to reveal its purple silk lining, and his bare feet snaking out of the tailored cuffs. He had done that for Aleksandra, put on one of the suits that belonged to her husband so she could see it filled again. She said it brought her comfort, even if it were an ersatz Ray lying there with his mind on another wife. She climbed over him on the bed.

"You do look like him a little bit," she whispered. She squinted as she stared down at him, perhaps to trick herself into seeing Ray below her. "You breathe the same way, out of your mouth instead of your nose. I can remember it now."

There were two days to his birthday. Sex, malaria, children, praying Muslims—that's what the world was screaming with and none of it would be missed. He buttoned the jacket to fight a chill. Aleksandra smiled. There was still time for kindness. He would do that for her. He'd give her some comfort even if it wouldn't last.

ON A JUNE day *in 1978, Trip is shingling the roof of a neighbor-hood bungalow, and the temperature is steaming past 103. There has been some fight among the workers, mostly Harley drivers with tattoos and pony-tails and with kids living with ex-girlfriends' relatives. There was a radio playing Bob Seger that one of the workers kicked off the roof. Trip tells everyone to take an hour off to cool down. He drives back to the house on his lunch break, parks his truck in the driveway, strips to his underwear in the upstairs bathroom, and removes his teeth. He dives into the pool.*

When the department secretary appears at the door of the classroom, Katherine has just scrawled "personal conflicts in the Bull Moose Party" across the blackboard for twenty delinquent summer students. The secretary's face looks sallow behind the meshed rectangular glass, and she can't get the words out. She waves for Katherine to follow her. Outside on the college lawn clicking with sprinklers, she manages "something's happened."

Katherine learns it happened so quickly he probably didn't feel it for more than a moment. But the coroner's report finds water in his lungs as well as a ruptured artery, making it difficult to determine if he felt himself drowning, taking in water, while he struggled against the pain driving through his chest. The cause of death should be heart failure—or rather it should only be heart failure—but he died of drowning before his aorta could do him in. The next door neighbor, Mrs. Emily Gehlert, says that she never heard a struggle or a cry for help.

The coroner says the heart would have burst anywhere—in a pool or in his sleep, lifting a hammer or lifting his son. The official report lists "aortic dissection," a surge of blood released from the heart, opening a rip in the lining of the main artery. Death was excruciating but rapid, blood spilling into the open cavity as water fed into his mouth. The ICU doctors feel the need to press the point that the tear wasn't caused by swimming, as if they are worried that Katherine might blame the death on her husband's decision to swim alone in the backyard pool during a workday.

Christine buckles her grandson into the front seat of her car. Fifteen minutes later, they walk through the automatic doors of Christ Hospital and find Katherine sitting alone in the waiting room. She wears a blue silk blazer and two silver beaded necklaces. Her lips tremble, as her hands massage her forehead. All she keeps saying is, "it's so hot," like she's been saying it over and over and now that two people are standing in front of her to hear it, she isn't sure if she is asking or telling it.

THEY WEAR BLACK. *They sing in the front row of St. Mary's, "Amazing Grace" and "Here I Am, Lord," and they follow a coffin that looks too small to hold a man as big as Trip Holbly. The hot June air scorches the church grass the color of rust.*

Trip Holbly doesn't exist in the house after the funeral. Not the man, anyway. In Joseph's mind, his father dove into the backyard pool and never climbed out. Katherine doesn't cry at the cemetery. She keeps counting with her lips, touching thumbs to fingertips. She looks like a woman trying to work out an intractable math problem, as if it will answer what she was doing on that field of stones wearing too many layers in the dead of summer.

JOSEPH HEARS THEM *in the kitchen. His grandmother is sipping coffee, while his mother walks around opening the freezer, closing the pantry doors, tapping her nails across the counter, turning the faucet on and off, checking the water pressure with her fingers.*

"Trip died of drowning," his grandmother whispers. "I saw the death certificate. I spoke with the doctors. It's not the same thing."

"He died of his heart," Katherine whispers back angrily.

"What difference does it make? He's not a blood relative. He's not a Guiteau, he was a Holbly, so it isn't the same." She takes an anxious sip of coffee and struggles as the wheels of her chair keep rolling her away from the table.

"How old was dad when he died?" Katherine asks, not expecting an answer but to prove a point.

"Don't bring your father into this mess," Christine replies gravely. "That was too long ago. What you need to do right now is grieve. Real grief, not this twisted mumbo-jumbo logic variety. Have you gone out to the cemetery? Have you taken his son out there? Who's going to pull the weeds if you don't?"

"I don't give a damn who's going to pull weeds," Katherine snaps. "Why is everyone in this family so concerned with weeds? And don't you dare lecture me about history."

"Please, honey, you must stop obsessing like this. There's no one to blame. Not you. Not your own family. Trip drowned, he's gone."

"Thirty-four, mother. That's how old Trip was. Just like Dad. Like Grandpa. On and on."

"He drowned." Joseph's grandmother bangs her coffee cup on the table and starts crying. They don't talk for several minutes, and Katherine finally runs upstairs, beating down the hallway and slamming her study door. Joseph hides in the dark foyer closet, like he does every day for hours that summer. In some way he believes that if he hides there, he might be saved, that the killer won't find him and will eventually leave them alone.

That summer is also the last of the birds. After Katherine has the pool filled in, Joseph stands in the greenhouse addition with his cheek pressed against the glass. He goes completely still, barely breathing, while birds fly into the windows. He feels the impact of the hit on his face, and watches them drop to the ground, one every hour, like clockwork. Finally, Katherine has thick tweed curtains installed, which cover all of the windows, turning the greenhouse into the darkest room in the house. She tells her son that they can't open the curtains anymore, that it's cruel to kill so many defenseless creatures like that just for a view of their own backyard.

At first Joseph thinks that it is her way of controlling death, of keeping more of it from touching them. That isn't it. It proves to be just the beginning of her descent, the trial run for what is to come. The counting gets worse too. Trip Holbly doesn't exist in the house after that day in June, but his ghost does. Two years later Katherine legally changes Joseph's last name to Guiteau. It isn't a widow's reprisal to strike the Holbly clan from memory. She's merely correcting a loophole in history. She's adding her son to the family count.

CHAPTER THIRTY-NINE

DEL DANCED LIKE she was drenched in gasoline and fire licked her knees. Her bare feet kept time, dirty heels crashing backward on the hardwood, and her hips dissolved that metronome in fast swaying. She lifted her arms over her head, hands winging like giant hunting hawks, and then dropped her hands on her face, black hair covering her eyes and nose.

If she can move, there is hope. If her blood beats, there is hope. If her tongue can form a word, there is hope.

Del danced alone for the length of two '70s rock albums, the turntable cranked to its highest volume. She never looked over at William on the couch, never asked him to join her, lost in her own drunken orbit of where the music took her as she sipped from a bottle of scotch. Nor was her dancing for William's benefit; she was dancing in spite of him—or, better yet, to spite him. The message: *This is my home, you aren't welcome here. This is my noise, my private rite, and you're not invited. The only thing you can help yourself to is the front door.*

She lit a cigarette and consulted her wristwatch. It was almost midnight, and Joseph wasn't home. He had left her alone at first, she thought, because she needed distance. But every hour tonight increased the feeling that maybe he had just left her, running off to his own secrets that he never let her in on. And here she was, trapped with this stranger whom she never liked, while clear across the island Raj kept his own vigil that no longer involved her. How alone she felt tonight in the solitary confinement of the living room, how many years she had thrashed only to end up here with her own arms wrapped around her. She had tried calling Joseph but his phone went to voicemail. She had wanted desperately to call Raj but feared the stalemate of silence on the end. What could she say to him if he answered? Drunkenly, she spoke the word in her native tongue: *oikía*, home. She could say whatever she wanted in Greek but no one would understand her.

The apartment was lava hot with the windows only cracked open an inch, and the air thick with her smoke. She was purposelessly hotboxing William, filling the room with her sweat and cigarettes until there was no oxygen left without her angry taint mixed in it. She jacked her body straight like a switchblade trying to find the pulse of the music but stopped as she caught her reflection in the lit glass of the window. Her hair hung in a tangle down her back. Her skin was phosphorescent but darkened with muddy clumps of eyeliner over swollen eye sockets. Dancing to the most contagious form of American culture, she looked like a foreigner marooned in a nightclub far from home.

The song ended and Del collected her breath with a hand against the wall, the bright lights of the room throwing her shadow across the ceiling. There was a jumpiness in her eyes and a sag to the lips that made her look lost, and sorrow burst forward like a crowd spilling out of an arena when a concert ends, running and screaming with pandemonium, unbeatable sorrow flowing from her eyes and mouth as she tugged on a silver necklace to pull it from the sweat of her neck. She lifted the needle from the record.

"I loved that album," she said.

CAB LIGHTS FLOATED down Broadway. She felt as if an invisible protective seal had fallen off of her, and, as she finally managed to wave down a cab, she realized that the invisible seal had been her youth.

It hit her like a piano falling from one of the penthouses laced in white Christmas lights, the sound of the keys and wood crashing onto the concrete, a boom louder than it could ever play when pieced together. The only action that filled her life was that of waiting— waiting for a green card, waiting for December, waiting through the last days of her job to see her into a future that held no other career. Waiting around like an old woman to make sense of what her life had become. Youth can handle its failures; it can wake from its botched love experiments wound-licked by its own survival mechanism— that there would be something else around the next corner. The survival mechanism of those who have lost youth: laziness, habit, the fear of falling down.

The cab sailed by club entrances lit red like ovens, dungeons of love with young women cooked in the haze of the doorways. Above them, apartment lights glowed, and bedroom televisions flashed unending blues and pinks. The whole city was pulsing with electricity. It had been all of this light that had first attracted her to New York, had brought all of the fresh arrivals beating around the same shine. But what happened when her eyes finally adjusted to the light? In the reflection of her living room window she saw a lonely married woman in a tiny apartment too tired to remember what she was waiting for. The alcohol was pushing thoughts through her head fast and jumbled, and the most reckless seemed the most illuminating. Madi would have told her that she was just feeling sorry for herself. But Madi wasn't around to tell her anything anymore. What was the survival mechanism to guard against self-pity? She rolled down the cab window and lifted her head out into the cool wind of Twenty-Third Street.

Wouldn't it be a relief if a tornado moved through Manhattan and wiped all of the garbage away? Wouldn't it be wonderful if a tidal wave cleaned all of the windows and watered the trees? Wouldn't it be magical if fire melted every skyscraper into pure molten liquid and eradicated all of the documentation on who was an immigrant and who was not, and they could all start over, in the scraps of what had been? It was a sick perversion of youth to romanticize destruction, but it was also perverse to wake up every morning and be repaid in such little happiness. She thought she could hear the city's message in the air curving around her ears: *I made you no promises. If you can't stand it, leave.*

Why was she so insistent on staying here anyway? Greece had been windblown lavender, the soft pebble beaches that cooled the palms of her feet, not new, very un-new, but un-terrible and sweet with uncomplicated currents. She could have lived all through Europe without having to sacrifice a single night's sleep worrying about a green card. And that was the brutal revelation, wasn't it? Maybe she had made a mistake to marry Joseph. She had loved him but not enough; they had known each other but not entirely. She had married him for the green card—that was drunken honesty in a cab ride late at night. She would have married Dash and she would have married Raj. It had been her own survival mechanisms that had led her down to City Hall two months ago with Joseph. But now survival was no longer on her mind.

The cab rolled over potholes, and Del noticed the condemned two-story buildings anchored on the West Side Highway, once home to strip clubs and adult-video emporiums that had long been raided and shuttered, their paper proclamations of HOT, NUDE, CHEAP still peeling from putrefied walls.

She paid the fare and climbed out the backseat, hurrying toward the bell. As long as she still can move, there is hope. As long as she still can speak, there is hope. She pressed the buzzer for his apartment.

"Hello?" the familiar voice boomed in the near-empty street. Streetlights flooded down on the green dumpster where two rats ran under its rusted wheels.

"Raj, it's me. Can I come up?"

She didn't know if she should expect him to open the door. She wasn't even sure what she would do if the door opened. But when it did, she almost cried.

CHAPTER FORTY

THE CHILDREN WHO *grow up in Cincinnati in the '80s learn about the world on the evening news. They sit night by night at dinner tables watching the Iran-Contra hearings and Reagan's assassination attempt and the epidemic of AIDS escalate from a disease that plagues viceless coastal cities to hospitals and dental offices in their own backyards. They learn such hard-hitting facts about their world mostly from one leading news anchorman. He sits at a news desk as a sincere arbiter of international affairs and closes his commentaries with a comforting message, one, it could be said, appropriated from a children's storybook: "Take care of yourself, and each other." Children love him, and they see the world.*

In 1991 this man takes a second job in television, hosting a daytime talk show in Chicago. No child accustomed to this venerated man beaming into their kitchens each night feels particularly reassured watching him heckle incest victims, interview closet plushophiles, or encourage punches in a nail fight between transsexual prostitutes. What is the truth and where did it go? The stories bleed together, two outposts of televised reality losing their sovereign glue. From 1991 to 1993, this leading anchorman reads the Channel 5 news and hosts The Jerry Springer Show *on the same network.*

Every fact depends on its source. If the source is corrupt, the fact should be disregarded. What we know depends on the veracity of who is telling it. Such obvious logic blurs in the prism of Cincinnati.

WHEN JOSEPH LOOKS *back, all he sees are conspiracies. Not just with his mother—that's too easy—but a bigger, more devious variety that collects over the sprinkler-clicking lawns of his upper-middle-trying-to-be-upper-upper neighborhood. Those Midwestern mothers and fathers hide facts every morning under the shirts they button and the skin-toned stockings they roll to their waists. They want their children to believe, no matter which reality Jerry Springer is spinning on the television set, that Ohio is locked-in, state-padded, farmland-pillowed, and as long as they keep office hours they can keep living in their two-story Tudors with the Sunday football games shouting over snacks fresh from airtight bags and the days can go on forever, they can, like this, on and on, magically, forever. Every wealthy neighborhood is a confluence of dreams, as bright and intangible as the dew that collects on the grass each morning. And it is a hopeful promise for those who could afford to keep it.*

How can you blame these deceitful mothers and fathers? Isn't this precisely what everyone wants? The right to unremitting peace, the assurance that nothing goes bump or blast, that families can be just what they are: families birthing more families on sprinkler-clicking lawns while football games go into overtime over bottomless chip bowls.

The gentle, infectious peace of Cincinnati gives Joseph's generation a mild headache, like riding too long in the backseat of a car. One look at Joseph's grade-school class and it's apparent that these offspring of so much protection and love have little chance as happy inheritors. Petty, mean, ruthless cabals of hostile socialites, sharp-eyed for easy weaknesses, they are mean, vengeful children, and Joseph fits right in. They are Ohioans. Proud, nasty, beautiful Ohioans. Because they don't have outsiders, they make each other into them.

So, by the local squint, Joseph grows up relatively normal. Except, of course, for his heart.

AFTER SCHOOL, KATHERINE *takes him to appointments with area specialists. The doctors draw blood, run him through scanners, x-ray his ribs and lungs, strip him down to his electric-blue underwear and bring in colleagues to stare in awe at his sunken breast bone and pale left nipple. A few expert cardiologists, aroused enough by the Guiteau family history to fly four hours from Cedars-Sinai Heart Institute in Los Angeles, talk to Katherine in pleading whispers, hoping to write treaties and present her son at regional medical conventions. One Xavier University documentarian even asks if she can periodically follow Joseph around with a camera until he turns thirty-four, recording the "paranoia and being choices" of an abbreviated human life span. Katherine dismisses all opportunities for early-death stardom. She wants to keep the paranoia close at hand.*

Katherine Guiteau remains a college professor in and out of the classroom. She is an empiricist in the old sense, constructing her lectures on American history the same way that she draws up the death warrant on her own son's heart: by observation and recorded evidence. Facts do not shift in transport on their way to the vague ether of the theoretical. The eight Guiteau birth and death certificates that she collects tell all she needs to know on genetic predisposition. Eventually when the doctors fail to find any physical aberrations in Joseph's heart muscle, Katherine stops scheduling appointments. She takes Joseph on as her own assignment.

The greenhouse addition is the first room to be sacrificed of sun. The rest go later, window by window, year by year. For Katherine, pulling the blinds is a way of killing free time. Darkening the house assumes the same gathering tactic that other families utilize by building a fire or calling their children to dinner. Initially, Katherine doesn't remove her husband's artifacts from the house, packing only the most obstinate possessions like his cross-country skis and Holbly Builders job files into the far reaches of the basement. She leaves most of his things where they last fell. His bathroom door is shut in the upstairs hallway, the bulb in the ceiling socket unscrewed, but it still holds his clutter of loose change, nail clippers, and open cans of shaving cream. Trip's winter coats mix with theirs in the front closet. His shoes line up single file in their shared walk-in off the bedroom, and ties hang according to color from a bar on the other side of the door. Joseph takes his father's teeth from his medicine cabinet and hides them in a sock at the bottom of his underwear drawer. If Katherine notices, she doesn't say anything. She continues on, rifling through the mail, pulling out advertisements and election notices addressed to Trip Holbly and collecting them in a brown grocery bag permanently stationed by the front door. Joseph didn't really know his father. He was too young when Trip died in a swimming pool that had since been filled with concrete and covered with teak lawn chairs that have never once been sat on. Katherine keeps those remnants of her husband around not so much as if he still lived but as if he just left. It is Trip's death that defines his character. It eats and sleeps in the house right alongside them. Katherine has the widow's habit of closing her eyes and rotating her wedding ring. She wears it for the remainder of her life.

TRIP HOLBLY (GUITEAU), 1944–1978, 34,
HEART FAILURE (BY DROWNING), CINCINNATI

THOMAS GUITEAU, 1923–1959, 34,
HEART FAILURE (SEE BROTHER, VINCENT), CINCINNATI

TYSON GUITEAU, 1894–1928, 34,
HEART FAILURE, CINCINNATI

JOHNSON GUITEAU, 1867–1901, 34,
HEART FAILURE, CINCINNATI

JOSEPH THOMAS (HOLBLY) GUITEAU, 1973–2007?, 34?,
HEART FAILURE?, CINCINNATI?

Not martyrs of coincidence, these names that Katherine prints across the dry-erase board in her study. Not saints or sufferers, these Guiteau males that she clatters out on her electric typewriter, pausing before adding the additional question marks on her son's entry. Each is a link, a ruler of time, a pixel in a pattern that crystallizes faultlessly through the years. The fact that Trip is not a Guiteau by birth does not negate the design. It only suggests to this tenured history professor that a larger law is in effect. Dates are her expertise, her religion, identifying a necessary plot point in the procession of events. Katherine grows her hair long until it touches her waist. She puts on her makeup every morning and irons the wrinkles from her blouses and skirts. For a long time she does not speak aloud about the chance pattern of those names and dates, but they weigh in her mind until she can't sleep, creeping down the long hallway from her bedroom to Joseph's to stare in at him in the dark.

The opening lines of her first and only book, Chain Reaction: Premonitions by Historical Patterning, *read as follows: "To believe that history is a dice throw of coincidental actions that could have gone any which way is to accept chaos as the governing principle of life. Let's suspend chaos theory for the sake of thinking logically. Reader, don't fall into the illusory trance that time is moving pawns without intent."*

Two planes crash in a field. In the first case, all on board die. In the second, everyone survives. For most, the difference rests on the impossible variable of luck. For Katherine Guiteau, the results are rational—the movement of the wind, the speed of impact, the pilot's responses under duress, a fate that can be figured. Trip Holbly's death did not depend on a ripped aorta or the inability to breathe under water. She sees history doing what it does: fulfilling a promise no one else has the perspective to comprehend. No coincidences. No random chances.

It is hard to isolate the exact moments when Katherine Guiteau's belief in a strange, invisible hand guiding the universe starts to impact her university lectures. At some point her personal fear of all of the men in her family triggers a reevaluation of all historical events as a coded pattern. At some point she takes the world for a system, each death for a clue. The bookshelves of her study once held the wonders of histories and atlases, biographies on capitalists and convicts, minutemen, and Donner survivors. But slowly these chronicles are lost to new titles that come delivered in brown wrapping paper every few weeks by UPS: Assassination Theory; Kennedy and the CIA: Who Knew?; Lincoln's Killers; Lee Harvey Oswald: From Moscow to Mafia; The Calibrations of Poker. *The outdated orange wallpaper of her study is tacked with stills of the Abraham Zapruder film, atomic greens and gun grays caught in pixilated freeze frame.*

"We came together because of this," she tells Joseph one afternoon as he stares tentatively at the photographs. "Did I ever tell you that? You owe your life to what happened down there." When Joseph tries to resist this birth rite, she stands behind him, swirling his blond hair through her fingers. "We know things that we don't even realize we do," Katherine says quietly, almost as if the riddle is a soothing gesture, a mother's voice. "We're so used to looking at them day in and out, we forget that they have anything left to show us. But we see it. It's only frightening because it offers something that will change us."

Chain Reaction *is published by a small university press in 1990. At the moment of what Katherine believes to be her greatest triumph, her validation of several years of rigorous intellectual labor, the deans cancel her first day of American History II. Arriving to her classroom, she finds not students but campus security. They escort her back to her car in the parking lot without allowing her to collect her personal items.*

This final humiliation, this sentencing of an overactive mind chained to a history that no one wants to hear, proves her final break with the world. Two small but searing articles in the morning paper expose her heretical teaching practices as a perverse form of religious mania. Joseph's civics teacher, an ancient Jesuit priest who continually applies Vaseline to his lips, places the clipping on his desk and shakes his head. "I won't bring this up with the counselors," he promises. Katherine Guiteau followed that signal cliché of history—those who forget it are doomed to repeat it—but it doomed her for finding it there.

Katherine remains in her darkened bedroom with all of the lights off, the blinds pulled over the windows, the alarm clock by her bed unplugged, and leaves it only to gather her husband's possessions that have blended into their own over the years. She collects them slowly in her nightgown, ignoring Joseph as he follows her around the house asking her to stop. Coats, ties, winter boots, wallets, condoms, an assortment of arrowheads, the grocery bag of junk mail, and everything else in her immediate line of vision. She brings them out to the backyard, climbs the hill with her slippers muddy and her long fur slung over her shoulders and drops them into the pit where Joseph's father once burned fall leaves and summer nettles. She pours gasoline and lights a match, watching the smoke waft over the house and tunnel upwards into the January sky. Katherine Guiteau disappears. She strings thick wool over every upstairs window to keep the sunlight out. She doesn't even leave her bedroom when the wailing alarms of tornado warnings tell her to take shelter in the basement. Joseph sits on the edge of her bed and talks to a woman he can barely see. She reaches for his hand in the dark and holds it, her skin soft and warm and safe. She rubs the calluses on her son's palm and smiles. If he ever mentions the possibility of her venturing out of the house, maybe just a walk for fresh air, she wrestles her hand away and turns over on a pillow.

FOR THE MOST *part Joseph avoids her bedroom. He lives like a teenage bachelor, playing host to his grandmother, Christine, who visits on weekends and pretends that her daughter's psychosis is a passing phase. School life at his all-boy's Catholic high school: Choir Boys with BMWs and Attention Deficit Disorder, or some other title of an after-school special that doesn't*

*explain the daily lull of punches and communal push-ups and acne-stained
necks splitting out of white oxfords lassoed with St. John's regulatory poly blue
tie. Joseph has a few friends, enough to fill a cafeteria table, enough to cheer
him on at dress rehearsals playing Tom alongside a talcum-powdered girl
shipped over from St. Ursula cast as his mother in* The Glass Menagerie,
*or a Caiaphas tied with pillows around his waist in St. John's all-male
review of* Jesus Christ Superstar *(a whorish freshman with long red hair
wins hearts and, unfortunately for him, minds as Mary Magdalene). Joseph
picks theater because it is the extracurricular that eats up the most hours after
school. But he also chooses theater because it allows him the temporary escape
hatch from being Joseph Guiteau. Off stage, Joseph has a quiet laugh that
terminates his sentences as if he isn't fully committed to the words he speaks.
He is tall, his cheeks are blotched rash red, and his scraggly blond hair is
shaved on the sides and sprouts roughly into a rumple of bangs.*

*Joseph usually learns about raging weekend house parties that involve
live, sexually curious girls on the Monday morning after the fact. For
obvious reasons, friends rarely receive invites to slumber parties at his house,
and like every other American high school, St. John's exists on a reciprocal
trade economy, so he is rarely invited in kind. The few friends who do make
their way through the doors on Arcadia Avenue never see his mother, largely
because upstairs is off-limits to guests. He often tells friends that his mother
has an incurable blood disease. He tells them that she is afraid of people. In
both cases, he doesn't think it a total lie.*

*In the end, he leaves. He wants to get away from the house and its ghosts
and all of the men chain-linked to the years written beside their names. He
goes where no one knows the history of a death-prone family. He follows
that great summer migration of losers and misanthropists on their flocking
journey to coastal cities on the promise of bright-light anonymity. He leaves
at eighteen, after his graduation pushes him across the stage in tasseled penny
loafers and a blue cap and gown. He has already received his acceptance letter
from NYU, arriving like a prize plane ticket from a nonsensical game show
called College Admissions Roulette. His grandmother takes his picture by the
hood of her car in the parking lot.*

*At least Christine Guiteau is there to care for her daughter. At least she
understands.*

"Don't go," Katherine says in the blackness of her room. Only scant

flashes of light burn between the vertical blinds above her bed. She has begun reading books again, but she can never finish more than a few chapters before turning to another in the hope of starting out on a higher spirit. "Or do," she reconsiders. "But don't go far. I'm sorry I wasn't the mother you deserved."

He tells her that she has been. He tells her that he loves her. He tells her that he isn't going far. He lies to her as he holds her warm hand on the edge of her bed.

"You know, there's nothing wrong with you," he finally says after a long silence, and they are left staring into the dark shapes of each other. "Even if you're right about me, that doesn't mean you can't go on."

"I hope you don't believe that," she replies. As Joseph stands up to go, she places her hand on his knee, so softly that, for a second, he merely mistakes it as a final sign of tenderness. "I have something for you," she says. "It isn't anything really. It's these earrings that belonged to your great-grandmother. She gave them to me for my wedding. I know you can't use them. But maybe you can give them to someone when it's right." She lifts herself off the mattress and digs through her jewelry box with amazing precision. It occurs to him that her eyes must have become supernaturally accustomed to see in the dark, and that maybe she had been able to look at him clearly all along. "It's important," she says, pressing the two pearls into his palm. "Please take something. Something more than you've already got."

Joseph leaves Cincinnati with pearls and his father's teeth. The pearls fit in the holes between the teeth on the retainer. He gives the pearls to his first serious girlfriend in New York, who loses one to the lawns of Central Park and the other to the drain.

The teeth remain in a box under his bed. They remain there next to a gun.

ON THE MORNING of August 19, Joseph turned thirty-four.

He wore Ray Andrews's three-button suit to greet the sunlight pouring through the hotel windows. He placed his hand on his heart to feel its metronome under thick Italian wool. Aleksandra coiled next to him on the bed, her own dress rumpled from sleep. She was already awake, rubbing the tiredness from her face and consulting her wristwatch on the nightstand.

He had no intention of sleeping over. The evening pulled down so fast he couldn't even remember closing his eyes. But he had a distinct physical memory of Aleksandra's arms covering him through the night. He had wanted to be home for his birthday, to meet the anniversary straight on, to wake up in his own bed with Del at his side surrounded by the comfort of his own belongings.

He tried to lift himself up but his muscles collapsed under the weight of heavy lungs. He clamped his fingers over his eyes and gave in to the weakness, falling back against a mattress damp with his own sweat. He looked over at Aleksandra, her skin pale and grooved from the pillow, and his voice came out hoarse like it had grown stubble in the night.

"I have to get back," he said. "I have to go home."

Joseph wiped the sweat from his forehead and tried to breathe, but the walls of the bedroom seemed to close around him. His lungs weren't filling with enough air, as if Aleksandra, her face now inches from his own, were stealing the oxygen from the room. Rain drizzled on the windows. Even the honking traffic on Madison Avenue seemed acutely aware of wasted time. He leaned forward to swallow, and Aleksandra pressed her hand on his chest as if to help him inhale.

"Thank you for staying over," she said softly, nervously, breaking up her words with pockets of air. "I know you didn't mean to. But it was a comfort to me." She grabbed his hand and placed her fingers inside of it. "I never got to say good-bye to Ray. So it felt like tricking myself into having him here again. For one more night at least."

"You're welcome," he replied, not entirely honored by the sentiment. Aleksandra looked older in the morning light, like the hours of sleep had taken an exhausting toll. He couldn't shake the feeling that she might have stayed awake in the night just to watch him—to see some earlier version of her husband. Joseph pulled his hand away and stopped himself from telling her that this morning would be the last time he could visit her. In his mind he was already hailing a cab to Gramercy, climbing the five flights of stairs to his apartment, opening the door, and crawling into bed with Del. He was already back there, surrounded by the familiar objects that he had somehow managed to compile in sixteen years of living in New York.

"I want to show you something," she said and climbed over the side of the bed to open the white dress box on the floor. She returned with a small plastic bag in her hand, which held a simple gold ring. "When the police showed up at the door, they told me Ray was gone. Gone, like he had taken a plane somewhere, like they had lost sight of him on the highway. They wouldn't let me identify the body. They said he'd have to be identified by dental records since the gunshot destroyed his face. I begged the detectives to let me see him one more time. The dead aren't dead until you see them that way. Those officers were right: they're just gone. After the investigation ended and the detectives finally ruled it a suicide, they returned some of his effects. Brown shoes, his ring, a wallet with all of his credit cards still in their holders, the St. Christopher medal he wore around his neck. I spread them all out on the dining room table and examined each one to find a single drop of blood. They said there was blood everywhere, all over the front seat, blood and brain matter and splinters of bone." Aleksandra placed the plastic bag down gently on the bed and bent over it. She looked up to invite Joseph to inspect it, but he didn't want to. She placed her fingertip softly on the edge of the band. "Do you see it?" she asked. He wasn't looking. "It's so small. Just a little speck. The tiniest drop. That's all I have left of Ray. The smallest trace of blood to prove he was more than gone."

"I have to go," he said urgently. "I have to be home."

Aleksandra gazed up, half-hypnotized, and her face suddenly crumpled as if his words only made sense to her now.

"Stay for a few more minutes," she said. "Don't go yet. There's a surprise for you."

"No. I have to." He waited. "Aleksandra." He didn't look at her. He couldn't watch the imperfect good-bye pass between them like two people waving on opposite sides of a car window. But there was no more time to spend mourning for Aleksandra Andrews. There was no more time to mourn for anybody else. Why had he not found her endless grief so frightening all along? The way she studied the ring sent a chill up his back, and all of his memories of Aleksandra holding her husband's photographs, suit coats, and even the pages of her script seemed tainted with the same specks only visible to his wife. "I can't come back here for a while," he said. "I have some things to deal with."

"But you will come back?" she asked. Joseph kept his eyes on the floor to prevent looking at her face, but he could hear the anxiety crowd her voice. "Just promise me that you will."

"Yes. I promise. But not for a while." He waited to say one more thing—*Aleksandra, I can't be your husband anymore*—but she was already crawling across the bed and leaping onto the floor, where she rearranged her dress over her thighs.

"Just another minute," she said. "It's a surprise."

She hurried to close the curtains and darted out of the room. He could hear a cabinet open, the clink of metal, and an empty box dropped onto a table.

Joseph unbuttoned the suit, pulling himself from Ray Andrews's sleeves. He shed the wool pants, slipping them from his legs by yanking the cuffs. He stripped off the vest, flailing his arms free. He found his jeans on the floor and pulled them up to his waist. Quickly he grabbed the plastic bag that contained the ring and held it up against the sunlight. There was no blood on the metal, not a single drop.

Joseph saw the light beating into the shadows, orange flares carving the blackness. "Are you ready? Close your eyes," she said as she neared the bedroom. He didn't close them. Aleksandra stood in the door frame carrying a birthday cake on a plate, thirty-four candles like a small bonfire over the white icing that swirled with blue roses. The flames lit her face. "Happy birthday," she said, bringing the cake toward him. They were both breathing hard, in and out. Her face disappeared behind the runny candles beating long bobbing flames. She placed it under his chin, and he smelled the sweetness of burning sugar.

"Thank you for coming back," she said.

CHAPTER FORTY-ONE

RAJ STOOD IN the center of the gallery rubbing his hands. Now that he had made the artwork and hung it on the walls, he wasn't quite sure what to do with his hands. He tried shoving them into the pockets of his pants, ripping out the thread that had sewn them shut. He tried holding on to an empty plastic cup that cracked down the sides from his grip. He tried pressing them into the eager handshakes of collectors and fellow artists who offered compliments like "masterful," "seriously moving," or "what a beautiful testament to your sister."

His gallerist, Mirabelle Petz, overdressed in a black vicuña gown, was busy distributing drinks and angry glances to the loud, drunk twenty-year-olds who had descended on the Thursday night opening. She looked over at him onerously, although he knew that it was part of her business to keep the young entertained and amazed. He returned her look with a frazzled smile. The truth was he was relieved that the greasy, pretty Lower East Side contingent had shown up in their dirty sneakers, ripped T-shirts, and proud, boisterous body odor, laughing and scratching what facial hair they could muster, turning spilled beer into slick black scuff marks on the white polished floor. They broke the melancholy he worried might overtake his first gallery show, which could be accused of indulgently providing the memorial for Madi that he had once promised to hold for her in New York.

In the bright warehouse space, twenty photographs of his sister, each a foot high and framed in black, hung in a square on the far white wall. A few older couples stood in front of the portraits, pointing out details in her face as if they were tracing their fingers over road maps for the fastest route through difficult terrain. Raj studied the shots taken not even a month ago in his studio, each one a different version of his sister staring into the lens, self-consciously sucking in her cheeks, carefully plumping her upper lip, concentrating all of her efforts on her forehead to ease the wrinkles. Twenty Madis looked out at him, so alive and loving and still asking him to go to India with her and ridiculing their self-pitying parents and trying to make sense of the fact that neither one of them had managed a successful romance. Twenty unblinking, breathing visitations of a woman whom he had loved most and lost the fastest, blind to the terrible event to come, but now, for the month-long run of the exhibit, staring across the room at what lay only days ahead of her, cutting all of her hours into unfinished things. Raj turned his head 180 degrees to catch a view of the opposite wall. Blown up so huge that the colors were a pixilated patchwork of sunburst reds and concrete grays was the cell phone picture that Cecile Dozol had inadvertently captured of his sister dying in the street. The single photograph papered the entire wall, and to stand inches in front of it was to see only the pop abstraction of digital bleeps. The way to make out Madi's body in her red sari on the wet cement and the blue car speeding down the street was to see it from the distance that the twenty Madis did, from the viewpoint of the only woman who could not witness how her own life had ended. Below the giant cell-phone picture, a humming fluorescent sign spelled out KEEP GOING in white cursive. Raj had chosen that as the name of his show.

The first guests had slowly petered in like morbid curiosity seekers, none of them men or women Raj knew by face, and their frail coughs and whispered voices echoed through the gallery. The uncertain hush felt like an affront to Madi's memory, as if the larger world had already lost interest in her death. Raj had resigned the work to obscurity in the first hour of the show, but soon the small pools of visitors collected into a current that spilled from the door until Raj couldn't walk three feet without jostling into someone. He smiled, nodded, and kneaded his hands nervously. Right now it wasn't the photographs that worried him. It was the large, glass bell jar placed in the center of room, the only piece of sculpture standing midway between the competing walls. Inside the bell jar, hundreds of houseflies scrambled over each other, their red eyes bloated like gas masks, their silver-green wings fluttering against the cylinder walls. They gleamed like freshly poured blacktop, and visitors stepped cautiously around it. Raj was uneasy about this macabre inclusion, causing him to rub his hands more furiously. He had improvised the insects in the transparent container to fill the air and unite all of the dead white space that floated around the photographs. It was a testament to his earlier attempts to reveal the living, breathing traces in cold architecture, but, of course, there was no denying the fact that the flies were instruments of death. At exactly 8 PM tonight, he would lift the glass top to infest Mirabelle's warehouse space with a dark pestilence swarming in every direction.

Mirabelle had nearly vomited at the proposal—not in *her* gallery. But a second later her hazel eyes lit up with entrepreneurial glee, imagining the placement they would get in the papers for such a feat. Then she checked herself to fall in league with art-world solemnity. Only now, standing on the sidelines of his own opening, did Raj worry that the sculpture, like a grisly circus spectacle, cheapened the portraits of his sister.

Raj combed his shaky fingers through his hair. He nodded appreciatively at the compliments given by guests, avoided questions about his sister and his family, and accepted business cards that were misplaced forever inside the pockets of his suit. Standing by himself at the reception desk, he wished Del had not decided to return home to change. She had refused his conviction that her T-shirt and jeans were appropriate attire for his first opening. His eyes skirted the crowd. He wondered what was keeping her. Del was the only person who would understand what the work on the walls really meant to him.

They had woken late that morning in bed, his arms roped around her naked body. In that first moment of blunt surprise that she was lying next to him, Raj felt happier than he ever expected he could. The sunlight poured across the pocked plaster walls, motors wailed down the Westside Highway, and Del's back rose and sank with each sleeping breath. *People change*, he thought. *When they get older, they do. They get weaker because they understand the stakes.* He realized that morning that it was possible to reclaim someone counted as lost. When she finally woke, raising her arms in a stretch and smiling back at him on the other end of the pillow, he wasted no time in pledging his love. He told her he didn't care that she was married. He knew from the first day she told him that it had only been for a green card. He told her that she could remain with her husband until her citizenship was arranged—people did it all the time, stayed married and divorced when the papers were signed. He'd wait for her. Then he'd marry her himself if he could. Del wiped the tears from her eyes and stopped his frantic declarations with a palm against his chest.

"Please, Raj," she said quietly, as stunned as he was by the momentum of his words. He had never been this man before, loud and open and willing to accept all compromises, and he struggled to adjust, flailing his hands in fear that she would leave him again. He knew if she did he'd never be able to get her back.

"Tell me you don't love me," he had dared her, sitting upright on the mattress. If she told him that, he'd believe it. She lifted her hand and covered his cheek.

"You know that I do," she said.

They had remained in his studio all afternoon, a couple moving tightly on their own circuitry, and Raj swore he could feel an electric shock every time he touched her.

He glanced eagerly as the gallery door opened, hoping to find Del in its frame. Instead two party photographers ran over to blind the latest arrival with a battery of flashbulbs. Everyone turned and waited to identify the recipient of so much attention, growing quiet for a second in the collective awe of a potential celebrity gracing their midst. The hurricane of hunched photographers ebbed, backed up, still shooting through film just in case they hadn't arrested every possible angle. Cecile Dozol, her brown hair messily strewn in a pony-tail, her short tight skirt barely reaching beyond a baggy motorcycle jacket, wrenched herself away from the cameras and raced up to Raj. She gathered his shoulders in her arms.

"Congratulations," she said in her exaggerated French accent. She unlocked her giant yellow teeth as she pointed to her cell phone picture blazing across the wall. "The first time I have ever done anything that was placed in a gallery. I'm honored that I could give you this."

"Thank you for everything," he said sincerely. She cupped his hands and kissed him on the cheek. In a second, flashbulbs flooded their embrace, catching the necessary shot of unknown artist next to a societal somebody. Mirabelle Petz, face flushed, exalting the god of celebrity appearances, materialized by his side, feigned old acquain-tance with Cecile, and soon the two orbited into the sea of partygoers all waiting anxiously for the flies to be released at the end of the night.

Raj dropped his head in defeat, wondering if any of this mattered. It had taken him several speeches in his bathroom mirror as he got dressed to convince himself that he wasn't selling out his love for his sister to the shocks and starts of a cold, inhospitable art world. Raj shook his head to drive off the despair. When he looked up he finally saw her, the only woman left who meant anything to him, standing with her hands on her hips, her lips disappearing and then cracking open in a smile.

"It's for Madi," he said weakly, scared to open his arms for fear that she wouldn't accept them. He stiffened his back even as his heart muscles weakened. Del reached her hand out, and he took it. She smiled at him in approval, and he knew that he had done something he could be proud of.

"This is the best way to celebrate her," Del said, the bright white overhead lights creating constellations in her eyes. "I want every single one of those pictures. Promise to make me a copy of all of them."

"I don't want to think what Petz is trying to sell them for," he replied. He had so much more to say to her, the throat that had finally opened that morning now choking eagerly to make up for lost time. But Del rocked anxiously back on her heels, as if a little splinter of uncertainty had already managed to wedge between them in the hours since they last saw each other. She smiled and asked him when he was releasing the flies.

He looked at his watch. Five minutes to eight.

"Soon," he said. "You don't think it's disrespectful, do you?"

"Come on," she replied. "Madi hated these places. She'd love to have one last joke on all these sophisticates taking her pictures so seriously."

Del wrapped her hands around his waist and kissed him softly on his lips, enough to convince him that, at least for tonight, nothing else mattered. Not art or theatrics. Not an unsolved traffic accident that would never find peace in the arrest of the perpetrator. Not messages from his father demanding justice or even the fact that Del was still married and they would have to deal with those consequences tomorrow. For now she was here with him. And his pictures had succeeded in doing all that photographs can be asked to do: honor a split second that the world has already let go of.

"I guess it's time then," he said, steadying himself for the finale, although Del was staring over his shoulder at a man in jeans and a black sport coat inspecting the blue pixels of the hit-and-run car.

"What is William doing here?" she asked as the color leaked from her face.

"Who is that?"

"No one." She tried to recover, swatting the annoyance away with her hand. "It's not important." Mirabelle interrupted, her fingers tapping her wristwatch.

"Raj, go do it, and let's close up shop," she ordered in her heightened state of polite hysteria. "The best openings end when everyone's still enjoying. I'm worried the flies are going to get stuck in the air-conditioning vents. It will be hell to clean up tomorrow. Do it before the Health Board comes and shuts us down. Or, at least, before I change my mind."

He walked over to the bell jar in the center of the gallery. The youngest, bravest guests were crowding around him, waiting with

cringing mouths and twittering feet. The flies were the end of everything. They were the agents that quickened the decay, that impreg-
nated the dying flesh with their own embryos, that spun through
summer rooms like reminders that nothing would last, not even
them, dying belly up on a windowsill in a few short hours. Raj
grinned painfully in expectation, holding the expression of a man
who liked the poetry of this act on paper but suddenly felt absurd
when braced with lifting the container and letting the small pestilence invade the room. But he suppressed any last apprehensions. For
him, it served as a ritual, not Sikh nor Christian nor Floridian Singh.
Just for him and Madi. Art only makes sense if you believe in it.

"Do it, man," one skinny kid said through his T-shirt, which he
had tented like as mask over his nose. Several women started running
for the front door.

Raj looked at the twenty portraits of his sister, each of their faces
staring attentively out at him. *Come on, brother, tell me what you're
thinking. I'm the only person who has the same blood that you do. I know
you like the palm of my hand. Tell me, and no sugarcoating it either. Tell me
what you really want from this world.*

He lifted the bell jar. The swarm cycloned the air, eating the white
from everyone's eyes, a thousand black molecules exploding in all
directions.

CHAPTER FORTY-TWO

WILLIAM WAS ON his hands and knees in the living room. A hamster's nest of newspaper drifted around him as he searched each metro section for the tiniest fragment of news on Quinn. There were so many lurid murders happening every day in New York, entire columns devoted to knife-wielding subway riders, raped and strangled college students last seen drinking at clubs, Craigslist male escorts found tied and butchered in outer-borough dumpsters. There were so many murders, it was possible that a single death would simply disappear into the collective pool. How could this city have ever seemed like a sanctuary to him when so many killers and victims cruised through its streets, each part of the equation looking for its missing component in an endless sequence of crimes? The city's garbage was sent to Fresh Kills, the garbage people to Rikers Island. That's where William would go if he ever got caught, locked up on an island created out of the waste of this one.

William twisted on his knees as he read through the newspapers, spending hours that no subscriber could possibly afford to waste each day on every square inch of information. The lack of discovery only slowed the movement of the clock and invaded the room with an excruciating silence. Every time the phone in the apartment rang, William jumped in panic. The answering machine recorded voices of friends wishing Joseph a happy birthday.

He picked up the manila envelope that Rose Cherami had given him. He hadn't decided yet whether or not to give it to Joseph. Perhaps it would make the perfect birthday present, a perverse reminder that he was not immune to those tragedies that awaited their coverage in the next day's newspaper. *We are all potential fodder for those grisly dispatches*, he thought. *In the news one day and then out of mind forever as if to prove just how insignificant any life here was.* It had occurred to William to take the file up to the Carlyle himself, demanding money from Aleksandra Andrews to keep the documents from Joseph. But even alone and desperate for an action on which to focus his energy, William didn't want to get mixed in any more trouble. What he needed now was a solution. He needed to borrow money—a lot of it—from Joseph, and every hour he waited for him to return home, the brutal heat and quiet of the apartment increased his conviction that leaving New York was his only safe bet.

When the lock finally turned and the door opened, he stood up expectantly with his hands clenching the envelope. Del stumbled down the hallway, her eyelids already dipping in the fatigue of finding him there. She mumbled as she shot past him into the bedroom, pulled a red dress from the hanger in her closet, and ignored his hello as she shut herself in the bathroom. She walked out a few minutes later, her wet, black hair gathered over her left shoulder and fresh makeup darkening her eyes and lightening her cheeks. She moved toward the sofa with her head bent to claim her purse.

"Are you going to meet Joseph?" he asked her.

"Why?" she snapped back at him as if answering an accusation.

"Because it's his birthday," he said pensively. Del froze and looked up in surprise. Her lips grimaced, and, for a second, she hid her eyes in her hand.

"Oh," she sniveled. She took a moment to catch her balance and then placed the purse strap purposefully on her shoulder.

"I thought maybe you would wait for him. I'm sure he'll be back soon."

Another wounded expression pitted her face. She stopped at the hallway as if fighting whether or not to leave.

"I'd like to see him too," he hinted. He guessed that Del must be on her way to meet him. She must have arranged a party for Joseph and resolved not to invite him. Of course, she wouldn't want him there. She didn't want him here. But William already decided there was no more time left to wait on asking for a loan. He couldn't handle another morning of newspapers to define the only actions of his day. And he couldn't ask Del for the money, not for another two thousand dollars on the same excuse he used on her the first time.

"Are you going to a party?" he asked to force a confession.

"Yes," she replied, more to herself than to him. "I mean, no. Not one for you, William. It's none of your business where I'm going."

"But it's his birthday," he found himself repeating, almost whining out the words, as if he truly had Joseph's interests at heart.

Del leaned against the wall, shook her head to gather some last ounce of strength, and then turned. She hurried to the door and opened it. Her heels reverberated down the hallway steps.

William sprinted into the bedroom closet and selected one of Joseph's black sport coats. He threaded his arms through the sleeves, slipped the manila envelope under his armpit, and ran after her down the steps. What difference did it make now if he showed up unexpectedly? What could Del do but smile at his arrival?

She was half a block ahead of him. Church bells counted to seven, and the sky was dissolving from orange to black, sending silver echoes on eastern balconies. Del headed west across Broadway, taking the looks of paunchy businessmen with her, men who were returning from work to their own wives but dreaming of mind-blowing sex in every apartment along the way.

William followed her, keeping fifteen feet behind, a stalker's distance, staying out of range in case she happened to look behind her. She walked quickly, surveying roadblocks way ahead of her and swerving in advance to maintain her hurried pace. She raced all the way through Chelsea. William didn't have to pass under awnings or loop around bus stops. She was a distance runner envisioning a finish line. She never once bothered to look back. A soft wind was sliding through the city, snuffing out candles on outdoor bistro tables, blowing trash across the sidewalk, licking William's ears and, with a slight tilt of his head, blow-drying his hairline of sweat. The half-deserted blocks in far West Chelsea were loud with echoes from where they had been, which emphasized the quiet of the street they moved down now, a woman and her fidgeting shadow. Blackened art galleries started mixing with closed car washes under the rusted canopy of the old Highline elevated train tracks.

He began to quicken his pace, concentrating on the bones of her back wavering under her red dress, her neck wisped with delicate black hair, her thin, white legs skipping over dog shit until they suddenly stopped in front of a glass door. Del reached for the handle, but the door opened before she could grab it, and the sound of laughter and conversations swelled as a young couple danced onto the sidewalk with unlit cigarettes hanging from their mouths. Del disappeared into the gallery, and he could hear the celebration of so many friends inside.

William shoved the manila envelope into the waist of his pants, polished his front teeth with his forefinger, and drove his hand through his hair. He plunged into the crowded white warehouse space, grabbing a beer bottle at the reception desk, and cased the party with a respectful frown.

He searched for Del, which would lead him to Joseph. She hugged an olive-skinned man in the center of the room. She hugged him tightly. The man was skinny and hawk-nosed with skin as smooth as a wet pebble, nervous as a lawnmower as he treaded his fingers over each other, and then William saw Del lean in to kiss this man on the lips. There was no sign of Joseph anywhere or any other scant indications of a birthday celebration. He looked around the gallery for familiar faces who might also be witnessing the public demonstration of two lovers under bright overhead lights, and that's when the air went out of the room. His breath stalled in his throat. William was left to his own beating heart, staring at the far wall, where he found the photograph he had been running from since the first day he saw it.

He dropped the beer bottle. It clanged on the floor and rolled

against his feet. A thousand pixels built color and from color shapes
and from shapes the scene of a hit-and-run on a Tribeca street corner,
the very picture that Quinn had brandished on a page of the *New
York Post*. There it was, blown as huge as a billboard, an advertisement of his own guilt, the woman he struck lying in the street
and the blue car with its white bumper sticker speeding not fast
enough into the distance. A thousand pixels were washing into his
retinas making one clear picture that moved past the moment they
constructed: William racing away in the car, turning a corner, foot
on the gas, tunnel ahead, police waving his dented, bloodied grill
underground until he had come out the other side with everywhere
to run. He tried to swallow and checked to make sure no one was
watching, connecting the dots just as his eyes were doing now. He
turned to look at Del who had led him here to see this, then brought
his eyes back on the wall. Nothing added up. His vision swarmed
with yellow lights, and he fought to keep from falling to his knees.

He advanced on wobbly legs, one foot in front of the other, until
the hit-and-run dissolved into shapes, shapes into colors, colors into
a thousand pixels of meaningless raw blue cells and inside of them a
man in the driver's seat checking his rear-view mirror to make sure
that no one was watching him go. KEEP GOING read the neon sign
in front of him. The light whined faintly with electricity. *Keep Going*.
He had already done that.

He turned around and saw the face of the woman in twenty black
frames, puffy eyes and puffed out lips, like a collection of discarded
passport photos, serenely watching as the man behind the wheel now
nearly collapsed on the gallery floor. *A setup*. The realization almost
came as relief. William's thoughts reassembled in a scrambled dream
logic. *They brought me here to catch me. This is a trap*. His eyes quickly
scanned the room, scrolling for indications that this entire gallery
had been constructed just for him. Yes, everyone looked too clean,
too orchestrated in their matching clothes and forgettable smiles like
background actors in an elaborate stage set. They were all part of it,
each one playing a part, just waiting for the police to materialize out of
the white walls or for William to fall on the floor with a confession.
He tucked his hands into his armpits to keep them from lashing out.

But not a single person seemed interested in him. Only Madi Singh stared with cool indifference from twenty windows on the opposite wall.

What do you want from me? William asked her with silent lips. He tried to find the answer in the dead woman's forty eyes, dark little orbs pinpricked with a camera flash. What could he do now but beg her for forgiveness? *I'm sorry.* He wanted to yell that through the room. *My life was ruined too. I'm sorry. Forgive me and leave me the fuck alone.*

Forty black eyes aimed directly at his forehead. *Too late for that*, she seemed to reply, half-smiling, half-not. William's knees lurched as he tried to move them toward the door. He needed to get out, to run until he was out of Chelsea, off this island, gone from the entire state, the whole eastern seaboard far behind him, never to come back. He should have done that in the first place. That's when William started screaming at the top of his lungs.

Flies swept over him, a hundred maggots burying into his hair and skin. Flies sense rot hidden underneath the flesh, and they were sticking to his face and neck. He screamed through his teeth to keep the insects from slipping down his throat. He slapped his arms and stomach as the flies covered his fingers like chain mail. She had brought this on him. Right here, next to the photo of his crime, he could actually believe that. He imagined them pouring from her eyes, nose, ears, and mouth.

William wasn't the only person screaming in the gallery. But he was the only one who suddenly believed in divine retribution. He begged for help, "God, someone, please," and no one in the gallery bothered to watch him as he fell.

WILLIAM SLAMMED HIS shoulder against the glass door and burst out onto the sidewalk. He ran blindly, knocking into a woman, and then twisted around as he fell into the street. He landed on his side, his hands scraping against the cement. He lay there for a minute against the concrete, still flinching from the flies as if expecting more to descend on him.

"Are you alright?" the woman asked. Her fingers gently touched his neck. He looked up with his hands guarding his face and found worried, mascaraed eyes. William glanced around and noticed guests from the gallery assembling on the sidewalk, choking with disgust and laughing as they rubbed their arms and legs. His heart beat erratically under his sweaty shirt, but he slowly realized that the flies had not been a figment of his imagination. He lifted himself onto the curb, and the young woman stood over him with wisps of brown hair falling across her face.

William pinched the tears in his eyes. Her long red lips opened to expose twisted yellow teeth, which bit down decisively on a cigarette. She cupped a lighter, and the flame softened her skin. He felt the jerk of beauty, that familiar wrench to the gut when being in the presence of someone astonishingly beautiful. It was stabbing William even as his brain was still busy trying to make sense of the moment the world opened and flies shot out to swallow him. She wore a black leather jacket, and her bare legs traveled up to a tight, short skirt that, from his angle, barely covered her underwear.

"No, I'm not alright," he managed, then burst into a laugh, hiccupping as he wheeled backward on the sidewalk. "I really wasn't. But I guess I am now." His hands were raw from the concrete, and they stung when he pushed himself upright again.

"What's your name?" she asked. It took him a second to remember it.

"William," he replied.

"William," she repeated in the foreign elongation of vowels. She pulled her skirt farther down her thighs. "With pleasure. I'm Cecile. They were just flies, you know. Do you always lose your mind like that?"

"Lately," he said as he studied her. He recognized her. She was a model, maybe, or an actress, or some other scarce visitation circled in a halo from the streetlight behind her. Anything was possible now. He would take anything as long as he was free from ever stepping foot in that gallery, from ever looking at Madi Singh in the face. "The bugs were all over me," he said, rubbing his arms. "From that woman in there."

"Ah, yes, Raj's sister," she surmised with quiet reverence. "Are you a friend of his?"

"A friend of a friend," he said. "It's too awful. I've got to get out of here. I can't go back in there again."

"Yes, it's so sad," she whispered, examining his face and finding something that she liked in it. Her eyes narrowed. She shook her head, as if simultaneously admonishing and celebrating her own impulsiveness, and reached her hand out to him. "Well, William, if you are a friend of Raj's, then why don't you come along with me. I have a car waiting. We go to a party at a friend's place. Just try not to fall over, okay?"

Before William could even comprehend his deliverance from the gutter outside the gallery into the arms of Cecile Dozol, he found himself in the backseat of a black Range Rover, being driven by a man who introduced himself as Cecile's bodyguard. As they pulled away, William spotted Del walking down the street with the olive-skinned man she had kissed in the gallery. He felt the jab of the envelope on his stomach as he relaxed into the leather seat. He didn't care anymore about Del or Joseph. He didn't want to remember anything, no more visitations, no more photographs or newspapers or a body hanging from a sheet yet to be discovered in a cottage ten blocks south. William had no more energy to devote to those crimes. He let them go as easily as he released the grip of his fingers. He turned his mind to Cecile Dozol, as he watched the lights of the city blur through the tinted windows. The dead were gone, at least for now. He felt the lightness of being driven, no longer at the wheel, carried off by strangers with smooth shock absorbers and beautiful, beckoning faces. The Range Rover drove east. Cecile's bodyguard watched him distrustfully in the rearview mirror, and Cecile smiled at every green light.

CHAPTER FORTY-THREE

IMITATION WAS A Darwinist trick to ensure survival. Western diamondbacks were the snakes responsible for the most fatalities in North America, and their diamond coats and maraca rattles warned anyone who got close exactly what kind of bite to expect. But when Del returned to the Gramercy apartment the morning after Joseph's birthday, she wasn't thinking about rattlers. She was taking lessons from the non-venomous bull snake two cases down in the exhibition hall at the zoo. The bull snake capitalized on its superficial similarity to the diamondback, duplicating its dorsal patterning, mimicking the same strike posture, even manufacturing a hissing sound that impersonated the percussion of the rattle. Bull snakes were method actors, all color and no bite. Joseph was an actor. Imitation as survival.

She had not expected nearly three months into her marriage to fall back in love with Raj. But the world had changed since the morning of June 14, the ground had come unmoored, and the people she had loved most had been swallowed in its fissures. Abrams phoned her on her walk east to ask her why she had not reported to work for the last two days. Then he told her not to bother showing up for her last week of employment. "You've disappointed us," he said sternly before informing her that he had already found her replacement. The only thing keeping her in the country was a marriage almost three months old and a meeting scheduled for December 1 at Immigration and Naturalization Services.

As she steadied her key in the building door, she understood that imitation was her only possibility for remaining in New York. She had made her bed, so far from the country gilded on her passport and stamped across her face, and now she would have to continue making it, pretending love and happiness for total strangers, filling photo albums with pictures that told of youthful devotion, which did not have their basis in reality. Maybe Joseph would understand. He must see how far they had fallen out of each other's reach. He would understand, and they could continue on toward the day of that scheduled interview, two actors who loved each other but not enough to believe their parts.

She wanted to blame him. How much easier to walk in and accuse him of wrecking their marriage with some excuse about not being the man she thought he was. But Del couldn't pinpoint any moment that Joseph had proven to be anyone other than who he claimed: quiet and compliant, willing to let her live her life however she wanted, asking for so little that she had been left needing someone who asked her for so much. *What about my happiness?* she wanted to scream at him as she climbed the steps to the apartment, her fingers trembling over the railing. Her happiness—she suddenly realized how hollow that demand was, as if she could claim it as an inalienable right. What were her rights in this country? She had somehow been led to believe that happiness was promised here more than anywhere else.

She let herself in and tiptoed down the hallway. She found Joseph in bed, his skin still torched with a fever, his eyes glassy but staring up at her tenderly as she hooked her purse on the doorknob. She wished she had kept it in her hands. They were shaking uncontrollably. Would this be the last time? The last walk down the hallway, the last keys placed on the counter, the last view of the windows leaking their slanted Twenty-Second-Street light, the last glimmer of a husband who still did not know that another man stood in his place?

"I'm sorry I missed your birthday," she said, sitting down on the edge of the bed. She placed her hand on his arm. Touching Joseph was a habit, and she quickly pulled her hand back. Joseph nodded his head as if he hadn't expected her to remember. He didn't ask where she had been or why she was wearing a red dress that indicated a life already being lived beyond the confines of this bed. She stared into the corner of the room, as he pressed his fingers on her knee to bring her eyes back to him. When she finally relented, she was startled by how forcefully he looked at her. The last blue eyes. The last time they searched for her in their bedroom.

"There are things I haven't told you," he said, as he propped himself up against the wall. "I haven't been honest with you."

We haven't been honest with each other, she wanted to reply.

"There is something I kept from you because I didn't want to admit it. I was afraid what it would sound like. I didn't want to tell it to myself."

Here it comes, she thought, the moment of confession. I lied, you lied, we married too fast and resented each other for that decision. She almost wished they could skip over the details and admit defeat without having to bare their worst selves.

"Are you ready to listen?" he asked.

She rolled a cigarette and lit it. It amazed her as the moment of ending approached how much love came pouring back in—almost enough to repair the break. Almost. Like the first days of warm weather arriving in late winter, the sun glassing the city and making everyone believe the worst weather was behind them, just before a new bank of storms chartered east and paved the streets in ice.

"Joe," she sighed in resignation. "You can tell me anything."

IN THE TIME-SAVING unions of City Hall, there was no clause for sickness and health. In fact, there were no promises offered at all, no end to loneliness, no eternal blessing to remain devoted as long as you both shall live, no richer or poorer, or even, amid the mind-absorbing bureaucracy of paperwork and money orders, a scant mention of love. So what exactly had Del and Joseph promised to be for each other that June morning almost three months ago? If it had only been about a green card, why the blue silk dress and the pinstripe suit and the fight about riding the subway home and the ancient Greek recipe and the anxious twisting of rings? Was that simply to make the deception easier to swallow? They had promised each other so little. They had only said *I do* to the lawfulness of husband and wife. *I do. I don't now. I did once, maybe.*

Del didn't believe him. When Joseph told her the story of his family, going back four generations, she laughed hysterically. But laugher was only the smoke in the engine. When Joseph recited the list of names and dates that had once hung in his mother's study, when he did the addition to thirty-four, when he explained the same moment repeated in flawless symmetry, she jumped off the mattress in rage, kicking her foot against the bed to jolt Joseph's calm, lucid expression. She wanted to punch that expression right off his face.

Her mind raced with betrayal—a far worse betrayal than simple adultery. It was the betrayal of someone she loved telling her a ludicrous story to stop her from walking out on him.

"You're crazy," she screamed. "Have you lost your mind? Listen to yourself. Your mother was insane, and that's what you inherited. Jesus, Joe, I wanted you to tell me anything. That you weren't in love with me. That we rushed into everything too quickly. Anything but this *bullshit*. My god, you really are sick."

Del opened the closet to make a show of retrieving her suitcases. She splayed them out on the bedroom floor and began rifling through the dresser drawers before pausing as more anger found flint on her tongue. Suddenly every fallen promise—of him, of a green card, of remaining in New York on infinite autopilot—was striking the same loud chord.

"You people," she yelled in disgust. "I'm so sick of everything about this country. You do whatever you want and then pretend you aren't accountable like everything is beyond your own control. Conspiracies," she hissed. "You've invented this twisted idea in your head until you've made your body believe it. Well, guess what, that's not how life works. There's no destiny. You make your own or you die."

"I'm just asking for you to listen," he shouted while reaching out his hands.

Del felt the adrenaline of escaping, of leaving Joseph just as she had planned, of closing the door on him and running off. *We were an accident. Let's just chalk it up to that, and we'll be more careful next time.*

"You think I wanted this?" he asked her, pleading as she tossed every article of clothing that she could find on the floor. "If I wanted this I would have stayed in Ohio. I thought I could get beyond it. I'm afraid."

He was insane. He was an insane person manipulating facts in an attempt to keep her here against her will. She rounded on him, fingers slapping his face, her nails digging into his cheeks. She wrestled over him on the mattress and grabbed his chin so he'd be forced to submit to the spit flying from her lips. Her knees jabbed his legs, and her hair fell over his face.

"It's bullshit," she screamed an inch from his eyes. "You should have warned me that I married a lunatic. You want me to believe some stupid prediction that even doctors can't find? You expect me to listen to any of this? You were right when you told me your mother was crazy. Fine, Joseph, if you really believe that, let yourself die. Why should I stop you? But don't expect me to wait around for it."

"Why should you stop me?" he repeated in astonishment. "Why should you wait around?"

"You can't tell me this," she whined. "It's not fair. Not now."

He stared up at her, and a shiver ran through him like he suddenly realized that Del hadn't returned this morning for a reunion but for its opposite outcome. His eyes contracted. "But you're my wife," he said, as tears lit the corners of his eyes.

"Joseph, come on," she cried. "You know it hasn't been right for a while. Please understand." She crawled onto her knees and placed her fingers on his arm. He yanked it back, and that same shiver tightened the muscles in his face, as if he was beginning to sense the kind of woman that kneeled in front of him on their bed.

"Forget it," he said. "I didn't realize—I thought you'd listen and believe me."

She shut her eyes to gather that last reserve of anger that would see her out of the apartment and in a cab across town, but suddenly that future was crowded out by the tiny bed, the two small bodies tossing on top of it, and the two eyes tracking her as if she were a total stranger mistaken for someone else. Who that someone else was had become entirely clear to her. Joseph hadn't told her his family history to keep her from leaving, he had told her because he still believed that she was his wife. Del tried to recall the moment when they first met, to find the rips and flaws long overlooked that would have made this ending inevitable. He had given her a way out—if she had known this about his family, she wouldn't have married him. He had given her an opening. Leave now and take what you can from this wasted marriage. Run. She was free to hurry back to Raj, who would take her in his arms and they could live in the quiet of his studio and he would never ask her how she had managed to cut her ties with Joseph, knowing too well what indignities she had performed to bring such an ending into effect. She could be that person. She could desert her husband at his weakest moment and live with that memory until it no longer stung.

But Del was frozen on the single question Joseph now asked her. "Who are you?" he said like he still didn't know.

"Joe," she replied quietly. "It's too much to ask."

"You once told me you wanted to hear the worst, whatever it was. Well, now you have. Why did you ask me to marry you in the first place? Why did you bother?"

She remembered that night four months ago and wished she could forget it. That night she had felt her own future slipping from her grasp and had stared down at Joseph almost in tears. She had asked him to marry her, and he had said yes without a single untrusting beat. He had done that for her, saved her from her own life when she was certain there was so little left to save.

She bent over him on the mattress and pressed her cheek against his chest. Maybe it was her only way of saying good-bye to him. To hold him one more time. *Pity isn't love*, she told herself. But neither was selfishness. She felt the tremor of his heart against her cheek, the faint drum she had slept next to for the past ten months.

"I know it sounds crazy," he whispered. "I want it to be crazy. I can't tell you how many times I tried to find the right words to explain it. I was so scared. I'm scared there's nothing I can do to stop it from happening. Maybe it's nothing like you said. But either way, what am I supposed to do? I needed you to hear it. To help me maybe. I don't know."

She tried to find the voice in her head, the one that said so confidently this morning that her own happiness was all that she owed herself. She tried to imagine Raj waving his arms for her across town. But the question returned: *Who are you?*

She unclenched her muscles and let the air flow from her mouth. Joseph had only told her a story and asked her to listen. He stared down at her with his eyes narrowed, and she knew that he expected her to make good on her threat and leave. Yes, the ones who love you know exactly the kind of person you are. It's you who are constantly deceived.

She thought of Raj waiting in his apartment. She stared up at Joseph, so much older and more exhausted than he had looked when they first met. He was waiting for her too.

There was a sacrifice in every decision. Stay or go. Faith requires the sacrifice of a single leap. One day she would look back at this moment and she'd have to say, *I did this. Yes, that was me.*

She pulled her hand from Joseph's grip and wiped her eyes. She lifted up and swung her feet to the floor. She tried not to think of the man she was losing. She reached over and pressed her fingers against Joseph's lips.

CHAPTER FORTY-FOUR

AT NIGHT JOSEPH dreamed of his mother.

He slept in his bedroom in the house in Ohio, his ceiling lit with green plastic stars and the snow beating against the curtained windows. There was a hole in the house somewhere, an opening that had come uncovered from the thick wool fabric that hung over every window. He heard her racing around the rooms, floor by floor, as she searched for the hole, because she must have felt it. He felt it too, a rogue current of air sweeping up the stairs and over his bed. His body shivered. Then his mother was sitting next to him on the side of his bed. She placed his father's teeth in his palm and cupped his fingers over them.

Every night now, Joseph dreamed of her, and every morning he woke to find Del next to him, pressing her palms against his forehead and running to fetch him a glass of water. She had stayed by his side, nursing him through his fever and forcing aspirin down his throat to control his temperature. He was so glad to find her there, kissing her palms with their glass-white scars and appreciating her yellow-flecked eyes between long black lashes as she sopped a wet washcloth over his cheeks. At first he tried to tell her more about his family.

Now that the valve had been loosened, he had no end to the stories set to the backdrop of riverfront lawns and messy suburban houses. But Del shook her head. He had promised to let the past go, to stop willing the connections, to leave the dead where they were buried, and to concentrate on their life now.

Every morning, the sheets were soaked in sweat, but the pain in his chest was dissipating. His fingers and toes were numb, but his feet fit his shoes and he climbed from bed without feeling the churn of his stomach. He walked around the apartment forgetting about his body, leaving it for whole minutes and finding it later operating with no warning symptoms. *Maybe it is possible*, he thought, *that it was all just a trick of the brain.* Aleksandra had listened to the story of his family and had believed, and by doing so she had encouraged the sickness along. Del hadn't believed him. She told him outright that the past only mattered if he met it halfway. Maybe now he could bring his own mind to let it go. Joseph forced that point: *Nothing will happen. You're crazy to think so. Concentrate on what is.*

Del seemed surprised by his slow resurrection, his Midwestern face rising out of its skeletal underpinnings and flying toward her with a drive that he hadn't possessed even in their first months as a couple. But it didn't surprise him. Joseph had sensed how close their marriage had come to its own fault line, and, even in her fitful silence as she spent hours staring out of the window, he pressed himself against her until she relented. She laughed as he slowly stripped her out of her clothes.

She said his attention to her was embarrassing. Yet Joseph couldn't resist following her as she shuffled around the apartment looking through old books on reptiles, searching for a reminder of her earlier interests. He clung to her so tightly that she employed a soft shove to push him back to bed. He didn't tell her that the bed frightened him. Lying down, he was too attuned to every beat in his blood and when he closed his eyes, they were there, his family, only seconds into unconsciousness, taped under his eyelids.

His agent, Janice, phoned with her battery of auditions, but Joseph didn't answer. He listened to her messages later, angrily optimistic, and then, when not hearing from him, just angry, threatening to cut him from the agency if he didn't get back to work. And then he heard a voice he had almost forgotten, terrified and demanding, filled with a brutal history he no longer wished to revisit. "Joseph, I know I shouldn't bother you, but I need to see you," Aleksandra said. "Please come. It's getting worse." Joseph pressed delete and ran to his wife. She smoked a cigarette against the windowsill as dusk fell early. Summer was finally losing ground to autumn.

Monday, Tuesday, Wednesday, Thursday. He counted each day as if checking it off a list.

The afternoon Del went to Madi's apartment to settle her belongings, Joseph decided to take the opportunity to settle his own. He dug underneath the bed for the metal box wrapped in a towel. He brought it to the coffee table and opened the lid.

He cupped the .38 special in his fingers, a weightless piece of metal with its stainless steel barrel and black rubber handle. Five gold bullets were still stored in the chamber, never fired, never registered in the State of New York because he had bought it ten years ago in the back of a Harlem porn shop. Joseph stared at the weapon in his hand. He had expected for so many years that he might one day use it, the muzzle against his temple with his finger over the trigger, the pain in his chest too unbearable to see beyond it. He imagined what his eyes would look like in that moment, streaked glass windows with no emergency exits. It seemed impossible to him now to think of killing himself.

Joseph needed to get rid of it, wrap it in a towel, and toss it into the East River. He placed the gun back in its container and grabbed the small blue ring box that was also stored there. Inside were his father's teeth, two incisors and a canine strapped to a wire. The teeth were cold, smooth, and yellowed, and they used to fit on the gums of a man who had no idea what his heart had in store for him, digging his own backyard ditch deeper and deeper, year by year. His father had been luckier for not knowing. He could face his mornings without any narrowing of the horizon over their backyard hill. Joseph placed the teeth on their cotton pillow and closed the lid. He heard Del's key turn in the door and rushed into the bedroom, wedging the box between the mattress and spring.

He had slept for too long over a gun and a set of teeth. How could he have ever lived in the present with those two items—one from the past, the other bent on the future—always within arm's reach? We don't have to become the people we've imagined for ourselves, he thought, those strange versions invented so young and held on to far past their expiration date. He could start over now as his own man. Del had promised to stay with him if he agreed to believe that.

As he ran into the hallway, he made a calculation by habit that he knew he should break. Perhaps it would go with the residue of his fever. He counted eight days into three-hundred-and-sixty five, the stretch of time until he'd be free of thirty-four.

His father had destroyed his mother, but Joseph had Del to save him.

CHAPTER FORTY-FIVE

"TAKE WHAT YOU want," Raj said. Del stood by the elevator bank in Madi's apartment. A layer of dust had settled over every inch of her place—the coffee maker, the answering machine, her black Mac laptop closed like a briefcase on the kitchen counter, the embroidered screens, the gold peacock whose feathered crown held up the glass coffee table; all of it looked outdated and decaying under the coat of grime. It occurred to her how quickly time took the living out of rooms. People had to fight to keep anything alive and present; otherwise it drifted into dust from lack of contact, resentful for not being used.

The same could be said for the quiet that hung between Del and Raj. He was standing behind a barricade of empty brown boxes, his arms crossed over a yellow T-shirt.

"Are you going to keep the place or sell it?" she asked him, removing her sunglasses. She wanted to keep them on but knew avoidance would be Raj's first point of attack.

"I haven't decided," he replied, scanning the loft with the indecision of a potential buyer, uncertain whether the four walls and the raftered ceiling would constitute a happy home. Not that a happy home had ever been a consideration for Raj before. "You know, it's funny," he said. "I feel a responsibility to settle her belongings. So I got these boxes. But it now strikes me, settle it how? I suppose that means get rid of it. Belongings," he whistled like he only just got their joke. "You buy this stuff and think you're going to own it forever. But you really don't leave any instruction on what anyone's supposed to do with it when you're gone. I really don't know what to keep."

"Whatever you don't want, you could just put on the street," she advised. "I'm sure there's still that great economy of garbage pickers who make sure it all gets a home. Or donate it to a charity. Madi did a lot of volunteering for Angel Outreach, which gives all the money it earns from estate sales to women living with HIV."

What was she talking about? Del listened to herself ramble on about charity mission statements to compensate for what she couldn't say, couldn't even find words for in the roaring stream of consciousness of her mind. Stream? More like a river. She hadn't wanted to see Raj, not yet. In the week since she last left his apartment, she had avoided his calls, answering only periodically to tell him that Joseph was very ill and she wasn't sure yet what she had decided to do. That, of course, was a lie. In the hot, incoherent days of late August, Del rarely left the apartment, sleeping next to Joseph at night, and when she did run out to the grocery, her body started to show signs of a stoop, a tightening and hunkering of the shoulders that seemed to remove her from the prospect of new possibilities. She often kept her phone turned off. But when Raj called asking if she'd help him deal with Madi's apartment, she had no choice but to consent. Now she forced herself from the entryway with such hesitant, careful steps, it seemed clear that she couldn't be expected to gauge the value of a single bookend.

"You don't want anything?" Raj asked.

"I guess I do. A piece of her jewelry would be a nice way to remember her. I don't know. I don't feel right picking through her things for myself. Wait. The gold peacock." She pointed to the obese metal bird standing guard in front of the couch. "I'd throw away the glass and just keep that horrible thing as a little Madi memorial."

"Yeah, I was thinking the same thing," he said smiling. "She really developed quite a taste for the gaudy at the end of her life, didn't she? She would accuse us of being brainwashed Western minimalists. I can hear her now. 'Oh, no, it has an ounce of character. It might actually suggest I have a personality. Banish it from my sight.'" He kicked a cardboard box to clear a path toward Del and brandished a package of neon paper squares. "I brought Post-its. Let's put them on the stuff we don't want and give that to the charities. You and I can fight over the rest until we've completely destroyed her legacy in a greedy wrestling match between the two people she loved most."

They worked for three hours attaching Post-its to Indian tapestries and teak dining-room chairs, to copper plant basins and cushioned wicker stools. They each took a side of Madi's long linen couch and carried it toward the elevator as the first essential piece to donate to Goodwill. Working this way, laughing as they wielded stained-glass lamps and overstuffed sequin pillows, Del could almost imagine a different reality, one where she and Raj were in a similar New York loft, moving things in and not out, choosing items to position on shelves and side tables and window ledges, arranging their lives together as a young couple in love with all of the unspoiled days ahead of them. Del couldn't resist acknowledging that a part of her wanted it. Wanted it desperately, even still. Bookcases filled with Raj's photo monographs and her biology encyclopedias, Greek bric-a-brac under black-and-white portraits, the insidious gold peacock standing in front of a new leather sofa. Her rock albums could go underneath the windows, and they'd put the speakers in the rafters, and the bell jar from Raj's fly sculpture could hold candles, which they could light at night for dinners. That's how their future would have been built.

They ran through an entire pack of Post-its before they set foot in the bedroom. Del entered Madi's walk-in closet, picking through hangers and sliding her foot over the army of shoes that lined up across the floor.

"Your jurisdiction," Raj said from the door frame.

"She's got all of these wonderful saris. We should send those to an Indian charity, don't you think?"

"Whatever you say." He eyed her from the edge of the closet. She held her breath as he watched her, keeping her focus confined to the hangers. "Hold on," he said. "I have something for you." He disappeared into the living room, while Del slipped a vintage party dress over her head, its tight black architecture barely fitting over her ribs, so much so it must have never fit Madi. She must have just wanted it, the black bodice curving into lace that swept down to her toes. Del walked out to model it for Raj. He was removing an item from the large oak dresser, which he had already claimed as the sole piece of furniture he wanted to keep.

"I have something for you," he repeated, taking a step toward her. "It was Madi's." He opened his palm and picked up the ring between his thumb and forefinger.

It was a simple platinum band she wore on her right hand. Del remembered Madi buying it with some of the first money she had made working in the financial sector, when the idea of doing anything with her literature degree had finally been dismissed as the dream of an impressionable student who didn't understand how little poetry suited real life. Raj grabbed Del's wrist and slipped the ring onto her finger. It fit perfectly.

"She was wearing it when she died," Raj said, still staring at it. "They gave it back to me. We put it on her at the funeral but these goons come out just before they close the coffin to take all of the jewelry off. Anyway, I want you to have it. She would have liked that."

Raj held her fingers in his palm and gazed into her eyes, dripping blue icebergs, once so inhospitable but now begging for her to tell him what he wanted to hear.

"I can't leave him right now," she said suddenly, terrified that if she didn't say it right then she would never find the courage. "Joseph's very sick. He needs me to take care of him."

"Is that how it is?"

"Yeah. That's it."

"Just right now or . . . ?"

"I'm not leaving him." She reached her hand up to touch his cheek, but he pulled his head back in defense, dropped her fingers, and turned around. "I'm sorry, Raj. I guess there wasn't going to be a part two for us in the end. I thought there could be for a while, but we were both just fooling ourselves."

"No," he said as he walked toward the oak dresser. "I wasn't fooling myself. You were. You were fooling both of us."

"Maybe," she replied. "I didn't know what was going to happen. I'm sorry." She struggled to lift the dress over her shoulders, fighting with the fabric until the lace skirt covered her head. In that second, when the room was blocked out by a curtain of fabric, she gave herself a moment to shut her eyes and let out a hard, silent cry that cramped every muscle in her face and left her jaw open in the volts of the loudest ache. Then she collected herself, snapping her mouth shut and pinching the water from her eyes, as she threw the dress on the floor. Raj stood by the dresser with his back to her, pretending to rifle through papers.

"You can come back another time and go through her clothes," he said with the coldness of a legal agreement. "Just take what you want and leave what you don't. I'll get people to move it all out this week. And take the peacock too or else it will go with the rest."

She picked up her purse from the dining-room chair. Clutching the strap, she walked quietly over to him, reaching out to touch his arm.

"There's so much I want to tell you," she said, trying to hold back her tears. "It's just not the right time for it. You have to believe me."

"There is never the right time for it. Is there, Del?" He didn't look up but flinched as her fingers pressed against his skin. "I think you should go."

She didn't take the peacock. She pressed the call button and when the doors split open she walked into the elevator and struggled to find any last words that would sum up everything she wanted to say. Only when the doors started to shut and she saw him rounding the corner, his neck craned sideways to watch her go, his skinny body casting a long shadow across the concrete floor, his eyes not angry or excited, only then did she find something to say. In the last inch of Madi's apartment she said "good-bye." Then the room and Raj disappeared into a crack, and the elevator brought her down.

THAT NIGHT, SHE and Joseph lit candles and ate from takeout boxes on the living room floor. Thunder made only a purr that trembled the windows, but lightning struck deep, momentarily turning the room into flashes of white and green. Del had bought two bottles of wine on her way home from Madi's apartment, and she ignored the Chinese food for the task of finishing one bottle all on her own. She hadn't told him about her interaction with Raj, and it hardly seemed worthwhile to speak about it now. She took long sips from her glass, as Joseph mentioned the appointment at INS.

"It's still set for December 1," he said. "That's three months away."

"Yeah," she replied from behind her glass.

"What's wrong?" he asked, dropping his fork into the container and staring worriedly over at her. "Don't you still want to go through with it?"

She took another sip and changed the subject.

"Did I ever tell you that rattlesnake venom is being tested to cure heart failure?" Del had been thinking about that irony all week, how the venom in her favorite animal was being studied to treat the disease that had wiped out Joseph's family. That had been only one of the many ironies that left her smoking cigarettes while staring out the window at the same tenement building across the street as if she were trying to commit the view to memory. She told Joseph of the advances Dr. Isely had been making in her underground lab up at Columbia, milking snakes to locate the molecules that slowed the blood supply and relaxed the muscles in the heart. "Maybe it will be a reality in five or ten years. Who knows?" she said, as she poured more wine in her glass. "Maybe one day rattlesnakes will be the cure everyone's been waiting for."

"Jesus," he said, reaching across the floor to wrap his fingers around her ankle. "I hope it's true. Do you know what that could mean?" She didn't answer. "That could be your next job, Del. Why don't you call up this woman and ask if you can be a part of it? There can't be many people around with your specialties. They could probably use you."

She put her fingers on his hand and smiled faintly as she pulled her foot away. It meant something that Joseph suggested it, but she had already signed off on that dream.

"No," she replied. "That's not going to happen."

She looked at him as she poured the last of the wine from the bottle. Outside, lightning flashed across the windows, bouncing off buildings, leeching through metal until its current dispersed deep below the sidewalk. Was it true that lightning couldn't strike a person if they weren't grounded, feet in midair, no part of them anchored to the earth? In midair, a person was safe. Lightning strikes weren't random. They hunted for things with roots to correct an imbalance between the land and the sky. Lightning was an atmosphere looking to settle a score.

She took a sip and smiled. How could she not smile now, not want to laugh out loud at the shit-spitting humor of the world? Up until a few weeks ago, Del had dreamed of a green card, and now a meeting at INS scheduled for December was the last option on her mind. *It was amazing what life gave you*, she thought. *Almost as amazing as what it took.*

The truth was Del had already said good-bye that afternoon through the closing elevator doors of Madi's apartment, and she meant to keep her word. She gulped the final remnants from her glass. It had been quite an experiment. She could remember watching 1999 turn into 2000 from a rooftop in Tribeca, feeling all of the promise of that new invisible century finally arriving. She had been looking north toward the glowing halo of Times Square, and Madi had grabbed her by the neck and said, "Stop staring at the place where some stupid ball dropped. It's not there, it's right here." Madi had been right about the future, for a while anyway, but now it was time to say good-bye. She could feel things dying, the power leaking out of her, leaking out of buildings and store windows and the trees lining the sidewalks, out of the new glass high-rises along the piers of the Hudson River and out of the back doors of the yellow cabs racing down FDR. It was all ending—her version of it, her time with it, that future they once waited until midnight for—washing quietly away.

She rose from the floor and carried the takeout boxes into the kitchen to dump them in the trash. After a few minutes, Joseph appeared in the doorframe. He leaned against the refrigerator, dropped his head, and calmly spoke.

"I don't want you to be unhappy," he said. "What can I do?"

She ran tap water over her chopsticks and then threw them in the garbage too. She would no longer need chopsticks. She would no longer need the plates in the cabinets or the pots hanging like rusted ornaments over the stove or the ceramic plant holders lined up on the sill.

"I don't want to stay here anymore," she said.

CHAPTER FORTY-SIX

WILLIAM FOUND HIMSELF in the first days of September the happiest he had ever been in New York. He watched Cecile walk from the shower with a towel tied around her waist, beating her hip with the palm of her hand, picking up a plum that matched the color of her nipples, and tearing her teeth into its meaty flesh. Joy tidal-waved over him at the sight of this woman, right here, no mirages, the frank tap of her feet coming nearer, her hair wet and her thin body wired. They had remained in her Bowery apartment for almost a week, having sex and sleeping until their bodies gathered the strength to do it all over again. William was happy to let go of the city outside her windows. He listened to Cecile play a ballad on her guitar, memorized her favorite films and the arrangement of the dresses in her closet, and clapped as she danced in only a pair of heels with a flag draped over her shoulders. He felt himself falling under a heavy spell and didn't resist.

By the fourth day, Cecile picked through a basket of needles and thread and handed him a spare key to her apartment, another of so many spare sets he had collected over the summer. He took it greedily and kissed her for the gift. But William didn't risk leaving her place for fear he would never find his way back.

Occasionally he woke in the middle of the night, his fists swarming through her pillows from a nightmare that starred Quinn in a lumberjack shirt turning around in a small woodland cottage with car keys in his hands. The keys transformed into a flurry of flies, and William came awake on the soft down comforter to hear the traffic roaring on the Bowery. Cecile's lips glided along his collarbone as she formed sleepy French phrases he didn't understand, guiding him back into the safety of the bed.

Se coucher. J'ai la photo tire demain. Translation: You are safe, don't think of the hell you passed through to find me. The world, this city, my arms, they're yours . . .

Such was the paradise of Cecile's loft with its old granary wheel forever bull's-eyed in the top window that William only left one early morning to mail the manila envelope that Rose Cherami had given him. He addressed it without a note or a return address to Joseph at his Twenty-Second Street address, no longer caring what effect it had on its recipient or even if it arrived. William simply wanted all traces of the past out of his hands, free to return to the vortex of Cecile Dozol's universe floating four flights above the street. Of course, her privilege was a clear attraction. William had even found the courage to call Janice and insist on arranging a meeting between her and Cecile if she'd consider letting him back into the agency. Her family name might open doors that otherwise shut in his face.

William walked up the street, located the nearest mailbox, and threw the envelope away into it. He headed back to the apartment as a cool fall wind curled around his ears, and so complete was his surrender to this magnificent dream state that he was taken aback at the sight of two middle-aged men in cheap dove-gray suits standing at the door of the building. The men eyed him, turned their attention to the buzzers on the door, and then swerved their heads in simultaneous double take.

"William Asternathy," the bearded, coffee-toothed man said. "Are you William Asternathy?"

"Yes," he answered. "Why?"

"I'm Detective Tasser. This is Detective Hazlett. We're from homicide."

In that furious second, William evacuated his body in search of an outdated version of himself that he no longer recognized.

"What is this about?" William asked, training his eyes on the shape of an urn that the detectives' profiles made against the cold sunlight.

"It's about your friend, Brutus Quinn. You know him, don't you?"

"Yes," he replied through a dry mouth. "Of course I know him. An old friend. Haven't seen him for a while. Has something happened?" His teeth chattered, ready to break into a full nervous crescendo. He clenched his hands, which were shaking in the air over his chest.

The two detectives shared worried glances.

"Do you mind coming with us down to the precinct?" Tasser asked. "Our car is just over there. We need to ask you a few questions."

"It would be better if you came with us," Hazlett confirmed. "It's not something you want to do right here."

"Should I bring anything with me? You see, I've got an audition in forty-five minutes," he lied. "Can this wait for another time? Perhaps tomorrow or next week?"

The two plainclothes detectives shared more worried glances, communicating some cop shorthand for suspect apprehended, suspect showing signs of resistance.

"You should cancel that audition," Tasser said, bracing his fingers around William's arm.

THE DRIVE TOOK eight minutes, an entire lifespan. William counted the minutes on the dashboard clock from the backseat of the Cadillac. He crushed his hands between his knees, wondering why they hadn't used cuffs. The interior smelled musty and sour, although scuffed paper mats from a recent trip to the car wash carpeted the floor. There was no metal netting separating him from the officers, no guns visible in their belts, no police cars trailing closely behind.

But William had seen enough cop movies to predict what he could expect. He knew they would take him into a bare, windowless room and work him over, picking at him slowly, politely, before rifling through him with violent accusations to pry out a confession deep in his chest.

William bent his head and forced himself not to look out of the tinted windows, as Houston Street sailed by in construction sites and mountain-high underwear ads. He stared at the green digits of the console clock, four minutes, five, six, seven, almost eight. The inside of this car was a network of windows and doors, but it was still the first of many cramped spaces he would have to share with law enforcement, a whole future of claustrophobically small enclosures. He was still simply a suspect, no confession, no lawyer, no Miranda rights. Cecile would be wondering why he hadn't already returned. He had told her he was running out to buy condoms and flowers, such embarrassing, fantastic items, purchases that told the shop clerk he was a well-loved human being, a man who cared about the body and mind of someone else, a man who wouldn't murder anyone. If he had gone to buy those items instead of mailing that envelope, would Tasser and Hazlett have let him out on the next corner?

William could hardly remember killing Quinn. But he had, way back when, at a point as faint now as an echo. His heart was pounding, and he sat on his hands to prevent them from lashing out. If the detectives were from homicide, shouldn't he already have asked if Quinn was dead? Wouldn't an innocent person have immediately asked that question? William dove forward between the front seats, but he was too late. Tasser spun the wheel, and the unmarked Cadillac found a parking space in front of a gray stone building.

Hazlett opened the back door, pulled him out by his arm, and tailed behind him, while Tasser led the way. They passed single file through the entrance, walked by the bulletproof glass humming with accident reports, and climbed a flight of stairs. Tasser punched open a swinging door on the second floor, guided him down a passage of filing cabinets and ringing cubicles and into a bare, white-walled room that held a brown Formica table and three metal chairs. It was exactly like the movies. Exactly like an episode of *Law & Order* that you turn off at the next commercial break. Exactly like a place that purposely existed outside of the real world, where it was just William and his soul and the detectives with their questions about what that soul was doing at the time some murders took place.

"Have a seat," Tasser ordered with a host's gesticulation. Hazlett carried in files under his beefy armpit.

"What is this about?" William asked as he sat across from them. "Quinn isn't in some kind of trouble, is he? That man wouldn't hurt a fly. He was like a father to me. *Is* like a father to me. Homicide? He couldn't have killed anyone."

More anxious glances flew between the detectives. They declined the chairs in front of them, preferring to stand. Tasser closed his eyes. Here it comes. The first accusation, delivered in the cheap deceit of friendship, making an easy pathway for trust, just before the punches started, the shouting, the turning over of every detail. His thighs beat together, his feet tapped on the linoleum tiles, he took long breaths, he fidgeted, his body was rocketing out of control, and he kicked his chair back to unleash the energy stored in his legs.

"We have some very bad news," Tasser started, gazing at him intently with coffee-stained eyelids that matched his teeth. "Your friend Quinn was found yesterday morning in his backhouse apartment."

"Found?"

"He was found hanging from his shower pipe."

William had intended to produce some effective tears, but when Tasser delivered the news, he immediately choked and tears streamed from his eyes. They had finally discovered his body. There were no more questions in the matter. The news that William had waited to hear for so long passed through him like an electric shock.

"That can't be. Not possible. Quinn couldn't have been murdered."

Tasser squinted.

"Why would you assume he was murdered?"

Trap one.

Six consonants hissed out of William's mouth, failing to produce a word. He swallowed and tried again. "Because Quinn would never kill himself. I know that. He was a fucking survivor. He had been HIV positive for twenty years. The man wouldn't let anything stop him. He loved life. He of all people had to fight to stay here with us, to keep himself going. Suicide. I'm telling you, he wouldn't have done that." Everything he was saying was so horribly accurate.

"Mr. Asternathy," Tasser said with a sigh, "we found him hanging in his shower from a cord. That would suggest a suicide."

Cord, trap two. He had used the navy sheet stripped from his bed. "Was there a note?"

"No," Hazlett replied, taking over from his partner. "We didn't find a note. The coroner estimated he'd been dead for more than two weeks. The super had come to collect the back rent yesterday morning and let himself in with his key. Did you have any contact with your friend in the last month?"

"I'm sure I talked to him on the phone. No, not recently, but maybe two weeks ago, yeah. I'd call to check in on him periodically. He didn't have many friends left, you see, so I tried to be there for him. I was meaning to stop by the cottage this week. Oh, Christ. I can't believe it."

Tasser bowed his head in sympathy. He had respectful silence down to a science: he waited ten seconds. "Can you remember the last time you spoke? It's very important. Was he acting peculiar in any way? Was he depressed or paranoid or did he mention anything troubling that had happened?"

"No. He was working on costumes for a play up in the Theater District. He hired a few tricks here and there, which kept him happy."

"Prostitutes, you mean?"

"I don't think they call them that, but yeah, basically. He didn't make much money. But, no, I don't remember him mentioning any problems."

"He didn't mention anything about his car?"

At Tasser's prompting, Hazlett placed a photograph in front of him. It was a shot of the Cressida parked exactly where William had left it. He could see the shoddy repair job on the hood, the hammered-out dents in the front fender, the mismatched blue paint that glimmered against the car's muted metal.

William took a breath and crossed his legs and arms to consolidate his body into the smallest amount of space.

"That's his car. He's had it for years. I never understood why he kept the thing. It barely worked."

"He said nothing about an accident?"

"No," William responded curtly in a pitch five octaves too high. Then he tried to reroute the conversation. "How can it take two weeks to find a body? What kind of city is this?"

"I'm not going to lie to you, Mr. Asternathy. The scene was pretty gruesome. A body decomposing for fourteen days in that kind of heat. You say that he could have been murdered, but from what we could tell, there were no signs of a struggle to indicate that he resisted in any way."

"I can't believe it," William repeated piteously. He looked at them for consolation but found detached detective stares. "I don't get the point of all this. If you think Quinn was a suicide, why are two homicide detectives investigating his death?"

Tasser nodded, and from a folder, Hazlett produced a copy of the *New York Post* sealed in plastic. Folded to the second page was the cell-phone photo of the hit-and-run, Madi Singh piled on the cement, the blue Cressida a blur in the background with Quinn's bumper sticker reduced to a white rectangle. Somewhere in the pixilated stew William was leaving the scene, driving away from the second-worst moment of his life.

William tried to access some deep reserve of composure, but instead his face turned white and his hands shook. He realized right then that he didn't have the strength to defend himself. The past was catching up, each action weaving and knotting into a web until there was no way to struggle out of it. The detectives knew. They were spiders familiar with the thrashing of doomed insects. They studied him as he stared at the paper, their shoulders bent forward, their eyes trained to catch the slightest tremor in his face. The bare room with its greasy Formica and hot white fluorescents didn't allow any retreat from the showdown. Hazlett tapped two nicotine fingers on the picture.

"Does that look familiar?"

"It's the newspaper."

"Does that story look familiar?"

"I think I saw something about it on the news."

"That's all?" he asked with surprise. "You never heard about it anywhere else? Never knew anyone involved?"

"No," he stammered.

"William, if you've got something to admit, you'd better do it right now. That way it will be easier on all of us." Tasser's voice was a masterpiece of reason and control, and William wanted to spit in his face for the fatherly manner in which he proposed a simple confession. They could hear him faltering, they could see the desperate acrobatics of his thoughts.

"I don't know what you're talking about."

Tasser straightened up and placed his hands on his belted hips.

"I find that hard to believe, Mr. Asternathy." He paused, then continued. "Don't you wonder how we managed to find you today? We got your whereabouts from your agent at Touchpoint. She said you were staying at the address of a Cecile Dozol."

"Yes," he whispered. "That's my girlfriend."

"Are you aware that Ms. Dozol took this picture with her cell phone the day of the accident?"

This information arrived like a bullet. William's eyes opened, and he collapsed backward in his seat. He had no idea that Cecile had taken the photo on her cell phone, and he assumed the detectives must be telling him a lie. Cecile had never said why she had been at the gallery. She hadn't wanted to discuss it, and neither had he. He stared up at them frantically, comparing their faces.

"That's not possible," he managed.

"You didn't know that? You said she was your girlfriend."

"The truth is, we've only been dating for a week." They had caught him. Out of one lie the truth would slowly be ripped out, each new deception placed on the table and dissected until it was revealed for what it was: a lie with a rapid heartbeat.

"So you do know one person involved with this picture. Do you know any others?"

"Hazlett is asking if you know the driver," Tasser prodded helpfully.

"No."

"We don't believe you." Tasser slammed a fist on the table and shot his eyes on him. "I think you know who was driving that car. I think you are the only person on earth that can tell us the identity of that man."

"I don't know anything. I'm telling you the truth. So what if Cecile took that picture? I wasn't there. Why don't you ask her?"

"We have asked her. And we might just go and ask her about you right now. She might be able to tell us some interesting things about your involvement with a particular hit-and-run. Do you think she'd like to hear our version of events?"

He couldn't follow their logic. He had been so careful about guarding his own crimes at the front door he hadn't notice them slip in from the back. It was as if they anticipated his answers and spun him around until he was jumping over one trap only to be caught in another. Now they were using Cecile against him. He drove his palms into the table and watched helplessly.

"We found this newspaper in Brutus Quinn's cottage. Odd that it should be there, don't you think, because there weren't any other newspapers found in his junk."

William sank at the realization that he had forgotten the newspaper when he wiped the evidence from the scene. His own fingerprints might be all over that paper. Had he touched it? Had it ever moved from Quinn's hands to his? Maybe he could grab it and rip the plastic off and contaminate it with his fingerprints before they bothered with a test. He swallowed and dropped his head.

"And isn't it also odd that Quinn owns a blue car that matches the one seen leaving the accident? Odd too when we performed some analysis on the hood that we found it had undergone a recent patch-up job. What do you think, Hazlett?"

"The kind of patch-up job to hide damage that could have been caused, say, by hitting a woman."

Tasser smiled in rage. "Makes sense to me. And now we have you, Mr. Asternathy, suddenly in the arms of our only material witness. That's a little bit odd too."

"I told you, I don't know who was driving the car."

"Of course you do. And you went over there to make sure the

driver would get away with killing an innocent human being. You had to be certain all the fires were put out. That way no one would ever discover the guilty party."

"No."

"Then why was this newspaper found at the scene of Quinn's suicide?"

"I don't know."

"Why didn't he leave a note? If it was just a normal suicide, you're right, where's the note?"

"I don't know."

"Because the Cressida was the car driving away in this photograph."

"No," William screamed, holding his hands up to shield himself.

"Tell us who did it."

"I don't know."

"Yes, you do. Quinn knew. You two talked about it before he died."

"No."

"You talked about it, and you'd do anything to keep it quiet."

"No."

"Quinn trusted you. He let you in. He opened his door to you."

His whole body convulsed, choking up spit as he sniveled into his palms.

"I won't say it. I won't say anything. I think I'm going to be sick."

Tasser and Hazlett retreated a step. Tasser whispered in Hazlett's ear and they both left the room, shutting the door behind them to leave William shaking and staring into the infinity of a white cinder block wall. The detectives were outside preparing for their final drive home. They were watching him. He spun his head around, looking for mirrors or cameras from which they were spying on him. He rubbed his hands and felt a warm stream of urine flood his underwear. There was no way out.

The detectives returned a minute later, Tasser smiling and Hazlett grumbling as they finally took the seats across from him. Now it was only a matter of one last accusation and they'd finally have William by the throat. What did they have? A positive ID from the desk clerk at the New Jersey hotel? The check that Madi wrote with his own name signed across the back? Cecile now crying in another room just like this one, suddenly realizing she could remember a young man at the wheel of the car?

"Please, stop," he begged. "Please. None of this happened like you said. I loved Quinn and now he's gone."

"We know that," Tasser replied solemnly, reaching his hands over the desk to offer a ceasefire.

"Jason," Hazlett snapped. "We can keep going. Come on." Hazlett didn't get the response he wanted and kicked the table leg in fury.

"We know what happened," Tasser said softly. "And we think all you were doing was trying to protect him. After all, you were his only friend in the city. You were the only person he loved. He was like a father to you, wasn't he? You were just trying to save him from trouble. Am I right?"

"What?" William's voice broke with confusion. He wiped his nose and timidly lifted his head to meet their eyes. Something had replaced Tasser's ruthless gaze, some unmuscled expression simulating kindness.

"William, we know Brutus Quinn was the driver of that car. He couldn't live with the guilt of hitting that woman, could he? He couldn't shake the shame of killing someone, and it weighed on him. He killed himself over it."

William sat frozen, waiting for Tasser to manipulate his logic or swerve back into another round of accusations. He almost fell to the floor when Hazlett hissed in anger, rebuking his partner for giving in.

"He must have confessed this to you. You were like his son, isn't that right? And you went over to make sure that Cecile Dozol couldn't identify Quinn as the man behind the wheel. Because that would mean a prison cell for a sick old man who was like father to you."

"No," William said quietly. "That didn't happen. Quinn never told me that."

Tasser nodded, and Hazlett gathered the newspaper back into his files.

"The kid didn't admit anything," Hazlett yelled.

"It doesn't matter," Tasser countered. "We don't need him."

"He's lying," his partner said. But Tasser continued to nod compassionately and pulled his open hand from the table.

"William, it doesn't matter if you tell us or not. We've got the evidence on Quinn. It's so solid I'd stick my mother on it. We were hoping for a little confirmation, but if we are wrong on that theory, I'm very sorry you had to go through this. It's our job to give the family of Madeline Singh some peace of mind, and even though this interrogation might have been troubling to you, we're here to bring relief to a brother who's been begging us to find the man responsible. If you really don't know, as you say, I'm sorry to tell you that the man we've been looking for is your friend. Quinn must have been very depressed about what he had done. It's not uncommon for the guilty to suffer as much as the victims. As you said, he knew how valuable life was."

"Yes," William replied, his brain spinning and his body so drained he wasn't sure if he could rely on his legs to support his own weight.

"I hope his crime won't stain your memory of him. If it's any consolation, your name came up for questioning because you're the only person we could track down in this city who was close to him. We had hoped you could tell us something." Tasser reached into the inside pocket of his sport coat and placed a business card on the table. "If you do remember anything, I'd appreciate a call."

"So I can leave?"

"Yes." Tasser smiled coyly. "You were free to leave at any time. We were never holding you. We appreciate your patience."

The detective stood and offered his hand. William shook it, said thank you, and he walked through the hallway, down the steps, past the bulletproof lobby, and out into the cold autumn sunlight.

William was so dazed by the sun, he shouldered into an olive-skinned man nervously rubbing his hands as he entered the police station. The man stopped and turned as if he recognized William, but William refused to pause, expecting hands to reach out from behind him at any second and drag him back into that room.

He walked a block without a single thought passing through his brain, just his feet echoing on the pavement, the chilly air whipping over his ears, his eyes squinting in the direction of home. When he got to the corner, he stopped to wait for the walk light. No cops had followed him out of the precinct. A group of pedestrians huddled around him waiting to cross, remote, staring distractedly at the speeding traffic, but unafraid to stand next to him. A pregnant woman pushing a grocery cart. An Asian skinhead with a skateboard stopped under his sneaker. A hirsute businessman yakking about an impending market crash on his cell phone. An elderly couple with matching Toledo sweatshirts and matching never-go-gray blond hair.

It was over. The dead had taken the fall for the crimes of the living. William watched the green traffic lights turn yellow and the impatient swaying of his fellow travelers preparing to cross. The city swam around him, his every glance filled with incalculable pools of information, every detail, every atom, bursting with activity, the whole town right now a raw shot of chaos flowing around him on this Tribeca street corner. He hugged himself tightly and let the cold sun pour across his cheeks.

The cross light told him it was safe to start walking, and he waited for the first pedestrians to begin moving. He went with the crowd, a gathering of strangers making their collective pilgrimage across two lanes of traffic, connected for an instant in the same simple purpose of reaching the other side. In a few seconds they would separate, never to be together in the same place again.

But not yet. They were only halfway across.

They still had time with each other, free, unnamable men and women of this city with rich, convoluted histories that had led them all to be here at the same moment, wandering east together in a colorful, unspeaking herd.

They were nearly over. The cross light changed from a solid white figure to a blinking orange hand. The cars began to creep forward in the release of their brakes. But they had made it across safely.

William broke from them and headed off alone. The beginning of a smile leaked across his face.

CHAPTER FORTY-SEVEN

THE NEWS THAT the police had identified the driver should have come as a relief, as if what was broken could be fixed. Raj extended a sincere thank-you to Detective Tasser, who informed him that since the perpetrator was already dead, there'd be no need to endure the duress of a trial. Raj relayed the information to his father by phone, and he exclaimed "praise the universe" in gratitude. Raj was part of that universe, and his father goaded him on the victory of justice over the wicked. "My son, you have avenged your sister by catching this evildoer," he avowed with paternal pride. Raj wondered if anyone outside of his immediate family and intergalactic science-fiction sagas ever spoke to their loved ones this way. Raj was happy for his father. The man could go on living now from the pages of his holy scripture, and the world he met at his doorstep each morning returned to one marked with equal measures of fairness and spite. Raj wished he could have shared in that consolation.

After he had cleared Madi's loft of her belongings, save for the gold peacock that remained standing in a tapioca shaft of Chinatown sunlight, he had expected to feel something amounting to closure— finality, resolution, the clasp of hands that could do nothing further.

But the opposite happened. The spaciousness of Madi's vacant apartment disturbed Raj's equilibrium. He tried sleeping on an air mattress there for a few nights as a trial run before moving in and had awakened terrified that intruders had cracked the locks and, finding nothing they could steal, decided to bash his head with a brick in retaliation. Raj couldn't remember the last time he had actually been scared of New York. He had grown too used to living in tight quarters, where every door and window could be inspected with a single turn of the head. After two nights, he gave up and returned to his cramped, gas-reeking studio on the tip of the West Side Highway. The ratty mattress and the mildewed Polaroid boxes comforted him as he chain-locked the front door.

Raj understood that if he fell now there would be no woman with a spare set of keys to march down the hallway and entreat him back into the world. He'd have to tread very carefully from here out. Mirabelle Petz had called a week prior with a bleak report. The art wasn't selling. It had merited a glowing paragraph review in *The New York Times* and a few prospects from European curators who were hoping he might reenact the interactive fly performance, preferably without the accompanying portraits. Collectors didn't want dead bodies piling up in their living rooms. It didn't take much convincing to persuade Mirabelle not to add his name to the stable of artists on her website.

He had become a relatively solvent man from his sister's inheritance. He had the money now to do anything, go anywhere. He could board planes and pit stop around continents like he had once done mercilessly as a freelance photographer. He considered his options as he paced the studio floor and climbed across his mattress, burying his head in a pillow. One morning, lying in bed with the newspaper, he found an article on the national elections in India one year away. Manmohan Singh would be up for reelection as prime minister, and grassroot politicos of every caste were vying to win the hot seat of the biggest democracy on earth. A band of rebel Maoists was threatening to chop the hands off of anyone who voted and machine-gun through the flamboyant fabrics that covered the poll booths. The morning he had turned thirty, Raj had hallucinated heaving, restless crowds. He had chosen to photograph bare modernist rooms but the crowds waited in the very country Madi had loved. He cut the article out and tacked it to his wall. One year from now, maybe he would go. He would take pictures of the voters in all seven territories gathering to cast their straws on the future of their warring, religion-whipped, atomic republic. He would do so without interfering, a mere foreigner capturing the country where his father had been born through the lens of his camera. Maybe he would even travel to Punjab and surprise his father with a call. *You'll never guess where I am.*

The afternoon sun folded in arcs across his walls. Night revived them in trailing headlights. Morning faded the walls white. He stared out of his window at the Hudson River, which licked the sides of ferries and sailboats. He mixed sour milk with the last of his granola and spooned it into his mouth as he sat on his stool, rocking in semicircles with his bare feet. He thought of Del but not as often. He remembered the last moment of seeing her in the elevator, and part of him wished he had fallen to that superior cliché of romance by saying, "I hope you find what you're looking for." Of course, that wasn't really the truth. He hoped she'd realize the value of what she left behind. He wondered if she had finally been granted her green card and if that had satisfied her into fondness for the man she had married. Or had she already moved out on him? He considered sending one of Madi's portraits over as a present, but no one needed to be reminded of the ghosts that haunted them. The twenty portraits were stacked in his studio, covered in brown packaging paper.

The light bouncing off the river aggravated his eyes. He placed the bowl on his desk and walked to the window to pull the chain on the blinds.

Raj knew he should put on his shoes and leave his apartment. He should will a habit out of the sun and the restless pedestrians and the fluting breeze drifting off the Hudson River chop. He should bring his camera out with him to begin a new series of photographs. But his muscles froze at the very idea of opening his front door. It would all be there waiting for him, a crowd outside his very window, as it always had been.

Sweeping the shredded quilt over his shoulders, Raj climbed into the darkness of his bed.

CHAPTER FORTY-EIGHT

JOSEPH AND DEL created two mountains in their living room. One small pile—books and sweaters, photographs and record albums—was devoted to items to take. The more impressive range, consisting of furniture, the stereo, lamps, and thick winter jackets, climbed toward the ceiling as a chaotic whirlpool of possessions they would not need in Greece. Joseph worked diligently at stripping and disassembling the Gramercy apartment, his skin drenched in sweat from the fever that still clung to him. He had not been able to shake that last symptom of his late summer sickness, but even in delirium, he taped up boxes and cleared shelves. He wanted to prove to Del that his body had been delivered back to health. He wanted her to believe him strong enough to make the trip. She watched from the sidelines, folding clothes neatly into her luggage. Even though they were leaving, there was meaning to the boxes they filled for Amorgos, his stuff and hers mixing in the messy mergers she had once envisioned for them inside these walls. She had already phoned Frank Warren, Esq., to let him know that they no longer needed his services.

His fever intensified at night, warping his dreams into hallucinations of his mother, so he tried not to sleep. He stared out the window from the bed, the single square in the apartment not given over to packing. Any doubt Joseph had about going with her only rose in the middle of the night. The darkness covered the city and then the city ate through that darkness with a radiation visible from outer space. That was the vision of New York Joseph stored in his head like a postcard. What happened here? The answer was everything, and he'd miss that vast proposition. But he pressed his wet body against Del, and the sacrifice became small in comparison.

The evening before they were scheduled to fly out of JFK, a storm ripped across the island. Rain swelled the streets and flooded the storm drains. Water splattered on the wood floor from the open windows. Red siren lights bled through the gray air as ambulances sped toward emergencies. Del brought up the last batch of mail from the downstairs box. Only one piece was addressed to Joseph, a large manila envelope scrawled in sloppy print. He opened it against the windowsill, and his eyes scanned the name of Aleksandra Andrews on a series of police files. Joseph flipped through the stapled pages, testimony briefs, evidence inventories, and photocopies of typed procedurals, all indicating that Aleksandra had been the prime suspect in the murder of her husband. "She wore rubber dish gloves, which later could not be recovered. Consequently she passed a forensic paraffin test on both hands. Fresh mud on boots suggests recent activity. Refuses lie detector. See defense sequester." Joseph slapped the papers against his chest and studied the envelope but found no return address, only the fact that it had been mailed in New York. So she had killed him all along, he thought. The memory of him lying in bed next to her dressed in Ray Andrews's suit sent a chill racing through his arms.

Joseph shoved the papers into the envelope, and he couldn't help feeling thankful to the anonymous sender. If he held any last doubt about leaving, this final discovery steadied his resolve. Maybe Aleksandra had mailed it to him as her way of saying good-bye, just as she had mailed that ridiculous letter to herself to convince him once to stay. In either case, he had spent too much time in this city mixing with the wounded and the deranged, too much time dressed as other men. Tomorrow he would be on a new island.

Del eyed him nervously from the pile of clothes in the middle of the room.

"What is it?" she asked.

"Nothing," he said, as he tossed the envelope on the bed. "Another thing to get rid of." He ran to her and wrapped his arms around her waist. He whispered against her ear. "I can't wait to leave and live around absolute strangers."

She pulled him softly back with her hands. He knew that Del was still trying to come to peace with him, as if he had cleared all but one last hurdle that prevented her from dissolving into him.

"I have to confess something to you," she said, staring up. "I never actually told my parents that we got married."

"So they don't know I'm coming."

"Not yet," she said. "I tried to tell them but I didn't know how. I'm their only daughter, you see. They wouldn't have forgiven me if I'd gotten married without them there to witness it."

Joseph laughed and nodded his head. They could forgive each other for their families. "It's fine. We don't have to tell them. We can do it again."

Del burrowed through the remaining clothes yet to be packed and yanked out a yellow rain slicker, which she drew around her shoulders.

"Last shopping trip," she told him. "I'm going to the pharmacy to buy a few things."

He tried to grab her wrist but she was too fast, darting for her keys on the dresser.

"Can't you just wait until we get there?"

"Joe, I don't think you realize how small Amorgos is. They barely stock enough soap for the two thousand Greeks who live there. You have to smuggle the quality American stuff in. Perfume, tobacco, toothpaste."

She waved a hand and stumbled down the hallway. Joseph walked into the bedroom and pulled the metal box from under the mattress. He placed it on top of the envelope on the bed. Two last items to get rid of. Two pieces of a puzzle that no longer completed his picture or any other. He opened the box and removed his father's teeth. Then he turned to the window, lifting the glass and gathering the diamond security grate at its hinges. He climbed out on the fire escape. Drops of rain spiked on the rusted bars. As he scaled the slippery metal steps, clouds of brick dust erupted from the scaffolding.

The rain slowed as he ascended to the roof but he was already drenched. Joseph took off his shirt and tugged his jeans to keep them from sticking to his legs. His feet were black from tar, and he jumped up and down as he waited, bouncing on his tiptoes. He could hear the rumbling, the shake in the sky like a jet passing low through the cloud cover. Up here it was possible to feel the ache of the storm, the physical desire to make contact with the city. The weather had come in from the Midwestern plains. Yesterday it had ripped through the Ohio Valley and had followed its sidewinding meteorological path through the flats of Pennsylvania, mowing down trees and upending trailers, before making its way into Manhattan—the last shelf of land before the ocean.

He saw the first strike, a narrow white tracer that forked like a tree root and evaporated. He jammed his fists straight up, taking to the airwaves. He was young and getting older, and the blood was pulling through his capillaries. When a second bolt of lightning spliced a rooftop farther south, shooting off sparks of singed iron, he screamed. *That was more like it. Make some noise.* He had been in bed so long, he never wanted to lie down again. He had wasted too much time waiting for the worst, pushing his body toward its own extinction. The lightning bolted in twos and threes, trying desperately to touch something that could take it. Every building was like a willing wire, every spire and antenna. The whole city was a conductor.

Soon he wouldn't be here anymore, he'd be gone, way east or west, farther away than he had ever been in his life, a tropical island he couldn't locate on a globe. He'd go with her because Del was the future, and a future was a place he could now imagine. Maybe he'd even take her name. He'd drop Guiteau like unwanted cargo into the Atlantic along the way. Joseph tried to stretch his body as long as his muscles could go.

The storm was running out to sea. The lightning tore through the clouds, whitening the city like an X-ray. The storm was losing its chance to correct the imbalance, to strike and settle an aching debt. The wind slipped through his armpits and over his stomach. He pulled the teeth one by one from their metal bridge and, in one quick toss, threw them as far as he could over the skyline, until they disappeared into the night. Towers blinked red to warn planes. Red signs flickered in the streets. Red glazed the puddles on the rooftop. Manhattan waited and continued to wait.

He would not think about the past anymore. That was his only promise. There was an old Cincinnati joke that went as follows: If the world blew up, Ohio would find out about it two years later. Deeming the news too distressing, they'd quickly change the channel. In that admission of willful ignorance, Joseph thought, there was a certain hopefulness, a protest against oblivion. It was enough.

Joseph climbed down the fire escape and crawled through the window. He was eager to see Del's island, where she had warned him only eight people spoke about eight words of English. That would do for him. Last night, she had drawn Amorgos across his back with her fingertips. "And here's the beach, and there's the goat hill, and that's the church with its ugly goat bells. And here's where my parents live." She had told him what the weather in Amorgos was like. Almost like New York, she said, in its seasons. But softer and lighter and yet much more extreme.

He could only listen to her. She would perform all translations for him now.

He put his foot down on the floor and brought his other leg over the sill. His jeans and hair were dripping with rain, and he left his T-shirt in a ball on the fire escape. The charge in the air had come with him into the apartment. He wiped the water from his eyes. In the dim light of the bedroom, he noticed papers strewn across the white mattress, ripped from the staple that bound them together. The envelope lay on the floor. The metal box was open and empty.

He saw her standing in the corner of the bedroom. Her wet body twitched like she was surrounded by hidden enemies, and her eyes rushed around his face as if she were searching for a point of entry.

"What are you doing here?" he yelled, trying to take a step back.

"What do you mean?" she pleaded. "I came because I need help. You're the only one who believes me."

She pressed her palm against the bedroom door and shut it. The bolt snapped into its lock.

He heard each drip of rain outside the window, each siren, each breath.

As she reached her arm toward him, he told her that he didn't believe her.

"What do you believe then?" Aleksandra asked him.

I'm completely out of stories, he thought. *It's over, and I have no more stories to tell.*

EPILOGUE

WINTER IN AMORGOS was brutal. Harsh winds tore across the island, slapping every shutter, picking up outdoor furniture and tossing it miles out to sea, sliding through clothes to look for loose sails that pushed people battling for foothold toward cliff edges. When spring finally arrived, purple anemones and flowering sage burst from plant boxes, and the smells of mint and rosemary drifted down from the mountains. Goat bells clanged day and night, and on Sundays church bells rang more hurriedly as the thick-ankled women made a moaning procession toward mass.

Del moved around the house with slow, lumbering steps. She surveyed the blue sky over the silver Aegean from the kitchen window and helped her mother skin a rabbit for dinner. The Kousavos house was like all others on the island, a featureless whitewashed slab that burned the retinas to blindness. Her childhood bedroom was decorated in inscrutable paper triangles from where her father had clipped her teenage rock posters from its pale yellow walls. On her shelves were some of her old college biology books, creased and dog-eared from the last time she lived at home, twelve years ago now after the death of Dash Winslow. Del could still remember her flight last

September over the Atlantic. She had watched the dark bank of storm clouds recede and the eastern sun break over the ocean. She had trouble remembering so many things lately, particularly English words that she would reach for out of habit—*holster, espionage, ink-jet, electricity*— only to draw her hand back empty. Her doctor said that forgetfulness was normal in her condition and in a few months the fog would lift. She preferred it to remain indefinitely. When she had finally reached the island port, her parents had been waiting. They had not expected Joseph to accompany her and they had not found him running with her into their arms.

Del left her mother with the stew and hobbled out into the front yard. Although it was only April, she felt the first tick of summer in the air. Soon vacationers would invade the island, filling the pebble beaches and dotting the horizon with cruise ships as high as hotels. She had begun counting months last October and she willed a new habit out of counting them with her finger and thumb as a substitute for cigarettes. When her mother caught her behind the smokehouse sneaking a ravenous puff, she flew into a rage. "You cannot think only of yourself, Delphine," she hollered in Greek. "There are others now."

Del had no memory of the shot being fired because she hadn't heard it. She was half a block away carrying two plastic pharmacy bags. She didn't see a woman run from the building, although neighbors were later able to describe her. She found Joseph lying in a fetal position on the bed, his eyelids closed like a boy asleep in her absence, a bullet wound blooming from his heart.

She couldn't remember the gun on the floor, but the police said it had been there the whole time. Del had only spoken to Joseph's mother once—a ten-minute conversation by phone where she delivered the news of her son's death. The old woman on the other end of the line hadn't seemed to understand what she was telling her, so Del repeated it several times into the silence of the receiver. Finally a low, steady voice said that she would see to the arrangements. Del hadn't gone to Ohio for the funeral. She wasn't even certain there was a funeral. If there had been one—as it had been with Dash's parents—she wasn't invited. Del felt no need to say good-bye to her husband in that part of the world from which he had wanted so desperately to escape. Still, it seemed fitting the body she kissed one last time in their apartment found its final resting place in Cincinnati. His future had always been buried there, among his own people, biding their time until his return.

She had been careful not to tell the case detectives that Joseph had predicted his death. They were too busy trying to determine whether his murder had been accidental or premeditated, a distinction lost on her as she sat gathered around the luggage bound for Greece. The neighbors had heard shouts and the sound of a brief struggle. Through William and Janice, the police traced the woman seen fleeing from the building to a room at the Carlyle hotel. They found all of her belongings, but Aleksandra Andrews never went back to claim them. It was as if she disappeared that night out of the horror of what happened, or perhaps she had simply been invented, an emissary from Joseph's nightmare to complete the task of killing him by heart failure at thirty-four.

Goats trailed along the hardened dirt road, and the goat herder whistled at her condition, beating his stick on the ground twice for good luck. Seawater drifted in the air, giving the sense that all objects could be pried loose and washed away in the slow salt winds. Del crossed the road and approached the cliff, where the view encompassed an entire stretch of coastline with its swerving coves and ragged crags jutting roughly into the sky. To walk quickly, Del carried her stomach in her arms. Was it a final betrayal of a widow to wish the father was Raj and not Joseph? In the days after she discovered she was pregnant, she counted months backward and forward as if a different answer could be cleaved from basic math. Del had not become impervious to the superstition of a bloodline. Joseph had fulfilled his own prediction, and she worried the baby growing inside her might also carry that bad inheritance into the channels of its life. Ultimately, there was no question that the child was Joseph's, and she was glad. At night it kicked against its walls and settled when she sang to it. It would arrive any day now, an infant with plenty of room to grow.

She could lose an entire afternoon to patterns. First Dash. Then Joseph. She could trace circles with her foot in the dirt, until one circle perfectly matched another. She could count up the coincidences that had shaped her years and echoed each death, until they formed a perfect sequence. She could gaze directly at the sun until its outline scorched her eyes and everything she looked at carried that faint red impression. But she preferred to stare out at the stretch of sea, where somewhere, thousands of miles beyond the curve, New York must still exist, and so must the people living in it. She didn't miss it, not more than some jittery, lightning-fast memory of youth.

One day, maybe, she would tell her son about it. Although nothing was decided. On that point, she was convinced.

ACKNOWLEDGMENTS

THIS BOOK WOULD never have been attempted had it not been for a hundred different people, but it surely would never have been completed without the support of a select few. I'd like to thank my agent Bill Clegg for his supreme trust and belief in the book through the wilderness of the middle to the end and back again (and again with expert understanding of characters even at their most irrational); for him, this novel would survive as a flurry of word files on a computer and nothing more. I'd like to thank Denise Oswald for braving lengths and seeing something possible in its lines. Without the support, creative endurance, and perfect ear of my editor Dan Smetanka, this story might have had bite but drawn no believable blood. The entire team at Counterpoint including Charlie Winton has been wonderful at giving a first-time author a first-rate chance. I'd also like to thank particular friends who doubled as tireless champions: Fabiola Beracasa, when introductions were due, Michael Martin for his diligent reading and honest responses, T. Cole Rachel for listening to me whine, Joseph Logan and Kelley Walker for turning their Orient Village home into an erstwhile writer's retreat, Danko & Ana Steiner, George Miscamble, Brian DeGraw for first alerting me through his art to the strange phenomenon of post-9/11 lightning-strike deaths, the Bronx Zoo for allowing me to tour its herpetology department and being undeserving of the fictional world I set therein, *Interview Magazine* and *V Magazine* for keeping me employed, Brooke Geehan, and Heather Bollen. I am grateful for the research provided when research was required by the *Economist, Assassination in America* by James McKinley (Harper & Row Publishers), *Rattlesnake: Portrait of a Predator* by Manny Rubio (Smithsonian Institution Press), and a fleet of conspiracy-theory websites that half-convinced me they might be on to something.

I'd also like to specially thank all of my friends in New York City, some still with us, others lost, who stayed up with me well past midnight on so many nights and made me believe I could one day wake up and put the words down on paper. This work is partly dedicated to them.